*The Marriage Bowl*

*By the same author*

Beggars Would Ride
Yesterday's Road

# THE MARRIAGE BOWL

MARY MINTON

C

CENTURY

LONDON MELBOURNE AUCKLAND JOHANNESBURG

First published in Great Britain in 1986 by
Century Hutchinson Ltd
Brookmount House, 62–65 Chandos Place
London WC2N 4NW

Century Hutchinson Australia Pty Ltd
PO Box 496, 16–22 Church Street, Hawthorn,
Victoria 3122, Australia

Century Hutchinson New Zealand Limited
PO Box 40–086, Glenfield, Auckland 10, New Zealand

Century Hutchinson South Africa (Pty) Ltd
PO Box 337, Bergvlei 2012, South Africa

ISBN 0 7126 9544 3

Typeset and printed in Great Britain by
WBC Print Ltd, Bristol

Dear Norma with love

# Chapter One

## 1923

Julietta van Neilson was halfway across the field when she stopped and stood, hesitant. She was running away from the problem again. If she did not make up her mind now what she was going to do with her life another day would be gone, another week, another month. It was no use approaching her parents again unless she had a definite plan of what she wanted to do. But what?

Her brother Richard had broken away from the parental reins by simply stating he wanted to go to London to join a firm of architects and study architecture – and it was done. His talk now was all of freedom.

In his letter of that morning he had written: '*This is the life, Julie, no parents breathing down my neck all the time, wanting to know where I'm going, what time I'll be back. Jake, the chap I room with, has a secondhand Morris and we go haring all over the place in it. One night last week we went to a pub in the East End where they were celebrating a couples' golden wedding. Boy, what a night that was! The Cockneys might be tough and their humour bawdy, but they're the salt of the earth, warm, generous . . .*'

Julie turned slowly and stood looking at the house at the top of the slope ahead where she had lived for the whole of her sixteen years. The house, shaped like a crescent moon, was a feature of the area. Every room was curved, the man who designed and built it being of the opinion that a house without angles would make for more harmonious living.

Although Julie had not been conscious of much disharmony during her childhood, her life recently had been a constant friction between her parents and herself.

Her mother had aggravatingly dismissed the restlessness she felt as something that would ease in time. To which Julie had retorted, 'If you tell me it's just a part of growing up I shall scream.' And she had slammed out of the room.

It was all right for her parents, their lives were wrapped up mainly in business. Her father dealt in optical glass while her mother had built up a business known as Leddenshaw Glass, with the famous peacock glass selling all over the world.

The wind was cold for late summer and there had been intermittent torrential showers. Although it had been dry when Julie set out a gust of wind brought a spattering of large drops of rain. She made for the forest on her left, where she could shelter.

As soon as she opened the wicket gate childhood memories came flooding back of Richard taking her by the hand and running her to the 'furnace room', where old William and Thomas and Ben had worked with the molten glass, rolling, shaping . . .

But there was no welcoming glow now, no gentle roar of the furnace, just a desolation. Leaves had blown in through the partly-opened door, making a damp carpet that stuck to Julie's shoes. She fingered the chair where old William had sat and run the rod over the arm, as he shaped the glob of glass.

But William was dead, so was Ben, killed on the Somme and not then sixteen. Thomas had been gassed in the war, but he had come home and married Ivy and they had set up a little general business near a pottery at Stoke.

Julie suddenly felt a faint stir of excitement as she thought of Ivy and Tom. They were responsible, hard-working people. Would her parents allow her perhaps to help them in their shop?

Although her mother was a wealthy woman now in her

own right she had come from a working-class background. She had been in service and met Ivy there. Ivy had lived with her parents when they were first married. She was a part of Julie's childhood, it was she who had disciplined her. Could this be the answer to her wish for freedom? Then her excitement suddenly dimmed. What was the use of hoping? Her parents had not even allowed her to go to a finishing school in Paris or Switzerland as some of her friends had done because she was 'too rebellious'.

But this was different, she argued to herself. She would be working, earning her own living. It was worth a try. She would put over the points carefully, let them see she could handle herself sensibly.

The last thing her mother had said to her before she had stormed out of the house half an hour ago was, 'Come and talk to me when you have found some sense.' But that had been in reply to a suggestion that she wanted to go to London – like Richard, but with no plan in mind.

Julie left the forest, feeling for the first time that she had a purpose in life, something that could combat the dreadful restlessness from which she had suffered for so long.

She walked up the long drive without stopping, pushed open the massive carved oak door, crossed the circular hall and went upstairs to her parents' room. With luck she might be able to have a talk with her mother before her father arrived home.

Without preamble Julie said, 'Mother, I should like to earn my own living.'

Kitty van Neilson, used to her daughter's mercurial moods and whims, sat down at the dressing table and took a brooch from her jewel box before replying.

'Oh, yes, Julie, and what did you have in mind?'

'I thought I would like to work in Ivy and Tom's shop at Stoke. It could be fun.'

Kitty turned quickly, an angry light in her eyes. 'Let me tell you, Julie, there's no fun in working the way Tom and

Ivy have to work to make a living. The shop is open from six o'clock in the morning until late at night, sometimes midnight. What is more you're too young, too irresponsible to leave home.'

'You were married when you were sixteen and fifteen when you went into service!'

Kitty's anger died. 'That was different, Julie. I worked because I had to, my mother needed the money. I was brought up to work. You've been brought up in luxury, been indulged. You would never fit into a working-class life.'

'How do you know I wouldn't? You adjusted to Daddy's way of life, why can't the situation be reversed?'

'Because I adjusted *gradually.*' Kitty spoke patiently. 'I graduated from scullery-maid to under-housemaid then Mrs Helder, or Aunt Helder as you came to know her, took me under her wing and taught me languages, deportment and introduced me to poetry. It was a slow build-up. You would be plunged into a totally different way of life – you've never experienced poverty.'

'And whose fault is that?' Julie demanded. 'You and Daddy wouldn't even let me play with the workers' children!'

'Because we wanted to protect you, wanted you to know the finer things in life.'

'The finer things in life!' Julie flung out her hands in a gesture of despair. 'You sent me to a local private school which I hated. You delivered me every morning and collected me every afternoon like a criminal put out for a day's work.'

'And from which you determinedly set out to "escape", by getting yourself expelled!' Kitty turned back to the mirror and fastened the brooch at the neck of her blouse, her fingers trembling. 'You broke every rule in the book.'

Julie came up and stood behind her. 'Don't you see that I had to,' she said quietly. 'Don't you understand me at all,

Mother? Haven't you ever been aware of my need to get away from the empty-headed young people I meet in the wealthy circle we mix with? They're all like lost souls because they have nothing to strive for.'

Kitty looked at the mirrored image of her young daughter. The eyes which had been rebellious moments before now held a desperate plea. They were lovely eyes, unusual, slightly slanted, changing colour with her moods. In this pleading mood they looked more a midnight blue than dark grey. Many people had remarked on the beauty of Julie's eyes and Kitty had marvelled that the girl had never become self-conscious about them. She was such a strange mixture – a rebel, a dreamer, lovable, exasperating . . .

It had never occurred to Kitty that she had not understood her own daughter's needs. She remembered now her own needs to continue with her glass-making business after marriage, and how she had had to fight to get Tyler to agree to it. What frustration she would have suffered if this had been denied her.

But how could Julie adjust to Ivy and Tom's way of life? She had never even washed up a cup in her whole life. On the other hand, if she was not given a chance how could she ever prove her capabilities? Kitty turned to her.

'Look, Julie, I'm not promising anything but I will talk to your father when he comes in and I will try to get him to understand the way you feel.'

Julie flung her arms around her. 'Oh, thanks, Mother, thanks a million, you won't regret it, I promise! I'll work from morning till night. I'll do *anything*, anything at all. I must go and tell Caroline!'

Although Caroline was one of the nicer girls in her circle of friends Julie was unable to make her understand her reason for wanting to work for a living.

'Why do you want to be different, Julie?' she asked in bewilderment. 'This is our kind of life – isn't it?'

Julie found it impossible to explain to her how boring she

found the conversation of the people in their circle. All the girls ever talked about were clothes, parties, dances and of course – men. And all the men talked about were horses, hunting, shooting – and the girls they had bedded. Even when her parents entertained, their guests were mostly clients whose sole talk was of glass-making. And Julie wanted to be miles away from where the word 'glass' would ever be mentioned.

She stayed with Caroline until she felt sure her father would be home and her mother would have had a chance to talk to him. This was one good thing about her parents – if there was something to discuss there would be no waiting. Her parents were close, still very much in love. There were times when Julie resented this. They had promised on two occasions when planning to go to London on business to take her with them. But each time they had made an excuse and left her in charge of Mrs Parker, the housekeeper. Although they had made the reasons sound valid at the time Julie had been left wondering if they had thought of the trips as 'second honeymoons' and did not want a daughter tagging along with them.

When Julie got back to the house Mrs Parker met her in the hall and told her that her parents wanted to see her in the sitting-room.

Julie said, 'Thanks,' took off her hat and coat, hung them up and after taking a deep breath forced herself to walk sedately up the stairs.

When she went into the room her father stood up and Julie, as she so often did, thought with a warm feeling of love how attractive and immaculate her father always looked.

'Ah, there you are Julie, we were just talking about you.' He drew up a chair for her. There was no gravity of expression on his face, which gave her hope. Nor was there any lecture, just a straightforward discussion, as a result of which it was agreed that her mother would write to Ivy that very evening. Julie could hardly believe her luck!

The letter was written and posted. By return, a reply came from Ivy saying that she and Tom would be only too pleased to have Julie – especially if she was willing to help in the shop and perhaps do a bit of housework and cooking.

Tyler van Neilson said laughingly, 'Cooking? Heaven help them!' which made Julie all the more determined to prove herself.

Kitty remarked, 'Ivy suggests you travel next Monday but as I have an exhibition on that day I won't be able to take you. It will have to be the following Monday.'

Julie protested. She wanted to travel on her own! Again to Julie's surprise both parents gave in. She smiled to herself. No lecture, no protest! The sky would fall tomorrow.

During the next few days she lived in a state of excitement. Her mother described the shop which was near a pottery. It was small but sold just about everything you could think of – groceries, vegetables, bread, hardware, cigarettes and tobacco, firelighters, paraffin and, at midday and evenings, which was their busiest time, they sold hot mushy peas, pease pudding, black pudding and small, home-made meat pies.

'It sounds lovely,' Julie enthused.

'Until you work in it,' Kitty answered wryly. 'I stayed with Ivy and Tom for two days once and I marvelled at the amount of hours and work they put in. Tom has good and bad spells. As you know, he was gassed in the war. Some days he can hardly get his breath. When that happens, a neighbour comes in to help.'

'I'm glad I'm going,' Julie said softly, 'even if it's just to help Tom.'

Kitty looked up in surprise. She had forgotten there was a gentleness towards sick people in her wayward daughter. And yet she should have remembered. Marguerite Helder had often remarked on it. Kitty got up. 'You'd better start sorting out what you want to take with you, Julie. Choose the simplest of your clothes. You *are* going to be a working girl. And travel light. Take only one suitcase. Another one can be sent on to you.'

Julie felt dismayed. She had already packed five cases and had been about to fill a trunk. Ah, well, she could buy more clothes if necessary.

But Julie soon learned that wanting to be a working girl meant just that as far as her parents were concerned. On the morning she was due to leave her father handed her an envelope to be given to Ivy. 'It's for your board and room, Julie. I've also put in extra for your pocket money. I've told Ivy to give you three shillings a week.'

Julie eyed her father in utter astonishment. '*Three shillings*? What can I buy for that?'

'Not very much, I agree, but I should imagine there are some girls who are not given nearly that amount. And I feel confident you want to live in every way suitable to your surroundings and the people you mix with.'

'Yes, but –'

'Julie, dear . . .' Her father spoke gently. 'I want very much for you to make a success of your project. I left home when I was seventeen, unwilling to go into banking as my father wished. I got a job with a glass-blower and that was the start of my career. I worked hard, it was heavy going but I got the utmost satisfaction out of saving my first money.'

Julie searched her father's face. 'I didn't know all this. Why didn't you tell me? Both Mother and you seem to have little secret things in your lives. Mother says she'll tell me *her* secrets sometime. When? When I'm ninety?'

Tyler laughed. 'Before then, I'm sure. Now we must go or you'll miss your train.'

Although Julie would have liked to be the complete traveller and go to the station on her own her parents insisted on accompanying her. And, as it turned out, she was pleased they had. There was an intimacy between the three of them as they waited for the train to come in, that she felt had been lacking lately. They talked generalities but her father had his arm across her shoulders and her mother had her arm linking through hers. Julie felt quite moved. Then the train came puffing importantly in and she felt a surge of excitement again. It brought back memories of her childhood and going to the sea on holidays.

Julie was pleased when her father handed her a third-class ticket but not so pleased when a carriage was found for her which held a vicar and his wife. Julie prayed her mother would not ask the couple to keep an eye on her and she didn't.

They said their goodbyes with even her father seeming a little emotional as he pressed some money into Julie's hand for a taxi to Ivy and Tom's house. Julie promised to write as often as she could.

There was a sudden commotion of a family arriving late to board the train, with onlookers willing them to make it. Carriage doors slammed, the guard blew his whistle, then the train was on the move with much huffing and puffing. Last minute instructions were being called from the people on the platform to those on the train, including her parents – 'Don't forget to give Ivy and Tom our kindest regards . . . Take care of yourself, Julie . . . Let us know if you arrive safely . . .'

Julie waved and tears filled her eyes then her parents became blurred figures getting smaller and smaller. She sat down, briefly acknowledged the Reverend and his wife, then leafed through a magazine, until she could get her silly tears under control. After all, she was not crossing an ocean to a new life, she could come back tomorrow if she wanted. Not that she would, of course.

She was actually quite glad of some company, as they helped to pass the journey. Julie wrote an imaginary letter to her parents describing the couple: *'They weren't a bit "churchy", not like some we know. Quite ordinary really . . . we shared our packed lunches . . .'*

Ivy was firmly fixed in Julie's mind as a thin, wiry woman,

always busy, rather plain until she smiled, then it transformed her, but she was unsure whether she would recognise Tom. All she could remember of him was that he was kind, rather gentle.

The first person Julie saw on the platform when she arrived at Stoke was Ivy, a trim figure in a navy costume and white blouse, wearing a navy felt hat with a tip-tilted brim. This gave her a jaunty look, which was not really Ivy. Julie ran to her, calling her name.

They hugged and kissed then Ivy held her away from her. 'My goodness, I hardly recognised you. Quite the young lady. Come along, let's collect your luggage then we can get a tram home.'

'No, we'll get a taxi,' Julie said. 'Daddy did give me the money for it. But after this I'll travel by tram. I want to live as *you* live, Ivy.'

Ivy grinned. 'You must be a nut, wanting to live our kind of life when you can have so much luxury. On the other hand, I don't think I'd want luxury now. But I did enjoy it when I was companion to Mrs Helder in your Dad's house. It's a lovely place.'

'I'm looking forward to seeing *your* house and the shop.'

'Don't think you're coming to Buckingham Palace. You'll be sleeping in a little boxroom.'

'Ivy, I wouldn't mind if I had to sleep on the floor.'

'Brave words!' Ivy sniffed. 'Tell me that in a week's time then I might believe you'll want to stay for a while.'

She pointed out places of interest on the way home in the taxi, but all Julie was interested in seeing was the shop. Ivy told her, 'You'll be a big help to me, Julie. I need an extra pair of hands, especially when Tom has one of his bad days. We have rushes when folks come in at midday and suppertime for the pies and peas and what-have-you. A neighbour has been popping in to help but she and her family are moving. Our boarder lifts the heavy stuff.'

'Boarder?'

'A young man – his name's Angus MacLaren. When I say a boarder, he sleeps in the house and has his meals but we hardly see him otherwise. He works at the pottery, but he has his own pottery wheel in our shed at the back and makes stuff for himself there. He's a man of few words but we like him.'

Ivy said the last sentence in an almost belligerent way, defying Julie not to like Angus MacLaren.

When the taxi began to slow past a line of shops Ivy sat up expectantly. 'Well, here we are and Tom's waiting to welcome you. He's so looking forward to having you with us.'

Julie saw a small man with sandy, thinning hair and a yellow skin standing in the doorway of a double-fronted shop. He was almost swamped by the big apron he was wearing. Julie felt shocked, not recognising Tom at all.

She paid the taxi driver and was scolded by Ivy for giving him such a large tip. The next moment Tom was there, saying shyly, 'Why Julie, I didn't recognise you!'

She put her arms around him and laid her cheek to his. 'How lovely to see you again, Tom.'

Ivy picked up the suitcase. 'Come along, we'll have a cup of tea and something to eat.'

They went into the dimness of the shop, which seemed to have a myriad smells, the dominant ones being kerosene and cheese. Julie would have lingered to look around but Ivy had a door held open and she followed.

Ivy set down the suitcase. 'Well, this is the kitchen.' The smell here was of meat stewing. A large wooden table scrubbed to whiteness dominated the room, but Julie was intrigued by just how much else was in it. A fire glowed in a black-leaded range which had an oven on either side. There was a gas stove in the room, too. She counted two small armchairs and four wooden ones. There seemed to be three or four cupboards which reached from ground-level to ceiling. The floor was covered with brown lino but a brightly-coloured homemade rag rug lay in front of the fire. The drape round the mantelpiece was red velvet with bobbles, and there were red cushions on the seats of the leather armchairs.

'Well,' said Ivy, 'it's not Crescent House, but it's home to us.' Again there was the slightly belligerent tone.

Tom had pushed the simmering kettle onto the fire and as the lid began to rattle he asked if he should make the tea. Ivy told him yes and reminded him to make a good strong brew. Ivy's voice held a different tone when speaking to Tom, it was almost gentle.

Ivy then took Julie up a narrow wooden staircase that led from the kitchen to show her her room. It was tiny, containing only a bed, a chest of drawers and a washstand, but the wallpaper was white with sprigs of rosebuds, there was a candlewick bedspread in rose pink – a little faded, and a sheepskin rug. 'It's lovely!' Julie exclaimed.

Ivy looked pleased. 'Well, I had to pretty it up a bit, but it didn't cost much. I got the wallpaper as a job lot for sixpence and Mrs Jenkins slapped it on for me. I bought the bedcover and rug too quite cheaply at Billy Barker's – he has a secondhand shop on the corner. They had to be washed mind, but I thought the rug came up lovely.

'Now then,' Ivy pointed to a piece of board on the wall holding some hooks. 'You'll have to hang your clothes there and if you can't get them all on you'll find some room in the big wardrobe on the landing.' She waved her hand towards the washstand. 'If you want hot water to wash in you'll have to come and get it from the kitchen. Bring the jug. What else? Oh, yes, I'll show you where the WC is.' She went to the window. Julie followed. 'That's it, just outside the scullery door. The shed is where Angus has his pottery wheel.'

The yard was large but was filled with empty barrels, cardboard boxes and all the rubbish of the trade, no doubt waiting to be taken away. Ivy remarked about the high wall facing them. 'They're stables – all right in the cold weather, but stink to high heaven in the summer. But there, you can get used to anything if you have to. I'll leave you to freshen up, come down when you're ready. The water will be warmish in the jug. Oh, one thing I've forgotten. A mirror. I'll find one somewhere. Remind me when you come down.'

But there was no opportunity for reminding Ivy. After they had had a cup of tea, some sandwiches and cake, Ivy was here there and everywhere – in the scullery, out in the back, in the shop, then back in the kitchen making pastry for the steak and kidney pies. She enlisted Julie's help. Ivy lined the small tins with pastry and spooned in the meat. Julie put on the pastry lids then passed the tins back to Ivy for the edges to be pinked with a fancy roller. Ivy worked at such a speed Julie was clumsy at first and found it difficult to keep up with her, but gradually she got into a rhythm and won praise.

'You're a quick worker, Julie, I will say that for you.'

One batch of pies went into the ovens of the black-leaded range and another into the gas stove. The mushy peas and pease pudding were warming in pans on top of the stove. When Julie asked what was the difference between them Ivy said the mushy ones were green peas done with a ham-bone to flavour them, while the pudding was made from yellow split peas.

Julie was about to ask if she could now go and have a look around the shop when there was the sound of a door slamming at the back, followed by whistling. 'That will be Angus,' Ivy said, and spread a cloth on a corner of the table and put out cutlery.

Julie looked towards the window and saw a man coming up the yard. He was big and strong-looking, with rough-hewn features, reminding Julie of a book she had once read about the clansmen of the Scottish Highlands in the old days, who fought with fist and sword.

The scullery door opened, slammed shut then Angus

MacLaren came into the kitchen, stopping when he saw Julie. Ivy said, 'Angus, this is Julie van Neilson.'

'Oh, aye,' he said, his quiet voice belying his warrior image. He held out a hand. 'Glad to meet ye, Julie. Did you have a good journey?'

She winced at his grip. 'Yes, yes, I did.'

Angus took off his jacket, hung it behind the kitchen door then sat down at the table. Although Julie had seen brawny men before at her father's works there was something different about this man, but she was unable to place what it was.

When Ivy put a plate of steaming lamb stew on the table Julie began edging towards the kitchen door, suggesting she'd better go and talk to Tom while Angus was having his meal.

Angus pointed his fork towards a chair. 'Set you down, lassie, ye'll no be bothering me.'

'Yes, stay and chat to Angus,' Ivy urged. 'Get to know one another. I'll take you into the shop later. You'll not be wanting to rush in after you've been serving when there's a crowd in! It's like Bedlam. I'll be back in a few minutes. Keep an eye on the pies.'

Julie sat on the edge of one of the hard wooden chairs, keeping her gaze towards the fire. She felt uncomfortable. Angus started on his meal.

After a moment he said, 'So you've come slumming then?'

Julie's head came up. 'No, I haven't come slumming! I've come to work, to earn my living. I want to get to know the people.'

'Oh, ye'll get to know them all right. They'll scoff at your accent for one thing.'

'And what harm would that do?'

'I thought you might be touchy, take it to heart. They're plain-speaking people.'

'And I'm plain-speaking too! If they don't accept me I

won't shed any tears over it. I'm staying, so they will have to put up with me. And that goes for you, too.'

'Oh, that'll be no hardship.' There was a roguish twinkle then in Angus' dark eyes. 'But then we're not likely to be seeing much of one another. I'm a busy man.'

'And I hope that I will be too busy to see much of *you*,' Julie retorted.

He shook his head at her, half-smiling, then the next moment he was sniffing. 'The pies, girl, can you no smell them? Get them out.'

For a moment Julie panicked, not quite knowing what to do, then she seized a cloth and was about to open the oven door when Ivy came in and took the cloth from her. She glared at Angus.

'What are you being so awkward about? You've taken pies out of the oven many times when they've been ready. Julie's never done any cooking before.'

Angus grinned. 'Then it's a good time to learn. She's anxious to find out and I'm no the one to take a girl's job from her.'

'Men – !' Ivy lifted out a tray of pies and put them on a tiered metal stand. To Julie she said, 'Go on into the shop, love, Tom'll show you around.' Julie fled before she changed her mind.

Tom, who was sitting on a stool behind the counter got up and gave her a shy smile. 'Have you come to get to know all the prices? You'll soon learn.'

The price of the goods on the shelves was marked underneath, so that was no problem, but there were many other things to remember. Tom showed her how to package sugar, and dried fruit in squares of strong blue paper, tucking the ends in to make the package secure. He demonstrated the bacon slicer and how to draw vinegar from a barrel and fill bottles with paraffin and kerosene . . . how to weigh potatoes on the big scales using heavy brass weights. She had to know the prices of the various kinds of cigarettes and tobacco, although Tom said that the majority of the workers bought Woodbines. Then there was hardware – loaf tins, cake tins, some tin mugs and enamel ones, billy cans – the list of goods was endless.

Tom said reassuringly, 'Don't worry, lovey, you'll get to know where all the goods are in time. We're not as busy on a Monday night as other times, especially towards the end of the week, but there's a bit of a rush when the shift changes at nine o'clock.'

Julie was trying to memorise the goods on the shelves when a hoarse voice said behind her, 'Hi, Missus, I want a packet of Woodies for me Dad and he says will you put them on the slate till the weekend.'

It was a small boy, so small that only a pair of large dark eyes and a snub nose appeared over the edge of the counter. Julie looked at Tom for guidance and he shook his head. Then he said to the boy, speaking gently: 'You'll have to bring the money, Jimmy. Your Dad owes us quite a bit already. Tell him, will you?'

The boy nodded and ran out. His knee-length trousers were frayed at the edges and he was barefooted. Julie was full of concern. 'Bare feet! In this weather! He'll catch his death of cold.'

Tom sighed. 'It's heartbreaking to see kids like Jimmy. He's one of eight children. His father drinks almost every penny he earns. His mother looks as if she hasn't the strength to drag herself around, yet she does washing at some of the big houses. It's terrible how some people have to exist.'

When Julie asked what the boy had meant by having his father's cigarettes 'put on the slate', Tom explained that at one time a piece of slate was used to record the money customers owed for goods. They usually settled up on pay days, but now the items were put into a book.

'The majority pay up promptly, Julie, but there is always the odd one who'll run up a bill then go somewhere else to shop. Eventually they'll come back, expecting you to have forgotten the debt, but of course we never do, we can't afford to. Either Ivy or I will keep you right about the good payers. Don't worry about it.'

A sprinkling of customers came in but Julie found herself waiting for the rush of shift workers. 'You'll hear them before you see them,' Tom told her with a smile. 'Most of them have to wear clogs for the mess of wet clay they work in.'

When they did come, the sound of chattering voices mingled with the clatter of the wooden clogs on the cobblestones. One moment the shop was empty and the next it overflowed with men and women who jostled and pushed and kept up a light-hearted banter. 'Get your bloody elbows out me ribs, Archie Sloper . . . Here, watch it! That's me toes you're trampling on, I need them to get me home . . . Hy, Netta Backworth, how did you get in front of me, you were miles behind?' To this last remark came a laughing retort, ''Cos I pinned on me fairy wings and flew here . . .'

Above all this some women were shouting their orders. Ivy yelled, 'Will you shut up the lot of you! Was it a pennorth of peas, Mrs Ashford, or pease pudding?'

'Peas, and I'll have a pennorth of black pudding an' all.'

Then they seemed to become aware of Julie and a man in a greasy cloth cap said, 'Ooh, you beautiful doll, where did you come from?'

Ivy introduced her. 'This is Miss Julietta van Neilson, my new assistant, and you lot see you treat her right, d'ye hear?'

A saucy-looking girl, a black shawl over her head said, 'Oh, Julietta, where did you get her?' And a man began to chant: 'I'll get Julietta, get her, get her.'

Julie, who had put a scoopful of pease pudding into a basin for a woman customer, smiled. 'Can we get on with the serving, please?'

The man swept off his cap and bowed, mimicking her accent. 'Can we get on with the serving, please?'

There was a burst of laughter and Julie, still smiling, held out the basin and said, 'Would you like this in your face, or over your head?'

There was a sudden silence and into it came Ivy's tart voice. 'And don't think she wouldn't do it!'

One or two people began to laugh then they were all laughing. Ivy said under her breath to Julie, 'It's all right, you're accepted, you're one of them now.'

Afterwards, Julie had a feeling that her mind had suddenly opened and was gobbling up impressions which would form a pattern of a different way of life once she had them all assembled. But at that moment excitement and exhaustion had them all lying jumbled in a heap.

She was too tired even to drink the cocoa Ivy made for her when the shop was closed. Ivy hustled her off to bed. 'I'll let you have a lie-in in the morning, love. I won't wake you until seven o'clock.'

'Seven? A lie-in?' Julie couldn't even find the energy to laugh. Ivy had put a stone hot-water bottle into the bed, wrapped in a piece of flannel. Julie hugged it to her. The prices of goods flitted under her eyelids, then faces – thin ones, gaunt ones, jolly ones, melancholy ones. Then she saw the rough-hewn features of Angus MacLaren and felt sure he was going to be a part of the pattern, but was not sure at that moment where he would fit in.

Julie slept.

# Chapter Two

Julie was roused from a deep sleep the next morning by Ivy shaking her. 'Come on, love, wake up. I've brought you some hot water and here's a cup of tea. But this is special just for this one morning. From tomorrow on you'll have to come down for them yourself.' Julie drew herself up in the bed and thanked her.

At home, she was used to awakening to a fire in her bedroom and she shivered in the cold dark room. It was like getting up in the middle of the night. She washed and dressed quickly, the sleep not yet out of her eyes. But as soon as she opened the door at the bottom of the stairs a wave of warm air met her.

'Oh, lovely,' she said, going to the fire and holding her hands out to the blaze. Tom came in from the scullery.

'Hello there, Julie, did you sleep well? There's porridge in the pan or I could cook you some bacon and egg.'

Ivy came in from the shop. 'She'll cook it herself. Mrs Tate wants half a pound of bacon cut on number six, Tom. I must get the pies started, I'm behindhand this morning. Julie, make a corner for yourself on the table. You can lend me a hand when you've had breakfast. Do yourself a piece of toast, if you want it. There's a long wire fork hanging by the oven.'

Julie had never toasted a piece of bread before but because everything was a novelty she speared a slice of bread on the fork and held it out to the blazing fire. And felt she had managed to achieve something when it turned out to be burnt at only one corner. She spread it with butter, put a thin layer of marmalade on top and declared it to be delicious.

'Humph,' Ivy said. 'You'll want more in your belly than that if you intend to do a day's work. Get yourself some porridge.' Julie was not fond of porridge, but helped herself to a small portion and poured milk on it. She was surprised to find she enjoyed it. Perhaps it was the change of air!

Suddenly, she wondered about Angus. He had gone out after his meal of last night and had not returned before she went to bed. When she asked about him Ivy told her he was at work, but would be finished today at about two o'clock. 'And then he'll be out in the shed,' she added. 'Pottery comes between him and his wits. You'd think he would get sick of the sight of it after working with it at the pottery.'

Ivy began mixing pastry in a large bowl. 'Julie, if you've finished your breakfast, pop into the shop will you? Tom had a bad night last night. There's a few folk come in about this time for their cigarettes and baccy and what-have-you. Just nip those dishes off the table and put them in the sink. Meg Jenkins will be here at eight o'clock to help in the shop. Then you can come in here and give me a hand.'

Julie felt disappointed. She wanted to stay in the shop, but she did as she was told. It felt strange to be starting work when it was dark outside and the shop gaslit. Tom was sitting on a stool behind the counter near a paraffin stove that gave out little heat. His skin somehow looked more yellow in the gaslight, but although his breathing was bad he gave Julie a warm smile.

'A bit early for you, love, isn't it?'

'Poor Tom,' Julie said softly. She laid her cheek against his. 'I'm sorry you're not so well this morning. Just tell me what needs doing.'

'Perhaps you can cut a few pieces of cheese, small pieces. Some of the folk from the clothing factory buy a morsel to have with their bread at lunchtime. They don't start until eight o'clock.'

Tom had shown Julie the night before how to use the wire cheese-cutter and she felt quite professional as she sliced up some portions. She wished her parents could see her.

The bell above the door tinkled and the girl with the saucy-looking face, who had mocked Julie the night before, came in, tightening the black shawl around her.

'Morning, Tom. Morning Julietta van Thingummy. God, it's a freezer this morning. I wouldn't have turned out but I didn't have a smoke.' She put five pennies on the counter. 'I'll have ten – Woodbines, if you don't know my brand, but I bet you know *everything* – bet you're a right little clever clogs!'

Julie, mimicking the girl's broad accent, said, 'A proper dunce until I came here. But I'm learning quickly.'

The girl grinned. 'You'll do. The name's Peg Smith. Haven't got a fancy title like you.'

'I'd be better off without it if I'm going to be scoffed at all the time.' Julie got the packet of cigarettes and handed them over.

Peg shook one out of the paper packet, lit it from the small jet at the end of the counter, took a deep drag and exhaled. 'Oh, I've been wanting that for the past hour.'

Tom said gently, 'You should stop it, Peg, won't do you any good.'

'But it does, Tom lad, it's one of me few pleasures. But for these I may as well be dead. I'd better go, me Mam's in bed this morning, got a hacking cough. Never slept all night. Ta-ra – be seeing you.'

Tom laughed and it set him off coughing. 'Oh, this wretched chest!' He thumped it. When the bout was over he wiped his eyes. 'Peg's quite a character. She's had a hard life, Julie. Her father died when she was five years old. There were three children younger, she bosses them all around *and* her mother, but they all love her. I've never once heard her complain about her life. Julie, will you hand me the debt book. There's something I forgot to put in and Ivy's a stickler for everyone paying their debts, which they should of course – she works hard for what she gets.'

Julie brought the book and opened it. 'Can I put the amount in?'

'Yes, you can. Put it against "Big Ed": two shillings and threepence.'

They were all mostly abbreviated names, 'Dot . . . A.L. . . . Jinny . . . Mrs B . . . Mrs W.R. . . . Frank . . . Simmie . . .'

Tom said, 'You'll get to know them all in time, Julie. There's one chap listed under "Dragon" – that's because he has a little dragon tattooed on the back of his hand. Then there's "Scarface" – *he* was burned when he was young and old "Blackie", who spent nearly all his working life in the pits.'

Julie kept turning over pages. 'I find it all so interesting, Tom. I'm sure there must be a lot of stories you could tell.'

Tom nodded. 'That I could. There's tragedy, Julie, but there's a lot of humour, too. And there's excitement. Only last week, one of the men at the pottery was left three hundred pounds by an uncle he didn't even know existed. All the people in the neighbourhood shared his pleasure. I think he would have spent the lot on treating the men to drinks, but they wouldn't let him. "You see to your family, George," they said.'

Tom had another coughing bout, which brought Ivy into the shop to scold him. She held out a small glass. 'Here you are, drink up your medicine. I have to follow you around like a hawk to make sure you take it. I reminded you earlier. I can't remember *everything* you know.' Although Ivy's words were scolding her tone had the gentleness in it she reserved for Tom.

The doorbell pinged and a plump little woman in black came bustling in, taking her coat off the moment she had closed the door.

Ivy said, 'Why, Meg, you're early, but now you're here I'll

leave you with Tom.' To Julie she said, 'This is Mrs Jenkins. You can come and help me now.'

Meg Jenkins beamed at Julie. 'Lovely you are, girl. My two boys would be taken with you. Neither of them is walking out with anyone.'

'And neither of them will be walking out with Julie!' Ivy retorted. 'She's here to work.'

'But you wouldn't be wanting her to be working *all* the time, now would you? You know the old saying, "All work and no play makes Jack a dull boy".'

Ivy sniffed. "Jack can do what he likes but I decide what Julie does, and right now, the pair of us have work to tackle.'

Meg gave Julie a wink. 'I'll be seeing you later, girl. We'll have a nice talk.'

Ivy started to say something about Meg as they went into the kitchen, but paused as she heard Tom coughing again. Her eyes took on a fierce expression. 'I would willingly stick a bayonet into any man who was responsible for poison gas being used in warfare *and* I'd find pleasure in twisting it in his guts! There's many a man worse off than Tom, although he's bad enough. Some were blinded, and some left complete wrecks.'

Julie nodded. 'I know. Two men in the village near us were blinded. Daddy wasn't gassed in the war, but he was wounded. Mother said he was like a scarecrow when he came home. It took him years to recover.'

'Yes, it did,' Ivy said grimly. 'I was there at the time.' She picked up an oven-cloth. 'Anyway, talking won't get the work done.'

She kept Julie on the go, helping with the pies, washing up, making up the fire, doing the beds, dusting, scrubbing down the table . . . Julie felt exhausted and was appalled to find it was only half past nine. She felt she had put in a full day's work. She longed to go back into the shop but did not get the opportunity until Ivy told her to go in with Mrs Jenkins and let Tom have a glass of milk and a rest.

Julie liked the little Welsh woman, who had nothing but praise for Ivy. 'A hard-working woman,' she said, 'and it's all for Tom. His dream was always to have a little cottage and keep hens, a few pigs and have a smallholding. This is Ivy's aim.'

Some customers came in then Meg resumed her story. 'It was your parents who gave them the money to get started.'

Julie looked at her in surprise. 'My parents?'

Meg nodded. 'And Ivy has paid it all back. Now she's saving every penny she can to give Tom his dream. She wants to *buy* a cottage, *buy* the land, says Tom must feel secure. No use renting something then be turned out at the whim of some landlord.'

Julie had a new respect for Ivy – and for her parents, who had been caring enough to help Ivy and Tom.

They were busy at lunchtime and Julie enjoyed every minute, loving the people, the variety, laughing at the quips, accepting the admiration of the men.

One young fellow with dark curly hair and a bold smile said, 'Julie, you're coming to the pictures with me one evening! Which night suits you?'

Julie gave him a pert smile. 'Any night as long as you'll take my boyfriend as well.'

There was a burst of laughter at this but the young man came back with: 'I will, as long as he sits five rows behind us.'

An elderly man teased Julie. 'You can't win, lass, not with a feller like Cal Coates.' But a woman standing next to him refuted this.

''Course she will! Julie had an answer for him now and she's only been here a day. Think what she'll come up with in another couple of weeks!'

Cal grinned. 'I'll ask her then and let you know.'

Julie felt a glow to be already a part of these people. When Ivy called her into the kitchen for a meal she talked about them. 'They're lovely people, Ivy and I'm really enjoying myself. I'm so glad I came. I don't think I'm very hungry, though.'

Ivy set a plate before her. 'Eat it. An engine won't work without fuel.'

Julie laughed. 'So now I'm an engine.'

Despite her lack of appetite Julie easily got through the two fried chops, roast potatoes, cabbage and turnips *and* the apple dumpling to follow. She patted her stomach. 'Oh, Ivy, I won't need another bite for the rest of the day. Trouble is, I feel sleepy now.'

'There's no time for that. You must write a letter to your parents to let them know you arrived safely, then I want you to pop along to Billy Barker's on the corner and see if he has a cheap mirror. Thought I had a spare one, but I haven't. Get the letter written, *now*. You can post it on the way to Billy's.'

Julie groaned. 'You're worse than Mother. If something wants doing it has to be done at that very minute!'

'It was her who got me working that way. She taught me a lot did your Ma. And Mrs Helder.'

Julie sat hesitant a moment, then said, 'Ivy, do you know who the Tiernes are?'

Ivy, who had been drying a jug she had washed, rubbed it, put it down then picked it up again. 'What made you ask that?'

'Because two days before Aunt Helder died she kept telling me I must meet the Tiernes. She was rambling a bit so I didn't take much notice. But that evening, when I was alone with her, and her mind seemed clearer she mentioned them again. "You *must* meet the Tiernes, Julie," she said, "you *must*, it's your right." I was about to question her but the nurse came in and no more was said. Later that evening Aunt Helder went into a coma, and the following day she died.'

Julie was silent a moment, reliving the grief she had felt at the death of the old lady. Ivy rubbed the cloth over the jug. 'Did you ask your mother about them?'

'Yes, I did, but not until after the funeral. She told me it was something she was unable to discuss then because it would involve other people, hurt them. She added that there might be a time in the future when she would be able to explain.'

Ivy set the jug firmly on the table. 'Then that's it – you must accept it.'

'All right.' Julie's head came up. 'Then let me ask you something else. Who is Violet?'

Ivy turned away and began poking the fire. 'Who told you about her?'

'No one, it was something I overheard. It was a time when Aunt Agnes and Aunt Mary were on a visit. I saw them in the woods and they both seemed upset. Aunt Mary was saying, "It couldn't have been our Violet you saw, you must have been mistaken."

'Aunt Agnes said, "It was her, I tell you, who could be mistaken with that face!" Then she added, "But for heaven's sake don't tell our Kitty, we don't want to bring all that up again." They moved away after that, and because of what had been said I couldn't ask Mother about it, nor could I ask Daddy – because I didn't know what was involved.'

Ivy turned and faced Julie. 'I'm only going to say that Violet is one of your mother's older sisters: she caused an awful lot of trouble in the past and I hope we've all seen the back of her, for good and all. Let her lie, she doesn't affect your life in any way. Now come along, get that letter written. You can just write a few lines for now and send another letter later in the week.'

Julie did write only a few lines, finding it too difficult to concentrate. Would all these mysteries be cleared up when she was older? She was sitting, chewing on the end of the pen when Ivy came up and stuck a twopenny stamp on the envelope. 'Come on, move, Angus will be in soon. Don't forget to go to Billy Barker's and get the mirror.'

'What sort of mirror do you want, Ivy?'

'It's to go in your bedroom. See it's a good one. I can't ever remember looking into a decent mirror when I was young. They were either cracked, which made your face distorted, or there were so many marks on them you looked as if you had a spotty complexion.'

Ivy took a sixpence from her purse. 'Billy enjoys bargaining. He'll probably ask you for a shilling for one, but you tell him you can't afford that. He'll probably shrug and say he can't let it go for any less. That's when you start walking away. He'll call you back, you'll get it for sixpence. Or perhaps less if you stick out.'

Julie was intrigued at this way of shopping, and thought suddenly, 'This is living – it's different, exciting!'

When she went through the shop she waved the letter at Meg and Tom. 'I'm going to post this and then buy a mirror.'

Tom laughed. 'If you're going to Billy Barker's we won't expect you back for an hour!'

Julie realised what he meant when she arrived at BILLY'S EMPORIUM. Set on a corner, the shop's two windows were crammed with bric-à-brac of every description. Inside, it was even more crowded – you had to edge your way between chairs, sideboards, pianos, sofas, beds . . . the list was endless. A tubby man in shirt-sleeves, his stomach hanging over the waistband of his trousers, came ambling out of a small office at the rear. A cap was pushed to the back of his head.

'Hello, m'dear, what can I do for you? Oh, you must be Julie, at Ivy and Tom's.' He wagged a finger, and gave her an amiable grin. 'Oh, I've heard all about you, heard you can hold your own with our lot.'

Julie smiled. 'I need a mirror – a cheap one, please.'

'Mirrors! I got them all shapes and sizes. Chevalier mirrors, Florentine ones, swivel, hand mirrors, tortoiseshell-backed and –'

'Just a small one, to hang on the wall of my room,' Julie said. 'It must be cheap.'

'Well, let me see. "Mirror mirror on the wall, who's the fairest of them all?" ' Billy gave her a huge wink. 'Not the old Queen, eh, but Julie! Come with me, gal.'

He was right about having a selection, there was a boxful of them. And Ivy was right about Billy's love of bargaining. He started off with a shilling, came down to ninepence then Julie said, 'I'll give you sixpence, take it or leave it.'

Billy roared with laughter, his double chins wobbling. 'You've got a good teacher in Ivy and you have the right outlook for learning. Here, keep your tanner, I'll make you a gift of the mirror, on condition you have a look around and spend your money on something else. That's a bargain, isn't it?' He held out his big paw and Julie put her hand in his.

'It's a bargain. I'll have a look and see what I can find.'

Julie could not remember a time when she had enjoyed herself more. She sorted through boxes of books, boxes of ornaments, then rummaged through one of battered toys and pulled out a shabby, one-eyed teddy bear. She held it up. 'How much is this, Mr Barker?'

He came ambling up and nodded his head slowly. 'I knew as soon as I saw you, you'd be a lass after me own heart. That there bear has been asking to be adopted. It's been crying for a cuddle, but me – I ain't got time to be nursing teddy bears. To anyone else I would have to charge a bob, but to you – a tanner. Take it.'

Julie left laughing, with a promise to come again.

Ivy, who was in the shop when she got back, flung up her hands in horror and said to Tom, 'I give her sixpence to buy a mirror and she comes back with a moth-eaten teddy bear, which is sure to be full of fleas.'

'Oh, I got the mirror.' Julie brought it from under her arm. 'Billy gave it to me, as a gift.'

Ivy stared at her. 'Billy? Gave it to you? Heavens above it'll rain frogs tomorrow. He's as tight as a pea in a pod.'

'Oh, I don't know,' Tom said. 'I've always found him a generous chap. Often used to stand me a pint in the pub and wouldn't have one back.'

'Two of Billy's chosen!' Ivy retorted. She gave Julie a push. 'Come on, that teddy'll have to be washed if you want to keep it.'

When they went into the kitchen, Angus, who was at the table having his meal, looked up and greeted Julie with, 'I hear you went to Billy's to buy a mirror. How did you get on?'

Ivy held out the teddy bear and told the story of it. She then took the kettle of hot water from the hob and poured some into a bowl with Julie hovering anxiously and saying she hoped the teddy bear would be all right.

Angus suggested to Julie that she pour herself a cup of tea. There was one in the pot and it would help her to bear the strain of waiting until the 'operation' was over. She bridled, thinking he was being sarcastic but his smile was friendly and warm. She poured a cup of tea and as she sipped it wondered about this brawny Scot, finding him difficult to weigh up. But then he probably found it difficult to understand her. He must be asking himself why a girl who came from a wealthy background should want to buy a sixpenny teddy bear. And why had she? After all, she had expensive dolls and animals at home.

With the teddy bear washed and rinsed Ivy wrapped it in a thick towel and squeezed the moisture out of it. 'There.' She laid it on a dry cloth in the hearth. 'It's out of the direct heat, so it'll dry slowly.' She straightened the teddy's ears, then with a sheepish grin said, 'I'm as daft as you, Julie van Neilson. Come on, let's have a look at the mirror.'

Ivy approved of it and after giving it a good rub she handed it back to Julie. 'Here, take it upstairs and get it out of the way. You'll find a nail above the washstand to hang it on.'

When Julie came down again Angus was in the yard. Ivy

nodded towards him. 'He'll be in that shed working until it gets dark. He never wastes a minute. You can go and see what he does later, but in the meantime go into the shop and let Tom come and have a rest.'

Although Julie was not particularly interested in seeing what Angus was making she knew she wanted to be with him. It was a strange sensation. She had never felt this way about any young man before.

It was nearly three o'clock before Ivy told Julie she could go and see Angus work. It was such a short distance to the shed from the scullery that Julie was not aware of the sharp air, but when, after knocking, she went into the shed she felt a clammy chill. She gave a small shiver. Angus, who was at the wheel making a vase said without looking up, 'You'd better put on my pullover, it's behind you.'

Julie pulled it over her head. It smelled of pipe smoke, but she had never seen him smoking. The vase looked completed but Angus kick-started the wheel, did some finishing touches then, drawing a wire under the base, lifted the vase onto a slab.

After wiping his hands on a cloth he gave her a quizzical look. 'I suppose you've come to have a go on the wheel?'

'No, I haven't. I'm not interested. My parents are glass-makers and I seem to have had glass rammed down my throat as far back as I can remember.'

'It must be cut to ribbons.'

'What? Oh – my throat. *Very* amusing.'

'No, it's not, it's corny. Why did you come?'

Julie felt the colour come to her cheeks. She turned away and shrugged. 'I think Ivy thought I might be interested in seeing you at work. And I am, but not interested in wanting to make anything myself.'

There were two shelves of items fashioned in clay – vases, jugs and bowls. But only one bowl, a largish one, was completed. It had a cream glaze with a variety of small figures and what appeared to be signs painted on it.

Julie pointed to it. 'What's that? Is it supposed to represent something?'

'It's a marriage bowl. I made it for a couple I know at the pottery who are getting married soon.'

'It's not very attractive, is it? You could have painted some flowers on it.'

'There *are* flowers on it, but not all of marriage is attractive. My father made one for my sister, which was presented to her on her wedding eve. He had made many beautiful designs before and I think she was disappointed when she saw it. Then he started to explain the purpose of the bowl and I, as well as my sister, became interested.'

Angus went to the shelf and lifted it down. 'My father said the first thing he painted on it was the two bears, named Bear and Forbear because they were two of the most important ingredients of marriage.'

'I would have thought that love would have been the most important.'

'Oh, there is a love-seat, here, with two people on it, but it was my father's contention that if two people married without love then it was going to be heavy going to make a success of it.'

Angus went on pointing out various figures – like a clown, doing a somersault. There had to be humour, laughter . . . There was a man dancing along a road playing a tin whistle, with notes of music all around him . . . clasped hands, for friendship . . .

'Friends? A married couple?' Julie looked doubtful. 'Lovers, yes, but –'

'To be good friends and be able to discuss things is most important.'

'How about forgiveness?'

'Here we are.' Angus pointed out a man standing with a woman kneeling at his feet, hands held up to him.

Julie was indignant. 'Typical male attitude! So it's the woman who has to ask to be forgiven.'

Angus grinned. 'I knew that would get you going. Here is the man on the reverse side, *he* doing the kneeling.'

'Good. And where does the romance come in?'

'Will you settle for a couple walking along a moonlit road, their arms about each other's waists?'

Julie said she would settle for it and queried a fairy tale type of castle on top of a mountain peak. Angus told her it represented dreams, for without them, life and marriage too, would be flat. There were figures of a man and a woman, giving gifts, as well as taking. There was a window box of flowers with Angus explaining he had added these after a comment from his sister.

'When my father gave Maddie the bowl he told her he had left a space for her to add another ingrdient for a successful marriage, but not until they had been married for a year. She painted in the window box, explaining that they lived in a rather drab neighbourhood, where they had no garden and lacked the money to buy flowers. Her husband made the box from scraps of wood and planted it with seeds.'

Angus paused and rubbed a hand over his arm, his expression mellow, as though remembering. 'Maddie said when the flowers grew she wept, wept because she realised that a few seeds planted with love could bring colour into a drab life.'

Julie said softly, 'What a lovely story and what a lovely man your father must be.'

'Was – he was killed during the war.' Angus turned away. 'I must get on with my work, Julie, you'll have to excuse me.'

'Yes, yes of course, and I must be going, Ivy might be needing me. I'll see you later.'

Julie was so quiet when she went back to the kitchen that Ivy commented on it. 'What cat's got your tongue all of a sudden? Angus say something?'

'I didn't know his father was dead – killed in the war.'

'His mother died two years later and four months ago he

lost his beloved sister Maddie, in childbirth. The baby was stillborn.' Ivy's voice trembled.

Julie stared as Ivy, shocked. 'How awful, why didn't you tell me?'

'I didn't know he was going to talk about his family.' Ivy picked up a cloth, opened the oven door, stuck a darning needle in the cake she was baking then closed the door gently. 'Angus is grieving I know, but life has to go on and he knows it.' She added softly, 'It's the living who matter.'

Julie, guessing that Ivy was thinking about Tom, changed the subject quickly by talking about the marriage bowl. Ivy, looking surprised said, 'First I've heard about it, but then Angus isn't very forthcoming about his work – nor about anything else for that matter. Not that I blame him, everyone's entitled to a bit of privacy.'

When Julie asked her what she thought was the most important ingredient for marriage Ivy stood thoughtful for a moment then looked up at her.

'I reckon that there window box is as good an example as any. I don't exactly mean flowers, but sowing seeds of other kinds. When Tom came back from the war he was in a right old state, but he said, "Ivy, when I get a bit better I'm going to work at something and take care of you." And he's certainly done his best to do just that. When he's well enough he gets up at four o'clock to put the fire on and brings me a cup of tea.' She sniffed and flapped the oven cloth at Julie. 'You're getting me as daft as yourself. Come on, there's work to be done.'

Julie laughed but there was a catch in her voice. 'You're talking just as Mother said Mrs Bramley did when you were both in service together. She was Cook, wasn't she?'

'She was!'

Julie had enjoyed hearing her mother talk about her young life and was delighted when Ivy began to reminisce about the 'old days'.

'Talk about work! You were run off your feet from morning till night, at everyone's beck and call.'

'Of course this isn't work you're doing now,' Julie teased.

'What? This is child's play in comparison!'

Ivy reminisced until Tom came in and asked with an amiable smile if he was to get anything else to eat that day.

During the next few weeks, Julie fitted into her new life, becoming so much a part of it that she felt she had been born amidst it all; the clatter of clogs in a morning, the summoning sound of hooters from factories and potteries, the chatter and ribald laughter of customers at busy times in the shop. And then there were the smells – the dominant aromas of cheese and kerosene, the appetising kitchen smells of peas, browning pastry and cakes cooking and the warm yeasty fragrance when Ivy made a batch of bread.

Lastly, there was the special, earthy smell of the shed with its wedges of clay. Julie had been to the shed again several times, but only when Angus was not there. An urge had developed in her to try her hand at throwing a pot, but it was something she was unwilling to admit to. She kept thinking that if she could see a spare piece of clay she would have a go. But there were only large lumps of clay that looked a uniform size. Perhaps at some stage Angus would suggest she make something and then she could accept, without appearing too keen.

The trouble was, she had hardly seen him during the past few weeks. She was either in the shop when he came in for his meals, or shopping for Ivy. Julie enjoyed going to the butchers because, as well as being able to look in the windows of other shops, she always had a browse around Billy Barker's secondhand store.

He unfailingly gave her a welcome. 'Well, here's me lovely girl to brighten me day! What are you looking for, Precious, another mirror?' His greeting never varied and he always laughed uproariously as he mentioned the mirror, but Julie didn't mind. There was always something exciting about digging into boxes, never knowing quite what you would find. She had bought some little pieces that were ridiculously cheap, like a piece of raspberry glass for Ivy for sixpence and a small, beautifully carved box for threepence, for Tom to put his pills in.

Tom almost wept when he thanked her for his gift. 'It was a lovely thought,' he said. Ivy sniffed when Julie handed her the little basket-shaped piece of raspberry glass and told her she ought to save her money. But Julie could see that she too was pleased with her gift.

Then, one morning when Julie was in Billy's rummaging through one of the boxes of bits and pieces, she came across the miniature. The glass was grimy and she dampened a corner of her handkerchief and wiped it. The next moment she was staring at a young man, dressed in an old-fashioned style, a lock of hair falling over his brow. Billy came up and after his usual greeting looked at the miniature.

'Oh, so you found that, did you? Wondered where it had got to.' He tapped it with a fat forefinger. 'One of my treasures, that is. Couldn't sell it for under five bob.'

Julie looked up. 'He could be my brother Richard's twin. Who is he, do you know?'

'I was told he was the son of an English Earl or a Lord, or some other bigwig. I did know his name –' Billy scratched his head. 'It's on me tongue end, but I can't get it out. Probably remember later. I tell you what, because it's you, I'll let you have it for four and a tanner.'

Julie looked regretful. 'I haven't got that much. I broke two cups and two saucers and a pudding basin last week. Ivy deducted the cost to replace them from my pocket money, which left me with sixpence.'

When Billy exclained, 'The mean cow!' Julie rose in Ivy's defence.

'No, she isn't mean. She warned me to be more careful when I was washing up and told me what would happen if I broke anything.' Julie grinned suddenly. 'It's a good lesson-learner.'

She looked at the miniature again, then up at Billy. 'I'll give you three shillings for it when I get my pocket money on Friday.'

'Four, and you can pay me the other bob the following week.'

'Three, take it or leave it.'

Billy gave a mock groan. 'You've become a regular Scrooge. Take it, before I change me mind.'

Julie gave him a quick hug. 'Thanks, Billy, you're a darling. I must run.'

'And you're a heart-stealer,' he called after her. Julie paused at the door to blow him a kiss, leaving Billy utterly bemused.

Back at the shop, Julie rushed into the kitchen and held out the miniature to Ivy. 'Here, take a look at this, who does he remind you of? It's Richard, isn't it? He could be his double.'

'Oh, Julie, what rubbish have you been buying now?' Ivy wiped her hands down her apron and took the miniature. After studying it for a moment she laid it down. 'I don't see any resemblance at all to your Richard. Well, perhaps a little but nothing to get excited about. Who is he supposed to be, anyway?'

Julie repeated Billy's comments and Ivy gave a derisive laugh. 'Don't you believe a thing Billy Barker tells you, he makes up stories as he goes along. He says today the feller is the son of an Earl or a Lord. If you were to ask him next week I'd like to bet he'd tell you he was a Duke's son.'

Ivy went over to the stove and stirred the contents of a pan. 'Now you'd better take that thing upstairs out of the way. And stop spending your money on bits and pieces! Your bedroom'll be overflowing with knick-knacks, all of them to be dusted.'

Overflowing? Julie thought, feeling indignant. *One* mirror

and *one* miniature. And she didn't care what Ivy said, the young man in the miniature was like Richard. She would show it to Tom later, and see what he said about it. Perhaps she would get him to knock a nail in the wall so she could hang it up.

Julie was trying to find the right spot to hang her prize when Ivy called up the stairs.

'Come on, what're you doing up there? Planning an art gallery?'

Julie threw the miniature onto the bed, ran downstairs and into the kitchen.

'You're making a slave of me! I never get five minutes to myself. You tell me I'm spending my money on rubbish, you make me pay for breakages – I never have any fun, never – I –'

'Hey, hold it a minute. What's brought all this on? What sort of fun had you in mind?'

Julie, who was on the verge of tears, sniffed. 'Well, I hear the girls who come into the shop talking about having been to the pictures, seeing Charlie Chaplin and Theda Bara and – I haven't been to the pictures for *two* years. I thought by coming to live in a town –'

'I can arrange for you to go to the cinema, if that's what's bothering you. Tom can take you one evening. *And* I'll pay for you. Now – are you ready to lend me a hand?'

Julie was all sunny again. 'Oh, yes, Ivy, I'm sorry for blowing off steam, it was just that – I wonder what's on at the Majestic this week . . .'

# Chapter Three

Tom usually went to bed before ten o'clock each evening and was asleep when Ivy came up, but that night he spoke as soon as she came into the bedroom, the flames of the candle casting flickering shadows on the wall.

'You're later than ever, love. What have you been doing?'

'Thinking.' Ivy dampened her fingers and nipped the candle flame before she started to undress. 'It's Julie, she's bothering me. Not because she accused me of being a slave driver but –'

'You do put a lot of work on her shoulders, Ivy.' Tom's tone was gentle.

'I know, but I feel it's necessary. If she wants to live as we do she has to experience everything. No, it's not that, it's all the questions she's started asking. First she wanted to know about the Tiernes and then about Violet. Now it's this resemblance to Richard. The fellow in the little painting is like him, not that I would admit it to her, but she's started probing – she even ran quickly to Billy's earlier on to see if he had remembered who the young chap's father was. Why? Could she suspect something secretive?'

'Oh, come on, Ivy, how could she? It's just any girl's interest at seeing a painting of someone who is like her brother.'

Ivy unhooked the waistband of her skirt, let it fall to the floor then stepped out of it. 'I have a feeling it's more than that. She was eager to know if *you* could see a resemblance to Richard. I was glad when you hedged a bit.'

'I had to when I saw your warning glance. I wasn't quite sure what you wanted me to say. Anyway, stop worrying, Julie will have forgotten the whole thing by tomorrow.'

'Don't you believe it! Julie is like her mother in that respect. Kitty will worry at a problem like a dog gnawing a bone, until she finds the answer. And, if Julie does the same she might unearth the family skeleton. I would hate it for both Kitty and Tyler's sake. And for Richard's too, of course.'

'Now Ivy, that's enough.' Tom for once spoke firmly. 'You're building a mountain out of nothing. Hurry up and finish undressing and get into bed. You get little enough sleep as it is. I thought today you were looking a little peaky.'

Ivy protested vehemently that she was as fit as a fiddle, but she felt touched at her husband's concern. When she got into bed she moved close to him and he put an arm under her shoulder. 'You will stop worrying now, Ivy, won't you, otherwise Julie will have to go home.'

'Oh no, Tom, no. I wouldn't want that. I might be a bit hard on her, but I love that girl and I would miss her if she went back home now.'

'So would I,' Tom said quietly. 'She's a lovely, warm-hearted girl who has the knack of making you feel you're important to her, that she's a part of the family. I hope she stays with us for a long time.'

Ivy said she hoped so too, and felt an ache that she had not been able to give Tom any children. He would have made such a good father. But there, she had been lucky he had come back from the war at all, so she must be thankful for that mercy.

In the room at the end of the small landing Julie lay in her narrow bed listening to the muted voices of Tom and Ivy. It was unusual for them to be talking at this time of night.

Were they discussing the miniature? When Julie had first seen the resemblance between the young man and her brother she had thought it to be just one of those strange coincidences in life, but Ivy's reaction had turned it into a mystery. After saying firmly she could see no likeness whatsoever to Richard in the miniature, she had kept stealing glances at it. Then there had been her warning glance at Tom when he had been asked his opinion. Oh yes, there was a mystery all right.

Julie had thought it might have something to do with the Tiernes, but her quick return visit to Billy Barker had squashed this idea. Although he had still not remembered the name of the young man's family, he was definite it was not Tierne. Julie decided she would ask her parents when next she saw them, and demand to know about the secrets in their lives.

This subject dispensed with, she began to think of the promised visit to the pictures. Tomorrow she must find out what was on at the various cinemas . . .

About the time Julie was dreaming of the film she would see, she herself was under discussion in Crescent House. Kitty van Neilson was saying to her husband, as they got ready for bed, 'Tyler, you really must read Julie's letter. It's so funny. Who would have thought that our rebel daughter would be thrilled at receiving the gift of a cheap mirror and overjoyed with a one-eyed teddy bear she had bought for sixpence – *and* which had to be washed in case of fleas?'

Tyler van Neilson chuckled. 'I don't believe it.'

'It's true!' Kitty waved the letter at him. 'It's all here. She says she works hard, but she enjoys it – and Ivy bears this out. Ivy says she's astonished at how Julie has adapted. Apparently, she washes up, scrubs, dusts, helps with the cooking, and not one complaint.'

Tyler slipped his arms into his blue silk pyjama top. 'It

seems incredible, doesn't it? I thought she would have been running back home after a week.'

'So did I.' Kitty was suddenly serious. 'Why should living with Ivy and Tom hold such an attraction for her?'

'The novelty of change, Kitty. When I was young I used to stay now and again, during school holidays, with an aunt and uncle. My aunt had scant time for children and my uncle less, yet I enjoyed myself. It was the change of scenery, meeting different people. It was a feeling of freedom away from parental control. Yet my aunt and uncle were fairly strict.'

Tyler buttoned up his jacket slowly, his expression thoughtful. 'Do you know something, Kitty? I imagined I would enjoy the peace and quiet without our wayward daughter and our effervescent son, yet I miss them both terribly. At times when I come home and you are not here either the place is like a morgue.'

Kitty nodded. 'I know what you mean. And yet, if I had to start our married life all over again I don't think I could do it any other way. I would still want to be involved in glass-making.'

'Hey, we're getting morbid.' Tyler threw back the bedcovers and gave her a wicked grin. 'How about consoling one another?'

'There's nothing I would like better at this moment,' Kitty said softly and held up her arms to him.

The following morning while Ivy was bustling around the kitchen she said to Julie, 'I asked Angus if he would take you to the pictures this evening and he's agreed. I decided that the atmosphere would be too smoky for Tom.'

Julie, who had been spooning porridge from the pan on the hob to her plate, paused and looked over her shoulder. 'Angus? Does he want to take me? I mean to say, he has his pottery to do.'

'He said he would take you and he wouldn't have done so if he hadn't wanted to. Hurry up and get your breakfast, you'll have to nip down to Georgie Fletcher's. He's forgotten to put the kidney in with the meat. And don't you linger on the way and start looking in Billy Barker's.'

'Oh, we are in a bad temper this morning, aren't we,' Julie teased. And had the handle of the carving knife thumped on the table in front of her.

'I am *not* in a bad temper! It just annoys me that anyone could forget an item for an order that's been regular for so long. It's sheer inefficiency. When I see him, I'll give him a piece of my mind.'

Julie touched her hand. 'What's worrying you, Ivy? Is it Tom, has he had a bad night?'

'No.' The anger went from Ivy. 'It's just a few other things. Forget it. When you pour yourself a cup of tea pour one for me.' Ivy got on with her tasks.

It was a bitterly cold morning with a sleet-laden rain stinging Julie's cheeks as she ran to the butcher's but it could have been a sunny morning she felt so excited. She was going to the pictures – and with Angus. 'Going with a feller,' as the girls from the pottery would say. She must ask them when they came in what films they had seen that week. Not that it really mattered – it would be lovely to see any picture.

Although it was not yet seven o'clock all the shops were open on the way and there were six or more customers in the butcher's. Julie, not wanting to keep Ivy waiting for the kidney, spoke to the elderly assistant, explaining what had happened.

One of the shawled women said, her tone amiable, 'Take your bloody turn, Julie, we're all in a hurry.'

Julie said eagerly, 'Have any of you been to the pictures this week? Is there a Charlie Chaplin film on anywhere? I've never ever seen him.'

The fact of Julie being served before her turn was

forgotten in the consternation of her never having seen a Charlie Chaplin film.

'What? Never?' exclaimed one woman. 'Oh, gal, you don't know what you're missing. *The Kid*'s on at the Majestic this week, you *must* see it.'

Another woman said, 'I've seen it three times, you'll laugh your head off and cry your eyes out. That little Jackie Coogan's a lovely actor, and when Charlie finds him abandoned when he's a baby, oh –'

The women were all adding comments now. 'And didn't Charlie love him! He was just a tramp but he brought him up proper, saw he was clean and said his prayers . . .'

'I tell you the part that fair pulled me heart out,' said an older woman. 'The part when Edna Purviance had to give the baby away. She couldn't keep it, see, she wasn't married and had no money. Oh, I cried and cried . . .'

The butcher's boy said earnestly to Julie, 'But it wasn't her who left the baby in all the rubbish. She put it in this big fancy car, wanting a good home for it, but then the crooks came and –'

The butcher, who had been standing watching them with some amusement, arms folded, interrupted with, 'If you folks are going to go through the whole film I'll just nip into the back and have a fag.'

Oh, no, they all wanted serving. And now! They'd be late.

Julie picked up the parcel of kidney and thanked the women for the information, adding, 'We are going to the cinema this evening so I hope we can see that film. I can't wait to know what happens.'

She was at the door when one of the women called, 'Who's taking you, love?'

'Me feller!' Julie went out laughing.

She ran all the way back to the shop, wanting to know if Ivy had seen the film, but Ivy hadn't and said she had no idea whether Angus had seen it or not. So, Julie was forced to wait until Angus came in for his evening meal. When he did arrive he said, 'So we're going to the pictures tonight. It'll have to be second house, I have some work to do.'

There was such a lack of interest in his voice that Julie felt annoyed. 'You don't have to take me if you don't want to. There's plenty of others who would be glad of my company. Cal Coates for one.'

'He's the last one Ivy would let you go with. If you want to go I'll take you. Make your mind up.'

Although Julie was fuming at his attitude and wanted to refuse she knew she would be reluctant to admit the following day she had not seen the film after all.

'I want to go.' She spoke quietly. 'And if you are agreeable, I would like to see the Charlie Chaplin film at the Regal. It's called *The Kid*.'

'That's no problem. Be ready at half-seven.' Angus went into the scullery and she could hear the tap running. Then Ivy came in from the shop to serve Angus his meal and Julie went to help Tom.

They were quite busy but Tom sent her off to get changed in plenty of time. It took her a good ten minutes to decide what to wear. She wanted to look nice but not too expensively dressed.

Eventually, she settled for a grey pleated skirt and a white, finely-knit jumper under a simply-cut grey coat with a velvet collar. After further debate she topped it with a white peaked knitted cap.

Ivy gave her a nod of approval. 'You have class but you're not overdressed.'

Julie, who had not seen Angus in anything but working clothes, stared at him when he came down, looking madly attractive in a brown suit with white shirt and brown tie under a trenchcoat. The brim of his brown trilby hat was pulled down at the front, giving him a slightly rakish look and reminding her of a film star she had seen once in a magazine.

Meg Jenkins, who came in just at that moment beamed

from one to the other. 'Going to the pictures then, I hear. Lovely you look the pair of you. It'll be circle seats tonight, I suppose.'

'No Meg, the stalls.' Angus spoke kindly. 'And we'd better be going.' Tom told them to have a good time. Ivy warned them not to be too late back.

Although Julie had been out many times in the early morning darkness, with the shops all open, the windows lighted and the streets busy, there was a different feeling coming out in the evening to the same scene. There was no clatter of clogs and people were wearing different clothes. The women had replaced their shawls with coats and hats, and most of the men had exchanged their morning mufflers for a shirt and tie.

The weather was better, too. The rain had stopped and although the gaslamps were reflected in the still damp pavements the sky was clear with a sprinkling of stars. Julie kept hoping that some of the customers would see her walking out with Angus but so far there had been no greetings.

'How are your legs?' Angus asked suddenly.

'What?' Julie looked at him, startled. 'My legs?'

'Do you feel like walking or do you want to take the tram?'

'Oh, walk.' How romantic, she thought wryly. Yet could think of nothing more enlightening to talk about than the weather. She remarked how good it was that the rain had stopped and that it was nice to see the stars come out. Angus said, yes it was, and that was that. After walking a short distance in silence Julie stopped abruptly.

'Look, let's go back home. It's obvious it's an ordeal taking me to the pictures. I can go some other time.'

'You wanted to see Charlie Chaplin, didn't you? And that's where we're going.'

'Not if you're going to be bored to death!'

'Listen, I've never seen *The Kid*. I *want* to see it, does that satisfy you? If I'm quiet it's because I've had a bad day at work. I spoilt several plates I was painting and that's a rarity for me.'

Julie eyed him in surprise. 'You paint plates? I thought you made pots.'

'Only for my own satisfaction. It's a hobby, a relief thing. It can be trying, painting plate after plate, day in and day out.'

'I do painting,' she said, 'but only spasmodically – when the mood takes me.'

'Lucky you.' Angus put a hand under her elbow. 'Come on, the second house will be going in soon.'

They heard the rise and fall of voices and small bursts of laughter before they reached the cinema. A shabbily-dressed man was standing in the gutter, making circles with his left hand to encourage a small dog to do somersaults. The man's right arm was missing and a wooden stump replaced his left leg. No doubt a veteran of the war. This incident and Angus' mood took some of the shine from Julie's earlier pleasure at the thought of a visit to the cinema.

As they walked along the line of waiting people to go to the back of the queue Angus was greeted by a number of people. One man, with a saucy wink at Julie began to chant, 'Who, who, who's your lady friend?'

Angus just raised a hand acknowledging the greetings, but went on walking. When they reached the end of the queue they found themselves standing behind Peg Smith and a fair-haired man in a raincoat that had seen better days.

Peg looked Angus up and down then laughed. 'Get him! All done up like a dog's dinner.' To Julie she added, 'Hey, how'd you get Angus Mac to take you out?'

'Sheer bribery and corruption.'

Peg's companion, his expression solemn said, 'I could do wi' a bit of corruption meself.'

Peg jerked a thumb at him. 'This is Alf. The life and soul of every party!'

She looked different this evening in a dark green coat and a red tam-o'-shanter – pretty, pert.

The man with the performing dog came along the line of people, his cap held out. Most of them, including Angus, dropped in a copper. Alf said, 'Poor bugger, he's never done a day's work since the war.'

A man in front called over his shoulder, 'You don't need to feel sorry for 'im, mate. He's here six nights a week, both houses *and* matinées. Bet he makes a hell of a lot more than the likes of me.'

'But you have both your arms and legs,' Angus said quietly.

Then there was a shout of, 'They're coming out!' and the people began to move up as the first house patrons spilled out of the cinema.

Peg said, 'I reckon you two'll be going in the posh end. Me and Alf'll be in the pit. Perhaps we'll see you afterwards for a cuppa at Lil Firth's. She keeps open till midnight.'

'Probably will,' Angus said, but he did not sound too enthusiastic.

The man with the dog had further depressed Julie but once inside the cinema her early-morning excitement returned. For seconds it was like a glorious madhouse with everyone pushing and shoving to get the best seats for viewing. Some seats were placed behind pillars. The cheaper seats were of wood and as the previous patrons had tipped them all up on leaving there was a continuous bang, bang, bang, right along the rows. The seats in the stalls were red plush and the dropping of them a little more subdued. Angus led Julie to the front row of the stalls, where there was a wide division between them and the pit, saying it gave him more room to stretch his long legs.

Overall a buzz of chatter mingled with the rustle of paper bags of sweets. A stale smell of cigarette and tobacco smoke mingled with that of oranges.

When there was a sudden burst of applause Julie realised it was for the man who was going to play the piano. Angus said, his tone slightly scathing, 'Now we'll hear *Hearts and Flowers* and *Entry of the Gladiators.*'

Julie glanced at him. 'I don't think you're going to get much enjoyment out of this evening.'

'I'll enjoy just sitting back and relaxing.'

'How romantic,' Julie said dryly. 'You might just as well be sitting with a wooden plank beside you.'

'What did you expect me to do – take you in the back seats and fumble you?'

Colour rushed to her face. She said in a low, furious voice, 'How vulgar you are.' She got up. 'I'm leaving.'

He pushed her back in the seat. 'Sit down. Stop being so childish. I thought you would have been used to a bit of plain speaking. You're not living with the filthy rich now, you know.'

'The filthy rich, as you call them, do at least have manners. Not one would have used that word to me.'

Julie sat tense. If only he had said touch her, or caress her. There had been boys who had touched her breasts. But although it had sent her pulses racing she had refused to let them go any further. She felt suddenly miserable at the spoiling of her night out and when the *Pathé News* came on she took no interest in it.

Angus found it impossible to concentrate, either. He was annoyed with himself for having said what he did. It was something he would not have said to any other girl – so why had he done so to Julie? Was it because she gave him a feeling of inferiority? Not that she put on any airs and graces. There was a sweetness about her, a naturalness . . . Deep down, he admired her for the way she had met every demand Ivy made of her, without complaint. Apart that is, from when she had exploded and called Ivy a slave driver. It was Ivy who had begged him to give Julie a night out. And what had he done but ruin it for her by his stupid remark.

He wanted to say he was sorry but the words stuck in his throat. It was Gwen who had changed him, made him hard.

He had been so crazy about her and he'd thought she felt the same way about him. But the bitch had been two-timing him, seeing another bloke on the nights they had not been together. *And* sleeping with him. He couldn't believe it. There had been such an innocence about her, and a wide-eyed wonder at anything new.

Angus realised then that this was why he was so down on Julie. She had the same wide-eyed wonder look. But there was more character in Julie's face. She could stand up for herself and she could also be hurt . . . not like Gwen who didn't give a damn that she had devastated him.

He stole a look at Julie. She had a crumpled look, as though someone had kicked her into a corner. He reached out a hand and laid it over hers. 'I'm sorry, Julie.'

In the flickering light of the screen he could see tears glinting in her eyes. 'It's all right,' she said. 'I know you didn't mean it.'

Angus felt then he had taken the first few steps away from the memory of Gwen.

The *News* had ended and there followed a short film about people at work in a bottle factory. Then came *The Kid* and Julie sat up, knowing now she would enjoy the film whatever it was. Angus had made his peace with her.

Right from the beginning of the film Julie found herself transported into another world of comedy and pathos. She laughed with the rest of the audience when Charlie, who was wearing gloves with big holes in them, took cigarette ends from an empty sardine tin, cried when Edna Purviance left the baby she loved in the big automobile and booed the crooks who stole the car but left the baby among a lot of rubbish.

Julie just knew that the little man with the funny walk would find the baby and bring it up. She lived every moment of their lives, including Edna's, feeling joyful that she had the lovely flower shop, and longing for her to get together with Charlie and her own little son.

After a lot of trials they did, but the end left Julie wondering and she couldn't wait to ask Angus what he thought of the outcome.

Although a few of the younger people sneaked out before the playing of the *National Anthem*, the majority stayed and Julie, in an emotional state after the film, felt a lump come into her throat. But once the music ended there was a concerted rush for the exits. Angus and Julie were caught up in the mêlée, yet despite the crush Peg and Alf managed to find them. They went to the little café and when they had their cups of tea Peg said to Julie, 'Well, and what did you think of the film?'

'I thought it was wonderful. I laughed, I cried, ached for Edna and loved Charlie and little Jackie Coogan. When Charlie disappeared at the end I was *willing* him to come back. Surely he would – I *do* hope so.'

Peg gave a nod. 'He'd come back, I know it. He couldn't stay away, could he? I mean to say – he loved Edna and Jackie and they loved him.'

Alf appealed to Angus. 'What d'ye make of this daft pair? They're treating the whole thing as if it was true, as if the actors were real people.'

Julie said they were to her and Peg agreed with her. Angus commented, 'Well, Julie, if you want to take it as a real slice of life then Charlie wouldn't come back. He was a tramp, Edna had money. He loved them both but made the sacrifice by leaving them, knowing he wouldn't fit into their lives.'

'Why shouldn't he?' Peg exclaimed. 'Edna had been poor once and Charlie knew they both loved him.'

Alf flung up his hands with a despairing gesture. 'He was a tramp, for God's sake, and always would be. He scavenged in dustbins. Don't you remember him picking cigarette butts out of a sardine can?'

Julie, who had been stirring her tea as she listened, dropped the spoon into her saucer with a clatter.

'Yes, but he wore *gloves* –'

'– with great big holes in them!'

'It showed he was fastidious,' she said earnestly, 'proved he would like better things. He did all sorts of jobs to get money to bring up little Jackie. He could adjust to Edna's way of life, I know it. I think it was a very clever film, with subtle undertones.'

Angus eyed Julie in a speculative way. Peg and Alf stared at her. Alf said, 'Clever? Subtle undertones? It was supposed to be a bloody comedy and it was to me! I laughed me head off, especially when the kid broke windows so that Charlie could replace them and get paid for the job.'

'That was subtle, too,' Julie said. 'It showed the boy's understanding of Charlie, his need to be independent. It was a way of showing his love without words.'

Alf said to Angus, 'You've got a right gal here, mate. I was going to suggest the four of us going to the flicks together next week, but I wouldn't want the film analysed afterwards, thank you very much.'

'Julie made some interesting points.' Angus spoke quietly, his gaze on her still speculative.

Julie laughed. 'Alf, I promise if we meet again I won't pass any remark about the film. I got carried away this evening!'

Peg, who had seemed a little bewildered with Julie's comments, now looked relieved. 'Oh, great, it'll be nice to have a foursome. Hey, how about us coming here next Thursday? *The Mark of Zorro* is on. I've seen it before but I'd like to see it again. It's all duelling and leaping about and Douglas Fairbanks is lovely, with swarthy skin, dark velvety eyes and he's all muscle. Oooh, I'd give me eye teeth for a night out with him!'

Angus got up. 'We'll discuss it another time. We must go now, Ivy warned us not to be late. Ready, Julie?'

They left Alf and Peg in the café, with Peg wanting to make arrangements with Alf to meet him on the Saturday evening.

As they walked along the now quieter streets Angus said,

'I'm not too keen about making up foursomes. Peg's all right, but Alf's a bit of a hothead. Still, I suppose it'll be all right to go with them next week. That is, if you'd like to go, Julie?'

'I'd love to! I only hope Ivy will agree to letting me go.'

'She will, knowing you're with me.' It was said more as a statement than a boast and Julie glanced at him. 'Did *you* enjoy the film, Angus?'

'Yes, I did, and I was interested in your remarks about there being subtle undertones in the film. You're quite perceptive – it was something I didn't expect.'

'You don't mince your words, do you?' Julie spoke tartly. 'What did you expect me to be, a featherbrain? Not that I'm clever academically, far from it, I –'

'Stop demeaning yourself. You've proved you're a capable girl by the way you've worked at Ivy's.'

Julie liked the way he said the word 'girl', as though there were three 'R's in it. She smiled at him. 'Well, that's life. Seeing the film tonight was a treat, because I'd been working hard. You really appreciate your pleasures, then.'

Angus put a hand under her elbow and urged her forward. 'Yes, well don't let yourself get too carried away by all these new discoveries. Alf works hard but he doesn't get much pleasure out of anything. Oh, he laughed at Charlie, but by tomorrow he'll be grumbling about everything under the sun. He's a born grumbler. I don't know why Peg goes out with him. She's a cheerful lass.'

'Opposites often get on. They strike a balance. Alf might grumble a lot more if he didn't have Peg. Right?'

'If you say so, but I think we've had enough psychology for one evening. It's nearly eleven o'clock and Ivy will be wondering where we are.'

As he began to hurry Julie had to take running steps to keep up with him. She said, 'Well, you can tell her we haven't been lingering under the stars!'

'It's not a pastime of mine.'

Julie wanted to snap, 'That's obvious,' but had no breath. By the time they neared the shop she had to slow down for a stitch in her side. She glared at Angus. 'It's the first time I've been out with a man and had to compete in a race against the clock.' Angus made no reply to this, but pushed her in front of him along the entry by the side of the shop and they went in the back way.

Julie, who had been fully expecting a reprimand from Ivy for being late was surprised when she greeted them amiably and asked how they had enjoyed the film. She was standing with her back to the fire, her fingers encircling a steaming mug of cocoa.

It was Angus who answered. 'We both enjoyed it, but I had to suffer a lesson in psychology afterwards from Miss Julietta van Neilson.' His tone was so scathing that Julie looked at him in bewilderment.

Ivy put down her own mug then began to pour boiling water into two mugs on the table with spoons in them. Angus said, 'Nothing for me, Ivy, thank you. I'm away to bed. Goodnight to the both of you.'

Julie stood listening to Angus' firm tread on the stairs. Ivy sugared the cocoa, added a spoonful of condensed milk, stirred it and passed the mug to Julie.

'What's put *him* out? What have you been saying to him?'

'Nothing. I just don't understand him. He was a bit snappy with me in the cinema, then he apologised and after that he was quite nice.'

'The trouble with Angus is, he likes you – but he doesn't want you or anyone else to know he does.'

Julie looked more bewildered than ever. 'Why not?'

'He probably thinks it's a sign of weakness to show his feelings. Some men like to appear tough, but many of them are as soft as mud inside. Angus has his tender side, all right. I saw him once with an animal that had been hurt, and he was just like a woman as he soothed it.'

Julie knew then why she had thought Angus different

when she had first met him. Although his face had a rough-hewn look, he had a tender mouth. Yes, that was it.

Ivy took her empty mug over to the sink and rinsed it. 'You haven't told me about the film, Julie, but I'll hear about it tomorrow. It's time we went to bed. Hurry up and drink your cocoa.'

Julie lay awake for a long time, mulling over the events of the evening, and in retrospect seeing things that had not completely registered with her until now. Peg's face, as she listened to Angus talking, a starry look in her eyes. Was she in love with him? Julie could understand it if she was. The pale-faced Alf compared very unfavourably with the strong-featured Angus.

And then Julie could hear the gentleness in Angus' voice when he apologised in low tones for using the word 'fumble' to her. She had a feeling it was not a word he would normally use. If so, why had he used it to her? Was there a feeling of aggression in him, like some people have against those of a different class – a desire to hurt?

Angus had made the point that Charlie would not want to marry Edna because she had money. They wouldn't mix, he had said. Had he been trying to tell her not to get any ideas about him because he was working-class and she came from a wealthy family? But if so, why had he more or less agreed to make up a foursome to go to the cinema again next week? Julie snuggled down in the bed. Why worry, it was something to look forward to.

As Ivy had once said, 'The past can't be altered, so live each day as it comes.'

# Chapter Four

The following morning, by first post, Julie had a letter from her parents, saying they were going to America on business for a week or ten days. Ivy had a letter from them, too. Kitty had written: '*I've given Ivy an address where she can get in touch with us, Julie, should any emergency arise.*' Tyler had written: '*I hope you're managing on your pocket money – being my girl, I feel sure you will. I'll bring you a nice present back from America. When we do come back we shall probably pay you a visit. Your mother will have more to say about this.*'

The letter was composed of paragraphs from each of them. Kitty enlarged on the proposed visit to Stoke. '*It will be so good to see Ivy and Tom again, and of course you, Julie. Both your father and I miss you terribly. But we won't bring you home with us unless you want to come. That I promise. According to your letters you seem happy enough. I will write to you from New York. Take care of yourself, much love, Mother.*' Tyler had signed it too, '*with love from Daddy.*'

'So they're going to America,' Ivy said, having finished reading her letter. 'And then talking about coming to see us. Now that would be lovely! I'd have to get in extra help, mind you, because your mother and me will have so much to talk about.' She grinned. 'You, Julie, don't know the half of what went on in our young lives.'

'No,' Julie said quietly, 'I don't.'

Ivy folded the letter and put it in her apron pocket. 'I'll let

Tom read it later, he'll be pleased to hear the news. Now I must get these peas on.'

Julie wasn't sure that she wanted her parents to come to Stoke. It had taken time for the customers to accept her. None of them owned motor cars. If her parents drove up in her father's big limousine it would certainly spoil her image of being a 'working girl'. Julie decided she would have to try and think up some excuse to put them off. But then, of course, Ivy and Tom would be disappointed.

Julie was still thinking of her problem when the second post arrived, containing a letter from Richard. Although he mentioned his parents' visit abroad he did so only briefly. The main point of his letter was to answer the one Julie had sent him, expressing her envy of his life in London and saying how she was longing to see all the places he mentioned.

'*How about coming for a visit?*' he wrote. '*I can promise you plenty of fun and sightseeing. If you can manage the fare it won't cost you anything otherwise. (I would have offered to pay your fare, but am running a bit short at the moment, so much to see and do.) Can you manage to get away for a long weekend? Far better to live it up for a few days than pare down the social side for a longer visit.*'

There was more about what he and Jake had been doing, where they had been and who they had met, then a postscript had been added.

'*Jake's aunt, who lives near, would be willing to put you up. So there's no problem there . . .*'

London? It would be marvellous. Julie sat dreamy-eyed for a moment then Tom looked in to say there was a bit of a rush on, would Julie lend a hand?

When the rush had ended and the shop was empty Julie told Tom about her parents' business trip to America then about Richard's offer to show her around London.

Tom's eyebrows went up. 'London? Now that would be a nice change for you, Julie. You'd enjoy it.'

'I would! I've wanted to go for some time, but I can see all the snags. There's the train fare for one thing – I couldn't manage it on three shillings a week pocket money, with some of it already owing to Ivy for breakages.' Julie grinned. 'I'm still ham-fisted where washing up is concerned. Then it would mean leaving you and Ivy without my help.'

Tom dismissed this as no problem. There was always an odd neighbour who would be willing to help. As for the train fare, well, he would be willing to lend it to her.

'I'm saying lend, Julie, because I know you wouldn't want it any other way. There's no need to say anything to Ivy about it.'

'It's very kind of you, Tom, but I don't think Ivy will be very pleased that I want to go to London.'

When Julie stood, twisting the corner of her pinafore between her fingers he said encouragingly, 'So what else is bothering you, love?'

'It's my parents.' She told him about their proposed visit to Stoke and why she had no wish for them to come, adding, 'If only they didn't have such an ostentatious-looking car. Richard drives around in his friend's car, which he calls a banger – I don't know why but –'

'It'll be because of the noise the exhaust makes.'

'I see, well, it makes it seem shabby somehow. The people round here I'm sure would accept that and accept Richard too because he can get on with anyone. He's so easy, so friendly.'

'Julie, stop worrying, love. The customers like you for *yourself*. They know you've come from a wealthy background, but they've accepted you as one of them. You don't give yourself any airs and graces.'

Julie sighed. 'Richard enjoys coming from a wealthy background, but I don't.'

'It's given you a lot of advantages,' Tom said quietly.

Julie studied him, as though weighing up his words then explained earnestly, 'Let me put it this way, Tom. In the past, I've enjoyed the comfort which money did give me, but after experiencing this kind of life I know I like it better. I feel there's more purpose to it.'

'That's because you've never known any *real* poverty, Julie. And by that I mean when a family has no food in the house and no means of getting any. This does happen and in this district, too. It's heartbreaking. But there,' Tom smiled suddenly, 'I'm moving right away from the immediate subject and that is, getting you to London. As I said, I'll speak to Ivy about it.'

Because Julie wanted to get a letter off to Richard as soon as possible she was impatient to know Ivy's reaction but it was two hours later before the subject was broached.

Ivy, looking tight-lipped, was busy making bread when she said, 'So, what's all this then about you wanting to go to London? You haven't been here five minutes before you want another change. What do you think your Mam and Dad would have to say if anything happened to you?'

Julie, who had been prepared to do battle with Ivy, raised her head in a defiant way. 'What could happen?'

'You could be knocked down by one of them London buses, or a motor car.' Ivy kneaded the dough, pummelled it, cut it into pieces and began shaping them to go into the tins. 'All sorts of things could happen in a big city.'

Julie pointed out that she could just as easily be knocked down in Stoke. Ivy told her this was not her only objection. What about this woman she would be staying with? What did Julie know about her?

'She *is* Jake's aunt and his family are wealthy, so –'

Ivy looked up. 'Oh, I thought you wanted to get away from the upper crust. Isn't that why you came here?'

Julie, who was getting more and more annoyed, snapped, 'If the only way I can get to London is being chaperoned by a wealthy woman then I accept the terms!'

'Typical, isn't it. You came here saying you wanted to be with the working people, to know how they lived. But all you wanted was a change and slumming to you *was* a change. That was it, wasn't it?'

'No, it wasn't! And I think you're being most unfair. I'm sixteen and in all that time the only change I've ever had in my life was coming here. Well, I no longer want to go to London now. You've taken all the pleasure out of even the thought of it. So, tell me what job you want doing next. I've filled up all the shelves in the shop, I've changed the beds, brought the dirty linen down, I've dusted, swept the floors, washed the dishes, helped to make the pies –'

'I could smack your face.' Ivy put two of the loaf tins in the hearth to rise then turned swiftly. 'And I would do had you been my own daughter and she was speaking to me in that manner!'

'Well – why don't you slap me? Mother told you to treat me as if I were your own. Go on, hit me, but stop punishing me because I want to go to London. And if you no longer want me here I'll go up and pack my case.'

'Oh, stop being so melodramatic. Of course I don't want you to leave, and not because of the work you do.' Ivy put the rest of the loaf tins in the hearth and threw a cloth over them. 'You forget that while you're living here Tom and I are responsible for you. There's a lot more could happen to you than being knocked down by a bus or a motor car.'

'Like being seduced?' Julie, who had been near to tears now felt a smile trembling on her lips. Ivy would never admit in so many words that she had affection for her, but it was there.

'And what do you know, Miss, about being seduced?'

'Enough to know I would never let it happen to me.'

'Oh, yes, it's very easy to talk big until such a situation arises. But see you remember when you go to London what you've just said to me.'

'When I go to – Oh, Ivy!' Julie, overjoyed, gave her a hug. 'Thanks, thanks a million. I won't let you down, I promise.'

'But only for a few days mind,' Ivy warned. 'And stop

fussing. You can get some potatoes peeled. There's plenty of jobs to be done.'

At that moment Julie would not have cared if she had been ordered to clean the house from top to bottom. *London.* She must get a letter off to Richard as soon as possible.

When the potatoes were done she nipped into the shop to tell Tom. They laughed together, both gleeful. Tom said, 'I felt sure that Ivy would give in.'

Julie wondered what Angus would say when he came home at two o'clock for his meal. If Richard could arrange things quickly for her visit, it might mean her missing the next trip to the cinema with him. Would Angus be disappointed? She still found it difficult to weigh him up.

When he did come in Julie was busy in the shop and afterwards when she was free she found he had gone into the shed. Ivy tut-tutted. 'Those pots! As I've said before, and I'll say it again, they come between him and his wits.' She poured tea into a mug, milked and sugared it and held the mug out to Julie. 'He wouldn't wait for a drink. Take that to him, will you, it's freezing out there. Put a shawl over you and don't stay gossiping!'

There was a layer of ice on the water butt in the yard and ice ferns on the shed windows. Julie knocked and went in. Angus, who was wedging clay looked up. Julie held out the mug of tea.

'Ivy sent you this. She said you were too impatient to wait for it.'

'I didn't particularly want a drink, but thanks.' His manner was cool. 'I hear you're off on a visit to London.'

'Yes, I don't know when, but I may not be able to go with you and Peg and Alf to the Majestic on Thursday.'

'That's no hardship. I wasn't keen on going, anyway.'

'Oh, thank you *very* much. It's lovely to be told by a man he was only doing you a favour by arranging to take you out. Well, I can tell you this, Mr MacLaren, you don't need to do *me* any favours in the future.' Julie turned swiftly to leave but Angus caught hold of her arm.

'Calm down. You didn't let me explain. I meant it was no hardship to be denied the company of Alf and Peg, especially Alf. I prefer a twosome. Perhaps when you come back from London we can arrange something.'

Julie gave a noncommittal, 'Perhaps', and was again on the point of leaving when Angus added, 'I noticed you slipping into the shed one afternoon. Did you want to have a go at making a pot?'

Julie looked at him in surprise.'I thought you were at work when I went in.' Although she had wanted to have a go on the wheel she denied her intentions. 'No, I have no interest in making anything. I just wanted to see what you were making.'

Angus, unexpectedly, threw her a piece of clay. 'Go on, see what you can make of that.' Julie dropped the clay onto the bench, repeating she was not interested in pot-making. Angus picked it up again and threw it back at her. 'Feel it, make a ball of it, dig your thumbs into it, shape it, you'll find it soothing, relaxing.'

'I don't need to be soothed or relaxed, thank you,' she retorted. But even as she spoke she was shaping the clay in her hands. She took it to the bench, pressed her thumbs into it, making a hollow. Then she began to draw the clay up at the sides between thumbs and forefingers, and as a shape began to form she had an odd feeling that the clay was alive and she was controlling its destiny. She worked swiftly and produced a bowl. It was crude but she felt satisfaction at producing a shape.

'Not bad,' Angus said. 'You'll have to have a go on the wheel.'

'I can't at the moment. Ivy told me not to stay gossiping and I must keep in her good books, otherwise I might not get to London.'

Angus turned from her and continued wedging the clay.

'You disappoint me, Julietta van Neilson. If you knew Ivy really well you would know she would never go back on her word.'

Colour rushed into Julie's cheeks. Hadn't he realised she was smiling as she made the remark, that it was intended as a joke? Why was he always so critical of her? She stood hesitant for a moment, wanting to explain it was a joke, then decided that explanations would only make it worse. Without another word she left.

Angus slapped down the lump of clay. There he was again, making snide remarks. What the devil was the matter with him? Why was he forever wanting to hurt her? He knew why. He had been looking forward to taking her out the following week and now she could be in London. Angus became impatient with himself, saying aloud, 'For God's sake, man, pull yourself together, she's only going for a few days.'

But it made no difference. Julie had really got under his skin.

Later, Ivy came out to ask him if he would bring a sack of potatoes and one of carrots into the shop. Angus dragged them in from the yard and stayed chatting to Tom, but kept one eye on Julie at the same time.

She was packaging currants and had become adept at it.

'You're quite the expert,' he said.

'I'm glad you've found *something* good about me,' she snapped.

Tom looked questioningly at Angus and Angus raised his shoulders. 'I don't know what's wrong with her. But you know women, they're not happy unless they can have a go now and again at us men.'

Julie came up and stood, hands on hips, glaring at him. 'You know perfectly well what's wrong with me, Angus MacLaren. You knew I was joking when I was in the shed, but no, you had to make me sound mean. You seem to revel in trying to take me down a peg or two. I don't know why – I've never said anything nasty to you!'

Angus said, grinning at Tom, 'She's cheeking me, Tom. What am I going to do with her? Put her over my knee and give her a good skelping?'

'Just you try it,' Julie warned, then she backed away as Angus moved slowly towards her. 'Now just you stay where you are, Angus MacLaren or else.' He reached out to her and Julie ran round the counter. Angus was chasing her with Julie yelping and laughing when Ivy came into the shop. She banged a fist on the counter.

'What d'ye think you're doing the pair of you? Acting like a couple of kids! Julie, you come here. Angus, you'd better get back to your shed.' Angus stayed.

Julie came round the counter and stood, her expression defiant. Ivy said, 'And you needn't look at me like that. For two pins I'd stop you going to London.'

'I don't think you will,' Angus said quietly. 'I've just told Julie you're a woman of your word. The fault was mine, for I was teasing her, promising her a good skelping for something she said to me.'

'I think you both want a good skelping,' Ivy retorted. 'There'll be no more shenanikans like this in the shop, is that understood?'

Both Julie and Angus agreed. Julie was now subdued. Angus said he would be getting back to his pots. He gave Julie a surreptitious wink and she acknowledged it with a brief smile. Angus then left and Ivy followed him.

Tom chuckled. 'It reminded me of when Ivy and I were courting and we'd have a bit of love play. Oh, yes, Ivy has a lot of fun in her, although she doesn't give people that impression. And Angus has fun in him too, which he's just proved, but I think it's been suppressed. He's had a hard life. *He* didn't tell me, it was a customer who used to know the family. Oh, I'll have to tell you later, here comes Mrs Oates. She'll buy two ounces of butter and want half an hour's conversation, poor soul.'

Julie didn't learn any more of Angus' life that day, but she did feel she was beginning to understand him a little better. Tom had given her a reason when he mentioned 'fun being suppressed' because of the hard life he had led. She was learning a lot of things. There were some children who had perky little faces and cheerful grins, but there were a lot more who seemed unable to smile and had young-old faces.

Angus did not go out that evening. Ivy said it was the first time he had stayed in for weeks. She was none too pleased at having him sat in the kitchen reading a newspaper. He was in the way of the oven, she grumbled. When he moved she complained she was unable to get round the table without falling over his legs. Angus took it all in good part. Once he teased her, 'Ivy, you wouldn't be wanting me to sit out in the back yard now, would you?'

'Well, you would at least be out of my way,' she retorted. 'Why don't you go and make some pots?'

Angus said because he was not in the mood and moved once more, to sit on a three-legged stool by the fireplace. He was not in anyone's way so there could be no complaint, but Ivy remarked with a sniff that he looked like a giant gnome sitting on a baby toadstool. This had Angus laughing and telling her she was just like his old grandmother used to be. She'd always had to have the last word.

It was a very busy night in the shop and Julie had no conversation with Angus until Ivy came to relieve her. Julie dropped into a chair and closed her eyes. 'I don't want to see any more mushy peas, pease pudding, black pudding and pies for a week!'

'There's some tea in the pot, would you like some? It might be a bit stewed, it's been made for a while.' Angus was up and had started pouring it when Julie said she would only drink it if it was strong enough to break the cup – one of Tom's expressions.

Julie wondered whether Angus would mention the

incident of the afternoon, but when he did speak it was to ask about her home.

'Ivy tells me that your family live in a house shaped like a crescent moon, and that there are no angles in it.'

'Yes, that's right. My father's eccentric relative who built it had the idea that rounded corners would make for harmony.'

'And has it worked?'

'I don't know whether it worked for him and his family, but I think people would need to be saints to live together without some occasional upset. My mother has told me often enough that I would try the patience of Job! But that doesn't mean we are not a loving family.'

Angus drew his fingertips down his cheek. 'I don't think that rounded corners would help people whose natures clashed. My father was a gentle person, my mother a tyrant. The only harmonious times in my young life were when I was with my father. It was not until he died that I learned that she had never loved him. The marriage had been arranged. Tragic, really.' Angus folded the newspaper and got up. 'Well, I'll away to my bed. I'll bid you good night.'

'Good night,' Julie said, taken aback by his sudden departure. She had thought she might have got to know more about his life.

When Ivy came in a few minutes later she showed no surprise that Angus was not there. 'He obviously has something on his mind,' she said. 'I knew he wasn't himself when he didn't go out this evening. He likes to go to the Hare and Pheasant and have a chat with his cronies. Angus isn't a drinker – a couple of half pints is all he has most nights, so Tom says. What Angus needs is a nice wife and a little home of his own. But there, that's his business.'

Angus was very much on Julie's mind until she had Richard's speedy reply saying he was delighted she was coming on a visit to London. If she could travel this coming Friday, he would meet her at the station.

Julie waved the letter at Ivy. 'It's all right, I can go! Richard says if I travel this coming Friday he can meet me. He has Friday afternoon off work, then we'll have Saturday and Sunday together and if he can't get more time off from the office Jake's aunt will show me around.' Julie had gabbled her news and Ivy told her to calm down and repeat, more slowly, what Richard had said.

With Ivy having digested this Julie then began to worry about what she would wear. If only she had brought better clothes with her. Ivy told her there was nothing wrong with those she had brought. Although they were simply styled they had the finish that would pass in any company. 'And anyway,' she added, 'your Richard is also earning his living so will certainly not be able to wine and dine you at expensive restaurants.'

Although Julie agreed with this she knew she would pack one of her favourite dresses. It was a jade green velvet with long tight sleeves and a high-fitting neck. When she had worn it for the first time, one man told her she looked chaste in it and another one demure. But when she put it on the next time for a twenty-first party, she had added a very long chiffon scarf in shades of cerise and jade, with one end thrown casually over her left shoulder. Then she'd had comments like, 'Darling, you look adoringly wicked . . . Sweet one, I could pick you up and carry you out and make love to you in the garden . . . Julie, you're driving me wild, stop tempting me or else . . . !'

Julie could not envisage such an occasion arising in London, but she knew she would pack the chiffon scarf, too. One never knew.

When Julie saw Angus on the Thursday evening, late, he told her that if he could have changed his shift at the pottery he would have taken her to the station the next morning. Julie thanked him for the thought but told him she would rather go alone, explaining that she wanted to be independent.

'I *must* be independent,' she said earnestly. 'I've nearly

had to go on my bended knees to persuade Ivy not to come with me to the station.'

Angus eyed her, his expression sombre. 'You're a strange lassie, Julietta van Neilson.'

'*You* are a strange man, Angus MacLaren. I never quite know how to take you. One moment you're friendly towards me and the next cold. I suppose I'm not experienced enough to understand all the complexities of the human spirit.'

'When a man's in love, he assumes complexities that he doesn't understand himself.' He paused. 'Yes, Julie, I'm in love with you. I must be – I'm not sleeping properly for thinking about you and wanting to be with you.'

Then Angus gave her a brief good night and left, leaving Julie staring after him, puzzled at first then bewildered. Had he told her he loved her on impulse and then regretted it? She decided it might be just as well if he had. Although she found herself attracted towards him she did not want any involvement. Ivy had said he needed a nice wife and to settle down. Well, that might be all right for Angus, he was older but she was young and just beginning to test out her freedom away from family ties.

But was she free – was one ever free? It seemed a person was always answerable to someone, family, or a boss . . . or God . . .

Later, when Julie went up to bed she stood for a moment at the window, looking out at the blank wall of the stables and thinking how different this view was from the one from her bedroom at home with the rolling fields, and the hills in the distance. For the first time since coming to Stoke, a wave of homesickness swept over her. Tom had often told her how well she had fitted into her new life, but had she? The old restlessness was on her again. The novelty of scrubbing and cleaning was wearing off. She had worked hard, tackled jobs she had never done before because she had promised her mother she would. 'If you let me go to Ivy and Tom's,' she had said, 'I'll do anything, *anything* at all I'm asked to.'

With a sigh Julie turned away from the window and began to undress. She liked the people, she had enjoyed going to the cinema with Angus, had been looking forward to going again. And if she left, where could she go? Although she felt homesick she had no wish to go back home to live. There would be the same old boring routine. What was more, her pride would not allow her to go home and admit she was fed up with all the work she had to do here. No, she would have to stick it out, for the time being at least.

Perhaps this visit to London had come at the right time. She would return feeling refreshed and no doubt full of all she had seen and be eager to see Ivy and Tom again . . . and Angus. Julie got into bed.

She was on the verge of sleep when she was fully aroused by the sounds of someone screaming and shouting. It seemed to be coming from Tom and Ivy's bedroom. Julie threw back the bedclothes, dragged on her dressing gown, ran along the landing and into their bedroom without knocking.

In the wavering light of the candle she saw Ivy holding Tom, smoothing back his hair and soothing him. 'It's all right, love, you've been dreaming, but it's over now.'

Then Angus came in, his trousers pulled over his pyjamas. He went straight to the bed. 'Can I help, Ivy? Do you want me to hold him?'

Ivy shook her head. 'No, Angus, he's calmed down. Will you fetch me that towel on the back of the chair.' To Julie she added, 'Slip down and make a cup of tea, just for Tom, I don't want any.'

Julie stood a moment, watching Ivy gently wiping the sweat from Tom's face, then she left, a lump in her throat. There had been such a look of love and tenderness on Ivy's face.

Julie had put some water on the gas stove to boil and was standing, thinking about Tom, her hands tucked into the

wide sleeves of her dressing gown when Angus came in.

'Tom's all right, Julie. He has these attacks occasionally. He relives the nightmares of the battlefield. Sometimes he's in such a state he has to be held down. This was a mild attack, thank goodness.'

'I'm glad,' she said quietly. 'Tom doesn't deserve to suffer in this way, he's such a nice person.'

'One of the best.' There was a silence between them after this and Julie, uncomfortably aware of Angus standing behind her, took the lid from the teapot ready to rinse the pot when the kettle boiled.

'You're learning,' Angus said, a teasing in his voice.

'Yes, I've learned a lot of things since I came here. I learned tonight, seeing Ivy with Tom that loving a person deeply isn't all cooing and kissing.'

Angus laughed. 'I like the cooing bit.' After a pause he said, his tone now serious, 'And that brings me to something I want to say to you, something I should have said earlier.'

The kettle came to the boil and Julie, after rinsing the pot made the tea, put the tea cosy on the pot and stood, her back to Angus, praying he was not going to say something stupid like he wanted to marry her.

He laid a hand on her shoulder and she was surprised to feel a tremor go through her at his touch.

'Julie, I want you to forget that I told you earlier I was in love with you.'

It was so unexpected she turned swiftly and snapped, 'It's the quickest declaration of love and retraction that I've ever heard of. It's almost an insult.'

'I didn't intend it to be.' He spoke gently. 'It's just that I think it would be more sensible for us to be good friends. I should like to take you out occasionally, to the pictures, or to a variety show.'

Julie's quick flare-up died. 'I would rather be just friends. I don't want to fall in love or for anyone to be in love with me. I'm too young to settle down, I have a lot of life to be lived.'

'And you live it, Julie, you enjoy your visit to London. Shall I carry the tray up?'

'Yes – I'll put the light out.' She had a flat, unhappy feeling.

When they went up, Tom was asleep and Ivy, who was still sitting up in bed, was dabbing hastily at the corners of her eyes with the towel.

Angus set down the tray and went over to her. 'Come on now, Ivy, down in the bed with you.' She obeyed and he pulled up the covers and tucked her in. 'There now, you try and sleep. I'll be up early in the morning and see to the fire.'

To Julie he added, 'And you get away to your bed, lassie. I'll attend to the tray.'

Julie, who was fighting back tears, sped to her room and lay in bed feeling chastened at such tenderness, such caring and wondering what she had to grumble about. What was a bit of scrubbing and cleaning compared to the suffering of Tom – and Ivy.

It seemed to her then that she had a lot more lessons to learn.

# Chapter Five

Julie did not see Angus the next morning. Tom, apart from looking a little drained after his nightmare, did not suffer with his breathing, for which Julie was glad, knowing if he had been ill she could not have left for London.

Ivy gave a last lecture on what and what not to do. She must get into a carriage where there were ladies or a family. On no account was she to talk to a man on his own. She must check with the porter the times of the changes she had to make. And be sure to eat the sandwiches and cake that Ivy had packed. At the end of all this she gave Julie five shillings and so did Tom, with Ivy saying she was not to go mad and spend it all at once.

Tom laughed. 'Take no notice of Ivy, love, spend it all in one go if you feel like it. Enjoy yourself, that's the important thing. You look very fetching.' Julie had decided to wear the grey coat with the velvet collar and the perky knitted white woollen cap with the peak. Ivy was still calling instructions to her when goodbyes were said and Julie was leaving. She went to get the tram to the station, her suitcase banging against her legs.

The young tram conductor helped her with her case, asking her where she was gallivanting off to, then when she arrived at the station another young man carried her case on to the platform. He was one of a party of six, three girls and three men, who turned out to be brothers and sisters all going to London for the wedding of a cousin. When they learned that Julie was going to London too and travelling on her own, they 'adopted' her.

They came from a middle-class family and were all in high spirits, one of the girls explaining it was the first time they had travelled anywhere without their parents. They had been put in the care of their brothers, who although in their twenties were in as high spirits as their sisters. They wanted to know where Julie was going and when she told them and that she was experiencing freedom too, the sisters were full of admiration that she had dared to break away from parental control.

They laughed and chatted and shared their food and the journey seemed to race over. They exchanged addresses in the train and promised to meet again, but when they arrived at St Pancras and the brothers and sisters were met by a stern looking middle-aged couple who ignored Julie, she knew then she had no wish to meet them again. They were feckless people who had simply helped to pass the journey away.

Julie looked for the slender figure of Richard among the people waiting beyond the barrier but there was no sign of him. Had he forgotten the time of the train? He was not a very prompt person.

When ten minutes went by and there was still no sign of her brother Julie began to get annoyed. Surely he could have made the effort to get to the station on time. He knew it was her first visit to London.

Then she saw him coming into the station. He was hatless and looked dishevelled, which was unusual. He paused, looked around him then seeing her, came sprinting over.

'Julie, I'm terribly sorry!' He just about squeezed the life out of her. 'We had an accident. Jake's in hospital –'

'What? Oh, no! How is he?'

'He's all right, just a bit shaken and bruised. Another car ran into us, and he caught it. They're keeping him in overnight for observation. His brother Fergus brought me to the station. He's in the forecourt.' Richard picked up

Julie's suitcase. 'He has a Rolls-Royce. Imagine! A *Rolls-Royce.*' There was a reverence in his voice.

As Julie and Richard approached the grey car with the big headlamps a tall, well-built man got out and came forward. He was in grey and although he too was hatless there was nothing dishevelled about this man.

Richard said, 'Fergus, this is my sister Julietta - Julie, Fergus Damant.'

They shook hands with Julie commiserating with him over Jake's accident.

'My brother is a mad devil,' he said, 'but I must admit he was not to blame for the accident in this case.' He smiled then and Julie thought what an attractive man he was. His eyes were a speedwell blue, thickly-lashed. 'What Jake *is* going to be upset about,' Fergus went on, 'is his beloved "banger". I doubt whether it will ever be the same again.' Fergus opened the car door. 'Shall we go? My aunt is expecting us for dinner.'

Julie climbed into the back and realised she had stepped into luxury. Her feet sank into thick piled carpet.

Richard sat in the front with Fergus, and Jake and the accident were forgotten as they discussed the merits of the car. To Julie it was like being transported on a magic carpet: there was no sound, no feeling of movement. It was the acme of luxury.

She looked from one man to the other. Richard, the excitable one, talked with his hands and every now and then pushed back the lock of dark hair that fell over his forehead. Fergus, completely at ease, moved his hands on the wheel, swinging it effortlessly. He had thick, chestnut-coloured hair which curled at the nape. Julie had a silly urge to touch it.

As though sensing this he said over his shoulder, 'Sorry, Julie, we're neglecting you. Did you have a good journey?'

'Yes, it went quickly. I had lively fellow passengers.'

Richard asked about Ivy and Tom and afterwards began

to speak of the various buildings on the route. He chatted about architecture until Fergus chided him mildly for 'talking shop'. Richard laughed.

'Yes, I'll wait until I take Julie to see the Houses of Parliament – then I can go to town.' To Julie he added, 'Don't worry, we have all sorts of trips planned. Buckingham Palace, the Embankment, the Bloody Tower. On Sunday we'll be going to the market at Portobello Road and to Petticoat Lane, too, if we have time. I hope old Jake's well enough to come with us, he was so looking forward to your visit – wanted to run you everywhere in his banger, of course. We'll have to go by bus and underground instead.'

Fergus then offered his services and Richard's delight was so infectious that Julie began to laugh. 'You men and your cars. Our father is always saying he must treat himself to a Rolls-Royce, but so far has kept his Cadillac.'

'The American car,' Fergus said. 'I drive one when I go to New York.' And so the two men were back onto cars again, but Julie didn't mind. She was fascinated just listening to Fergus Damant's beautiful voice. It had the timbre of a singer – a baritone, rich and warm.

Julie knew nothing about Jake and Fergus' aunt and hoped she was not like the stern-faced woman who had met her travelling companions at St Pancras. They drew up into a square of beautiful Georgian houses with a park in the centre. Small shrubs on the balconies of the houses looked a bright green against the white stuccoed walls.

A maid answered their ring and as they went into the hall a small, fair-haired woman came running down the stairs, greeting them in a trilling voice.

'Oh, here you are, safe and sound. Julietta, my dear, how lovely to meet you. Poor Jake, isn't it terrible? I've been so worried since I knew about the accident, but when I phoned the hospital a few minutes ago they told me he might be allowed home tomorrow. He must come and stay with me for a while, and you too, Richard.'

Julie wondered if Fergus lived here with his aunt and if so, why Jake didn't?

Klara said that dinner would soon be ready and a maid showed Julie up to her room. There was an air of genteel poverty about the house. The carpets and curtains were worn, faded. The furniture was all dark oak, heavily carved, but everywhere was spotlessly clean, with brasses gleaming and the oak surrounds of the floor having a mirror finish.

Julie wanted to change for dinner but knowing that Richard would not have a dinner suit with him, chose a sage green celanese dress with a cowl neck. And felt right when she came down and found Klara in a simple black dress and Fergus in the same grey suit. Richard, after freshening up, had lost his dishevelled look and with his tall, slender figure, looked just as distinguished as Fergus, although of course, younger. Fergus, she judged would be in his late twenties.

No cocktails were served before dinner and no wine accompanied it, and although the food was wholesome the meal was unimaginative. Julie was puzzled by the situation. Jake earned his living and lived in lodgings, Klara was obviously impoverished, yet here was Fergus driving a Rolls Royce!

Klara questioned Julie about her life in the potteries and said she thought her very courageous. 'What made you do it, Julie dear? I understand you work in a little general shop.'

Julie bridled at what she thought of as Klara's patronising tone but she forced herself to say calmly, 'Yes, I do – and enjoy it. I find it so much more satisfying than living in luxury.'

Klara sighed. 'I'm afraid I don't understand young people nowadays. There are Jake and Richard, who seem to find pleasure in going to the East End and talking to the people in a public house, and you, Julie, going to work among the poorer classes. What do you get out of it?'

'Education.' Julie was aware of a humorous smile

touching Fergus' lips and felt angry. 'Yes, education! It's surprising how much one learns being with working people. There's a great warmth, an understanding of one another's needs and problems. They help one another. If someone in the street dies neighbours will follow the hearse, on foot, no matter how bad the weather. To them it's their way of showing respect. Respect . . .' Julie nodded slowly. 'That is something I've come to appreciate. If I can earn the respect of the people I serve in the shop then I'll feel I've really achieved something. You can keep all your universities and degrees. This is life I'm learning about, and I'm happy, happier than I've ever been.'

She looked at Fergus in a defiant way and found him eyeing her, his expression serious.

'That was quite a speech, Julie, and I'm glad you made it. It's made *me* think.'

Richard laughed, a little self-consciously. 'But you wouldn't give up your Rolls, Fergus, would you?'

'No, I've earned it. And you too could own one eventually, if you work as hard as I have done. The trouble is, Richard, you're like Jake, you enjoy talking about being wealthy one day, but you spend most of your weekends lazing when you could be studying. That won't get you anywhere.'

Richard accepted the rebuke amiably. 'You're quite right, Fergus. My real trouble is, I've no incentive. Both my parents are wealthy in their own right and –'

'That's no excuse,' Julie said hotly. 'They're my parents, too. I think you find the East Enders a novelty and nothing more. They're good company, they make you laugh, but would you live among them, work with them – and by that I mean doing a menial job?'

Richard rubbed his chin. 'Now that I don't know, Sis. I don't know that I would like to rough it. I enjoy my comfort.'

'So do I,' Klara said. 'I enjoy what little I have. I wouldn't survive if I had to live in poverty. But, it's just as well we're not all alike, isn't it, or there would be no people like Julie to serve in shops or people to make your Rolls Royce, Fergus, would there? It would be a strange world.' Klara gave a little infectious giggle, dispelling the feeling of tension that had been building up. Julie suddenly found that she quite liked this little fair-haired woman with the fragile look.

Fergus drained his coffee cup, dabbed at his mouth with his table napkin then said, 'So, what plans have you for this evening? Perhaps Julie would enjoy a drive around London. It's a good time to see it, when the rush-hour traffic is over.'

They were all more than agreeable, with Klara saying she only hoped her friends would see her driving in a Rolls-Royce.

Julie realised how lucky she was to have had this opportunity. She saw parts of London she had not even thought about, like the lovely open spaces, and the private gardens within squares bordered by mansions. She was impressed with Buckingham Palace, felt moved to think that her King and Queen and family were behind the walls.

But the place that impressed her the most was the Houses of Parliament. She saw it in the moonlight with a hoar frost on the grass outside and understood Richard's dedication to architecture. He too was moved by the beauty and talked softly about his work.

They drove on now to Piccadilly Circus and there Julie found a different kind of beauty, an animation in the milling crowds, who seemed bent on pleasure and in the flashing red, green, blue and orange neon signs of the advertisements.

Klara suggested they went to the Embankment and there Julie was aware of a peace and a timelessness. It seemed to her that the little tugs chugging up and down the river had always been there and always would be. She admired the black and gold Victorian lamps and when they crossed to the other side of the river and saw the whole magnificence of the Houses of Parliament once more she said in a rapt voice,

'Oh, thank you all for making this possible. I shall never forget it.'

'Hey, this is just a start,' Richard teased. 'There's a dozen and one places you have to see yet.'

'But right at this moment,' Fergus said, 'we are going to have a coffee at an all-night stand. There you will see all the humanity you want – the rich, the workers and the down-and-outs. And I can promise you humour, too.'

Julie found the smell of coffee appetising as they reached the stand. A small group of people had congregated and there was a burst of laughter as they listened to a youth telling the proprietor about his mother going to a fair.

'Me farver intended to go wiv 'er, but 'e was on 'is back, see. Not his lumbago, no, 'e 'ad a skinful at dinnertime. Me mam went on 'er own, and she came back wiv a coconut she'd won. When we cracked it open it were black. Talk about murder! It'd cost 'er nearly five bob to win it!'

The pugnacious-looking proprietor said, 'More fool your ma, for throwing five bob away. There's your coffee, Sam, let's see the colour of your money.'

An old woman next to the youth said in wheedling tones, 'How about buying me a cuppa, Sammy? The Chancellor of the Exchequer ain't sent me the ten bob 'e borrowed off me last night.'

The youth threw some extra coppers onto the counter. 'All right, Maisie, but you stop making an 'abit of this, see.'

She gave him a toothless grin and reached out a mittened claw for the extra cup poured. The two of them departed and other people moved up.

When Fergus and Richard managed to get to the counter the man behind it said to Fergus, 'Well, 'ello there guv, 'aven't seen you for a few weeks. Been away?'

'Yes, Biff, I've been abroad – on business. Can I have four cups of coffee, please.'

The coffees were passed to Julie and Klara then the four of

them stood aside to let others in. There was a constant movement of people and Richard said, 'Your friend seems to have a flourishing little business.'

'Biff works long hours. He used to be a boxer, knew him in my younger days. It was expected he would reach the top of his profession, but a broken wrist finished his career. It was a compound fracture that never properly healed.'

Klara, who was running her handkerchief round the rim of the cup said, 'You do seem to know some odd people, Fergus.' To which he replied wryly that it took all kinds to make a world. Julie wondered then what line of business he was in. She must ask Richard later.

A party of four came up now in evening dress and it was surprising how they were accepted by those less fortunate. There was no mimicking of their cultured accents, albeit some cajoling from the down-and-outs to be bought coffee and food – but this was not readily forthcoming from the wealthy ones. It was the workmen who treated their less fortunate brothers.

'Well?' Fergus said to Julie as they eventually moved away. 'Have you learned a little bit more about life?' There was nothing patronising about his tone and she told him yes, she had learned that it was the poor who helped the poor!

Fergus caught hold of her arm, bringing her to a stop, then he pointed back to where the evening dress people were hailing a taxi. 'Shall I tell you something, Julie? Those people probably had less in their pockets than the working men. They live on credit, they dine out and sign chits and face the music when they're unable to meet the bills.'

'I see,' Julie said. 'I'm sorry for sounding as if I knew it all. As Ivy would say, "You're getting too cocky, girl, too big for your boots".'

'I don't think you would ever do that, Julie,' Fergus said quietly. 'Not when you can admit to making a mistake.'

They saw more of London, Klara wanting Julie to see the lit-up shops in Regent Street, and Richard enthusing about the varying styles of architecture. Klara then said, 'I don't have much money to spend, Julie, but in the morning I'm going to bring you here. You'll enjoy a good browse around. In the afternoon we must go hospital visiting, that is if Jake is not allowed home.'

Richard raised his shoulders. 'Women! They're taking over. All my plans are going by the board.'

Fergus said, 'Not altogether. If Jake does get home I shall take you all to dinner tomorrow evening as promised, at the Savoy.'

'The Savoy?' Klara drew herself up. 'Now that certainly will be a treat. Oh, Julie, my dear, I'm an out and out snob. I love high living.'

'And that goes for me too,' said Richard over his shoulder, his face one broad grin. 'I can bear to rough it if I can have a bit of luxury in between. Old Jake will be out of that hospital even if we have to kidnap him!'

When they got back Klara invited Richard to stay, saying it would be nice for him to have a long talk to Julie. He accepted and it was then Julie learned that Fergus had his own place, rooms in Lower Regent Street. He refused Klara's offer of a bedtime drink, saying he had to get back, there was a neighbour's cat he had promised to feed. Julie wondered if it was just an excuse to get away.

He promised to be in touch the next day, once they found out about Jake. If he was not allowed home then they would have to make it Monday evening for the dinner as he would be out of town on the Sunday on business. Julie became more and more curious. What business could be done on a Sunday that would take him out of town?

Julie was hoping to have a short while alone with Richard as there were several things she wanted to ask him, but Klara was in a chatty mood. The maid who had been summoned brought three mugs of Ovaltine. Richard pulled a face at this but then he smiled and started to drink it.

Klara talked of the problems of being left a widow. Her

husband had left her the house and an income which just enabled her to run it, but the money did not allow her any luxuries. That was why she was so looking forward to having dinner at the Savoy.

Julie asked if she had children and Klara said yes, one son, but he was married and lived away. She heard from them occasionally. Then she added, 'Jake and Fergus have been more like my own boys. They visit regularly, remember my birthday and at Christmas. Fergus would do a lot more for me, if I would let him, but I'm a very independent person.'

'What line of business is Fergus in?' Julie asked, hoping she sounded casual.

Klara put her mug on its saucer and sat back. 'Do you know, my dear, I just don't know. Neither does Jake. When we ask Fergus point blank he simply dismisses it with a smile and says, "Very private. I'm unable to discuss it".'

'Well, whatever it is,' Richard said, 'he's certainly making money.'

Klara cocked her head. 'I don't think it's anything – illegal. I certainly hope not. No, I'm sure it isn't! I know Fergus, I helped to bring the boys up when they were children. My sister ailed a lot. She died five years ago. Her husband married again, six months later. Can't say I blame him. But it was a bit quick. More Ovaltine, Julie, Richard?'

They both thanked her but refused. 'I'll get Bertha to show you your room, Richard, then you can come down and have a little chat together. I know you haven't seen one another for a while.'

When Richard had been shown his room and Klara had bid them good night and gone up to bed, Richard drew up his chair to the dying fire and held his hands out to what warmth there was.

'God, this is a cold house. Heaven preserve me from poverty. Our rooms are not luxurious but our landlady always has a roaring fire for us to come in to. And at breakfast time. I'll have to take you there tomorrow and let you see where we live.' Richard sat back. 'So, tell me all about you, Sis. How do you enjoy being a martyr? No, you don't feel a martyr, do you? What are Tom and Ivy really like to live with? She used to boss us round as kids. And Tom, does he still suffer from the effects of gas?'

Julie gave him all the details of her new life, enthusing about it and her new friends, then she brought up the subject of the secret in their parents' lives.

'I know there have been some funny goings-on,' Richard mused, 'but I think it had to do with the three aunts. I've never questioned Mother or Dad, I haven't really been interested. It's what's happening now that I'm interested in.'

'Well, I want to know what's happened in the past,' Julie said. 'I want to know who the Tiernes are.' She told him of Mrs Helder's remarks. 'She said I must meet them, that it was my right to do so.'

Richard pulled at his ear-lobe. 'Now the Tiernes have something to do with Mother's side of the family.'

'How could they? She was known as Harvey, then later Leddenshaw. Yes, I know the Leddenshaws were her foster parents, so where do the Tiernes come in? Look, there's something I want to show you.'

Julie brought the miniature out of her handbag and explained how she had come across it. 'There's certainly a likeness to you. Is he some member of the family? Billy Barker said he knew the name of the family but it had temporarily slipped his memory. I was hoping that you could identify the man.'

Richard shook his head. 'Haven't a clue.' Then a slow grin spread over his face. 'He's not bad-looking, whoever he is. I don't mind resembling him.'

'Bighead,' she teased. Richard stifled a yawn then apologised.

'Lord, I'm tired, Sis. It's been quite a day. I think I'm just beginning to feel the effects of the accident. I'm aching.'

When Richard was overtired his skin took on a transparent look. It had done since he was a child. Julie got up. 'You must go to bed. We can talk some more tomorrow.' She kissed him on the cheek. 'Thanks, Richard, for letting me come here. I've so enjoyed it.'

'There's a lot more,' he said. It was a catch-phrase of their childhood when he was telling her a story and he would keep her on tenterhooks. They both laughed and Richard gave her a hug. 'You can dream about one of our ancestors being a Duke or an Earl.'

'It would be much more interesting if he had been a highwayman.'

'And hanged on the gallows! Who said that men are the blood-thirsty ones? Come on – bed.'

In spite of all the events of the day crowding into Julie's mind she had a dreamless sleep and was awakened the next morning by the maid bringing her a tray of tea, and telling her that breakfast would be ready in half an hour.

When Julie was washed and dressed she went downstairs and was greeted by Richard, who told her that Jake was coming out of hospital that morning. Fergus was going to collect him.

Richard was his old exuberant self. 'It's great news, isn't it? They wouldn't have let him come home unless he was well enough. He'll be able to come to the Savoy with us this evening.'

Klara came bustling in. 'Oh, there you are, Julie, and you too are looking brighter. Richard has told you the news about Jake? I'm so pleased. Breakfast is ready. Come along.'

They went into the dining room where a fire burned fitfully, giving out little puffs of smoke. But a more than adequate breakfast made up for the chill and discomfort in the room. There were luscious slices of grilled ham, eggs, sausages, kidneys and mushrooms. They helped themselves from dishes on the sideboard and Richard kept giving little grins as he raised the covers on each dish. They both did justice to the meal, with Klara nibbling toast and marmalade in between talking about the various places Julie should see. The Crown Jewels in the Tower were a must, so was Madame Tussauds and the Zoo at Regent's Park. Richard said he would like to take her to Covent Garden Market, if they could manage to get up at about four o'clock on the Monday morning. 'It's quite a sight,' he added, 'seeing all the flowers and other produce arriving and being sold.'

Julie, who could think of nothing worse than getting up on a cold dark morning at four o'clock said she thought she would like to go to Madame Tussauds.

They lingered over breakfast, with Klara talking about her youth and saying how young people today had so much more freedom. Richard teased her and said that parents must have been saying that since the Stone Age - and no doubt it would still be said in the twenty-first century! Klara laughed. 'I suppose so. The older ones always tend to think they were badly done to. More coffee?'

They had started on their second cups when there was the melodious sound of a car horn outside the window. Klara jumped up. 'That could be Fergus and Jake.' She drew back the curtain. 'It is, and Jake is barely limping. Isn't that splendid?'

Julie for some reason had imagined Jake to be slender like Richard, so was surprised to find a tubby young man with fair curly hair and a cherubic face. At this moment, it was stretched in a broad grin.

'Well, here I am, folks, at death's door one minute and rarin' to go for a new adventure the next.'

Fergus said wryly from behind him, 'You just calm down, Jake, and forget about adventures. You've been told to take it easy.'

Although Fergus was more casually-dressed this morning in a brown sweater over beige corded trousers, he still managed to convey an air of wealth. He had what her mother called *panache*.

Jake greeted Julie with outstretched hands. 'So this is the beautiful Julietta! Your ears should have burned at times when Richard was talking about you. It's lovely to meet you.'

'And lovely to meet *you*, Jake. How are you feeling?'

'Great, apart from the fact that my shoulders feel as if they're encased in cement. Hey, I hear we're dining out this evening. Marvellous, I'm ready for a good nosh-up. The food in hospital! Aunt Klara, I can smell bacon! Is there any left?'

'Plenty,' she said, and drew up a chair for him.

While Jake talked with more enthusiasm than sense about the accident Julie found herself watching Fergus. Klara had poured him a coffee, but although he had a finger hooked through the handle of the cup he had not yet taken a drink. She thought this morning that the speedwell-blue eyes had a thoughtful look. What was he weighing up? The possibility of Jake making a claim for the damage to the car . . . or whether Jake was really fit enough to go out dining that evening?

The only resemblance Julie could see in the two brothers was in their noses, which were both beautifully modelled, Grecian noses. Jake's eyes were brown and his mouth small, soft-lipped. Fergus had a rather large mouth, well-shaped, firm. Julie wondered what it would be like to be kissed by him then blushed furiously as she found Fergus' gaze on her.

She switched her attention to Jake but was conscious that Fergus was still watching her. She was glad when he said, 'Well – now I've delivered the patient safely, I must go, I have some work to do. I'll pick you all up at seven o'clock. See that Jake takes it easy. He *must* rest all day, if he is to go out this evening.'

Richard promised with a laugh that he would tie Jake down if necessary. Fergus raised his hand in a general farewell and left without having drunk any of his coffee.

Although Klara had been determined to show Julie the

shops it seemed as though there was a lethargy over them all which Julie put down to the fact that as far as she and Klara and Richard were concerned, they had done and seen so much the night before. She was content, for the time being at least, to just sit and chat.

In spite of Jake's seeming obsession with adventure he had a keen brain and a knowledge of architecture that kept Julie interested for most of the morning.

After lunch, when Jake showed signs of exhaustion Klara insisted he went upstairs to lie down. Richard said he would stay in and make sure that Jake was all right, while Klara took Julie to the shops.

Many of the shops in the West End were closed on the Saturday afternoon but Julie, like Klara, enjoyed window-gazing, especially on Bond Street, both of them drooling over clothes they were unable to afford. And then, feet aching with all the walking they had done, they found a little café in a side street where they sat down thankfully to have a cup of tea.

And over their tea Klara questioned Julie further about her life in the potteries. Was she able to enjoy any social activities? Julie said, oh, yes, and spoke enthusiastically of the cinema and Charlie Chaplin. Then she began to talk about Angus and the marriage bowl he had made. Although Klara had seemed a little shocked that Angus was a lodger in the same house as Julie she was very much interested in the bowl, remarking that now she came to think about it, she had not put very much into her own marriage.

'But then I never had much chance,' she said. 'I seldom saw my husband, he was a gambling man, you see. I think I was a dutiful wife, I never queried any of his actions. This, of course, was something I had drummed into me from the time I was nearing marriageable age. I more or less considered it an honour that Hector had asked for my hand in marriage.'

'Did you love him?' Julie asked.

'If I'm honest I must say no. I liked him but only at times. Not all the time.' Klara toyed with the spoon in the bowl of sugar for a moment then looked up, a wistful expression in her eyes. 'But after I had been married for about five years I – well, I did fall in love with someone else – and then, Julie, I realised what I had been missing.' She leaned forward and added earnestly, 'I'm telling you this, Julie, so you won't marry a man you don't love. I never had what you could call an affair with the man I fell in love with, but sometimes I wish I had. He tried to persuade me to leave my husband but I couldn't, there was my small son. He left the district and the last I heard of him he was married and had a family.'

Klara sighed and gave a wry smile. 'The story of my life. Not too happy a one, but there, we must take what the Lord sends.'

Julie laid a hand over Klara's and said softly, 'I think it's a very sad story. I couldn't marry anyone I was not deeply in love with and he deeply in love with me.'

Klara smiled. 'Then make sure you marry into your own class. Now, let us change the subject. What are you planning to wear this evening?'

Julie wore the jade velvet – with the flimsy chiffon scarf, and had all the men complimenting her. 'You look great, Julie . . .' this from Richard. 'Utterly charming,' from Fergus, and Jake said, 'I claim the privilege of walking with you into the Savoy. I want all the men to envy me.'

Julie laughed and remarked that all these compliments would turn her head. Yes, she said to Jake, she would be happy to walk in with him.

She did, but Fergus was on the other side of her, cupping her elbow. Richard accompanied Klara. Their party drew quite a few glances but Julie noticed only the women eyeing Fergus. He certainly was an imposing figure in evening dress.

Fergus suggested they had a drink first and they went into the lounge. Julie was impressed, not so much by the opulence, but by the masses of flowers everywhere.

After the drinks were ordered Julie noticed a woman staring across at their table. Her companion was an elderly man but she herself would perhaps be in her early forties. She had golden hair, an exquisite beauty and was elegantly dressed in ice blue with an ermine stole around her shoulders. The person who held her attention seemed to be Richard, who was sitting in a direct line to her. Fergus had his back to her. When the woman continued to stare, Julie asked Klara in a low voice if she knew who she was.

Klara said she knew her face, but was unable to place her. A moment later, a waiter came up and handed a note to Richard, saying it was from a lady, and indicating the beautiful stranger's table.

Klara frowned while Julie, Jake and Fergus all watched Richard. He scanned the note, looked across at the woman then back to his table companions.

'She wants to meet me, says I remind her strongly of someone.'

'The miniature!' Julie said, excitement in her voice. 'She might be a relative. Here, I have the miniature with me.' She brought it out of her bag. 'Take it with you. Go on, the sooner you go the sooner you'll get back and we'll know what it's all about.'

Richard put the miniature in his pocket, stood hesitant for a moment then said, 'Well, here I go.'

Julie, Klara and Jake all watched him cross the room, but Fergus still sat with his back to the woman. When Klara said she wished he would take a little peep and see if he knew her, he remarked they would soon know who she was when Richard returned.

Before Richard reached the table, the elderly man got up and left.

'The plot thickens,' Jake grinned. '*Why* did he leave? And what is all this about a miniature, Julie?' When she had explained how she had come across it he said, 'Talk about intrigue! I wouldn't have missed this for the world.'

Richard was now seated. There was some earnest conversation between him and the woman then Richard brought out the miniature. She studied it for some time and when she looked up Julie thought she saw a glint of tears in the woman's eyes, but could not be sure. The miniature was put back in Richard's pocket, they talked some more, then the woman and Richard got up. They stood another moment talking then the woman left, leaving Richard standing looking after her. He turned towards the table, hesitated, then came over slowly.

Jake said, 'Well, come on, give. What's the mystery?'

Richard ignored this, looked at Julie and said, 'Her Christian name is *Violet.*'

Klara suddenly sat up. 'Violet! Now I know who she is. She passes herself off as Lady someone or other, but according to what I was told, she's not married. What is more – she's supposed to have once owned one of the wealthiest brothels in Paris!'

'Is that so.' A white pinched look had come around Richard's nostrils. 'How interesting. She tells me she is . . . my mother.'

# Chapter Six

In the stunned silence following Richard's statement Julie felt physically sick. Klara, her hand to her mouth, was staring at him in a stricken way; both Jake and Fergus were motionless, their gaze on her brother. Richard, who was standing behind his chair, gripping the back, said he must leave.

'Please try and understand. I'm sorry to spoil the evening, but I couldn't stay. Excuse me.' He moved away but before he had gone far Julie jumped up and went after him.

'Richard, you can't leave. I want to know what's happened. I want to know what she said – did she mention me? Am I involved in her life? You *must* tell me. I have a right to know.'

Some of the tension went from Richard. 'Yes, you're right. Can we talk somewhere alone for a while? There's a table over there in the corner. Explain to the others will you, that we'll come back to them. I don't want to face anyone but you at the moment.'

When Julie had explained how Richard felt Fergus said he understood, they all understood and if they wanted to go back home after they had had their talk he would take them. It was left at that.

Richard seemed a lot calmer when Julie returned to him. The pinched look had gone from his nostrils. Julie said, 'Right, now start at the beginning. What did she say to you when you first went over?'

'She thanked me for coming over, told me I bore a strong resemblance to her first husband and asked my name. When I told her she was silent for a moment then said, "I once knew your parents."'

'Knew them?' Julie exclaimed. 'Didn't she tell you that she was one of Mother's sisters?'

'Not then. I brought out the miniature, explained how you had come by it and after studying it for some time she looked up, tears in her eyes and said it was her first husband as a young man, and added how strong was my resemblance to him.'

'Was it then she told you that you were her son?'

'No. She explained how her husband had died leaving her penniless and how, unable to keep her baby she had taken it to her sister and her husband and left him in a basket on the doorstep. And then, when she went to claim him later, she was told the baby had been adopted by a couple who had emigrated to Australia.

'Then she said, "I know now, Richard, it was all lies. The proof is in having you sitting in front of me. *You* are my son".' Richard spread his hands. 'You can imagine how I felt. I sat staring at her stunned, then I asked what proof she had.'

'And what did she say?'

'She told me she had proof, asked me where she could get in touch with me and when I gave her Klara's address she said she would arrange for us to meet again soon. Before she left she explained she was Mother's sister then told me to tell you that –' Richard paused then added, 'No, that's all.'

'What do you mean, that's all? If she told you something about me I want to know.'

'It was nothing, forget it. In fact, I'm beginning to wonder if she hasn't fabricated the whole thing. There are people like her, who make up stories for excitement. Take the miniature – she sat looking at it for an awful long time. If there had been such a strong resemblance to her first husband, surely she would have mentioned it right away. No, the more I think about it, the more I'm sure there's something fishy about the whole thing.'

'Richard – stop trying to convince me she was lying. Tell me what she said about *me*.'

'All right, all right. She said that you ought to look into your background, too.'

Julie felt a numbing coldness creeping over her. What did that mean? That she was not her parents' child? If not, who did she belong to? The thought that she might belong to someone else was too awful to contemplate.

Richard spread his hands in a despairing gesture. 'Oh, Lord, why did I tell you? What a fool I am. Look, Julie,' he leaned forward, 'we're going to forget this for the time being. Yes, yes, we must. We must get some sanity into the evening. There are three people sitting over there who are waiting to go into dinner. We may not feel like eating but we must make an effort not to spoil the evening for the others. It might help us to talk over our problem. They *are* friends. Do you think you could try?'

Julie responded to the coaxing in his voice, knowing he was right. If they did leave, what could they do but sit at Klara's and go over every possibility of Violet's statement.

'Yes, I'll try,' she said.

When they arrived back at the table Richard said, with a forced cheerfulness, 'Well, as it's impossible to solve the mystery of the stranger until the parents return next Friday, I suggest we start enjoying the evening.'

Julie looked up. 'Mother and Father coming home on Friday? I didn't think it was so soon. Where will the ship be docking?'

'At Southampton. They're travelling on the *Aquitania* and I think she's due in about five o'clock.'

When Fergus confirmed this Julie said, 'We'll go and meet them. I don't feel I want to go back to Stoke until we've all had a talk. I'll send a telegram to Ivy and Tom, then write a letter explaining the reason for my staying on.'

Richard looked embarrassed. 'Look, Julie, it's a question of – well, accommodation. Klara has been kind enough to offer to put you up but I thought it would be only for the weekend . . .'

Klara waved a hand at him. 'Stop worrying, Richard. Julie can stay as long as she likes, I love having her.'

Julie, smiling, thanked her and after that the evening passed with a certain air of conviviality, with Julie even laughing heartily at some of Jake's and Richard's feeble jokes.

When Fergus drove them back to Klara's he said to Richard, 'I'm afraid I won't be able to see you and Julie tomorrow. I have a business acquaintance to meet, but if it's possible I'll drive you both to Southampton on Friday. I'll be in touch before then.'

Julie wondered again what line of business he was in to keep him occupied on the Sabbath. When she asked Richard later he said, 'Don't know, Julie, but there is something I want to say to you. Don't you think you are being a little irresponsible wanting to stay in London until Friday? After all, you do have some obligation to Ivy and Tom, you are working there. Also, it means I would have to ask for another day off. I think I could get it, but I don't like taking advantage of the fact that Mr Faverly and my father are friends.'

Julie, who had always thought of Richard as being the irresponsible one eyed him in surprise. 'I don't think of it as a proper job, not like the one you have. Ivy and Tom are friends and will understand. Ivy once said she could always get a neighbour in to help out. Anyway, I regard what has happened as a crisis in our lives and the sooner we get something sorted out the better. Where are we going tomorrow? Have you anything planned?'

'Not yet,' Richard said shortly. 'I'll tell you in the morning.'

Julie ignored his abrupt manner – no doubt he would be in a better mood in the morning.

Unfortunately, the weather was appalling the next morning, deluging rain without a break in the clouds. When Julie went down for breakfast she found an air of gloom. Richard said, nodding towards the streaming windows, 'Just look at it! Where could anyone go without a car? Jake has the right idea – he's gone back to bed. Mind you, I don't think he's too well.'

Julie took a seat at the table. 'I don't want to stay in all day. We could travel by Underground or bus and if Klara would lend us an umbrella –'

Richard immediately dismissed this. There was a gale blowing, an umbrella could blow inside out, they could get drenched to the skin. Julie said no more but was determined not to sit and mope. She could only hope the rain would ease eventually, then she would go sightseeing on her own.

At ten o'clock when the rain was still deluging down she jumped up. 'I want to go to the Portobello Road to see the market. Klara, can you direct me?' Klara, who had appeared to be more apathetic than Richard, got up too. 'I'll do better than that, Julie, I'll take you. I can lend you a macintosh that belonged to my husband, and his souwester, if you will wear it.'

Julie declared she would wear a pudding basin on her head if it meant her being able to go out. Klara laughed; Richard told them they were quite mad. He was stretched out on the sofa, a Sunday paper across his chest, looking half asleep.

When Julie caught sight of herself in the hall mirror she began to giggle. Klara's husband must have been an exceptionally tall man, for her hands were halfway up the macintosh sleeves and the hem touched the ground. She turned up the sleeves and finding a belt in the pocket, fastened it round her middle, pouching the top half of the mac up over it. She then anchored the over-large souwester by tying the strings firmly under her chin.

'My best friend wouldn't know me,' she said aloud to her mirrored image.

'Nor mine, me,' Klara exclaimed, giggling with her. Klara was wearing a bell-tent shaped cape that must have belonged to another age and had a red woollen scarf tied over her hat.

They went out into the driving rain and a wind that took their breath away. Klara took Julie by the arm and they set off at a jog-trot to the nearest Underground station, where riding on a train in the bowels of the earth was another new experience for Julie. When they eventually arrived at the Portobello Road she became excited at the cosmopolitan milling crowd, the cries and quips of the stallholders, with everyone in such a good mood in spite of the dreadful weather.

Julie loved the Cockney dialect and kept stopping to listen to various stallholders promoting their wares. One man who held out a cupped hand catching raindrops said to the group of women who had gathered, 'Listen, girls, all this wa'er might be good for your gardings, but it ain't for your complexions. It gets dry wiv all this 'ere soot and everythink floating arahnd.' He held a bottle aloft. 'Wot you need is my magical elixir! A teaspoonful morning and night'll mike your skin bloom like a desert after rine!'

'You bin in the desert then, Jack?' one woman called.

' 'Ave I been there, gal? I've lived there, where d'ja think I got me secret formula from? Lived wiv a royal family I did, as their very own son. C'mon now, who wants a bottle of this 'ere elixir, I'll not charge you ten bob, not nine nor eight –' He came down to a shilling a bottle and Klara, who had been eased to the front line opened her purse and said eagerly, 'I'll have one, please.'

Hands were shooting out from all directions with their shillings and Klara came away clutching her bottle, a bemused look in her eyes, in spite of one woman in the crowd telling her it was nothing more than coloured water.

Julie was surprised that Klara could have been so taken in, but she said nothing to spoil her pleasure.

It was a big market, catering for all tastes. There were fruit and sweet stalls, ones selling new and secondhand clothes, furniture, antiques, jewellery both cheap and valuable, jellied eels . . .

Julie, having heard Richard say how delicious jellied eels were, asked Klara if she would like some. Klara was willing and so they stood with their little dishes and forks, the rain dropping from their chins mingling with the vinegar-soaked eel. Julie had just finished hers and pronounced it excellent when someone peeped under the brim of her souwester and said, 'I thought it might be you.'

'Fergus!' Julie eyed him in astonishment. 'What are *you* doing here? I thought that you . . .'

'My business acquaintance was unable to come.' He turned to Klara. 'I called at the house and Richard told me where you both were and what you would be wearing.' At this last remark his lips trembled momentarily in a smile. 'Richard came with me, he's waiting in the car.'

'Oh, please let's stay!' Julie said quickly. 'We've only been here a short while.'

'Yes, I know. I don't want you to leave and Richard is prepared to wait. What shall we look at, what interests you?' When Julie said everything, Fergus laughed. 'Then come along, you lovely ladies, let us get started.'

Although Julie knew she looked a sight she was not bothered, but felt strangely happy to have Fergus with them. He was wearing a trenchcoat and a grey tweed cap, both of which had seen a good deal of wear, yet he still managed to look immaculate.

Fergus bought them each a packet of popcorn and they all munched happily, children again, as they browsed round stalls, walking as leisurely as if it were a sunny summer's day, Julie ignoring raindrops that dripped from the stall awnings, each time she leant over to examine some item.

She was looking for something to take back as presents for Tom and Ivy, yet knew she would have to be selective as far as price was concerned. If Fergus was unable to take them to Southampton on the Friday there would be train fares and perhaps a meal to buy.

Remembering that Ivy had once said she would like a string of imitation pearls, Julie beat a stallholder down from five shillings to two shillings for some, much to the embarrassment of Klara and the amusement of Fergus. For Tom she bought three white handkerchiefs for a shilling. Fergus teased her, wanting to know where she had learned to bargain. She told him about Billy Barker's 'emporium' and said how much fun it was, never knowing what bargains you might find there. Then, thinking about the miniature, she changed the subject.

Fergus stopped at an antique jewellery stall and asked Julie and Klara to each choose a bracelet for his two sisters. Price, he said, was no object, which warned Julie she must not attempt to do any bargaining. Her choice was a simple gold circle with a chased gold clasp in the form of a pagoda. Klara chose a gold chain bracelet, hung with numerous tiny charms. She then suggested they ought to leave, for Richard would be getting impatient and it was nearly lunch-time.

By the time they reached the Rolls-Royce, which was parked in a side street, the rain was beginning to ease. Richard was sitting in the driver's seat, his hands on the wheel, ignoring the small urchins who were peering in at the window and clamouring for pennies. Fergus handed out some coppers then chased the children away.

Before Julie got into the car she took off the macintosh, turned it inside out then, putting the dripping souwester with it, rolled the coat into a bundle. And had Richard snap at her. 'Get in for heaven's sake, Julie. Since when did *you* become so fanatically tidy?'

'Since living with Ivy and Tom,' she said, wondering what

on earth was the matter with him. Richard could be moody at times but she had never known him to be really nasty. Klara, who had stepped into the car wearing her soaked cape, looked a little self-conscious and made to take it off.

Fergus put out a hand restraining her – she was to keep it on, it would do no damage. Richard, his colour high, relinquished the driving seat to Fergus and when they drove away he stared straight ahead.

Klara broke the uncomfortable silence by saying in a bright voice, 'Well, I have enjoyed the morning and I hope you are all as ready as I am for lunch. Wasn't that man with the performing monkey funny? The little animal seemed to adore him.'

Julie responded to Klara's continued chatter but Richard's behaviour had spoiled the morning for her. And when they arrived back at Klara's she asked Richard to come upstairs with her, saying she wanted to talk to him. Before she had a chance to open her mouth he flung out his hands. 'All right, I behaved like a boor. I'm sorry.'

'So you should be,' she said in a furious undertone. 'I think you forget we are guests of these people. Your manner was unpardonable.'

'I know, I know! It was just that things got on top of me. While I was sitting in the car waiting I went over all that had happened last night and then those awful kids came demanding pennies –' Richard touched Julie's cheek and added softly, 'Forgiven?'

'Yes, of course, but do try and be pleasant. It's embarrassing for us all if you go all moody. We had better go down.'

Lunch passed more pleasantly than Julie had expected. Jake was up, looking more like his amiable self, Richard set himself out to be his most charming and Fergus, who turned out to be a passable mimic, entertained them by taking off the voices and mannerisms of various stallholders.

After lunch, Fergus said he would have to leave them but would call to take them out to dinner that evening.

Klara looked dismayed. 'Oh, Fergus, I would love to come but I have an old friend calling. I just couldn't put her off.'

Jake added, 'And I'm sorry, old chap, but much as I would enjoy an evening out I don't really feel quite up to scratch.'

Then to Julie's annoyance Richard declined the invitation, too. He thought he had better stay in case there was . . . a message.

Fergus raised his eyebrows enquiringly at Julie. 'And do you wish to stay in, Julie?'

'No, I would love to come, that is if Richard doesn't mind.'

Richard grinned suddenly. 'Thanks for acknowledging my superiority, Sis. You have my permission, enjoy yourself.'

Julie felt a lovely warm glow. Dinner alone with Fergus, it was certainly something to look forward to.

Just before Fergus arrived that evening Richard confessed that he now regretted having turned down the invitation, but Fergus gave him no opportunity for changing his mind. He whipped Julie away within seconds of arriving, saying he had booked a table at the Waldorf for eight o'clock and they were a little late.

They actually sat down to dinner at eight o'clock promptly, and when Julie pointed this out Fergus smiled briefly. 'That is how it should be. I'm afraid I'm a stickler for punctuality. If a business colleague makes an appointment for two o'clock and arrives at ten past without a good excuse, I'm annoyed.' Julie made a mental note of this in case of any future meetings with Fergus.

For some reason he was not so easy in his manner towards her as he had been that morning and after giving her the history of the Waldorf, in detail, she said, 'Have I said something to offend you?'

He looked at her with some surprise. 'No, why should you ask?'

She shrugged. 'Oh, I don't know. Your manner, I think. You were so friendly this morning and now you're treating me like a stranger who you are trying to impress with your knowledge of the Waldorf's history.'

'Julie! You really are embarrassingly honest. We were in a market this morning where anything goes. I ate popcorn from a packet but you would not expect me to stand in the middle of the floor and do the same thing now, would you?'

'No, but you were easy with me last night at the Savoy. Would you rather that the others had come with us?'

Fergus spread his hands with a gesture of despair. 'What have I done to deserve this? I bring a young lady out to dinner hoping for a pleasant evening and I get a lecture on my behaviour!'

This made Julie realize how stupidly she was behaving. 'I'm sorry, Fergus. I think I'm vulnerable to moods today. There was Richard this morning, so unlike himself –'

'Forget it, Julie. Now tell me more about this shop where you work. I understand you thoroughly enjoy it.'

She gave a rueful smile. 'Not all the time. I'm beginning to dislike the scrubbing and cleaning, yet I do enjoy the shop work, meeting people. So many of them live in poverty yet they always seem to be able to joke about things. You should hear them when they come in at lunchtimes from the potteries and factory, it's like going to the cinema. They're so funny, I have to laugh. Well, most of the time. Often there's an underlying pathos, like in a Charlie Chaplin film. Do you know what I mean?'

'Yes, I do, Julie. Do you often go to the cinema?'

'No. When I went recently it was the first time in about two years. It was quite an experience.' She amused him with funny little incidents that had happened in the cinema and in the shop and Fergus held her interest with his talk of visits to foreign countries where he went in connection with his business. He gave no indication of the kind of business he was in and when Julie asked him he skirted round it by saying he was involved with various projects.

Then Fergus asked Julie what her ultimate aim was. Did she intend to go on working at the shop, or had she some other plan? The waiter came then with the next course and Julie had time to think about it. What *was* her aim? Where would she go eventually? She looked up to find Fergus watching her with his attractive, speedwell-blue eyes. 'Well, Julie?'

She raised her shoulders in a helpless gesture. 'I don't know. I really don't know what I want to do with my life. I only know that whatever I plan ultimately it will have to be something to keep me busy. I couldn't go back home and just laze around as I did before. I hadn't realised until I came away to work just how desperately bored I had been.'

Fergus teased her, saying that most girls wanted to get married, run a home, have children – surely she had this in mind for the future?

'Eventually, yes,' she said, 'but I'm not ready to settle down yet. I want to do something with my life. If I had masses of money I would build better houses for people, see they had plenty to eat, make sure that children did not go barefoot or wear ragged clothes.'

Fergus laid down his knife and fork. 'Now this might be achieved to a certain extent if men could be persuaded to stop spending their wages in pubs and to curtail the size of their families.'

'But don't you see,' she said earnestly, 'it's because of the awful conditions under which some men have to work and live that they turn to drink. As for having so many children – it's their only . . .' Julie paused, feeling she was getting into deep water. She had been going to say, 'pleasure', having heard Ivy give this reason why the poor had such large families. She ended lamely, 'It's – well, it's marriage, isn't it?'

'So that's the reason?' Fergus' amused smile made Julie flare up.

'It's all right for you, Fergus! You have plenty of money, you can buy what you like, travel, drive a Rolls-Royce, dine out in expensive restaurants.'

Fergus, still looking slightly amused, said, 'May I point out, Julie, that you too are sharing in this luxury.'

She sighed and her shoulders went slack. 'You are right, of course. If I were a true philanthropist I would have asked you for the price of my meal and given the money to a poverty-stricken family.'

'Poor Julie, stop tormenting yourself.'

'I'm not,' she confided, 'that's the trouble. I'm enjoying myself! So what does that make me?'

'A very appealing and caring young lady, one whose company I'm enjoying. Oh – by the way, I have a present for you.'

It was the bracelet she had chosen that morning and she looked at Fergus, puzzled. 'You said it was for one of your sisters.'

'I know. I thought it was a good way of buying you something you really liked. I shall give Klara the bracelet that she chose, later.'

Julie fingered the emblem on the bracelet then looked up. 'It's beautiful, Fergus, but why a present for me? I've done nothing to merit it.'

'Oh, but you have. You made a very wet Sunday morning in London memorable for me. I don't think I shall ever forget you in your funny souwester and macintosh.'

'I looked dreadful.'

'You looked quaint and adorable, because you were so unconcerned with your appearance,' he said softly.

'I was happy this morning, very happy.'

'I know and you made me feel happy – something I've not

really experienced for a long time.' He gave a sudden boyish grin. 'But then I'm not in the habit of wandering around market stalls with lovely young ladies and eating popcorn. We must do it again.'

Julie had drunk very little but at that moment she had a heady feeling as though she had overindulged, a feeling that lasted until they were ready to leave. Klara had lent her a black swansdown shoulder cape, which, although it belonged to Klara's girlhood, did not seem out of place at the present time. When Fergus draped the cape about Julie's shoulders his fingers touched her skin, and she gave a pleasurable shiver. Would Fergus kiss her good night? She certainly hoped he would.

When Fergus drove her back he came into the house, gave his aunt her bracelet, which had her beaming at the unexpected gift then, after saying he really must go because he had some papers to look over, he took Julie's hands in his and thanked her for an enjoyable day. To Richard he remarked, 'I'll see what I can do about Friday', then was gone, leaving Julie completely deflated.

What had happened? Why the sudden change of mood?

In bed she called herself all kinds of fool, realizing how gauche Fergus must have found her for criticising his manner towards her. In his sophisticated world of travel and commerce she must have seemed a child . . . 'a quaint, adorable one'. She was Richard's kid sister, so give her a good time. Let's eat popcorn! Make the evening romantic, take her out to dinner, just the two of them . . . but once the evening was over that was it, no further involvement.

For the first time in her life Julie experienced humiliation and was glad she was in bed so she could indulge unseen in a few tears of self-pity. Then, as a sudden image of her parents flashed into her mind she realized how a casual meeting with a stranger had clouded the more important issue in her life, the question of parentage of both Richard and herself.

Violet's remark must have been eating into Richard's soul all that day, yet she had gone out twice, leaving him without someone close to talk to. She must try and make it up to him during the next few days.

# Chapter Seven

On the Monday morning, Richard and Jake left Klara's house to go to work, with Jake having announced he felt as fit as a fiddle. Klara said after they had gone, 'Now then, Julie, we are going sightseeing, and it's to be my treat. Tomorrow and Wednesday I have social commitments so we'll make the most of today. We'll take in the National Gallery, Madame Tussauds and perhaps a cinema. We shall need to sit down after all that tramping around!'

The visit to the cinema was the highlight of the day for Julie. They went to the Marble Arch Pavilion and saw the film *Where the North Begins*, starring the beautiful alsatian dog Rin-Tin-Tin.

'He was just so clever,' Julie enthused to Richard and Jake that evening after she had described in detail about half of the film. 'I wept when the poor thing –'

'Yes, well, don't tell us any more, Sis,' Richard interrupted, 'Jake and I might want to see it. We're taking you to visit friends later, by the way. It's not a party, just a get-together with coffee and talk, but I think you might enjoy it.'

The flat they went to was in the basement of a four-storey Victorian-type house. The room was large, sparsely furnished, cold, the coffee lukewarm and the talk over Julie's head. The majority of the twelve or fourteen people who were there were intense, including Richard. They discussed Freudian principles, the works of Carl Jung, then progressed to politics. Julie had the impression they considered only people like themselves had any brains and would be able to save the world from disaster.

During a pause in the conversation she found herself saying, 'Wasn't it Mark Twain who said that when he was seventeen he thought how little knowledge his father had, but when he was twenty-one he was surprised at just how much his father had learned in those few years?'

This was received in dead silence, with the gaze of all upon her.

Then a tall, bespectacled young woman said, 'Yes, well, as I was saying –' and they resumed their conversation as though Julie had never spoken.

Not long after this, Jake got up asking to be excused. He was not feeling well. Richard and Julie, concerned, left with him but once outside Jake gave a shout of laughter.

'Julie, you were great. I don't know how I didn't explode. I was told we were going to listen to gramophone records, but –'

'I thought so too,' Richard said, 'but quite frankly, I found the discussion interesting.'

'Not to me, it wasn't. Come along, let's go home and have a game of something, Ludo or Snakes and Ladders. Anything! We will at least have the comfort of a warm room. I was frozen in that ice-box.'

Julie thought – here she was in the Great Metropolis, teeming with wonderful things to see and they were going to play a children's game! But later she had to admit that the game of Snakes and Ladders was responsible for a lot of fun and laughter.

Over their bedtime drink while Klara was upstairs, Julie asked Richard and Jake if they would take her to the pub in the East End where the Cockney people were but Richard shook his head. 'I'm afraid not, Julie. It's not for you. The parents would never forgive me if they found out. We'll find somewhere to take you tomorrow evening, perhaps a show.'

During the next two days Julie went sightseeing on her

own, walking miles in the process, not only to save bus and Underground fares but because she did enjoy walking. On the Wednesday afternoon she was strolling along Piccadilly when suddenly she came face to face with Violet who was coming out of Fortnum & Mason's.

For a second Julie froze, then as she made to hurry on Violet spoke.

'Julie – it is Julie, isn't it? Yes, of course. I'm glad we met, I must explain about my not being able to contact Richard.'

'I don't want to know, and neither does he. Now, if you'll excuse me –' Julie was afraid of this golden-haired woman, without knowing why.

'Wait, it's important.' Violet's tone had changed from a coaxing note to a peremptory one. 'It would be foolish of you not to listen.'

A sleek-looking car drew up at the kerb and when the grey-liveried chauffeur got out Violet called, 'Perkins!' in an imperious way and held out a small package. He came up, his manner deferential, and after taking the package he returned to the car.

Julie had to admit that the beautiful and elegantly dressed Violet could have belonged to an aristocratic family, instead of once owning an expensive brothel in Paris.

Violet threw an end of her fur stole over her shoulder and addressed the girl. 'Take my advice and find out the truth of *your* birth. I must stress that Richard is my son and I shall have him accept me even if it takes years. Tell him I do apologise for not having contacted him: I have been genuinely unwell. Soon, I hope, we shall meet again.' With that she walked to the car and Julie walked on, her limbs trembling and her heart pounding.

Should she tell Richard of the meeting or would it be best to keep it to herself? Julie decided he had a right to know. It would at least prepare him for the fact that Violet was not going to let him go out of her life.

But after Julie had told Richard she regretted it. His face

took on the pallor it usually did when he was upset and he was withdrawn for the rest of the evening. In answer to her plea to discuss it he said no, there would be plenty of time for discussion on Friday when they met their parents.

Julie felt she could hardly wait for Friday to come, not only because of seeing their parents, but to see Fergus. However, there was no word of any kind from him so it was decided that she and Richard would travel by train. Mr Faverly had been very understanding about Richard's family commitments.

The day was dull and cold when they left the house to go to the station but a weak sun was trying to break through the clouds. Richard, who had remained in a withdrawn mood, resisted all Julie's efforts to make conversation on the way to the station, but once they were on the train and discovered that all the people in the carriage were on their way to the docks too, he began to show an interest.

One man said, 'If you haven't seen the *Aquitania* come in then you haven't lived. It's an experience you'll never forget.'

'I've been there three times,' exclaimed a middle-aged woman, 'and I cried each time I saw her coming down the river. What a beautiful ship, so luxurious, so dignified, a regular floating palace.'

Julie was surprised that only one of their fellow travellers was going to Southampton with the purpose of meeting someone arriving on the ship; the rest were simply on an outing. Before they arrived at Southampton it was agreed they would all stay together as a party, it would be more fun.

Although the *Aquitania* was not due for another two hours the quayside was crowded and there was a carnival atmosphere with everyone out to enjoy themselves.

There was the sound of champagne corks popping as one small group decided to celebrate early. A large group began to sing popular songs of the day like *It Ain't Gonna Rain No*

*More*, *When You and I were Seventeen*, *Chilli Bon Bon*, then they went on to the music hall songs and the crowd began to sway to the tune of *Lily of Laguna*.

Richard, who appeared to be enjoying himself said, 'Look, Julie, I don't think we can tell the parents the real reason why we are meeting them, not right away. We shall have to wait. After all, they will be full of their trip and will want to talk about it.'

Julie agreed, but pointed out they would not be able to delay it too long, since she was planning to travel back to London and then Stoke that same evening.

Richard dismissed this as being ridiculous. His sister would not be allowed to travel on her own so late at night. The parents were putting up at an hotel and that is where they too would be staying. Julie gave in but for the first time felt guilty about Tom and Ivy. Saturday was their busy day and she had told them in her letter that she would be back by then to help.

With all the lively chatter going on around them the time passed quickly. About twenty minutes before the ship was due to arrive a boy came pushing through the crowd calling, 'Get yer balloons, folks, tuppence a dozen, strings provided. If you ain't got no wind me little bruvver'll blow 'em up for yer.'

There was no sign of the little brother but nearly all of the people bought balloons. Richard bought two packs and Julie laughed, asking where they were going to find breath to blow up twenty-four balloons.

It certainly caused plenty of fun and once Julie collapsed into giggles as she watched the puffed-out cheeks of young and old, some of them trying fruitlessly to blow up dud ones. Then of course, there were the jokers who would put a lighted cigarette to balloons and all around there would be loud 'plops!'

Some of the balloons were kept tied in bunches but others were released and overhead was a cloud of red, blue, green and orange spheres drifting in the wind. Julie said to Richard, her eyes shining, 'Don't they look lovely? I'm glad we came.'

As she spoke, the late afternoon exploded into sound with the hooting of ships and small boats and above it went up the cry that the *Aquitania* had been sighted.

Dusk came suddenly and when Julie caught her first glimpse of the illuminated ship, with her pennants flying and small tugs chugging so importantly around and in front of her, she felt a surge of emotion. Cheering broke out on all sides. Richard gripped her hand. 'A magnificent sight, Julie.'

She felt so choked at that moment she could only nod.

Later, Julie found herself laughing at the tugs which, although powerful, looked like fussy little beetles, gently nudging and guiding the beautiful 'floating palace' to her moorings.

The decks were crowded with passengers who threw paper streamers to the people on the quayside below, and soon Julie was caught in a web of them. She searched the sea of faces, wondering if it would be possible to find her parents among so many and then, miraculously, she saw them.

'There they are,' she shouted, gripping Richard's arm. 'Mother and Daddy. Look! They're standing next to the big man in the light blue suit and white Stetson.'

It took Richard only seconds to locate them then both he and Julie began to wave their arms frantically, but there was no response from their parents.

Then Richard said he had an idea. He picked up a cardboard carton, tore a large piece from it and after writing on it in bold letters, RICHARD AND JULIE he held it aloft.

Tyler saw it first and drew Kitty's attention to it. Then they began a frantic waving.

Their eventual meeting was an emotional one, with Kitty saying, a catch in her voice, 'What a wonderful surprise! I can't believe you are here. How sweet and thoughtful of you both.'

'Come along,' Tyler said, 'we can talk at the hotel. We have a suite of rooms booked. We were expecting two friends to come back with us, but at the last minute their plans were changed. It seems like fate, doesn't it?'

Kitty put an arm around Julie's waist. 'We shall freshen up then have dinner bought to our rooms, all nice and cosy. I'm dying to hear all your news.'

All nice and cosy . . . Julie wished there had not been such a loving note in her mother's voice. Whatever cosiness they might enjoy at first would be gone before the evening was out.

In the taxi, Kitty wanted to know how Julie came to be in London, and after this was explained Richard told them about Jake's accident and about them all staying with Klara. Then Julie followed with an account of their visit to the Portobello Road market and became aware that she was laughing a great deal and talking in a feverish way.

Kitty said, 'I'm so glad you enjoyed yourself, Julie.' She turned to her son. 'And you, Richard, how is your work progressing?'

Little mention was made of Tyler and Kitty's trip to New York until they sat down to dinner and then it was Richard who kept firing questions. Had they suffered from vertigo when on the top of the highest skyscrapers? How about the density of the traffic and what was the most popular expensive car? Was the Statue of Liberty as impressive as travellers stated?

Julie realized that Richard was talking in the same feverish way that she had done and guessed it was to prolong the moment when the unpleasant incident with Violet would have to be broached.

Tyler had answered Richard's questions at some length but when he began to launch into an account of the voyage itself Kitty interrupted.

'Tyler dear, shall we leave that until later? I want to know all about Ivy and Tom, now it seems that our new business contracts will make a visit to Stoke impossible at the moment.'

Julie relaxed. Her fears were not to be realised.

Kitty sighed. 'It would have been so nice to see them and talk over old times . . . And you could have travelled back home with us, if you wanted.'

'But I don't want to come back home with you,' Julie protested. 'Not yet.' She saw her parents exchange disconcerted glances then her father asked how long she intended to stay, another month, two months, six months – ?

'I don't know,' she said, 'it depends.'

'On what, Julie?' Tyler spoke quietly. 'On the man called Angus who lodges with Tom and Ivy? You mention him quite a lot in your letters.'

'As though you had become very fond of him,' Kitty said.

Julie's mouth set in a mutinous line. 'You really are determined to rule my life, aren't you? You were both very indulgent and allowed me to go and live with Ivy and Tom, but the moment you think I might have become involved with a *pottery worker* you decide I have to return home. Well, you can forget about Angus, I can give you something much more important to worry about. Last Saturday evening Richard met –'

Richard called a warning, 'Wait, Julie –', but she shook her head. 'No, it has to be told and it might just as well be now as later.' She took a quick breath then said, 'Richard met your sister Violet in the Savoy and had a talk with her.'

When Julie saw the stricken look on her mother's face she wished she had broken the news more gently. Kitty mouthed the word 'Violet' but no sound came. Tyler put his arm around her and looked from Julie to Richard.

'Where did you meet her? What did she say?' His tone was harsh.

Richard had gone pale and there was a slight tremor in his voice when he spoke. 'She told me she was – my mother.'

'It's not true.' Kitty's voice was little above a whisper.

'Violet has lied her way through life, causing trouble and a great deal of heartache on the way. I had hoped she was dead.' Her voice had risen on the last sentence. 'Yes, *dead*. I mean that and I have never wished it about anyone else!'

Richard said, 'She told me that when I was a baby her husband died and left her destitute and as she had no means of supporting me she left me on your doorstep. What reason had she for lying –'

Kitty's head came up. 'Because she hates me, has done since I was a child.'

'Why?' The word was rapped out.

'Because I – because she – well, apparently she was jealous of me.'

'It could not be because of your looks, Mother,' Richard went on in a cold, relentless way. 'Although you are a very attractive woman, your sister is exceptionally beautiful.'

'Yes she is, with, unfortunately, an almost evil streak in her.'

Tyler said, 'Take my advice, Richard, and avoid Violet like the plague. She has a way with her of involving people in her web of deceit. When your mother once told me, long ago, of how she had nearly lost her life when she was young because of Violet's cruelties, I didn't believe her. But when I eventually learned the truth, by overhearing Violet taunting your mother with what she had done, I was appalled. So, if you should ever meet her again, *don't believe a word she says*!'

There was a silence after this then Kitty drew a hand across her brow with a weary gesture. 'I think I must go to bed. It was a wonderful trip to America, but quite exhausting.'

Julie said, on a note of pleading, 'Mother, will you tell me one thing before you go; who are the Tiernes and how are they connected with my life? Aunt Helder told me I must find out about my background, then Violet said the same thing.'

Kitty sighed. 'It's a long story, Julie, but I will tell you this. My mother was married twice, first to a man called Harvey and they had four children, Violet and your three aunts. Then she married Richard Tierne and I was their only child.'

Julie stared at her. 'Then why make such a secret of it? I've asked several times about the Tiernes and you've always put me off.'

'Yes, I know, because my story involved other people.' Kitty got up. 'I'm sorry, but I can't talk any more.' She swayed and Tyler caught her in his arms.

'Come along, darling, bed, and right now!' He picked her up and carried her out of the room.

Julie looked at Richard. 'And so we are still left with the mystery. I'm beginning to wonder if we will ever get to know what happened in the past.'

'We will.' Richard looked grim. 'I'll get it out of Father when he comes back.'

But Tyler was away for some time and when he did return to the sitting room said at once that he did not want to discuss any more family matters that evening, they would have to wait until the next day. But Richard would not wait. He wanted an answer to a quite uncomplicated question. He and Julie had been led to believe that both sets of grandparents were dead. Was this true?

Tyler sat eyeing them for a moment, his slender, steepled fingers pressed against his mouth, then, as though reaching a decision he took his hands away.

'Your mother's parents and my stepmother are all dead, but my father is still alive and lives in Italy. We became estranged when I was seventeen. I left home and travelled around, then found work with a glass-blower. Your mother and I have discussed, in the past, taking you and Julie to Italy to meet my family, and we've also talked of trying to trace the Tiernes. Your mother has never met them, Julie. She never wanted to meet them because they ignored her when your grandfather died, but now she knows that you both have the right to meet our respective families. That is for the future. Right now I want to hear from you, Richard, about your work and from you, Julie, about your life in the potteries. You talk, I shall listen.'

Although Tyler did appear to be interested in what they had to say it was not long before he was fighting to keep awake. At last he said, 'I'm sorry, terribly sorry, but I'm afraid that exhaustion is catching up with me, too. Still, we shall have plenty of time to talk over the weekend.'

'No,' Julie said quickly. 'I won't be here. I want to travel back to London tomorrow and then on to Stoke as early as possible.' When Tyler protested that they had so much to talk about and it was such an opportunity, she reminded him with a wry smile that she was a working girl, with obligations.

'Yes,' he said quietly, 'and I'm glad you recognise it, Julie. It is important in life. I'll find out the times of the trains for you.' Tyler then put his arms around her and held her close. 'I want you to know, Julie, that your mother and I love you very much. Never forget that.'

'I won't,' she whispered, near to tears then. 'I promise.'

# Chapter Eight

Julie left for London with a promise from Richard to write and tell her all the news after another talk with their parents. She had quitted the hotel so early to begin her long journey that there had been no opportunity for any further discussion. And anyway, her father had said, 'Your mother is not at all well, Julie, she had a bad night. I'm going to try to persuade her to spend the day in bed.' An excuse to avoid any further confessions?

Goodbyes had been brief, with her mother a little tearful, saying they would keep in touch. To be fair she had not looked well, but then the fault was hers. If she and Tyler had only been open and told Richard and herself about their past life there would have been no unpleasant incident. Richard especially would have been saved all the worry had he been told about the devious aunt Violet. Julie had accepted the story of this aunt she had never known because she had not liked her when coming face to face with her in Piccadilly, but Richard would not accept all that had been said about her.

'I can't, Julie. You didn't see her when she spoke of having to desert her baby – there was such pain and despair in her eyes.'

Julie refrained from reminding him that a woman in Violet's profession would be well schooled in the art of play-acting.

As the train carried her towards London, her thoughts progressed to her father mentioning he might take Richard and herself to Italy to meet his family. In spite of all the other unpleasantness Julie could not help a stir of excitement. Italy? How wonderful that would be. Then there was also his promise of trying to trace her grandfather's family, the Tiernes. Who were they, what line of business were they in?

Speculation of this and dreaming of a visit to a foreign country kept Julie's thoughts occupied for some time. Then Fergus Damant came into her mind. He had sent a message saying he would see Richard and herself before they left for Southampton, but he had not shown up, nor had there been any further message. When Klara remarked on it Jake dismissed it in a casual way. Fergus could be on the other side of the world, she should know by now he was here, there and everywhere. But Klara would not accept this, pointing out that Fergus was meticulous in keeping promises and appointments.

Julie thought it was perhaps just as well she had not met him again, since she had found him a disturbing influence. Not that he would think of her as any more than a casual acquaintance. How could he? She still squirmed when she thought of her gauche behaviour the evening he had taken her to dinner at the Waldorf. And yet – he had seemed thoroughly to enjoy the morning they had spent at the Portobello Road market. And he had bought her the gold bracelet. Julie sighed. It was no use trying to build the gift into anything, he would probably have bought one for any other girl he was with.

In spite of this the image of Fergus Damant lingered in her mind and she felt regret that she had not seen him again before her return to Stoke.

After a hurried trip to Klara's house in a taxi, to collect her small amount of luggage, Julie was on her way back to St Pancras, to catch the next express to Stoke. In Klara and Jake's absence, she left a huge bouquet of roses, along with an affectionate Thank You note.

When Julie did arrive at Stoke station she was surprised

at the strong feeling she had of coming home. She caught a tram that dropped her off near the shop and when she finally smelled the aroma of cooked meat pies mingling with that of the mushy peas she broke into a run, the suitcase banging against her legs.

Tom was alone in the shop and when she went in his face lit up. 'Julie, love! You're later than we thought! Come on, let me give you a big hug.' They met at the end of the counter and Tom nearly squeezed the breath out of her. 'Oh, it's good to have you back.'

'It's good to be back, Tom.' There was a tremor in Julie's voice. 'Where's Ivy?'

'In the kitchen, cooking. It was only about an hour ago she was saying she doubted now whether we'd see you for another week. Go on, give her a surprise!'

When Julie threw open the kitchen door and announced, 'I'm back!' Ivy, who was at the table rolling pastry said, without looking up, 'Three hearty British cheers, Princess Julietta returns!'

Julie laughed. 'Ivy, I love you. Who else but you would give me such a greeting? Have you missed me?'

'Of course I've missed you!' Ivy picked up a pastry cutter and began stamping out pie lids at an enormous rate. 'I've had everything to do, haven't I? Cooking, cleaning, shopping, serving – and then we get a telegram that frightened Tom and me to death. We thought something terrible had happened.'

Julie, serious now, said, 'It was terrible to us, in its way.' Ivy paused in her cutting, her eyes full of curiosity. Then she went on again, bang, bang, bang. 'You'd better tell me about it later, Angus will be in soon. He wants to do some work in the shed. He had a meal earlier, but I'll cook you something if you want it.'

'No, thanks, Ivy, I don't feel hungry, but I will make myself a cup of tea. I'll just nip upstairs with my things.'

When Julie came downstairs again Angus was standing,

his back to the fire, his fingers wrapped round a steaming mug of tea. He greeted her as casually as Ivy had done. 'Back again then, Julie, back to the old daily grind. Did you enjoy London?'

'Yes I did.' Julie poured herself a mug of tea, milked and sugared it, stirred it slowly then looked up. 'But do you know something, Angus? I discovered it's a nice old daily grind. I found myself wanting to be back.'

Angus smiled then. 'And *we* are pleased to have you back. What impressed you the most in the big city?'

'I think my most memorable experience was seeing the *Aquitania* arriving at Southampton.'

'Stop right there,' Ivy exclaimed. 'Don't say another word about it until I fetch Tom. He loves hearing about big ships.'

Tom came in beaming. 'So you saw the *Aquitania*, Julie. That must have been a sight to behold. Tell us about it.'

Julie described the scene from the moment of arriving on the quayside, the crowds of people, the popping of champagne corks, the cloud of coloured balloons and the emotional moment when she caught her first glimpse of the liner. 'I think what impressed me the most,' she said, 'was that anything so huge could have such beauty and grace. I should like very much to have a trip on her someday.'

Tom said softly and so would he, then he went on to talk about the time when he was twelve years old and he went out with the fishing fleet on a trawler where his uncle was skipper.

There was a dreaming in his eyes. 'It was the North Sea. When it was rough it was magnificent; when it was calm it was magical, especially in the late evening. There was this vastness when the only sounds were the swish of the water and the throbbing of the engines. I wanted to go to sea, but then the family moved and when I left school I had the chance to learn glass-making and that was it!'

There was a silence then Ivy said, 'You never told me you wanted to go to sea, Tom.'

He raised his shoulders. 'It was just a boyish dream, Ivy.'

Angus drained his mug and set it down. 'All youngsters dream, but few have them come true. Well, I'll away and get some pots made. See you later.'

Ivy gave a sniff. 'Yes, and we'd better get moving! The evening rush'll be starting soon.'

When the people did come in with their basins for the mushy peas, pies, black pudding and pease pudding Julie was greeted from all sides.

'You're back then, gal . . . Where you bin, London, was it . . . ? It weren't the same wi'out your lovely smile . . . Did you bring us a stick of rock, Julie . . . ?' One man said, 'She brought herself and that's good enough for me.'

Ivy kept warning Julie in a tart voice to take no notice of them, they were all buttering her up, hoping to get an extra dollop of peas. At this a woman shouted, 'Straighten your face, Ivy love, you grumbled all the time the lass was away and you're still as sour as an unripened gooseberry!'

Ivy sucked in her mouth and cheeks as though she was sampling a gooseberry which brought a laugh and eventually a broad grin from her. 'Come on,' she called, 'stop messing, give us your orders.'

Tom was in bed by nine o'clock and Angus looked into the shop half an hour later to say he was going to have an early night too. No, he said, he didn't want a drink or anything to eat. Julie was glad that both men would be out of the way when they closed the shop, wanting to have Ivy on her own for their talk.

After all the preparations had been made for the next morning they sat over the embers of the fire with a mug of cocoa each and a buttered scone. 'So,' Ivy said. 'What went wrong in London?'

'Nothing actually went wrong, it was – well, Richard and I met mother's sister Violet in the Savoy Hotel.'

'Oh, Gawd!' Ivy stared at her in dismay. 'So *she's* back in circulation again. What lies had she to tell this time? Where Violet is there's always trouble.'

'She asked to see Richard and told him he was her son.'

'The bitch! She should have been strangled at birth! She's the worst kind of woman because she puts on such charm when she tells her lies. I've seen her, heard her silvery tongue that sows poison. I only hope Richard wasn't taken in by her.'

'I think he was, despite the fact that we were reliably told she used to keep an exclusive brothel in Paris!'

Ivy's eyebrows went up. 'She did, did she? And Richard is sympathetic towards a woman like that? He must be out of his mind. You know what she's after, don't you? She realises she's getting a little older and has no family who care about her. She was in love with your father – did you know that?'

When Julie shook her head Ivy went on, 'She wanted him badly, and when she failed to get him she disappeared. She probably brooded that your father had turned her out of the house and this story could possibly be her way of revenge. How were your parents coping with this latest news when you left?'

Julie explained the situation then told Ivy of the proposed visit to Italy and also that her father was going to make enquiries about the Tiernes, adding, 'And about time too. It's all been such a mystery.'

Ivy did not approve of this at all. In her opinion, they should let sleeping dogs lie. To this Julie demanded – why? If there were skeletons in the cupboard she wanted to know about them and she was sure that Richard would, too.

'Perhaps,' Ivy said wryly, 'but who would be the one to suffer? Your mother. She's already suffered enough. I'm sure every time the name Violet is mentioned it must be like turning a knife in a wound.'

'I'm sorry about that, but . . .' Julie concentrated a

moment on running a finger round the rim of her mug then she looked up. 'Ivy – did Mother ever talk to you about my grandfather?'

'Not for a long time, then one day she told me about her mother's marriage to Richard Tierne.' Ivy's expression softened. 'It's one of the most beautiful love stories I've ever heard, but it's up to you, Julie, to ask your mother about it.' Ivy got up. 'It's bed for both of us, *and* right now!'

Julie was unable to sleep at first. Her over-active brain kept flashing scenes under her eyelids of everything she had seen and done in London, with the image of Fergus Damant interposed on each one. It took an effort to banish them and to think of Richard. Had there been a discussion with their parents? Would he write soon and let her know . . . ?

It was a week before Julie had a letter, and the contents were more or less what she had expected. Nothing more had been discussed at Southampton, and he had returned to his rooms in London on the Saturday evening, none the wiser.

*'I felt so frustrated, Sis. It was as though they were determined to draw a veil over their past life. I still have a leaning towards Violet, she seemed so sincere. If she does get in touch with me again through Klara and asks to meet I shall accept. Hope you had a good journey back and that you are settled down again, although I doubt it! Once you have tasted London life every other place seems deadly dull . . .'*

Julie looked up from the page. No, he was wrong. In retrospect there had been something insubstantial, unreal, about her visit. She thought of the strange wax figures at Madame Tussaud's, the fairy-tale world of the elegant liner at Southampton and then Violet, appearing out of the blue, with her witch-like influence to persuade Richard he was her son. Her thoughts travelled on to the mystery of her parents' lives and the changing attitudes of Fergus Damant. One moment he was a cheery, hail-fellow-well-met friend at the Sunday market and then, a well-groomed, sophisticated man who would claim the attention of waiters with a lift of his little finger. He was a man who also kept his business life a mystery.

Back here at the shop was reality. The people were hard-working, plain-speaking and big-hearted . . . And there was Angus, solid, reliable, making no fuss of her but letting her know he was pleased to have her back.

The following morning, a letter arrived from her mother, full of apologies to Julie for not insisting on her staying with them for a few days.

*'The trouble was, of course, I felt so dreadful, Julie. It was the shock of hearing about Violet again after all these years and bringing to the surface so vividly all the unhappiness of those days. I can only pray she does not pester Richard. But enough of Violet. Your father has set plans in motion to visit Italy and he is also making enquiries about the Tierne family. We may not be able to get away for a couple of months but the weather should be better then. I shall write to Ivy in a day or two. I hope you were not too upset when you left to return to Stoke. It was so unfortunate that on your one visit to London such a thing should happen. You are in our thoughts every day, darling. We both send our love, and give our love to Ivy and Tom . . . Your loving mother.'*

This was followed by a row of crosses.

Although Julie wanted to go to Italy she was glad that it could not be arranged right away, for she would have felt she was letting Ivy and Tom down if the trip had been in a couple of weeks' time. It would at least give them an opportunity to arrange extra help. Julie also knew she wanted to be with Angus for a while. A warmer relationship had developed between them since her return. He had taken her to the cinema a few evenings before to see a Theda Bara film and when she had come out drooling over the romance Angus had teased her.

'It's a celluloid world, lassie, but dream on, it colours the drudgery of everyday life. We all need a magic carpet.'

Julie was glad he had not been like Alf who had said to

Peggy, 'A load of bloody rubbish! Life's not like that.'

'That's why we go to the pictures,' Peg retorted, 'to get away from floor scrubbing and washing loads of dishes. Someone said that marriages are made in heaven, well, if I married you it would start in hell!'

An argument ensued between them but by the time they reached the corner where the two couples parted, Peg had her arm linked through Alf's and was laughing up into his face. After arrangements had been made for the four of them to meet again the following week Peg called, 'Ta-ra then, you two, be good!'

Angus put an arm across Julie's shoulders and said laughingly as they walked in the direction of the shop, 'It takes all kinds to make a world, doesn't it? But then it wouldn't do if we were all the same.' In a more serious vein he added, 'Do you mind them joining up with us, Julie?'

'No, not really. I like Peg and although I used to think that Alf was absolutely insensitive I realised he can be compassionate. When I went to the Co-op for Ivy on Tuesday I saw him helping old Mrs Waters across the main road. I heard afterwards he had taken her home.'

Angus nodded. 'Yes, it's easy to misjudge folks. By the way – how long are you staying with Tom and Ivy? Have you come to any decision, yet?'

Julie glanced at him, wondering at his over-casual tone. 'I don't know,' she said. 'I may be going to Italy with my parents in two months' time but I don't know what will happen after that.'

'Och, two months is a long way away. A lot of things can happen in that time.'

'Such as?'

'Let's wait and see, shall we?'

There was a light-heartedness in him then that Julie had never heard before and it marked a new warmth in their relationship. It seemed to Julie that he made opportunities to be with her. One evening he told Tom to go and have a rest and he would help Julie in the shop. Tom seemed about to protest, then grinned and said he had got the message. Then there would be odd evenings when he invited her out to the shed to show her some special work he had done, the invitation having been given in the nonchalant manner he had adopted. Sometimes it would be an intricately-designed vase or jug, but mostly it was an item he had painted, and it was then that Julie became aware of just how talented Angus was.

Although Julie had by now mastered the art of throwing pots and had made a few jugs and bowls, she was not so much interested in this side of it as the decorative part. She had become fascinated with the blending of paints, the designs themselves, and the making of transfers that could be used over and over again. Angus talked about it as 'pouncing': a design was drawn on a piece of paper, pin holes were made in it and charcoal put over it so that the dotted outline of black was left.

Julie, being impatient, wanted to make short cuts but Angus insisted she must learn the groundwork first. There were times when he would get annoyed with her impatience and tell her to leave. Then Julie would go storming back to the kitchen and declare she would not go near the shed again.

Once Ivy said, 'Chance is a fine thing! And don't blame Angus if he doesn't let you work there again.'

'He's cold, soul-less, doesn't care about anyone or their feelings!'

'Listen to me, Julietta van Neilson –' Ivy wagged a forefinger in front of her. 'You're getting too cocky by half. You should feel privileged that Angus is bothering to teach you his trade. And don't you call him cold and soul-less. Angus is a great big softie where people and animals are concerned. He sat up with Tom for two nights when he was ill and while you were gallivanting in London!'

'All right, all right, he's wonderful, but he can fart off for all I care!'

There was a split second's silence then a stinging slap on Julie's face had her staggering back. She put a hand to her cheek, too astonished to speak.

Ivy was standing, hands on hips, eyes blazing. 'You might hear those kind of words in London, but not in here! There's not a factory or a pottery worker or any neighbour who would use that kind of language to Tom and me. And do you know why? Because they have too much respect for us. And by God, Julie, respect has to be earned.' Ivy waved a hand dismissing her. 'Get out of my sight for half an hour!'

Julie grabbed her coat, shrugged herself into it then she ran through the shop and out into the street. She heard Tom call after her but she ignored him and kept on running, fuming at the indignity of having her face slapped by someone like Ivy. Julie's footsteps slowed as she realised what she had been thinking. For the first time, she understood that deep down she was a snob. This fact shocked her much more than the slap.

A bitter wind was blowing and when she came to an empty shop near a piece of waste ground she went into the doorway and stood, her coat collar held close to her throat. After all her talk of wanting to be with working people there was this niggle of wealth, her rich background making her feel superior. Or did she really feel superior? If it was in her she had really not been aware of it until now.

Julie felt suddenly ashamed at what she had said to Ivy. It was not something she would have said to her own mother. But although Julie knew she ought to go back and apologise she still stood, unsure now of whether she should go on staying with Tom and Ivy – or in fact, whether Ivy would want her to stay. But where could she go? She had no wish to go home, her life there had been so boring. London? If she could get a job would Klara accept her as a paying guest? But then again Julie thought how pleased she had been to return to Stoke, how it had felt like home.

This was a quiet part of the street and when she heard firm footsteps coming in her direction she shrank further back into the doorway, thinking it might be a policeman. She had no wish to explain why she was in the doorway of an empty shop at half-past nine at night.

The footsteps slowed then stopped. 'Julie?'

Julie came out of the doorway, said, 'Oh, Angus,' and burst into tears.

He wrapped strong arms about her, but there was no gentleness in his tone when he scolded her. 'That was a daft thing to do, tearing out of the shop as if there were monsters chasing you. Didn't you realise that Tom and Ivy would be worried about you?'

Julie's tears stemmed. She drew back, head up. 'Ivy told me to get out of her sight.'

'Yes, to go upstairs, not out into the streets. And get that mutinous look off your face, lassie.' He took hold of her hand. 'Come on, let's go.' When Julie made no move he said, 'Now look, I've had a full day, I've been working all evening and I'm not in the mood to coax a spoilt child.'

'I'm not a spoilt child. I used a swear word but there was no need for Ivy to go up in the air.'

'Julie, you should know Ivy by now! You've known her long enough to know she flares up then the flame dies. And you ought to know me too. I've told you over and over again that I won't put up with shoddy work, but no, you haven't to be told anything, you know it all!'

'I don't know anything,' she said miserably, 'and I don't know *anyone*, not even myself. I've just discovered I'm a snob.'

'Ay, that's true enough.'

Julie stared at him. Although she had admitted her fault to herself she was surprised that Angus had become aware of it. 'What made you think I was a snob?'

He took hold of her hand again. 'We can talk while we're walking. It was after you came back from London. You talked to the three of us in the kitchen about the Sunday market, Madame Tussaud's, and going to the cinema, but when we were with Alf and Peg it was the Rolls-Royce you mentioned, the wining and dining at the Savoy and the Waldorf, the dressing-up, wanting to impress them with the fact that you were completely at home in such places.'

'I didn't do it for that reason,' Julie protested. 'You must believe me. Peg loves to hear about beautiful clothes and how the wealthy live.'

'Well, let's forget it, but I must warn you not to expect Ivy to crawl to you when you apologise to her.'

'Who says I'm going to apologise?'

'I do. And you'll do as you're told, lassie. Is that understood?'

'Yes, sir,' she said with mock humility.

Angus grinned. 'It's as well to understand now who the master is. It will save a lot of fighting later on.'

Although he had made light of this last remark Julie found herself thinking that Angus would always have to be master and she thrilled at the thought of having him master her. Was this an indication that she might be falling in love with him? She would not want a man who was weak. Although Tom at times appeared to let Ivy boss him, on certain issues he would be firm and Ivy knew he had to be obeyed. On these occasions she would say with pride, 'Tom might have suffered in the war but he has great strength. Tom's a *man*.'

Ivy was preparing to close the shop when they returned. 'Oh, you found her then,' she said to Angus. 'You'd better go and make yourselves a hot drink. Tom's gone to bed.'

When Julie stood silent Angus gave her a dig in the back. She glared at him over her shoulder then turned to Ivy. 'I'm sorry for swearing.' Then after another dig from Angus she added, 'It won't happen again.'

'Good, I'm glad to hear it.' Ivy threw a tea towel over the bacon slicer. 'I can imagine what your mother and father would have to say if you went home with that kind of talk.'

'Well, don't go on about it, I've said I'm sorry!'

'I'm not going on about it, it's all finished as far as I'm concerned. Go and get your cocoa then you can get off to bed. I'll finish what has to be done.'

Julie had a sudden forlorn feeling. She had done wrong, she had been slapped and sent off to bed, but what she missed was her mother's arms around her, the kiss and cuddle to let her know she had been forgiven. In the kitchen Angus said, as though aware of her thoughts, 'Ivy is like me, she can't use flowery words, but you can take it that she's sorry for having slapped you. The fact of telling you to get off to bed proves that. There's jobs to be done and she's tired. I don't think I've ever seen Ivy looking so weary.'

Julie looked up at him. 'I hadn't noticed. I'll stay and help.'

'Good girl. You make the cocoa and I'll go and fetch some firewood and coal for the morning.'

Julie, who had made cocoa for Ivy too, handed her the mug when she came in. Ivy said, 'Thanks, love,' and squeezed her shoulder, which coming from Ivy was as good as a caress. The choked feeling eased in Julie's throat.

During the following month, Julie went with Angus several times to the cinema, had a long walk with him one Sunday afternoon and spent what time she could spare learning the art of painting in the shed. By this time she had become known to the customers as Angus' girl, which did not displease Julie, although he had never attempted to kiss her.

During their Sunday afternoon's walk Julie had told him a little more of her life and in a burst of confidence mentioned Violet and the meeting with her in the Savoy Hotel. To Julie's surprise Angus' sympathies were with Violet: if Richard *was* her son then the poor woman must have suffered having to part with him. If it wasn't true, then she should also be pitied. She must have known great unhappiness in her life to prompt her to say such a thing. Julie pointed out that there were wicked people like that in the world who said such things to hurt, mostly through jealousy, but when this brought the comment from Angus that it was all the more reason why Violet was to be pitied, Julie said no more . . . In fact, she was annoyed with herself for having brought it up. It was family business and ought not to have been discussed.

The dampness and fog of November drifted into December. Everyone but Tom seemed to be in a bad mood and Julie found herself looking forward to going home for Christmas. She seldom saw Angus now. He worked late every evening in the shed and when he did come in for his supper he had little to say, then went to bed. Julie remarked tartly one evening that he might just as well live on a desert island and had Ivy snap at her.

'You watch your tongue, girl! He's making pottery pieces to sell, to get money to give to the church to help provide a Christmas dinner for the poverty-striken.'

Julie apologised, said she had not known about this then added, with some spirit, 'I wish people would tell me these things.'

'You would know if you listened,' Ivy retorted. 'I told you last week, but you sit in a dream world at times and don't listen.' Ivy went out and slammed the kitchen door.

At that moment Julie decided she would not come back to Stoke after Christmas. Ivy and Angus could go to the devil!

But the evening before she was due to travel to Crescent House they all exchanged gifts, which brought a warmth back to the household. Julie had bought scarves for the men – beige cashmere ones, which had Tom declaring they would be 'proper toffs'! For Ivy there was a bottle of eau de cologne, an item she considered a luxury but would not buy for herself.

Ivy and Tom's gift to Julie was a white woollen jumper with a Fair Isle yoke. Julie had seen it in a shop window and told Ivy she was going to save up for one.

Angus gave her four china marmalade kittens in a row, the expression of each different and so lovable that she laughed. 'Oh, Angus, they're adorable.'

There were hugs and kisses all round and when Julie felt Angus' strong arms tighten around her she wished they could all spend Christmas together.

Her parents' and Richard's welcome when she arrived home was no less warm. They talked non-stop, exchanging news. Julie learned that Fergus, with Jake and Klara, was spending the holidays with friends in Paris.

Crescent House was ablaze with lights, there was a huge Christmas tree in the hall and one in the sitting room decorated with baubles and tinsel and coloured fairy-lights. An appetising smell of cooking hung in the air and a lovely aroma of cigars, which Julie always associated with Christmas.

The van Neilson family had a constant stream of callers and numerous invitations to various houses and although it all seemed most enjoyable Julie was aware that something was not quite right. It took her three days to realise what it was. Although Richard joined in the fun she found his jollity a façade. In unguarded moments a bleakness came into his eyes. Was he disappointed that he had not gone with Fergus and Jake to Paris? When she asked him, he said no. He had wanted to accept an invitation to spend Christmas in a country mansion, but his parents had said that he ought to turn it down, as families should be together at this time of the year.

Then he added on a bitter note, 'I particularly wanted to go. There was someone I wanted to be with.'

'A girl?' Julie teased. 'Oh, tell me about her! What is she like?'

'She's not a girl, she's a woman.' Richard excused himself and left the room, leaving Julie to wonder if he had fallen in love with a married woman.

Later, Richard apologised for his behaviour and although he would not give her any further information he was more like the brother she knew after that.

Although Julie enjoyed being at home, being made a fuss of and having breakfast in bed she knew a longing to be back with Tom and Ivy *and* Angus; and was glad when the time came for her to leave Crescent House.

Her parents and Richard came to see her off and although her mother was a little tearful at the station Tyler assured her it would not be long before they would all be together again. Each one promised to write.

It was like another Christmas when Julie arrived back at the shop, handing out all the presents that her parents had sent, and the food. Angus said softly, 'I've missed you, lassie, we'll have to go to the pictures one night.'

Julie smiled to herself at the promised date. The pictures . . . not a romantic moonlit walk! But it was something to look forward to.

As it turned out, they never got to the pictures. Four days later she had a letter from Richard that sent her into a panic.

*'Dear Sis,'* he began, *'When you receive this I could be dead. I've had several long talks with Violet and I'm now convinced that she is my mother and Tyler my father. I feel I hate my father for having lied to me on such an important issue and I'm so deeply ashamed knowing I am a bastard that I don't want to live. If I do decide to kill myself forgive me, Julie, for my weakness. Your loving brother, Richard.'*

Julie, with her heart hammering against her ribs, ran to call Ivy, who was in the shop. Ivy came running, demanding to know what was wrong. Had she burnt or scalded herself? Julie held out the letter. 'It's from Richard, he says he's going to kill himself!'

Ivy scanned the letter then looked up. 'Folk who talk

about committing suicide seldom do it, but –' She grabbed a shawl from a hook and flung it around her shoulders. 'I'd better let your parents know. I'll get in touch with your father at the factory. I'll go to the bakery – Mr Peters will telephone for me and he'll keep his mouth shut.' She was away running.

Julie was still standing in the passageway, shocked when Tom came out of the shop. 'What's going on, Julie?' She told him through stiff lips and he took her into the kitchen and made her sit down.

'Now, it'll be all right. Richard must be in a depressed state but he's basically a sensible fellow. I bet after he sent the letter he regretted it.' Julie nodded but could not control the trembling of her limbs.

It seemed ages before Ivy came back yet the clock said it was only five minutes. She looked pale. 'I've spoken to your father, Julie. He's going to get in touch with the firm where Richard works. He'll telephone Mr Peters as soon as he knows anything.'

It was two hours before Mr Peters came with a message, and they were the longest two hours Julie had ever known. The news was bad. Richard *had* attempted to take his life and he was in hospital, seriously ill. Could Julie come to London? If she let her parents know the time of her arrival someone would come to meet her. Mr Peters, who had already found out there was a train to London in half an hour offered to take Julie to the station in his van.

Julie, who suddenly found herself quite calm said she would be ready in a few minutes. Ivy packed her a small overnight holdall; Tom gave her the money for the train fare and in less than ten minutes Julie was sitting in the back of the van with Ivy, who had decided to go to the station with her.

Ivy said, 'I wish I could have travelled all the way with you, Julie. You need someone with you at a time like this, but it's impossible. I couldn't leave Tom.'

'No, I know you couldn't. Don't worry, I'll be all right.' She clasped her hands tightly. 'I wonder if Violet knows what she's responsible for?'

'I shouldn't wonder,' Ivy said bitterly. 'It's probably what she set out to do, to get her revenge. I can tell you this, if ever I come up with her she'll know about it. I'll beat the living daylights out of her! If only Richard would have accepted she was a liar. If it could have been proved that she told only *one* lie, he would have known her for what she is.'

Julie gave Ivy a quick glance. 'I've been a fool. I should have gone to Billy Barker's and found out if he remembered the name of the young man in the miniature. If it's *not* the same as that of Violet's first husband – then there would be the lie!'

'You're right! I'll go straight to Billy's when I get back and if I have any news for you I'll send a telegram to Crescent House. They'll know where to find you. This news could perhaps be the turning point for Richard.'

They parted on the station platform with a hug from Ivy that told Julie of a grief shared. After all, Ivy had played a big part in moulding the early years of Richard and herself. In spite of being strict with them she had always been fair, and although Julie knew that Richard had been her favourite, she had never minded.

She went over those early years during the journey, then relived her first visit to London. She mused over the recent upset with Ivy about the swearing and had to smile a little wryly to herself, remembering her mother saying that Ivy used to swear such a lot when they were in service together. Julie went painstakingly over all the things her mother had told her about those years, needing desperately to keep her mind from the fact that Richard could be dead when she arrived at St Pancras.

The strain told on her, and by the time she reached London Julie was in a state of nervous exhaustion. She looked for one of her parents to be there to meet her, knowing they would have reached the city some hours earlier, but was astonished to see Fergus Damant coming towards her, his expression sombre. He raised his hand acknowledging her then took off his hat as he reached her.

'Julie, how are you? Jake promised your parents at the hospital that he would come to meet you, but he was in such a state he asked me to come instead. Richard is still unconscious, but holding his own. Here, let me take your bag, I have my car outside.'

'Wait, tell me what happened. What way did Richard – ?'

'I'll tell you in the car, Julie. I think your parents are anxious for you to be there in case he regains consciousness. Apparently, he wrote and told them he wanted nothing more to do with them.'

'Oh, no,' she said on a despairing note. 'How deeply hurt they will be. No matter what faults they have their love for him is sincere.'

# Chapter Nine

When they were in the Rolls, Fergus explained about Richard's attempted suicide. 'He had taken a large overdose of a sleeping draught which had been prescribed for Jake, who has not been sleeping properly ever since his accident before Christmas. The two of them had been invited to a party but at the last minute Richard backed out. Jake went on his own and this is where he blames himself for what happened. He said he knew Richard was not himself and ought not to have been left. But of course with hindsight we would all behave differently, wouldn't we?'

Julie asked about her parents and how they had taken the news. Fergus said they were shocked, naturally, and they too had asked themselves if they could have prevented it happening. He added, 'I don't think anyone should feel responsible. Richard is a sensible person in many ways but he is over-sensitive. It matters greatly to him what people think.'

'Shouldn't it matter to all of us what people think?' Julie asked. 'After all, our behaviour has a bearing on our lives.'

'If a man steals then he couldn't expect respect from his fellow men, but if something happens over which he has no control then it's foolish of him to let it ruin his life.'

Julie became a little annoyed at what she thought of as Fergus Damant's unfeeling attitude, pointing out that it was impossible to prevent the public from ostracising people in cases where a parent had committed a misdemeanour or a crime. To this Fergus said that was exactly what he meant – so why grieve about it? Get on with life, prove your worth. If one society could not accept you, then live in another.

Julie remarked that this was easy enough for him to say, when he was living comfortably in a wealthy society where he was obviously respected. Fergus agreed with this, adding, 'I think I tend to forget that I've lived a privileged life.' He then mentioned Klara, saying how much she had missed Julie, but made no mention of the fact that he had broken his promise to call and see Richard and herself before they left London for Southampton that last Friday.

The talk had done one thing for Julie, it had helped to relieve the strain of the journey so that when the hospital did loom up she was prepared to meet whatever she had to face. Even then, the subdued sounds, the nurses moving on silent feet, the smell of disinfectant and the moaning of a patient on their way along the corridors gave Julie a feeling of death lurking around corners.

Richard was in a private room. Fergus saw Julie to the door and after learning that his friend was still holding his own he left, with a promise to return later.

Tyler and Kitty each held Julie wordlessly for a moment then they went to the bed. Richard's skin had a greyish pallor and his dark hair, usually so springy and gleaming had the appearance of straw. Julie said to her mother, an anguish in her voice, 'Richard *must* get well. He will . . . won't he?'

'We pray so.' Julie saw then that the faces of her parents were ravaged with worry. Tyler took Julie by the arm and asked her to come outside for a moment.

He led her into a small ante-room and there said, 'I feel confident that Richard will recover, Julie. When he shows the first signs of regaining consciousness your mother and I will leave him. Yes, we must. You see Richard is so against us both, he said in his letter he wanted nothing more to do with us *ever*, and that is why we feel it will be best if it is you he sees first, Julie.'

She told her father about the conversation she had had with Ivy and how the older woman had promised to send a telegram to Crescent House if she found out that Violet had lied about the miniature. Tyler, who was immediately interested, said he would phone home. Julie waited and when he returned she could see that he was quietly jubilant.

He took her hands in his. 'There *was* a telegram, Julie! The message read: *The man in the miniature was not Violet's husband*.

'So we have the lie! Oh, Daddy, that's marvellous news. If only we can let Richard know this. Come along, we must tell Mother.'

The news created a different feeling among them, a feeling of hope. Once Richard did regain consciousness and knew that Violet had lied he would make a quick recovery.

But the hours went by without him showing any change. Fergus had returned by now but it was Tyler who went to talk to him, as Julie was unwilling to leave her brother's side.

It had turned midnight when Richard stirred. It was no more than a slight movement but it was enough for Kitty to summon a nurse. The Night Sister, a woman who was much more compassionate than the Day Sister, came with the nurse. She took Richard's pulse then gave a confident nod and a smile. 'Your boy is going to recover, Mr and Mrs Neilson. Nurse Brentwood will keep an eye on him.'

When Richard was making more movements and the colour began to come back into his face, Tyler and Kitty left the room. Although the nurse kept looking in, Julie was alone with her brother when he opened his eyes. He stared at her, puzzled. 'Julie, what are you doing here?' He turned his head, taking in his surroundings, then his gaze came back to her. 'What happened? What am I doing here?' Then as realisation dawned he said in a ragged voice, 'The sleeping draught, I took an overdose.'

'Yes, but you're all right now, Richard. You're not to talk, but I want to tell you one thing, one important thing.

Violet was lying when she said that the young man in the miniature was her first husband. He was a stranger to her, do you understand, Richard? Violet lied, and if she would lie about such an important issue she would lie about other things.'

When the nurse returned she pronounced it a natural sleep and suggested that Tyler, Kitty and Julie go to their hotel and have a good night's rest. They needed it, all admitting to exhaustion and although there was some discussion about Richard on their way to the hotel, once they arrived they went straight to bed.

They had all hoped that once Richard knew the truth about Violet they would be a close family unit again, but although he was polite to them the following morning and apologised for the trouble he had caused, he was not at ease with any of them.

'Give him time,' Tyler said, when they left the hospital. 'He's been ill, very ill, and his brain is not working at full pitch yet.'

And there was no change in Richard's attitude when he was ready to be discharged three days later. He had wanted to go straight to his flat but the doctor would only allow him to leave on condition that he put himself in his parents' care.

There was still the strained atmosphere the following day and it was actually Fergus who healed the breach, but what he had said to Richard to bring it about was never divulged.

When Tyler and Kitty talked about returning home and taking Richard with them to recuperate, Julie said she would go back to Stoke. 'Oh, come with us, Julie,' her mother begged. 'You'll be company for Richard.'

Company for Richard? Was that the only reason they wanted her at home? Julie had a sudden rootless feeling. She was in a No Man's Land without a permanent place to live. She was welcome to go to Crescent House, she would be company for Richard! At Ivy and Tom's she was the shop assistant, the servant. And here she was in London again and no one had offered to take her anywhere! It was all what was best for Richard. He must stay in and rest, he must have people around him. Jake had called and they made such a fuss of *him*. Poor Jake, he had not been well. Sit down, Jake, would you like a drink? Even on the occasions when Fergus called she had been ignored. Talk to Richard, show him the error of his ways.

Julie worked herself into such a state she was on the verge of tears, then realising how utterly selfish she was being she felt ashamed. Jealous of her own brother, who had tried to end his life because of the viciousness of a woman. He could have died, then how would she have felt? Devastated, bereft. She and Richard had always been so close, but not any more . . . He had distanced himself from her, Julie suddenly realised. Why? Was it shame at what he had done? It could be . . .

She remembered when one of her father's workmen had hanged himself and Richard had said, 'There's something degrading about a man taking his own life. It's the coward's way out. That man gave no thought to the sufferings of the family he left behind.'

Julie wondered if she should go home to Crescent House and try to get close to Richard again. They could talk, thrash things out as they used to do. She had more or less decided that this was what she would do when Richard settled the issue by saying if he *did* go home he wanted to be free to do as he pleased and go where he pleased. If he wanted to spend a day walking on his own there was to be no fuss, no protests.

After exchanging glances, Tyler and Kitty agreed. And so Julie made plans to return to Stoke.

The night before she was due to leave Kitty said, 'Your father and I have been talking things over, Julie, and we've decided that you, Richard and I will go to Italy in three weeks' time. We shall have a week in Venice, a week in Florence, then your father will join us and we shall go on to

Rome. Will you tell Ivy that you'll be away for several weeks? I shall write to her myself, of course, but it will warn her and give her enough time to find some other help.'

Julie was torn between excitement at the thought of the holiday and resentment at the offhand way in which she felt her mother was treating Tom and Ivy. She decided she must say something.

'You know, Mother, Tom and Ivy have been very kind to me. I don't think you'll ever know just how good it's been for me to be with them, and I don't want them to be dismissed in your mind after they've served their purpose.'

Kitty eyed her in bewilderment. 'Served their purpose? Oh, Julie, I'm sorry if I gave you that impression. I love Ivy like a sister. She's been a good friend to me from the first days I went into service.' After a slight pause Kitty went on, her manner suddenly brisk: 'Now then, Julie, I shall write to you, letting you know the date we shall be leaving for Italy, but I want you to come to London two days earlier, so that we can go shopping for clothes.'

Thoughts of the shopping spree and the discussion later about the trip to Italy, with Richard talking with some enthusiasm on the beautiful architecture, gave Julie a feeling of togetherness again with her family.

But the next morning, when she was in a taxi with her parents and Richard, who were to see her off at St Pancras, she felt detached from them once more. Her parents were discussing business and Richard was sitting slumped in the seat, arms folded, staring straight ahead of him. When Julie tried to say something her father interrupted with, 'Just a minute, darling, I want to remind your mother about something.' Their discussion was still going on when they arrived at the station.

Tyler went to buy Julie's ticket while Kitty sent Richard off to get her some magazines then she said, in a distracted way, 'We shall leave for home today. I do think that Richard is looking much better, don't you Julie? What a dreadful worry it's been. Poor boy, what a state his mind must have been in. Oh, here is your father and good heavens, here is Richard with enough magazines to satisfy a trainful of passengers.' Kitty laughed, but there was no mirth in it.

Tyler came up. 'Well, here is your ticket, Julie. We must get you into a carriage with some decent people. I would have preferred you to travel first, but if you want to travel third –' he raised his shoulders as though to say such a thing was beyond him.

Julie said quietly, 'Please don't come with me on to the platform. I would rather find a seat myself. I know the kind of people I want to travel with.'

'The seasoned traveller, eh?' Tyler teased. 'Well –' he glanced at the station clock. 'We do have a lot to do. If you are sure you can manage?'

'Yes, I'm quite sure. I'll say goodbye, we'll be meeting again soon, then perhaps we shall all have time for a long talk.'

They kissed, gave messages for Ivy and Tom, then Richard said, 'I'll show you some beautiful buildings in Italy, Sis. Take care of yourself. And thanks . . .'

Julie went through the barrier and onto the train without once looking back to give a wave, but she could see her family in her mind's eye – her father and Richard both tall, imposing figures, her brother less well-groomed than Tyler but well-dressed for all that, her mother in silver grey, a slender fur stole draped over her shoulders, a hat turned up at the front giving height to the small, elegant figure. She got into a carriage without bothering to find out who her fellow passengers were. When she was seated, she found two spinsterish-looking ladies sitting opposite her and a middle-aged man with a stern-looking face. She hoped they were not chatty people.

When Julie was out of sight Richard said to his parents, 'If you two want to leave I'll wait until the train goes out. Julie might wave.'

Kitty said, 'I feel terrible. I just realised when I saw her walk away how badly we had behaved, talking business when she was about to leave us.'

Tyler laid his hand on his wife's shoulder. 'I think perhaps Julie understands that we don't love her any the less because we talk about our work.'

'Can you be sure of that?' Richard asked quietly.

Tyler and Kitty exchanged glances then they both looked towards the train that was due to leave. When the train drew away a number of people waved from carriage windows, but Julie was not among them.

When the train was out of sight Kitty was left with an image in her mind of a forlorn-looking figure with a small holdall in her hand, a holdall too insignificant-looking to belong to the daughter of wealthy parents. Kitty vowed then that when they went to Italy she would make it up to Julie . . . It was a silent trio which left the station.

Julie had her wish, her fellow travellers were not talkative. When she had first taken her seat her throat had ached with unshed tears. But although she now had her emotions under control she still had a dreadful feeling of aloneness as she recalled two incidents.

There had been talk of taking Jake along with them to Italy, as extra company for Richard. That was the first thing. Then, last night when she was about to come into the sitting room, she had overheard her father saying softly to her mother, 'It will be like a second honeymoon, darling.' They had kissed and Julie had gone away and come back. In those moments she had thought how romantic they were after all their years of marriage, but now she saw it as shutting their children out of their lives.

There was a sudden desperate need in Julie to belong to someone, to be important to that person, to be loved, cuddled and caressed. That was why, after what seemed an endless journey, when she arrived at the shop she gave Tom and Ivy an extra big hug and even hugged Angus, something she had not done before. He seemed startled for a moment then his arms went around her and as he held her close she could feel his heart pounding. When she pulled away from him he drew the back of his hand lightly over her cheek and said gently, 'It's good to have you back, lassie.' Julie felt a lovely warmth stealing over her. She was loved.

Ivy, of course, wanted to know about Richard – the drama of the near-suicide, what had happened at the hospital and his reaction to the news that Violet had lied to him.

Julie said, 'He seemed to accept that the young man in the miniature was not Violet's first husband when he was younger, but we had no details to prove it.'

'Didn't you get my letter telling you about it? I sent it straight away. Well, would you believe it! Anyway, the miniature, according to Billy Barker, was painted in the early eighteen hundreds, so it *couldn't* have been her first husband, now could it? Oh, what a liar that woman is, she's wicked, she's evil. And is poor Richard all right now?'

Julie told her then about the intended holiday in Italy, which brought the tight-lipped comment from Ivy that some folks were lucky, being able to flit here, there and everywhere whenever they felt like it. She then demanded to know what she was supposed to do while Julie was away – struggle along on her own, doing all the jobs, or train a new assistant?

Tom immediately protested at his wife's attitude, pointing out that Richard must have been in a terribly depressed state to do what he had done and depression was not something that could be got over just like that. In his opinion, Tyler and Kitty were doing the right thing by taking Richard abroad and getting him away from his usual environment. Ivy tried to say something at this point but Tom went on, saying to Julie, 'We could get help, that's no problem. Mrs Dodd's daughter Aggie would come in on a temporary basis while you're away.'

'She would if she didn't have a bellyache,' Ivy snapped,

'or a toothache or pains in her head! She's always got something wrong with her, that girl.'

'If that happens,' Tom said sensibly, 'there are plenty of other neighbours who would help out and be grateful for the extra bit of cash. Depression is a dreadful thing, don't I know it.'

Ivy, who had opened her mouth to make another retort, closed it. She stood looking at her husband for a moment, then nodded slowly. 'Yes, you do Tom, don't you.' To Julie she added, 'We'll manage, love, we'll manage. You go when you have to, and there's one thing certain – you'll have a lot to tell us when you come back.'

Later, when Ivy and Julie were alone Ivy explained the reason for her outburst. 'You see, love, I was disappointed when I knew you would be away for such a long time. The thing is, Billy Barker told me about a house with a piece of land that's coming up for sale very soon. It's on the north-east coast, in a little fishing village. The air is so invigorating up in that part, it would do Tom the world of good!'

'You mean, you'd be selling up here?'

'That's right, selling the goodwill of the business. I think I've got sufficient money saved now to buy instead of renting. I want Tom to have a feeling of security. I was hoping –' Ivy paused. 'Well, I was hoping you would not only be here to help us pack up but that you might think of coming with us. We'd both like it, Tom and me.'

Although Julie knew that Ivy would never openly beg her to go with them there was a pleading in her eyes. She sat silent, not knowing what to say. She was beginning to feel established in Stoke, for she had made friends – and then there was Angus. She asked about him, what would happen to him if Tom and Ivy left. Would the new people be willing to keep him as a lodger, be willing to let him use the shed at the back for his pottery-making?

'That I don't know,' Ivy said, 'but I have had a little talk with him and I get the feeling that if this fishing village was the kind of place that would draw tourists he might come with us and start up a little pottery business on his own. I was thinking of doing teas for visitors, that sort of thing. You would be a great help, Julie. But that is something to be discussed properly another time. Right now, I must get some fresh cheese out and cut up. You can tell me what you decide to do tomorrow, or any time this week, Julie. But please don't think I want to push you into anything. You might feel like going back home on your return from Italy.'

'No, I won't,' Julie said fiercely. 'Quite definitely I won't. I think it's more than possible that I would go with you and Tom. But I'll think it over and let you know.'

'Do that, love.' Ivy paused and stood eyeing her with some curiosity. 'You haven't had a row with your parents, have you?'

'No,' she replied, a bitterness in her voice. 'It might have been better if I had.' Ivy said no more then but at bedtime when Angus came in from the shed she stifled a yawn and admitted, 'I'll have to get to bed! Will you two see to the locking-up between you and come up quietly, will you – Tom's sleeping lightly these nights.'

Julie saw through Ivy's strategy. She wanted her to talk to Angus, perhaps persuade him to go with them when they moved. Angus was a useful man to have around. He was strong, and Tom would surely need some help if he was to run his small market garden business.

Ivy said good night and left. Angus went to the sink to wash his hands and Julie made cocoa for them both. 'Anything to eat?' she asked. 'Bread and cheese, a buttered scone, a piece of rice cake?'

'No, thanks, I had a good supper.' As Angus dried his hands he watched her. 'Shouldn't you be in bed too, Julie, you look done in.'

Julie brought her mug of cocoa to the table, pulled out a

chair and sat down. 'I did feel sleepy earlier but I think that Ivy's news about them leaving here snapped me awake.'

Angus hung the towel on the back of the door, came to the table, and sat down opposite her. With Angus, all his movements were deliberate. He sugared his cocoa, stirred it slowly then looked up. 'The move has been on the cards for some time. I'm surprised it hasn't come sooner.' When Julie suggested that lack of money had been the stumbling block Angus shook his head. 'No, Ivy had the means of raising it. Mrs Helder left her a William IV tea set. She had told her she was leaving it to her in her will and advised her then to sell it if ever she needed money. Well, I think Ivy should have sold it to get Tom away from the murk and filth of a town sooner. I had the tea set valued for her and she could have had a hundred and eighty pounds for it. So, with the money she had saved she could have bought a cottage and land a whole year ago.'

Julie hesitated a moment then said, 'Ivy told me that you might go with them when they moved, that is if you found there was a tourist trade and you could find somewhere to set up a small pottery.'

'We have talked about it but I would need to go to this Echo Cove first and have a look around.'

'Echo Cove? What a lovely name. Do you know why it was so called?'

'According to what I was told the name comes from the harbour. It's small, so small that the old fishermen sitting on seats on either side of it can talk to one another. At certain times in the evening, their voices even echo from the cliffs rising at each side.'

'Most intriguing.' Julie smiled. 'This tempts me to go. Surely this alone must attract holidaymakers and people wanting a day out, like cyclists, walkers and people having a car-ride. Quite a few people own cars nowadays. If you did decide to live there and set up a pottery business, what would you make? Small items people could buy with a message on them saying, *A present from Echo Cove*? Women collect this type of thing – *A present from Brighton*, *from Blackpool*, *from Margate* –'

'I don't know yet what I would make. I'll let you know if I decide to go with Ivy and Tom.' Angus set down his mug and got up. 'I'm ready for bed.' He paused and stood watching Julie, his expression thoughtful. 'Would you be willing to move to Echo Cove?'

'I think I might be tempted but not straight away. You see, my parents are taking Richard and myself to Italy for a few weeks.'

'I see.' Angus turned away but not before she had seen the disappointment in his eyes. He said, 'After a visit to beautiful Italy I doubt whether you will want to rough it in a cottage at a small fishing village on the Tyne.'

Julie flared up, 'Why do you make such a statement? I've roughed it here, and I don't see how it's going to be any harder doing teas for visitors. Why do you always try to belittle me?'

'I don't.' Angus turned slowly to face her. 'It's just that I can guess the effect a holiday of this type could have on you. You will be travelling first class, living in luxury hotels –'

'Angus, I was living in luxury at home! I left to come here to earn my own living. I've scrubbed floors, baked, dusted –' She flung up her hands. 'Oh, what's the use! I've gone over all this with you before. You're just determined to put me in the category of "pampered daughter of wealthy parents comes slumming in pottery town".'

'No, Julie.' He sounded sad. 'It's simply that I've lived a little longer than you and seen more of life, both sides of it. I know how people react to changes of environment.'

'Well, you don't know how *I* would react and I'm telling you now I shall go with Ivy and Tom whether you do or not. That is, when I come back from Italy. And now, if you will be good enough to see that all the doors are locked I'll damp down the fire.' Julie picked up the mugs to take to the sink to wash but Angus stayed her hand.

'Now listen to me, Julie. Don't go and make rash judgements because you're in a temper and are determined to show me that I'm wrong. Think this over carefully about going to Echo Cove. You will find a totally different life there, much more leisurely. There might be a good trade in the summer for people wanting teas, but the winter could be deathly quiet and you need to be busy. I know that much about you. Am I right?'

Julie gave a grudging 'Yes'. Then, with a sudden grin she added, 'I could help you to make pots.'

'Ah, but I need to be busy too and there might not be enough work for the both of us.'

Julie eyed him, her head cocked on one side. 'Do you know something, Angus MacLaren, *you* are a pessimist. That's no way to run a business. If trade is slack at Echo Cove you look for another outlet for your work! You experiment, find out what is needed. The sale of pottery is not just a summer trade.'

Angus was smiling now, too. 'And shall I tell *you* something, Julietta van Neilson? I think you have an idea there. We could work together: I will be the potter, the steadying influence – and you will be the inspirational. You have a flare for design. You could do some of the painting. How about it?'

Julie gave a quick nod. 'It's worth a try.'

'So that is settled then. Providing, of course, that there will be sufficient trade for a tea-room *and* a small pottery business and allowing for accidents or –'

'I won't change my mind, if that is what you're thinking,' Julie said quietly. 'I give you my word now and I never break my word.'

'So Ivy said. Oh, she gives you quite a good character, apart from your temper.' There was a twinkle in Angus' eyes. 'But I can cope with that, I think.'

'And I see I'll have to cope with a man who could drive a saint to drink!' Julie retorted. 'You can be most infuriating at times.'

'I promise to be on my best behaviour, cross my heart. Now come along, get the pots washed up and the fire damped down.'

'Orders, orders, you're worse than Ivy!'

Angus flicked an imaginary piece of fluff from her shoulder. 'You'll have to get used to taking orders from the boss.'

Julie had never seen Angus in such a light-hearted mood before. It was in his eyes, in his expression, but in spite of his mood she was firm. 'There will be no bossing, is that understood?'

'There's no partnership in my world without the man being boss, is *that* understood? If you don't do as you're told you'll be punished.'

There was a half-serious note in his voice now and Julie's heartbeats quickened. She played up to him, fluttering her eyelashes at him. 'What punishment, boss – bread and water for a week?'

'No, this.' He came up to her, caught her to him and covered her mouth with his. His lips were soft, sensuous, demanding, his breathing ragged. Julie knew she would have responded to him had he not drawn away.

'Now get those chores done and off to bed with you!'

She put her hands behind her back and cocked her head, giving him a cheeky grin. 'What if I refuse, sir? I rather like your kind of punishment.'

A slow smile spread over Angus' face. 'Ah, but that is where the suffering begins. Punishment is only meted out once a month.'

Her first instinct was to call him a conceited oaf but she could see how she could use his words to her advantage. He was enjoying playing this game and so was she. He had aroused emotions in her that were very pleasurable. She picked up the empty cocoa mugs and carried them to the sink. 'So, if the punishment for one disobedience is a kiss, what is it for ten disobediences?'

She heard him chuckling behind her. 'You might not get another kiss for ten months.'

'Oh, you rotten so and so!' Julie turned laughing, and Angus laughed too.

'You can't win, you know,' he said. 'I know all the angles.'

'You think you do. In my opinion you have a great deal to learn, especially about me.' Julie ran the tap and rinsed the mugs, then was aware of Angus coming up behind her. She waited, breath held, not quite knowing what to expect. He pulled her collar away from her nape and blew warm air gently down her back, making her gasp as an excited shiver ran up and down her spine. He laid the collar back and patted it, saying, 'That is in lieu of the next punishment.'

The next moment she heard the shooting of the bolts in the back door. Julie leaned weakly against the sink. Who would have imagined that such a simple thing could have sent tremors all over her body, tremors that would not be stilled.

She half-wished then that she was not going to Italy, for life here was beginning to take quite an exciting turn.

# Chapter Ten

During the following week Julie only caught glimpses of Angus. According to Ivy he was trying to pull in as much overtime as possible because he was planning to travel to Echo Cove at the weekend. He would travel overnight on the Friday, find out what the summer and winter trade was, look over the cottage, then seek somewhere suitable for a small pottery, that is, if everything else was favourable.

Tom talked about the project to Julie. 'It would be wonderful if it comes off, Julie. It's something I've dreamed about. A piece of land to work and also to be by the sea.' He covered her hand with his thin one. 'And having the bonus of you coming with us, love – what more could we ask for? It's like having a daughter, Julie. We love you.'

Julie dropped a kiss on his head. 'And I love you both, too. I only wish I could have come with you to see you settled before I go to Italy.'

'You might be back before we make a move. Not that I expect you would feel like packing everything up after returning from such a wonderful holiday.' Julie laughed and told him she would probably be glad to be energetic after several weeks of lazing.

During that week, Julie had letters from her mother and Richard. Her mother wrote that it would be the end of March before they would be able to leave. Richard was recovering and looking very well for the rest. He spent most of the time out of doors. Items of news about the business followed, but little else.

Richard's letter gave even less information. He had been tramping around, visiting their old childhood haunts. It had been quite rewarding. He was pleased to say it was all settled that Jake would be coming with them to Italy. Fergus had arranged with the firm for Jake to be away. Fergus would, Julie thought wryly. No other mention was made of him.

Richard's talk of childhood haunts had Julie dipping into their early years, and she recalled how she had always been Richard's slave, doing his every bidding until the day he kept her out of one of his games. The next time he ordered her to fetch something for him she told him to get it himself. She was then about four years old, and this was her first attempt at independence. Oddly enough, in its way she had earned Richard's respect and after that they had become closer, despite the differences in their ages. She was seven years old when he taught her to play tennis; when she was eight she could hold her own with him and a year later, she could have beaten him at every game had she pleased, but she had come to learn that one did not make a man or a boy feel too inadequate. This was one of the things that Aunt Helder had taught her.

When Julie was a child she had never tired of hearing how her parents had first met. It was a fairy-tale story, with Tyler the wealthy glass-maker and Kitty a scullery-maid in the house where he was a guest.

'Not a downtrodden, tongue-tied little scullery-maid,' Tyler would say, 'but a pretty girl with lovely big eyes and a mind of her own. Oh, she was always respectful, and she was a worker; very soon she was promoted to parlourmaid.'

Then Julie would ask, 'And when did you fall in love with her, Daddy?'

'When I saw her in the hall one day standing looking up at a glass chandelier I had made for Mr and Mrs Earle, as a present. There was such a look of awe and admiration in her eyes I had to speak to her.'

At this stage in the story Kitty would interrupt to say, 'I

ought not to have been there, of course. Upstairs was forbidden to me. I had sneaked up and got such a shock when your father spoke to me. I was sure I would get the sack.'

'A little scullery-maid with a love of beautiful glass,' Tyler would say softly, then add, smiling, 'And look at her now, an eminent glass-maker in her own right.'

It was not until Julie was older and heard more of her parents' story that she always felt that the full story had not been told. But always when she questioned this she was told, 'You will know when you are older . . .'

Would she and Richard get to know the mystery at last when they went to Italy?

Julie was in bed when Angus left on the Friday at midnight to travel North. She had not seen him earlier and wondered if he had purposely kept out of her way because of their kiss. And yet, she saw no reason why he should avoid her. If he had regretted it he could have told her so, as he had done the previous time when he told her he loved her.

During the weekend Julie, Ivy and Tom were all on edge, waiting to know what the outcome of Angus' journey would be. Tom kept saying it was no use speculating, and if nothing came of the visit to Echo Cove there would be other cottages for sale, in other places. Yet Julie knew his disappointment would be intense if Angus returned with negative news.

He was expected back at five o'clock on the Sunday evening and at ten minutes to five Julie put on her hat and coat, saying she would go outside and wait for him. A few people she knew said as they passed, 'Waiting for your feller, Julie?' and she replied smiling, 'Yes, he's late.'

But Angus was not late. As a distant clock began to chime the hour of five he turned the corner. Julie's heart leapt. How attractive, how strong he looked. He was wearing his best suit but he had on a cap instead of the trilby he wore for social occasions. To Julie the cap was set at a jaunty angle, which gave her the impression that the news was favourable. He was looking across the road and calling to someone so he had not seen her yet. Everything about him suggested strength – his features, width of shoulders, large hands, even his purposeful stride. She wanted to run to him but walked slowly towards him. She was almost up to him before he noticed her. Even then he did not quicken his step. On reaching her he said, 'I thought you might have been at the station to meet me.'

'Typical, isn't it?' she exclaimed. 'You left without saying a word to me then you expect to be met.'

Angus grinned. 'I love to see the fire in your eyes when you're mad.'

She gave him a dig in the ribs. 'Come on, tell me what happened. Did you see the cottage, did you find a place suitable for a pottery?'

'Wait on, girl, wait on. I'm not going to repeat myself when I see Tom and Ivy.'

Julie mentally rolled the word 'girrrl' over her tongue, loving the way Angus said it. But she admonished him to hurry up, to stop dawdling.

'Dawdling?' he exclaimed. 'I've never stopped walking since I arrived at Echo Cove, I had no sleep on Friday night and very little last night. As Ivy would say, "I'm fair worn out"!'

Julie laughed. 'You look fresh enough to walk another hundred miles.' She ran ahead and opened the shop door calling, 'He's here, Angus is here!' The kitchen door flew open and Ivy was there with Tom right behind her.

'You're prompt,' Ivy said. 'The tea's mashed and I have your meal in the oven. I saved some roast beef and Yorkshire pudding. Here, give me your bag. Did you have a good journey? Never mind, you can tell me that later. Sit you down.'

With what seemed to be maddening deliberation Angus washed his hands, and talked about the weather as he dried them. Julie said, 'It's not about the weather that Tom and Ivy want to know, it's about Echo Cove and if there are possibilities for setting up a tea-shop and a pottery!'

Angus nodded, 'Oh, aye, there is that, the news is most favourable.' He sat down, undid his tie, then looked from one to the other. 'Couldn't be better. There's an all year trade, because folks come to hear the echo. They're even getting visitors from abroad.'

Julie had poured the tea and Ivy brought the meal to the table. Ivy said, 'And the cottage? Did you see it, Angus? What are the rooms like? How much land is there?' Julie asked about a place for the pottery and Tom suddenly laughed.

'Let the man have his food! We know that things are favourable, that's the important thing. Go on, Angus, eat up, we'll wait.'

But Angus did not keep them waiting. He talked between mouthfuls of food.

'The house is larger than I expected. The people are still living in it, of course – nice folks, I stayed with them overnight. It couldn't be in a better position, as it's on the main road running into Echo Cove.' To Tom he said, 'There's as much land as you'll want to handle, and you're never going to believe this but there's a two-roomed cottage with a brick-built shed not a hundred yards away that will do for me. The small cottage and shed are a bit derelict but I can soon put them right. I found I can rent them for a few shillings a week!'

'Well, isn't that splendid,' Tom said, beaming.

'And our house,' Ivy prompted. 'What state is it in, how many rooms are there?'

Angus described it. There was a large kitchen and a small parlour downstairs, three bedrooms upstairs and a boxroom. But the most important feature as far as Ivy was concerned was the extension that had been built on to the cottage. It would be perfect for a tea-room.

Small patches of excitement coloured Ivy's cheeks. And was everything in good condition? Well, no, no, Angus said, the roof leaked a bit, the bricks needed pointing, there were some damp patches, some window-panes were broken . . .

By the time Ivy had pinned him down there was a long list of repairs that needed doing. Angus also admitted that the garden was in a bit of a state, being overgrown. The present owners were kind but a little, well . . . feckless. In the next breath he was repairing everything.

'With a little help I can soon get it ship-shape. Stop worrying. I'll have it right in no time, no time at all.' He chewed contentedly on his roast beef and Yorkshire pudding. Julie sat staring at him.

'I'm sure it was only a week ago that I called you a pessimist. Tell me just one thing: are you pushing this deal through for Tom and Ivy, regardless of the condition the property is in, because you have found what *you* need to set up a pottery?'

'It's an insult to even suggest it,' Ivy declared, bristling with indignation. 'You don't know Angus as we do and you have no right to say such a thing, he's the most –' She would have gone on but Angus held up his hand.

'Julie has every right to say what she did, Ivy. She has the interests of Tom and you at heart.' He sat back and addressed them all. 'I saw the possibilities of the property within minutes of setting foot in it. I put a deposit on it before I even caught a glimpse of the other cottage and shed. You can thank Billy Barker for getting the chance of buying, because he's the only one who knew that the Telfers are selling and moving away. In spite of them being a harem-scarum family, they love the place and want to have nice people to live in it. One is always getting surprises about folk.'

There was a moment's silence then Julie said in a low voice, 'I'm sorry, Angus, for suggesting what I did.'

He patted her hand. 'Think nothing of it.' He turned to

Tom and Ivy. 'Now the way I look at it is this . . .'

By seven o'clock Angus had both properties 'restored', the garden dug and planted, a greenhouse built and a promise made to Ivy that her tea-room would be in full swing by the beginning of July. 'I believe you,' Ivy said, an aura of radiance about her. Then she added softly to Tom, 'A dream come true for both of us, love, and getting you well again, with all that lovely invigorating air.'

He squeezed the hand, 'Thanks to you, Ivy.'

Julie felt so emotional she had to get up and potter around or she would have been in tears. Such love, such devotion.

When Angus had finished his meal he asked her if she fancied going for a walk. Julie agreed at once.

'We'll walk to the park,' Angus said, when they left the shop.

Since coming to Stoke Julie had been little further than the local shops and the cinema. When they passed Billy Barker's she said, 'Well, we have Billy to thank as well as you for setting Tom and Ivy on to a new life. You really surprised me, Angus, with your drive. I didn't know you had it in you.'

'There's a lot you don't know about me and a lot I don't know about you, lassie.'

'Oh, I'm like an open book.'

'You're not, you know. I think there's a great deal you don't know about yourself. The complexities of human nature are many.'

'Who could be more complex than you?' she demanded. 'You kissed me nearly a week ago then avoided me ever since.'

He glanced at her. 'Is that what you think? If I seemed to avoid you it was circumstances. Like most girls you expect too much of a man. Did you think I would follow you around like a little lap dog? I have work to do. You are the type, Julie, who would make a nagging wife. "Where have you been?" you would demand of your husband, "Who have you been talking to?" Then you would say, "I expect it was to some dumb thing who works with you, well, let me tell you . . ." and so it would go on.'

She stopped abruptly, her eyes blazing. 'What colossal cheek you have to assume what I would be like if I married. Have I ever given you any cause to suggest I would be a nagging wife?'

'Oh yes, plenty,' he said amiably. 'Take this evening for instance when you came to meet me. You told me to hurry up, to stop dawdling. Now what is that but nagging?'

Julie opened her mouth to reply then closed it again and when Angus asked whether he was right she met his gaze squarely. 'I'm not sure whether I was nagging or not. If I seemed to be then I must check it. There's nothing worse than a nagging woman.'

Angus said softly, 'That is one thing I do like about you, Julie, your sweet reasonableness. You will discuss things.'

'Oh, I'm glad I have one asset you admire,' she said tartly and made to move on. Angus caught hold of her arm and apologised. He was baiting her, it was wrong.

'Are we still friends?' he enquired.

'Oh, yes, we're friends, *very* good friends,' she said, wishing she could understand him. He had the ability to arouse sensual feelings in her, to make her want him, but he seemed reluctant to give more. She sensed a fear in him to express his feelings. She was sure he loved her. Was her background the stumbling block? Would things be different with a change of environment? They would be in closer contact, as he had promised she could work with him when there was an opportunity. Or was he perhaps reluctant to commit himself until she had been abroad, afraid that when she did return she might decide to go back home to live? She had assured him that this would not happen but *he* could not be sure about it. That was the most obvious reason. Well, they would just have to wait and see.

Angus had arranged for a solicitor to deal with the buying

of the cottage and to handle the shop business when the time came. An advertisement in the local paper offering the sale of the goodwill brought a number of prospective clients, and a storm of protests from the customers. The shop wouldn't be the same without Tom, Ivy and Julie. Couldn't they even leave Julie behind? The next people to come in might be glad to engage her as assistant.

Ivy explained they were leaving because of Tom's health and Julie told them she wanted to go with Tom and Ivy, as they were friends. At first an air of gloom seemed to settle over the shop, but as the people began to get used to the idea the lively chatter and joking began again. They would come up for a holiday and sample one of Ivy's special teas. 'Chance would be a fine thing,' declared one of the more pessimistic customers. 'Where's the money coming from? I didn't even have a honeymoon! In fact, the only time I travelled anywhere out of Stoke was to me Gran's funeral, and then it was sitting in the back of a wagon on a sack of tatties!'

'Oh, cheer up, Annie,' chided her companion. 'One of these days you might be left a fortune by a great uncle you didn't know you had.'

Annie sniffed and repeated that chance would be a fine thing. Ivy said, 'Will you stop talking about death! I can tell you this, if any of you did happen to get our way you'd be made more than welcome.'

A man called, 'Free teas, would it be then, Ivy?'

She grinned. 'I didn't say that, now, did I?' They all laughed.

A middle-aged, homely couple with a grown-up son and daughter were the third clients who came to look over the shop, and they were the ones who decided to buy. Ivy and Tom were pleased. 'They're the right people to take over,' Ivy said to Julie. 'I feel happier now at leaving, knowing that the customers will like them.'

The day following this, Julie had a letter from her mother saying that plans had been changed again and they were now leaving for Italy on the fourteenth, so would she travel to London on the twelfth? She would be met. The letter ended, '*In great haste, love from us all, Mother.*'

Julie waved the letter at Ivy. 'The twelfth! That's tomorrow. I wanted to help you prepare for the move, help with packing things –'

Ivy said, 'Don't you worry your head about that. You get ready. With the Liggetts wanting to come in daily and learn the business before taking over I'll have plenty of help. You'll probably be back from Italy by the time we're ready to move to Echo Cove.'

'Yes,' Julie said, that was at least one compensation.

With the prospect of going with her mother to buy clothes for the trip to London all Julie had to pack was her small holdall, so when the shop was quiet that evening she had time to have a long talk with Tom. He went over his early years working with glass, how good Julie's parents had been to him, and how he had fallen in love with Ivy.

He laughed softly. 'She always had a sharp tongue, but do you know something, she brought me out. I was a shy lad. Life has never been dull with Ivy –' His expression changed, became serious. 'Few people ever get to know the real Ivy. She's soft underneath but she hates people to know it. I think it's her defence against the world – she had a hard life as a child.'

'I know,' Julie said. 'Mother told me all about her and what a good friend she was to her when she first started in service.'

Tom studied Julie for a moment then said gently, 'I wonder if you understand your parents, Julie love? You always seem so aggressive towards them. They're good people – kind, generous and very much in love.'

Julie nodded. 'Yes, I know that too, Tom, but I think they've been too wrapped-up in one another and their respective businesses. It's not that Richard and I were ever neglected, and I'm sure they love us both, but I feel we have always been secondary in their lives.'

'You're wrong, you know, Julie. There was a time some years ago when your mother had a chance to go to America. It would have been a big breakthrough for her, but you developed measles the night before she was due to leave and you were so poorly she cancelled her trip. That was one sacrifice she made and there have been others. So don't condemn her. I know she's looking forward to having you and Richard with her on this Italian trip. Make the most of it, love. You'll have lots to tell us when you get back.'

Angus said to Julie later that evening, 'I think you'll be back just about the time we'll be making the actual move, Julie. It'll be nice for Ivy to have you with her to lend a hand, as it's a big task making a move like that. I'll be handing in my notice soon at the pottery. I would have liked to hand it in now and go to Echo Cove to do some work on the pottery shed, but I need all the money I can get.'

When Julie asked about the repairs that needed to be done on the cottage Angus said he could not attempt that until the Telfers had moved out, and they were not moving to their new house in Leeds for another three weeks.

'They're such a likeable family, Julie, but so disorganised. I dread arriving at Echo Cove to find they are still in the throes of moving out.'

'We'll help them to get on their way,' Julie exclaimed, feeling cheerful and excited at the thought of the coming holiday. Then she became aware that Angus was watching her. 'What is it?' she asked.

'I was wondering if you'll be changed when you come back from Italy.'

'I'll be full of all the things I've seen, but I promise you won't find me changed in any way.'

Angus got up. 'I'll say goodbye now, Julie. I'm on early shift in the morning and might have left before you're up.

Behave yourself and don't fly into tempers.' His smile was teasing.

'I won't, I'll be meek and mild and scare my parents to death.'

He laughed. 'I bet you would. Well, goodbye, Julie, have a good time.' Angus, his expression serious now, cupped her face between his hands and kissed her gently on the lips. When he pulled away he drew the back of his fingertips lightly down her cheek in the gesture she loved. 'Have a good time, lassie.'

He turned quickly away to go upstairs. Julie wanted to call him back to say, 'I love you,' but she stood mute. That must come from him. At that moment, to be parted from him seemed like an age.

The next morning as Ivy bustled around she said, 'I've never heard of any young girl having so many train journeys as you, talk about being a seasoned traveller! Come on, get your breakfast or you'll miss your train. Give your parents our regards, and love to Richard. I'm glad he's getting over that terrible time. Did you say that his friend Jake is going with you?'

'Yes, and I can imagine what their conversation will be all the time – architecture! Mind you, I understand that some of the buildings are really magnificent. Both Richard and Jake are dying to get to Rome, but I'm looking forward to seeing Venice. Did I tell you that some people have to travel to their homes and hotels in boats on the canals?'

'Yes, you did, five or six times. Now will you sit down and get some breakfast!' Ivy undid her apron. 'I'm coming to the station and don't say no, no, no. I want to see you safely on the train.'

When it was time to leave Julie said goodbye to Tom, was at the shop door and ran back to give him another hug, saying, 'I'll write and tell you all about Venice and I'll send you some picture postcards.'

'You do that, love, don't forget now. Hurry or you'll have

Ivy dragging you to the station.' They both laughed and Julie ran to Ivy who was waiting in the doorway, bristling with impatience.

Julie called gaily, 'Italy, here I come,' and was rewarded with a push from Ivy and an admonition that if she missed the train she would know all about it.

Julie did not miss the train and she felt a little choked when Ivy kissed her and told her gruffly to take care of herself, they would miss her. But once on the train and well under way, she began to think over the clothes she would like to buy, that is, if her mother was willing. A customer who had a daughter who worked at a big house had brought Ivy a catalogue and Julie had pored over the styles, fancying herself in flimsy chiffon that would float when she walked.

Her travelling companions were two middle-aged ladies and a man who had opened a book when they left.

Ivy had all but pushed Julie into this particular carriage and as it turned out it was the right choice for Julie. She needed time to think, and neither of the women had addressed a single word to her, nor to each other. There was the cottage to think about, the tea-room they would open, the move from the shop and Angus . . . He certainly was cautious in his dealings with her. She felt sure he was in love with her, but although he had shown tenderness towards her, he had not said he loved her. Perhaps it was just as well. In a way she did not want any commitments but, on the other hand, it would have been nice to go away feeling there was someone who really cared to come back to.

Richard and Jake met her at London. Richard lifted her off her feet and swung her round. 'Great to see you again, Sis.' Jake gave her a smacking kiss on each cheek and asked if she was prepared to put up with them both for a few weeks.

Julie, delighted to find them both looking so well after her previous visit said with a breathless laugh, 'I'm prepared to put up with anything and anyone to go abroad!'

Richard took the holdall from her. 'Come along, we're staying at the Ritz this time. Father hasn't come down from Crescent House yet to say goodbye, as he's madly busy and he knows that you and Mother will only spend tomorrow shopping. We have lots of surprises for you. Guess where we are going tonight?'

Julie said she had not the faintest idea and Richard told her triumphantly, 'To see a pantomime!'

'Pantomime, in March?'

'That's right,' declared Jake. '*Jack and the Beanstalk*. It's at the Hippodrome with Nellie Wallace and Tom Walls.'

'That is, if you're not too tired,' Richard interrupted.

'Tired? I feel on top of the world! What a marvellous beginning to the holiday.'

Richard and Jake chattered so much on the way to the Ritz that Julie began to wonder if the gaiety was put on for her benefit but came to realise it was a natural exuberance at the thought of the holiday to come.

She found her mother brighter, too. 'Lovely to see you, darling. Did you have a good journey? You must tell us all your news. You said in your last letter that Ivy and Tom are thinking of moving from Stoke. But there, you can tell us about it after you've freshened-up. I've ordered tea to be sent up.'

Julie did not want to tell her mother at this stage that she intended to go with Ivy and Tom and wondered how she could avoid it, but she need not have worried, as Richard and Jake dominated the talk with all they were to do and see in Venice.

Kitty remarked at one stage to Julie, laughing, 'And they say women can talk.' To which Richard replied that they could talk all they wanted to the next day when they went shopping.

Seats had been booked for the second house showing at the Hippodrome. It started at seven forty-five and when Julie went to get changed she had a feeling of high adventure about to begin. Although she had been to local pantomimes at Christmas this would be her first visit to a West End show.

Her mother told her she had brought her one of her dresses from home but when Julie saw it she wailed, 'Oh, Mother, it's too childish, it's a party dress.' The dress was white muslin with a flounced hem.

Kitty said firmly, 'It will not look childish when I'm finished with you.' She put up Julie's hair, threaded narrow emerald green ribbon through it, clasped an emerald necklace about her throat then brought out a white velvet three-quarter length evening coat which had a feathery trimming at the neck and round the edges of the wide sleeves. Julie was so astonished at the transformation she gave her mother an impulsive hug.

'Oh, they're all beautiful!'

'The necklace is a gift from your father,' Kitty said, 'and the coat is from me.'

'Thank you a million times. I must phone Daddy later and thank him for the necklace.' Richard called then to tell them to hurry up or they would be late.

When they went into the sitting room both men jumped up, Richard declaring that Julie looked marvellous. Jake echoed this then remarked that he and Richard would be envied by every man in the theatre for having two such beautiful ladies to escort.

'Jake, you are so kind,' Kitty said smiling. 'Extravagant flattery, but very welcome.'

'It's not extravagant at all,' Jake said softly, his gaze on Kitty. To Julie's surprise there was adoration in his eyes and she suddenly saw her mother in a new light. Kitty was wearing black velvet with diamond earrings and a matching necklace. Although not tall, she looked elegant and carried herself well. For a moment Julie felt uneasy, afraid that Jake's feelings for her mother might spoil the holiday, but then he held out an arm to Julie, Richard held out an arm to his mother, and the uneasy moment passed. Although Jake had a round, almost baby face and was fun-loving, there was a sensible side to him.

Julie was enchanted with the crowds, the flashing coloured lights of the advertisements and the elegantly-dressed men and women going into the theatre. She looked at Jake as they went in with shining eyes. 'Isn't this exciting!'

He agreed and patted her hand. 'And we have Italy to come. Aren't we lucky?'

Julie made up her mind that no matter how late she went to bed that night she must start a letter to Tom and Ivy and tell them all she had seen and done.

It was after midnight when she sat in her bedroom describing the pantomime, and Nellie Wallace with her funny little hat and the bobbing feather in it. She had forgotten some of the jokes but she wrote down those she could remember, knowing that Tom would enjoy himself repeating them to the customers. Julie concluded the letter by saying there was the shopping spree with her mother to look forward to and she would leave the letter open so that she could tell Ivy what clothes had been bought.

Julie went to bed, ready for sleep and feeling extremely happy.

# Chapter Eleven

The following day proved to be even more exhausting than the previous one. Not only did Julie and her mother try on numerous dresses, coats, shoes, hats and go from Harrods to Selfridges, to Marshall & Snelgrove, but they all went on later to a cinema in Leicester Square to see the film *The Americano*, featuring Douglas Fairbanks. Back at the hotel, Richard and Jake leapt about from chair to chair, brandishing imaginary swords and fighting off the baddies: Julie the 'heroine' was being saved from a fate worse than death.

Kitty, who had been laughing at their antics said at last, 'Enough! I'm worn out just watching you all. Come along the three of you and get packed. There will be no time for any delay in the morning.'

Although Julie had seen all classes of people travelling during her recent train journeys, there was a totally different atmosphere when they arrived for the boat train at Victoria the following morning. It was in the apparent wealth of passengers and friends and family seeing them off, the women dripping furs and jewellery, the men immaculately groomed with precious stones glistening in tie-pins and cufflinks, and the trolley loads of expensive luggage being wheeled by porters. Their own luggage was quite impressive. Even the carpet in the carriages was deeply piled, the upholstery expensive and pink-shaded lights on the tables.

When they were seated Julie watched various groups of people from the carriage window, fascinated by their actions. A tall, austere-looking man appeared to be holding court over a number of middle-aged women who were gazing adoringly at him; six children stood in a half-circle while an attractive man and woman talked to them. Five of the children appeared to be listening intently, but the sixth child, the youngest, was watching two beautiful Borzois, held on a leash by a man standing nearby. The child reached out a hand to pat one of the dogs and immediately a prim-looking woman in navy blue stepped forward from nowhere and slapped her hand. Julie ached for the child who was trying desperately to hold back tears.

Then into Julie's view came a party of people, at the centre of which was a thin, ageing woman, a white fur stole slung carelessly over one shoulder. The group stopped a short distance away and a number of men came rushing up, one a photographer. The woman waved a languid hand dismissing some of the men, who were obviously reporters, then posed for the photographer with a young man in a fur-collared coat by her side. The woman brought out a cigar, put it to her lips and at least four young men in the party rushed to light it. Although Julie had seen women in restaurants smoking cigarettes she had not seen one smoking a cigar. When she brought her mother's attention to this Kitty glanced over her shoulder and said, 'Oh, she's an actress, dear,' as if that explained it.

'An actress?' Julie exclaimed, impressed. 'And is the young man who's having his photograph taken with her her son?' The beautiful young man was kissing her cheek.

'Not her son,' Richard said, his lips twitching. 'He's her lover.'

Julie's eyes went wide. 'Her lover? But she's old enough to be his mother, his *grandmother*!'

Richard explained carefully that older women, wealthy ones, often had lovers, and although Julie was aware that her mother was shaking her head in warning at him, he concluded, 'The young men are known as gigolos.' He added to Kitty that it was best for Julie to know about such things now, as she would see plenty of gigolos in Italy.

'I suppose so,' Kitty said, and drew Julie's attention to some magazines that Richard had bought. But there was more to interest Julie than magazines. 'Gigolos . . .' she repeated; she must tell Tom and Ivy about them.

There were some late arrivals now, hurrying along the platform. One was a man in light grey, a porter beside him pushing a barrow with two large leather suitcases on it. Julie was thinking to herself what a striking-looking man he was when suddenly she jerked up in her seat and peered out of the window. Her mother said, 'What is it?' and Julie pointed.

'It's Fergus – Fergus Damant!'

'It can't be,' Jake said. 'He's on the other side of the world.' Then he was on his feet, tapping frantically at the window. 'It is! What on earth is he doing here?'

Fergus, who had seen them, raised his hand in greeting and made towards the carriage door. The next moment he was smiling from one to the other. 'I thought I was going to miss the train!'

Kitty said, 'That was why I didn't mention you might be coming with us.' She spoke as calmly as though it was an everyday occurrence for a busy tycoon to accompany them on holiday. To all the questions being fired at Fergus from Richard and Jake he said, 'If you wait until I get seated I shall tell you the story.'

Richard moved up to let him sit next to Kitty. He sat down, flicked up the knees of his trousers and once more smiled from one to the other. Julie sat gazing at him, her heart racing like mad.

'This really is a delightful change for me,' he said, 'to be going abroad on holiday instead of business. At least, most of my holiday will be spent sightseeing, but I do have some other matters to attend to. I also have an invitation to a wedding in Rome.'

'Whose wedding?' Jake asked, looking none too pleased at the intrusion of his brother. Julie thought that perhaps he was jealous of her mother's indulgent smile at Fergus.

Carriage doors were slammed, the guard shouted something and the train began to move. Fergus shot his cuffs down then continued, 'It's the wedding of the daughter of one of my most important clients. He told me he would not take a refusal so – here I am.'

'But how did you know that we were going on holiday if you were on the other side of the world when it was arranged?' Julie asked, speaking for the first time.

'Your father mentioned it when we were on the phone discussing some business. I told him about my wedding invitation and when I found that your dates coincided with mine I decided to take a well-earned holiday.'

'Holiday?' Jake exclaimed. 'Your life is one long holiday – you are rarely at home.'

'When I'm dealing with business, Jake, I'm unable to relax.' Fergus spoke softly. 'I needed this change and I was glad when the wedding invitation cropped up and delighted when I found that your break coincided with mine. I have been to Rome during the past three years but it must be six years since I was in Venice.'

'So you are going to be with us in Venice too,' Julie said, a suspicion forming in her mind.

Fergus nodded slowly. 'Yes, I am, *and* staying at the same hotel, I was lucky enough to get accommodation there.'

Kitty said, speaking quickly, 'It was your father's idea, Julie. Knowing that Richard and Jake would be spending most of their time studying architecture he thought it would be nice for us to have an escort in his absence.' She smiled briefly at Fergus, 'And – as Fergus was willing . . .'

'More than willing, Mrs van Neilson. How lucky I am to be entrusted with the care of two such beautiful ladies.'

Kitty laughed softly. 'All this flattery we are getting lately will be going to our heads. First Jake and now you.'

Jake said to Fergus, 'Don't think you can have the company of Mrs van Neilson and Julie all the time. Richard and I are here for pleasure as well as study.' His aggressive manner brought another gentle smile from Kitty.

'I think we shall all be together most of the time, Jake – that is the purpose of the holiday.' After this Jake seemed happier.

Julie, however, was not so happy, having by now convinced herself that Fergus was here to try and wean her away from Stoke, and from Angus. When she had mentioned to her mother in a letter about the proposed move of Tom and Ivy to Echo Cove, she had also mentioned that Angus was hoping to set up a small pottery there. She had deliberately said nothing definite about going with them but it would, she knew, be on her parents' minds.

It was not that Julie objected to having Fergus Damant with them, in fact she had felt a pleasurable thrill when she realised they would be spending the holiday together. It was just that she hated anything underhand and would be wary of him. It would have been different if they had met by accident in Venice or Rome.

She had to admit he was certainly an asset to the party, with his talk of classical music, theatres, the current plays and his wide knowledge of people in other countries, their customs and cultures. There was some discussion on architecture, but Fergus kept this to a minimum, no doubt on account of Kitty and Julie. And yet, Julie found herself becoming absorbed. It was the way Fergus talked, not showing off his knowledge, but managing to convey the impression that they too knew the subject well.

Julie had had lunch on a train before but never dinner and she found it rather romantic to be travelling in the dark with red sparks and curls of smoke from the engine seeming to be flying past the carriage window. Kitty had reluctantly allowed Julie to have wine with her meal, after Richard had pointed out that as they were going to a wine-drinking country, it would be just as well to let her get used to some. But the wine went to Julie's head and in the rosy glow of the lamps on the tables, and Fergus talking about the canals in Venice and the haunting singing of the gondoliers, she began to see herself in a gondola not with Angus but with Fergus, his arm around her, her head resting against his shoulder.

'The Italians are a very happy people,' Fergus continued. 'Noisy, brash, warm, lovable and generous. They would give their last piece of salami to a stranger. I can take you to narrow alleyways where lines of washing are stretched, there is dirt in the gutters, but the people laugh and talk and sing. I can take you to markets where –'

Jake said grumpily, 'Mrs van Neilson and Julie don't want to see poverty, they want to see the artistic side of Rome, the –'

Julie interrupted, saying earnestly, 'I also want to see how the working people live –'

Kitty began to talk then about places in Venice and Rome that Mrs Helder had once described to her, speaking in a bright, quick way. Later, she said privately to Julie, 'Listen, darling, forget about the working-classes while we are here. I want you to see the beauty of paintings and the architecture.'

Julie studied her mother. 'I know you are not ashamed of your working-class background because you talk about it – so why should you want to stop me from discussing the people I mix with?'

'Because, Julie, although you may not be aware of the fact, it has become an obsessional thing with you. No matter what is being discussed, at some point in the conversation you mention Stoke, or talk about some customer who has come into the shop.'

'So what is wrong with that?' Julie demanded.

'You will marry someday and –'

'If I marry a factory worker it will be more important to me to know how the working people live than to see all the beauty in places abroad.'

'You are wrong there, Julie.' Kitty spoke gently. 'If you see beautiful buildings, study art treasures, know the history, you will pass this knowledge on to your children. You were always asking your Aunt Helder questions, begging her to tell you about this place or that. She taught you some French and Italian, as she taught me when I was younger. She put beauty into my life and when one is poor dreams are so important.'

Julie was silent for a while then she looked up. 'I'm sorry, Mother, I hadn't realised that I was forever talking about myself. At the same time I'm glad that Fergus understands the working people, too. Will you tell me something? Why was Fergus invited to come on this trip?'

'Well, I did say earlier it was to escort us if the boys wanted to go off on their own, sightseeing and studying, but there is more to it than that. When Richard asked for Jake to come with us your father phoned Fergus to ask his permission – he is Jake's guardian. Apparently, a long conversation followed with Fergus eventually accepting your father's invitation to join us on the holiday. Apart from the wedding in Rome, he said he would be glad of the opportunity to spend some time with Jake, who he felt was not taking his studies seriously enough and needed some guidance. And we were very pleased because Fergus is so level-headed and Richard respects him. Although Richard is much better he does have days of depression. Fergus will be good for him. A young person is more inclined to take notice of advice from someone who is not family.'

Julie, relieved that she had not been the reason for Fergus' invitation said smiling, 'Then Jake should take more notice of *you*. You do know he's in love with you?'

'Unfortunately, yes, but I'm hoping he will get wrapped up in other interests once we reach Italy.'

'Does Father know he's in love with you? Would he be jealous?'

Kitty leaned forward and said in a confidential way, 'I

don't think he's noticed and to be honest, Julie, I don't think he would be worried. I like Jake, he can be great fun, but,' a sudden impish look came into Kitty's eyes, 'I can't see myself running away with him, can you?'

Julie laughed, feeling a rapport with her mother she had not experienced for some time.

The most exciting part of the journey for Julie was the Channel crossing that evening. It was rough, very rough and although Kitty, Richard and Jake were not seasick they all felt queasy and kept to their cabins. When Kitty eventually fell asleep Julie, dying for some fresh air, sneaked up on deck – and met Fergus, who was among the few who were enjoying the storm.

'Julie –' he grabbed hold of her as the boat dipped. She laughed joyously, enjoying the feeling of having a foot suspended in mid-air then the deck seeming to come up to meet it. She had tied a scarf over her head but the wind snatched it away and her hair whipped around her face. Fergus drew her into shelter and lifted a strand of hair from her mouth saying, 'It will get sticky from the salt.'

'I don't care,' she said, 'I can wash it. Isn't this marvellous? Exhilarating, exciting! Can we go to the rails?'

'No, just look at it!' Waves were running along the side of the boat then rising in spumes of spray and breaking on the deck. 'You would get soaked to the skin.'

'Wouldn't it be worth it?' Julie had to shout to make herself heard over the roar of the storm.

Fergus, shouting back at her told her it would not be worth it if she caught cold and had pneumonia in Italy. She grinned at him and nodded. They did go along the darkened deck but held the rail all the way. The storm grew worse and a seaman came and told them they must go below.

Afterwards, Julie was glad she had. By the time she reached the cabin she was feeling more than a little queasy.

In Paris, by contrast, the weather was sunny the next morning and it stayed sunny during the rest of the journey.

Leaving Paris she thought was like leaving London and in fact it was not until they reached Switzerland that she began to find a totally different kind of scenery. Julie was awed by the magnificence of the snow-clad Alps, the valleys, the still lakes. Then there were the lovely painted chalets. Fergus told her about the Simplon Tunnel, through which they would travel presently. It had been cut right through the mountain linking Switzerland and Italy. The tunnel was just a small hole in the distance now but it grew bigger as they rounded curves and then they were in it – and Julie marvelled that at the end of it was Italy!

She had thought the Alps magnificent but gasped when they came to a range called the Dolomites – mountains with needle-sharp pinnacles rising from them, glaciers in between, then more pinnacles.

Kitty said softly, 'They are well-named the Glass Mountains.'

It was late when they arrived at Venice and for once Julie was too tired to appreciate anything she saw. Mrs Helder had talked to her about Venice but then they had been only images in her mind. The following morning, however, when she was fresh, the images sprang to life the moment they stepped into a gondola to go to St Mark's Square. It was a world where the sun put dancing golden coins on the water, and gilded derelict buildings. All was movement and colour; movement on the canals with the ever-receding waves of passing boats, colour in gondolas, especially those piled high with fruit and vegetables; the incredible blue of sky and lagoon and a kaleidoscope of colour in the dresses and parasols of the women strolling with their escorts in St Mark's Square.

Then there were the sounds – the hum of conversation, the quiet talk and soft laughter of the more genteel, the raucous voices and bursts of laughter of vendors, then a wild fluttering of wings as pigeons swooped and picked up the crumbs thrown to them. There seemed to Julie to be clouds of them.

Fergus drew her attention away from the birds to the four beautiful bronze prancing horses on the top of St Mark's while at the same time Richard was urging them to join a group of people on a conducted tour of the Doge's Palace. They agreed to the tour.

The interior of the Palace was dim, the atmosphere one of reverence. Fergus told Kitty in a low voice that the best time to see the paintings was very early in the morning, when the light was at its best. Jake confirmed this.

Kitty studied the paintings with rapt attention and at times had to be urged on to the next point of interest. Every piece of architecture that she saw and every historical detail explained by the guide impressed her, but it was the paintings that stayed vividly in her mind.

Richard and Jake had drawn up an itinerary of places to visit that morning. Julie soon found her mind a-whirl with words and phrases. *Byzantine* architecture . . . the moulding of the plinths is of *Gothic profile* . . . There were types of marble – *Brocatello*, *Porphyric*, *Veronese* . . . They saw more exquisite paintings and gradually she became familiar with the names of some of the artists by repetition, like Canaletto and Tintoretto.

Kitty said at last she must have a rest and Fergus told her he knew just the place. They left Richard and Jake lost in the world of treasures and Fergus guided them through a maze of alleyways to an archway that led them to a quay that was no more than a corner, where tied-up boats bobbed on the sun-shimmered water.

'Oh, how lovely,' Kitty said softly, sinking onto a wooden bench. 'A sanctuary.' Julie sat down for a few moments then was up and walking to the edge of the quay. Fergus strolled over to her.

'So what is your impression of the morning, Julie?'

'There was so much to absorb I haven't yet got it all sorted out in my mind, but I think it all so beautiful, so awe-inspiring.' She shaded her eyes with a cupped hand. 'Just looking across the lagoon I can picture it in the olden days, the sailing ships coming from the Far East, laden with silks, satins, brocades and spices.' She laughed softly. 'I can even smell the spices. What an imagination!'

Fergus said wryly, 'You would need a vivid imagination in the height of summer when the water stinks in parts.'

Julie was indignant. He was spoiling it all. Kitty laughed and said to him, 'And I thought you to be the romantic type, Fergus.'

He turned to her. 'I am and I shall prove it to you tonight. I shall take you both on the lagoon and canals this evening, and have a gondolier sing haunting love songs.'

Kitty pulled a face. 'You can take Julie. I am going to rest this evening, otherwise I shall not be able to keep up with you all sightseeing.'

Fergus smiled at Julie. 'And would you like to be serenaded by a handsome gondolier?'

She was excited at the thought of it, but tried to treat the offer in a casual way. 'Why not? It will be something to tell my grandchildren.'

'Well!' Kitty complained, teasing too. 'Now my daughter wants to turn me into a great-grandmother.'

Fergus swept her an extravagant bow. 'May I say you would make a very beautiful one, Mrs van Neilson.'

They kept up this light-hearted banter all the way back to the hotel but at the back of Julie's mind was the thought of the coming evening alone with Fergus, which had a rather daring touch about it.

Julie tried on every one of the dresses that had been bought in London and decided on a delicate rose-coloured chiffon with trimmings at the neck and cuffs of tiny velvet pieces, shading from pale to leaf-green. When she went to get her mother's approval, cheeks flushed, Kitty stood looking at her in silence. Julie felt alarmed. 'Don't you like it, Mother?'

'Yes, I do, Julie. I was surprised at how grown-up you look. You are a very beautiful girl.'

Julie, relieved, laughed and dropped a curtsey. 'Thank you, ma'am.'

Richard and Jake played a game with her when they came in, walking around her, pretending to be old men and saying, 'Um, ah, yes, well, perhaps. I think, um, ah, yes . . .' Then they both burst out laughing and congratulated her. Richard came over and held her hands.

'You look lovely, Julie. I'm proud to have you as a sister and Fergus should be proud to be escorting you.'

'I am, very proud,' Fergus said from behind them. Julie felt her colour rising at the warm appraisal of his dark eyes. He said to Kitty, 'I shall take good care of your daughter, Mrs van Neilson, and fight off all the men who come rushing to pay court.'

'Oh, stop it, all of you,' Julie wailed, 'you are making me feel like an object instead of a person!'

Fergus whipped out a posy from behind his back and held it out. 'Flowers for a *lady*, not an object.' They were tiny pink and yellow rosebuds.

Julie felt inordinately pleased at the gesture, which added to the romance of the evening. To go with the dress was a gossamer-fine evening stole in pale green and when Fergus draped it around her shoulders she felt once more the thrill of his touch on her skin.

With a bright face she called to her brother and Jake, 'Have a nice evening you two, be seeing you,' and her heart was pounding as she and Fergus turned to leave.

Kitty said, 'Have a lovely time, I know you will both enjoy it.' Julie was glad she had not made a fuss about what time they should be back.

The mild March evening certainly seemed made for romance with a blue velvet, star-studded sky and the waiting gondola, with its red velvet cushions, gold braid and tasselled canopy, the attractive gondolier with his beaming smile poling away from the landing stage, a sensuousness in his rhythmic strokes. Julie had been unable until then to understand the quick-speaking Italians but when their boatman spoke to Fergus she understood he was asking if he wanted him to sing to them. Fergus answered in Italian.

Later he whispered close to Julie's ear, 'I think he expects us to act as lovers. I don't think we should disappoint him, do you?' And so saying he slid his arm across her shoulders. She sat tense, refusing to belive he was doing anything more than playing a part to make her evening romantic. Even when he caressed her throat with a fingertip, sending her pulses racing, she refused to respond. Instead she concentrated on looking into the water. At times when their boatman stopped poling and the boat glided over parts of mirror-smooth canal, buildings and lights were reflected in it as though they were underwater. It was all so beautiful.

There were couples in gondolas that passed, several of them being serenaded by their boatmen, the love songs hanging hauntingly on the evening air. Fergus' arm moved down Julie's arm, drawing her closer and when their boatman began to sing softly she no longer resisted. Even though it was a 'pretence' romantic evening, she would enjoy it.

With her head resting against Fergus' shoulder he whispered in her hair, 'Sweet Julie. How lovely you are,' and she wished the evening would go on forever.

They branched off into the quieter canals where lamp and candlelit rooms of houses added to the romance. When they came to a stretch where there appeared to be a few derelict warehouses Fergus asked their boatman to stop. Julie tensed again and sat up. Fergus laughed softly and told her not to worry, they would walk for a short distance. She had still not relaxed when she was helped out, not knowing what was in Fergus' mind.

'Julie, you're trembling,' Fergus exclaimed. 'You have nothing to worry about – my intentions are honourable, I assure you. I simply wanted you to see a house where I serenaded a Senorita in my mis-spent youth.'

She relaxed. 'Was she very beautiful?'

'Yes, she was, and unattainable! Her father came down and threatened me with a gun.' Fergus laughed. 'That cooled my ardour. The house is further along.'

'I think it's sad. Was she in love with you?'

'I like to think she was, but then I was very young. She married an old man with plenty of money. Although the marriage was arranged I was told afterwards that she seemed content with her position.'

The story brought to Julie's mind her mother's sister Violet and she gave a sudden shiver.

'You're cold,' Fergus said with concern.

'No, not really. Sad little love stories are like ghosts from the past, but in spite of the sadness I want to see the house.'

It was empty, with the stonework crumbling and broken steps leading to the front door. Fergus pointed to the second floor. 'It was from that balcony she blew kisses to me while, like Romeo to Juliet, I "wooed" her. And now there is only dereliction.'

He laughed suddenly. 'Heavens, this is supposed to be a romantic evening. Come along, if we walk a little further I shall show you a small oasis, like the one we saw this morning, only this one is an island.' But the island had gone and Fergus said, a sadness in his voice, 'It was there six years ago. It has sunk into oblivion, as all of Venice is doomed to do in time. It's so tragic, all that magnificence, that beauty lost to the world.'

Julie had labelled him in her mind that morning as a man without a soul, when he had teased her about the smell of canals, but now she realised he was a man with a deep love of beauty. They walked to the canal edge and stood looking at the reflection of sky and buildings in the water.

'The sky will always be above us,' Julie said softly. 'It's like dark blue velvet studded with diamonds.'

'Oh, a poetic young lady.'

A small silence followed in which Fergus became serious

and stood looking into her eyes. Then he put his hands on her shoulders and kissed her on the lips. Julie wanted to believe he meant it, but commonsense told her it was just another gesture to make the evening romantic for her. She drew away.

'Julie?' His tone was questioning. There was another silence then he made to draw her to him again. She pushed both hands against his chest and said, 'Please don't.'

'And will *you* please stop looking at me in that hurt way!'

Julie met the dark eyes, her gaze unwavering. 'I was not hurt. I know why you kissed me, it was because of it being a special evening –'

'It had nothing to do with it being a special evening, or my conferring any *favours* on you. I kissed you because I wanted to. You are a most attractive girl and you have a charisma . . .' Fergus put a finger under her chin and added softly, 'And a very provocative way of looking at a man.'

'I've never ever attempted to be provocative,' she defended herself.

'I know, Julie, that is why I find you so attractive. Shall we go?'

Julie felt annoyed with herself for having taken the romance out of the evening and was thinking up ways to make amends for her stupidity when Fergus said in a teasing tone, 'May I put my arm around you? If I don't we are going to disappoint our boatman. As you know, they are all romantic.'

'Of course you may.' Julie smiled up at him. 'I should hate to disappoint our man.'

They were met with a beaming smile and the gondolier sang his love song, as he took them back to St Mark's Square. Julie offered no resistance this time when Fergus drew her close to him.

The illuminated Square was teeming with people and an orchestra was playing in the centre. Julie felt little shivery tremors of cold and excitement chasing up and down her spine. 'What a lot of people,' she exclaimed, 'and they all look so bright and fresh it could be midday.'

Fergus smiled. 'That is what Venice does to you. Shall we have a coffee? It's too early to go back.' He had started to lead her towards a table for two outside a small café when Julie protested that it was late and her mother would be worrying.

This was dismissed with a wave of the hand. Not at all, her mother had said she would not expect them back until the early hours.

'The early hours?' Julie stopped and looked at Fergus wide-eyed. 'Mother said that?'

'She knows that you are in good hands.' There was a hint of mischief in Fergus' dark eyes. He cupped a hand under her elbow and led her to a table for two. 'Your mother wants so much for you to enjoy yourself.' He drew out a chair for Julie and they sat at the table with its spotlessly-white tablecloth, a small bowl of flowers in the centre. After the waiter had been to take their order Fergus said: 'I find myself curious to know why neither you nor Richard have followed in your parents' footsteps. Glass-making is a fascinating business.'

'Yes, we both found it fascinating when we were young, and in fact we did make small objects in glass, but I think we went off it because we heard so much talk about it. Glass was our parents' sole topic of conversation . . . or so it seemed at that time. Mind you, I did have some quite grandiose ideas of what I would make when I grew up.'

'And what were these grandiose ideas?'

'I wanted to make beautiful coloured glass eggs. This stemmed from the time Aunt Helder told me about the famous Fabergé eggs that the Tzar of Russia gave to friends and relatives as gifts at Easter-time. She told me that some of them were made of gold and studded with precious stones and that the items inside were most unusual and costly.'

'Yes, they were, they were works of art.'

'I planned to put simple gifts in mine, like a tiny doll, an animal or a brooch for a loved one.'

'So why did you not make your eggs?'

Julie shrugged. 'I think perhaps the idea died on me. Recently, I have felt I would like to make ceramic eggs. No, not to make them, but to paint them. Angus could do the making, if he was willing.'

She explained about Angus, and the work he did in the shed at the back of the shop at Stoke and about the marriage bowl he had made.

Fergus showed great interest in this. 'What an excellent idea! He ought to market them – think what an interesting talking-point they would make.' Fergus teased Julie, wanting to know what ingredient she would add to make a successful marriage.

'I'm not sure. Angus has covered so many things.' She smiled. 'Perhaps I would be better able to tell you after a year of marriage.'

Fergus eyed her thoughtfully. 'I think it important for a couple to be able to sit in a companionable silence at times. I stress the word *companionable*.'

'I agree, but –' Julie grinned, 'how would you portray that on a bowl?'

Fergus made various suggestions, none of which proved satisfactory, then they began to talk about the ingredients Angus had already portrayed and their conversation was animated one moment and serious the next. In the end Julie made a protest.

'Here I was, feeling young and all beautifully romantic and now I feel like an ageing grandmother!'

Fergus said softly, a smiling appraisal in his eyes, 'I am sure you will still be beautiful, Julie, when you are old and much loved by your husband, your children and your grandchildren.'

For a moment they sat in silence, not the comfortable, companionable silence of a couple long married, but one in which love and romance were the keynote, with the orchestra in the background playing a Strauss waltz.

The spell was broken by a middle-aged man, who came rushing up to them and slapped Fergus on the back.

'Fergus, my boy! Fancy meeting you here! What a small world it is.' To Julie he added, with excitement, 'The last time Fergus and I met we were sharing a shell-hole in France.'

The two men were now pumping one another's hands, Fergus as excited as the man Julie was introduced to as Joseph Hendry, who had been a war correspondent. Joseph insisted they come to meet his family and they ended up drinking coffee together.

'Sorry for having our evening interrupted,' Fergus said when they left the Hendrys to return to the hotel after midnight, 'but I felt I couldn't do anything else under the circumstances.'

'Of course you couldn't and I enjoyed meeting them.'

'Joseph is a fine man, Julie, he saved my life during the war, but –' Fergus smiled down at her, 'no more talk of war. What are your plans for tomorrow? I know your mother wants to visit the island of Murano to see the glassworks at some stage. Perhaps we should decide on that in the morning.'

At first, Julie had been a little disappointed at the intrusion of the Hendrys into the evening, but afterwards she came to realise it could have been for the best, knowing it would be all too easy to become emotionally involved with Fergus. His attraction for her was so strong she dreamed about him that night, a dream that left her trembling with desire. When she thought about it the next morning her face burned.

# Chapter Twelve

Because of her dream the night before Julie felt sure she would feel guilty should her mother ask her probing questions about her evening with Fergus, but when Kitty came into her bedroom the next morning to take early morning tea with her she spoke of the three men spending some time together.

'I think it's wise, Julie. I know that Fergus wants to have a talk with Jake and I feel sure that Richard would benefit by Fergus' sound business sense.'

Julie, who had been unwilling to discuss Fergus moments before now found herself asking what line of business he was in. Kitty shook her head. 'I have no idea. He doesn't talk about it when I am there and as your father has never mentioned it I suppose it's something Fergus wants to keep secret.'

Kitty was wearing a delicate blue negligée trimmed with fine lace and Julie thought how attractive her mother looked in it, how seductive, and tried to imagine herself wearing it. Then she felt a wave of shame, knowing she was thinking of Fergus seeing her wearing the negligée.

She was about to ask her mother what plans had been made for the day when she noticed Kitty, a far-away look in her eyes, swirl round the dregs in the fragile porcelain cup, then turn the cup upside down on the saucer. Curious, Julie asked, 'Why did you do that? It's what you do if someone is going to tell your fortune.'

Kitty stared at the cup, as though seeing it for the first

time. 'Well, how strange, I can't ever remember doing that before. Not unless a fortune-teller was there. Aunt Harriet was a great believer in having her cup read.' Kitty picked up the cup and appeared to be studying the inside.

When Julie asked eagerly if she could read the leaves Kitty shook her head. 'Not really, I know some of the signs but I'm no expert. Abel used to get mad with Harriet for believing what she was told.'

'Have a look,' Julie pleaded. 'See if you can read any of the signs.' She got up and going round the table stood looking over her mother's shoulder. 'There's a bridge, look, right at the bottom of the cup, and a dog sitting underneath it.'

'A bridge means an approaching journey. Normally a dog means loyalty, friendship, but because it's at the bottom of the cup it indicates some treachery or envy, jealousy.'

'Oh, dear,' Julie said. 'And what does a crooked arm mean? It is a crooked arm, isn't it – there, on the rim?'

Kitty put the cup down. 'It means underhand dealing and I think that is enough for one day.' Julie was disappointed that nothing indicated any connection to Fergus. 'We must get ready for breakfast, Julie. Oh, by the way, did you enjoy your evening with Fergus?'

'Yes, I did, very much. It was lovely in the Square with an orchestra playing and crowds of people milling around. Fergus met a man he had known in the war who had been a war correspondent. We had coffee with the family.'

'That was nice for you. You must tell me about it later.' Kitty was at the door when she stopped and turned. 'Julie, I think you ought to know now that your father and I have been discussing buying a small family house in London. We'll staff it and Richard and Jake can live there. So can you – it will be more of a social life for you. Your father and I will come for the occasional weekend.'

Julie was silent. She pleated the edge of the sheet then looked up. 'I'm sorry, Mother, but I promised Tom and Ivy I would go with them to Echo Cove.'

'I see.' There was no doubting her mother's disapproval. 'I doubt whether your father will accept that, Julie, but we shall talk about it later. Get ready, or you will be late for breakfast.'

Julie lay for a moment then flung aside the bedclothes and said to the empty room, 'I am going to live at Echo Cove, no one can stop me!' She picked up the teacup. 'A long journey, envy, treachery, jealousy! Could you call trying to inveigle me to come back into the family fold treachery?'

At breakfast Kitty mentioned that she and Julie had decided to do some shopping, so the men could make their own plans. Richard said he was glad they were not being drawn into window-shopping then turned to Jake and suggested another look at a monument they had been discussing the night before. Fergus when asked, said, 'Fine, fine,' but later when Julie happened to look up at him he was watching her. She glanced away then stole another look at him, and this time he gave her a conspiratorial wink. She tensed and hoped her mother had missed it, otherwise she might have put the wrong interpretation on it.

Fergus showed some concern that Kitty and Julie would be without an escort but Kitty dismissed it. She was perfectly capable of taking care of herself and daughter. Before the two of them left the hotel it was arranged they would meet the men in St Mark's Square for a pre-lunch drink.

At first Kitty showed some alarm at the amount of attention that she and Julie were receiving from men of all ages, but after a while she began to giggle. 'I should love to see your father's face if he could see what was going on. To be perfectly honest I wouldn't mind having a little flirt.'

Julie encouraged her. 'Why not? As Ivy would say, "what the eye doesn't see, the heart can't grieve over".'

'No, no.' Kitty tried to compose her face into serious lines. 'This is terrible. It's bad enough that I am saying I would flirt, without my own daughter encouraging me. I must be serious, very serious.' Her lips began to tremble and she was giggling again.

'I like you better when you laugh,' Julie said. 'We used to laugh a lot together at one time when you told me about your young days in service and the funny things that Ivy used to come out with.'

'Oh, Ivy was a devil, I remember once –'

Julie listened fascinated as she always did when her mother talked about her past, and felt again the closeness they had shared at those times.

They strolled along the narrow lanes, gazing into windows, looking for presents to buy. Tyler and Kitty had given Julie spending money and had been quite lavish on this occasion. There were so many lovely things it was difficult to choose.

Kitty bought several pure silk squares, for Julie, for friends and for herself. Julie bought one for Ivy and a tie for Tom. She also bought as a special gift two small pictures with chased silver figures of children, a boy and a girl on a background of crimson velvet.

Later Kitty became alarmed again when they found themselves with two persistent followers, two Frenchmen judging by their accents, who were well-dressed, young and attractive. No matter how Kitty and Julie hurried or went down various lanes to try and avoid them the men where there. Once, when Kitty paused to catch her breath she said, 'What are we going to do?' Julie teased her, reminding her that she was the one who had wanted to flirt.

'I know,' Kitty suddenly grinned. 'It was all bravado – I would never have dared. Come along, we'll go into this shop, explain what is happening and ask if there is another way out.' The proprietor was sympathetic and allowed them to leave by a back entrance. But the Frenchmen caught up with them again and were so doggedly persistent they were there when they reached St Mark's Square. However, when Kitty and Julie went straight to a table where their men were waiting for them the Frenchmen melted into the crowd.

Julie and Kitty were so breathless they had to explain what had happened with Kitty saying with a laugh to Fergus, 'And don't you dare say I told you so.'

Jake was all male aggressiveness and protective towards Kitty. Had they hurt her, if so – He glared at Julie. 'I hope that *you* were not encouraging them.'

Julie was indignant. 'Of course I wasn't, and anyway they were not interested in me, it was Mother they were after. She's had men of all ages and nationalities making eyes at her. Daddy should be very pleased he has such an attractive wife.'

'And daughter,' Fergus said softly. 'I'm sure your father does appreciate you both.' He wagged a finger, 'But let this be a lesson to you both not to go out without an escort.'

Kitty smiled sweetly and Julie said, 'You try stopping Mother! She has a mind of her own.'

'And her daughter takes after her,' Fergus said, his gaze teasing.

Richard and Jake began describing what they had seen earlier but when they began to go into technicalities Julie looked idly around her, her gaze going from one group to another. How she loved this cosmopolitan scene, the colour and gaiety. Would England seem drab after it?

An elegantly-dressed woman, escorted by three equally attractive men came into view. Julie sat up slowly, a prickle of apprehension touching her spine. It couldn't be – couldn't *possibly* be Violet. But it was and Julie panicked. If Richard were to catch sight of her, heaven knew how he might react. She was wondering what to do for the best when two things happened simultaneously. The party of four stopped to speak to people at a nearby table; and Richard and Jake, having apparently spotted two girls they had met earlier, asked to be excused.

Kitty had just said, smiling indulgently after them, 'Love's young dream,' when she caught sight of the group and went pale. 'Violet,' she whispered and looked frantically from Fergus to Julie. 'We must leave at once.' She made to get up but Fergus laid a restraining hand on her arm. 'Don't make yourself conspicuous, Mrs van Neilson. Richard and Jake are out of your sister's view. There's a constant movement of people, and when the moment is right we shall make a move.'

A minute later he said, 'Now – and don't hurry.'

Although they had not hurried Julie had a breathless feeling by the time they stopped a few feet away from Jake and Richard, who were standing with their backs to them, watching the girls move away.

'What do I say to Richard?' Kitty asked in a low voice.

'That you have the beginning of a headache and want to go back to the hotel. We can make further plans when we get there.'

Jake was most concerned about the headache but although Richard commiserated with Kitty his main interest lay in the girls, whom they had met earlier with their parents.

'Aren't they attractive?' he said. 'They just slipped away from their parents for a moment to say goodbye. Unfortunately, they're leaving for Rome today. What a pity, just when we had met.'

'Rome?' Kitty said, looking thoughtful.

When they arrived at the hotel she said she would go up to her room and lie down for a while, assuring Jake who was fussing over her, that it was just a *slight* headache, but she thought it was best to get away from the crowd. He agreed.

Julie went up with her mother but they were only moments in the room before Fergus arrived. Kitty thanked him for coming and Julie, not having heard her invite him looked from one to the other, mystified.

Kitty said, 'I asked Fergus if he would come and discuss our problem. Violet could be here by coincidence or design, but whichever it is, she will surely make trouble once she knows where we are. We must get away from here and the sooner the better. I suggest we go to Rome now, sooner than we had planned. Richard gave me the idea when he was talking about the girls who were leaving today to travel there.'

'But would it be enough incentive to suggest we leave?' Julie asked. 'Both Jake and Richard are taken with Venice and have a great deal more to see and study. And we had planned to spend a week in Florence, too.'

Kitty nodded slowly. 'Yes, you are right. So what do we do?'

Fergus said, 'Would Tyler be able to leave quite a lot earlier than he had intended? If he said he would meet us in Rome tomorrow or the next day then that would be the answer.' Kitty got up immediately. She would telephone Tyler.

Twenty minutes later she announced it was all settled. Tyler would send a telegram saying he would be arriving in Rome the following day and would meet them there. He would alter their hotel arrangements.

Kitty moved around the room, her palms pressed together. Once the telegram had arrived and could be shown to Richard and Jake they would prepare to leave, and trust they could get away without coming into contact with Violet.

The plan worked well. When the telegram arrived both Richard and Jake were excited and went into an animated discussion of what they would study first in Rome.

Kitty gave a nod of satisfaction to Fergus and Julie, but she looked strained, and did not relax until they had safely boarded the train that evening.

Their arrival in Rome had none of the leisurely feeling of arriving in Venice. There was a mêlée of voluble, gesticulating people, happy people who, it seemed to Julie, had no awareness of class distinction. Their taxi driver, who gave his name as Mario, chatted away to them as if they were old friends and was a mine of information. They were Engleese, yes? He had been to England, when he was young. London was very good, but Roma! Ah! He spread his hands and they all caught their breath seeing that they were caught up in traffic where cars, bicycles, carts and wagons fought to get in front as though they were competing in a race. The drivers shouted to one another but there was no aggression.

When they were forced to a standstill by two barrow men getting their wheels locked, solicitous enquiries were made from people stuck in the jam as to the health of the latest bambino, a wife or a grandmother. Fergus remarked that the Italians were wonderful people.

When they were on the move again Mario began to describe all the places they must visit. There were so many beautiful churches, but they just *had* to visit the Santa Francesco Romano. So small – he cupped his hands – but so *elegante* – there were steps and a gate to it, and many famous weddings were held there.

Then there were the monuments, the arches, mausoleums, which were so much a part of Roman history. And the fountains! But, of course, how could they possibly miss them, they were everywhere.

Mario was such a delightful character Julie was sorry when they arrived at the hotel, but it seemed they were not going to lose him. He was to be their guide and would call every morning to see if he was needed.

That night Julie had little sleep, partly due to all that had happened, but also because of the sounds of a wide-awake city. It seemed to be about four in the morning before the revelry ended and soon afterwards there were the sounds of a city coming to life for a working day.

Tyler was to arrive that morning and when after breakfast Richard and Jake were itching to go sightseeing, Kitty urged them to go, not wanting them to be there when Violet was being discussed.

Fergus went to meet Tyler at the station and while Kitty and Julie waited Kitty said in a worried tone, she was sorry she had to ask Tyler to leave his work but it was important for him to be here. Richard's future could be at stake because of Violet.

When Fergus and Tyler arrived Julie's first impression was how attractive and distinguished-looking both men looked, but when she saw her father's face, with lines of worry and his eyes tired through lack of sleep she felt a sudden wave of love for him.

Over coffee, with Fergus there, they discussed the problem of Violet. Tyler said they were perhaps making too much of something that could be pure coincidence, but Kitty had been right to get in touch with him. If Violet did show up in Rome, then they would have cause for worry. In the meantime, they would enjoy their holiday. Tyler laid his hand over Kitty's and said with a smile, 'You'll be pleased to know I've cast off the reins of work and am going to have several weeks enjoying myself . . . with you all.'

'Oh, Tyler –' Kitty's eyes were shining. 'That will be wonderful.' Her eyes suddenly clouded. 'That is, if Violet –'

'Forget her.' He got up. 'I'm going to have a couple of hours sleep. You three go and enjoy yourselves. Where were the boys planning to go?'

Fergus glanced at his watch. 'I told them we might go fountain viewing and if we didn't see them in the vicinity we would all meet for lunch back here.'

They found Richard and Jake at the Fountain of the Naiads. Julie, entranced by the magnificence and beauty of the work, remarked on it and Jake said, 'It's tragic that the sculptor, heartbroken by the adverse criticism when it was unveiled, took his own life.'

'Oh, how terrible,' Kitty said. Julie was indignant and wanted to know how anyone could possibly be against such beautiful work.

'Not everyone was,' Fergus said. 'One faction thought it

to be a fine work of art, while another proclaimed that the nymphs were artistically disreputable.'

'What exactly did they mean by "artistically disreputable"?'

'They thought the figures of the women wrestling and those posing on the various sea-horses erotic.'

Although Julie knew the meaning of erotic from secret conversations with girls at school, it was not a word bandied about, yet none of the others seemed to notice it.

'I think it a fine work of art!' Jake enthused, his eyes shining.

Richard added his contribution, a smile on his lips, his head inclined. 'There is a rather naughty air about it, but just look at those figures reclining in their shower baths.'

Kitty said, 'Yes – well – shall we be walking on?'

Julie enjoyed visiting all the fountains but the one that impressed her most was the famous Trevi Fountain, where people threw coins into the sun-sparkled water to ensure a return to Rome.

It almost filled the tiny square and was talked about as a 'water fantasy'. Here, there was an air of gaiety as people of all ages and nationalities threw their coins into the bowl and made their wish. From niches in the wall, three figures looked down from their lofty perches to where two tridents rose from rock pools on either side of the central cascade, each a sea horse at his side. One represented the ocean in an angry mood, Jake said, while the other was known as the sea of tranquillity.

'So who is going to throw a coin into the water and make a wish?' Fergus enquired. To Julie he added, 'Come along, what are you going to wish?'

She looked up at him and laughed. 'If I tell you it won't come true.'

'If you tell me it *will*! I am a magician.'

'All right, I challenge you. Magic the fountain to turn into a beautiful desert oasis.'

Fergus shook his head regretfully. 'Alas, that cannot be,

it's only on a Thursday that I can make an oasis.' It was his solemn expression that made Julie chuckle with delight. She told him they would return on Thursday so he'd better be prepared! Fergus smiled then – it was a date. Some people tossed in a coin as soon as they arrived at the fountain while others stood hesitant. Kitty was among the latter group and Julie wondered if she were wishing they could be rid of Violet. This was what Julie wished as she threw in her coin.

When they went back to the hotel for lunch, Tyler was up and looking refreshed. He asked what plans they had for the afternoon and Jake suggested visiting the Temple of the Vestal Virgins. They were all agreeable.

Julie had heard of the Vestal Virgins but had no idea what rôle they played in history. She decided to ask. After all, none of them had turned a hair when the word erotic had been mentioned.

While her father was pouring the wine she said, 'Who exactly were the Vestal Virgins?'

Fergus explained while Tyler mopped up the spilt wine. 'It was an Order girls joined when they were young, from six to ten years old. There were six resident Vestals, who were cut off from the world and lived a life of extreme simplicity.'

'In a house the size of a palace, with over fifty rooms on the ground floor,' Kitty said wryly. 'I've read about them and they did have privileges. Only the Vestals and the Empress were allowed to drive in carriages and everyone made way for them.'

'Ah yes,' said Jake, speaking gently. 'But they also had the power to plead for the reprieve for a condemned criminal, should this be pleaded for in the streets. And they *were* responsible for keeping the sacred flame alight in the temple, and with a hole in the roof and the weather uncertain, the flame was doused at times.' Jake paused, then said, 'At these times they were severely whipped by the Pontifex Maximus!'

'They also had to follow a strict code of personal

morality,' Richard offered, 'and if they broke this vow of thirty years of virginity they were buried alive.'

Julie shivered. 'How awful, how absolutely awful.'

Fergus said, 'They were told the penalties when they joined as novitiates; no girl was forced into this against her will and although they could resign the priesthood on retirement no one ever did.'

Julie said with great feeling, 'I only know that I would *not* have wanted to be a Vestal Virgin,' to which Fergus replied in a low voice, she would not have qualified, she was not the type. Julie was not quite sure how to take this but had no opportunity of asking because Tyler changed the subject by discussing the next course.

They went to visit the Temple of the Vestals but after a while Fergus and Julie wandered away with Fergus describing the size of the gardens and how they had been in their heyday.

During a lull in the conversation Julie stopped and faced him. 'Tell me, what did you mean when you said I was not the type to be a Vestal Virgin?'

'Because you have no longing for power.'

Julie cocked her head. 'How do you know I haven't?'

'If you had you would not be working in Tom and Ivy's shop.'

Julie moved away. 'Perhaps I shall leave when I go back. I'm enjoying this life. I loved Venice and I know I'm going to love Rome. This morning has been wonderful. The fountains – I want to see everything – the wonderful paintings, the Coliseum, the Sistine chapel –'

'And so you shall. We have several days and what we can't see in that time we shall finish when we come again. If not in this visit then at some other time in the future.' Fergus linked his arm through hers and smiled. 'I would enjoy having you on your own, seeing everything through your eyes, Julie. One gets a little jaded after travelling so much.'

Julie glanced at him and said with a teasing smile, 'And how many "fresh eyes" have you had with you on your travels?'

He laid a hand over hers. 'Well, let me put it this way. I haven't had anyone with me who has been quite so appealing, nor who has haunted my dreams.'

Although Julie laughed softly and accused him of overdoing the flattery she could not help but be pleased at the compliment. And was sorry when her parents and Richard and Jake came to join them.

They had a full day's sightseeing and at the end of it, all of them were ready for a quiet evening. Julie hoped that her parents would then discuss her mother's earlier life, but again this was put off. 'Tomorrow,' Kitty said. 'I feel I haven't the strength to talk.'

But the following morning she was lively again as they set out for another sightseeing trip. And that evening when Fergus suggested visiting the working-class district, Julie was surprised when her mother also agreed with it.

Julie soon realised what Fergus had meant by the atmosphere being brash, noisy and friendly. She had thought the party might have been conspicuous by their dress but they were accepted as a part of the community with people calling greetings. The narrow alleyways with their lines of washing were also exactly as Fergus had described them. Children played on the cobbled streets, and women looked out of windows adorned by pots of flowers.

One mother called to her child, 'Marco – *vienni dentro – e' ora di cena!*' Fergus remarked 'Supper-time.'

The boy called, '*Un' momento*, Mama,' but when he was called again, this time sharply, he obeyed and was away like a streak of lightning. The nearby market was a delight to Julie with its colourful stalls, the fruit, the vegetables, cheeses and clothing. There was a great deal of voluble and good-natured haggling between customers and stall-holders and everywhere they went there was music and people singing.

One man cheekily serenaded Julie. He had bright eyes and a lovely tenor voice.

Julie had written a letter to Tom and Ivy in Venice and sent cards; late that evening she put her impressions for that day down in a letter. *'It's almost impossible to describe all I've seen, impossible to describe the magnificence, St Peter's Basilica, the frescos, mosaics, the beautiful figures, so much gilt, so many jewel colours. We went into several churches and at times I felt so overwhelmed there were moments when I could hardly speak.*

*'We went to the Coliseum, where games used to be held. Terrible games, with men slaying lions and gladiators fighting to the death. As I stood there I imagined I could hear the roar of the crowds, the vicious shouting of "Kill him, kill him!" And yet, how could I help being impressed by the size alone. The Coliseum is a huge round structure, which goes up in tiers and held over 50,000 people, people who found so much pleasure in cruelty.*

*'But there is also the beauty. I saw the magnificent ceiling in the Sistine Chapel, painted by Michel Angelo. It took him four years and he spent that time on his back with his eyes being constantly blurred by splashes of paint. Poor man, it's a wonder he was not blinded. Jake said it was a labour of love. It must have been, and thousands and thousands of people must be grateful that he did so and we can all appreciate his beautiful work.*

*'Tomorrow Mother and I are going shopping on our own. Apparently there is a long, long street, full of art shops, I shall tell you all about it in my next letter.'*

She made no mention of Violet . . .

# Chapter Thirteen

Julie was with her mother the following morning in a fine arts shop, where Kitty was practically drooling over a painting of a country scene when Julie's attention was caught by the carved wooden head of a man. She had moved over to it and was standing studying the face when a voice said from behind her:

'Don't you think he resembles your friend Fergus Damant?'

Julie turned slowly and found herself staring into the insolently smiling face of Violet. Although Julie's heart was beating in slow, painful thuds she managed to speak calmly.

'Do you think so? Quite frankly, I cannot see any resemblance. This man has strong features but very little expression.' Julie glanced quickly to the left and saw with relief that her mother had gone into another section of the shop.

Violet drawled, 'You really ought to study Fergus Damant, darling. If you do you'll find he gives nothing away in his expression. But then it would be unwise to in *his* work, wouldn't it?'

A dapper little man came fussing up to Violet and after giving her a bow, a beaming smile and bidding her good morning in Italian, he asked in heavily-accented English, 'May I be of assistance to you, Lady Godell-White?'

Violet dismissed him with a wave of the hand. 'Not now, not now.' The man apologised and withdrew. Violet turned to Julie and smoothed down the fingers of her black suede gloves. 'I think it might be a good idea to have a word with your mother.'

Julie stepped in front of her. 'I think not! My mother has suffered enough from you in the past.' When Violet made to brush her aside she caught hold of her arm. 'If you don't leave her alone you will suffer from me, and I mean it!'

Violet laughed softly. 'Quite the little virago, aren't you. How appealing you must be to Fergus Damant, such a change from the hard-faced bitches he usually escorts.' Her expression changed, she pushed Julie. 'Get out of my way, *child*.'

Julie retaliated by pushing Violet with two hands. Violet lost her balance and ended up sitting on a brocaded sofa. Her expression now was one of comical astonishment. 'I warned you,' Julie said.

Julie could hear her mother's voice. She was apparently talking to an assistant. Then Kitty appeared and seeing Julie said, 'I've bought that painting for your father's birthday. I'm sure he'll be delighted with it, he –' She paused, having caught sight of Violet, and the colour drained from her cheeks.

Violet rose from the sofa with a careless grace, as though she had just been resting for a moment. 'Good morning, sister dear. Your daughter has been doing her best to prevent my meeting you. She's quite a little rebel! You'll need to watch her or she'll end up having – I won't be crude, so shall we simply say – having a *love child*, just as her mother was.'

The colour rushed back to Kitty's face, but although Julie knew her mother was angry she said in a calm voice: 'We've gone into all this years ago, Violet, and you know I'm not a bastard. Yes, I can use the word, I'm not like you, I don't forget my humble upbringing. You would be wise to remember it too, because one day it will catch up with you. Now, if you will excuse us. Julie –'

Violet stepped in front of Kitty. 'Before you go I should like to say something. You will never be rid of me. I won't give up tormenting you until I get Richard, and I will. He happens to like me, was sympathetic towards me – did you know that? One more evening with him and I could have him eating out of my hand.'

Kitty's head went up. 'If that's what you would want from a son I feel sorry for you, Violet, very sorry.'

Violet's smile was deceptively disarming; her eyes held hatred. 'And I shall feel sorry for you when Richard comes to me, which he will. I think deep down he knows that he is my son.' With that Violet turned and walked away from them, poised, elegant . . .

When she had gone from the shop Kitty said in a low voice, 'Come along, Julie, we must get back to the hotel and let your father know what has happened.'

Tyler was with Fergus when he was told about Violet. He said at once they must make arrangements to leave. He was white with anger, Julie had never seen her father so angry. Kitty agreed with him, saying she could not bear to be in the same city as Violet.

'That is exactly what she wants you to do,' Fergus said quietly. 'She enjoys tormenting you. The fact that she has not attempted to approach Richard proves she intends to prolong the torment. You left Venice in a hurry, and if you leave Rome just as suddenly he is bound to want to know the reason.'

Tyler drew thumb and forefinger over his chin as though stroking a beard. 'You're right, Fergus, we must think this over carefully. Yes –' he nodded slowly, 'I think perhaps the best thing to do would be to go on with our sightseeing as planned, ignore Violet and see what happens.'

'No, Tyler, we must get away, we *must*.' Kitty began to plead. 'Don't you see, we would never feel free from her, she could get to Richard –'

'Not if we all stay together, Kitty. We made what seemed

a valid excuse for leaving Venice but what explanation could we give to them this time?'

'We have planned to visit your family,' Kitty said eagerly. 'We could say we wanted to go earlier.'

'It wouldn't work, Kitty. Richard would naturally ask why there was all the rush, when we've waited years to meet them. If we want to leave it would have to sound like an emergency.'

'Then try and think of something that sounds like one!'

Tyler raised his shoulders in a gesture of despair. 'But what? It's not easy, not easy at all.'

Fergus who had been looking thoughtful now said, 'I think I could provide a strong enough reason for wanting to leave but I would need to work it out. Will you leave it with me? In the meantime I suggest we visit the Catacombs this afternoon as planned and behave normally. Mario will be waiting for us. As we go to the taxi we will laugh and chat. Is that agreeable to you?'

Tyler gave a quick nod. Kitty said, a desperate note in her voice, 'I'll do anything, anything at all to leave here.'

Julie was aware that her mother was under a strain over lunch but Richard and Jake were so full of what they had done that morning neither seemed aware of it.

And when they left the hotel later to go to the Catacombs it was enough to see Mario's beaming face to have them all laughing and chatting.

Mario was so full of little anecdotes to tell that it was some moments before Julie became aware that Fergus kept glancing over his shoulder. Jake seemed to become aware of it at the same time and said, 'What's wrong, Fergus?'

'I think that I am being followed.'

Jake shot up in his seat. '*You*? Followed? Why?'

'I'm afraid I can't tell you.' Fergus leaned forward and spoke to Mario, who was already on the alert. 'Mario, there's a car behind us, I want you to lose it.'

'*Si, Signore, si*, at once, *Signore*!' There was a gleeful note in Mario's voice.

Driving at any time in Rome was a hazard, but with Mario, plus the present situation it was a hair-raising, heart-stopping nightmare. Tyres screeched, gears crashed and there was a cacophony of blaring horns as they went around corners and dodged vehicles with inches to spare.

When Fergus said eventually he was sure they had now lost his pursuer it was not only Mario who showed regret but Richard and Jake, with Richard declaring it was as exciting as a 'Fantomas' film. Jake agreed.

Mario enquired of Fergus in coaxing tones, 'Perhaps you will be followed again, *Signore*?'

Fergus told him gravely it was possible, he would keep a sharp lookout. At this stage Julie was not sure whether Fergus was being genuinely followed, or whether it was all part of the plan he had in mind. Later, when they arrived at the Catacombs and got out she decided it was a part of the plan. Richard and Jake were excited and asking questions like who was his pursuer, why was he being followed . . . was the man dangerous?

'He could be,' Fergus replied, 'but I cannot say any more. I may have to leave Rome.'

'If you have to,' Richard said eagerly, 'we'll go with you, won't we, Jake?' Jake nodded vigorously. 'Of course. Just try and stop me!'

Kitty had lost her look of strain and when the opportunity came she thanked Fergus in a low voice. 'You're very clever, Fergus, it worked. Now I think I shall enjoy the afternoon.'

But although both Kitty and Julie found the Catacombs impressive they also found them depressing and were glad to get out in the fresh air again. From there they went to the Vatican Museums, with Mario constantly looking over his shoulder and being very disappointed to find no pursuer.

At the museums Julie experienced a constant feeling of awe at so much beauty. The item that remained vividly in her mind was the masterpiece known as the Belvedere Torso. It was a shattered fragment, which Jake said illustrated the superb craft of the Greek sculptor.

The torso was of a powerful man of mature age and was leaning forward. Michel Angelo, a great admirer of the sculptor's work, was known to have said of it, 'It is the work of a man who knows more than nature'. This deeply impressed Julie, who had by now become a fervent admirer of Michel Angelo.

Back at the hotel, while they were having afternoon tea, Fergus announced he would have to leave Rome. Tyler said, 'I suggest we all leave. We had planned to visit my family so why not now? They live on the outskirts of Rome and I feel sure that Mario would be able to evade any follower. The invitation did extend to you, Fergus, and to Jake.'

After a discussion it was settled that Tyler would telephone his family and if it was convenient they would leave the following morning. Once this had been confirmed, and Fergus and Jake had retired to their rooms, Julie said to her parents that now they were going to meet her father's family, it really was time that she and Richard were told something about them, and about the Tiernes. Violet's remark about a love-child had confused and upset her.

Tyler repeated what they already knew about him leaving home at seventeen and becoming apprenticed to a glass-maker, very much against his father's wishes, adding that he was sure his father had never forgiven him for not having followed him into the banking world.

'Nor had he forgiven you for marrying me,' Kitty said wryly, 'the daughter of a poor family.'

Tyler smiled and patted her hand. 'He was impressed that your father was the son of a man who had a name in the ceramic world.' He paused and added, 'Incidentally, I heard from the Tiernes before I came away.'

Kitty stared at him. 'You heard from them? And you never mentioned it? Why?'

'Because, my love, they are in Germany at the moment and that does not come into our plan. They are there for a number of weeks, holidaying. They did invite us to visit them at Monchau but I thought it more sensible to wait until they return home to Dorset.'

'Why shouldn't we go to Germany?' Richard demanded. 'You are always making excuses for us not to meet them. What are you hiding?'

'Nothing, nothing at all, Richard. It just seemed foolish to me to go all the way to Germany when we could meet them in England.'

'Who was it who wrote to you?' Kitty asked, looking annoyed. 'I think I ought to have been told.'

Tyler spread his hands. 'Be reasonable, Kitty, I didn't see the point. It was your father's cousin who wrote. He was the one who apparently inherited the estate. To be honest, I believe I thought it might be a good thing if we *didn't* meet.'

'Why?' Julie said. 'Are we allowed to know? Or is this something else that is to remain a secret?'

Kitty gave a deep sigh. 'My mother, as you know, married Richard Tierne, who came from a good class family. He died before they had hardly any married life together, and before he had a chance to provide for my mother. There was an old will, making a cousin heir to his estate. Mother sent it to the address of the solicitor she had found in Richard's papers and also told him about her marriage. She heard nothing from the cousin, who was the only living relative. She was left destitute with me to bring up. I wanted nothing to do with them, nor would I now – had you and Richard not wanted to meet them.'

'Well, I feel you ought to meet them,' Richard said, a stubborn thrust to his jaw. '*You* have a right to know why the cousin ignored you. The solicitor might never have mentioned about the marriage, or the letter to him could have gone astray. There are all sorts of possibilities and quite frankly I'm astonished that you haven't made any contact with them until now.' Richard turned to Tyler. 'Why didn't *you* insist, Father?'

Tyler sighed. 'Because your mother didn't want me to, it's as simple as that. What is more she had every right not to meet her father's family if she had no wish to. It's still up to your mother to say yea or nay.'

'We *shall* meet them,' Kitty got up, 'I promise. But I'm not promising that you shall meet them in Germany. Now, I must go to bed.'

Tyler, after saying he would follow her in a few moments, turned to Richard and Julie. 'Well, there it is. I wanted to protect your mother from any more hurt. It's up to you two to decide what you want to do. Good night.'

Julie looked at Richard. 'So what does that make us? If we insist on meeting the family we'll seem like the meanest people alive, but if we don't meet them we shall always go on wondering about our grandfather Tierne and his family.'

The stubborn expression came over Richard's face once more. 'I *want* to meet the family, I want to know first-hand why they left my grandmother destitute. Mother has a right to know and I think that *we* have a right to know. What do you think?'

Julie looked up. 'I've always been badgering Mother to know about the family, but now I'm not so sure that we would be doing the right thing. Supposing it discloses some skeleton in the cupboard?'

'If there is a skeleton then it needs to be brought out and given an airing. Anyway, we're not likely to be going to Germany, so we have plenty of time to think about it. Actually, the most important thing at the moment is to get Fergus away from Rome.' Richard's expression became animated. 'I wonder who it is following him? Jake doesn't know, he hasn't any idea what business Fergus is supposed to be in. Astonishing, isn't it?'

'I wouldn't say so,' Julie said wryly, 'considering that our own grandparents' lives have been kept more or less a secret from us, and that from our own parents! You would think that our grandfather had been a criminal.'

'There are worse stigmas than being the grandson of a criminal,' Richard replied, bitterness in his voice. He got up. 'I'm off to bed.'

He was away, leaving Julie staring after him. He obviously still thought of Violet as his mother. Was he right? Would they ever know? With a sigh Julie got up. So many questions still to be answered.

The next morning there was definitely a car following them and Julie guessed it was Violet who was responsible. But Mario soon lost the car and exclaimed, beaming, '*Perfetto*!'

Soon they were on the outskirts of Rome, where villas were partially hidden from the tree-lined road by high hedges. Here was a froth of spring blossom, and pink and scarlet oleanders were opening their buds.

Julie had asked her father about his family's house and he had described it as a villa built on vine slopes with a tall-columned portico. He had told her about the gardens with bougainvillaea spilling over arches and trellis, but when they arrived at the villa she saw that he had forgotten to mention the small waterfalls and the streams.

Kitty said, 'Oh, Tyler, it's beautiful, you didn't do it justice! How could you bear to leave here?'

To this Tyler replied softly, 'If I had not left, my darling, I would not have met you.' And there was something between her parents then that made Julie long to know the same kind of love.

A group of people were waiting outside for them as the taxi drew up at the door. There must have been eight to ten in the group but the person who dominated was a tall, aristocratic-looking man with greying hair and a Vandyke beard. He came forward as Tyler got out of the taxi. The two men embraced and although Julie's first impression of the elder man had been one of austerity, she now noticed there were tears in his eyes. They spoke in Italian for a moment then the rest of the party were being introduced to the van Neilson family.

Although Julie knew that her father's ancestors were of Italian and Dutch extraction she saw the whole family as pure Italian and her father looking the perfect English gentleman.

There were so many names being offered and relationships mentioned that she found it difficult to take them all in. A woman about her parents' age embraced Kitty saying she had longed to meet her, and it was not only Kitty who was emotional.

They went into the house, into a long room that was all elegance, chandeliers, settees and armchairs in delicate pink and pale blue velvet, the marble floor covered by beautiful rugs; there were statues, flowers in tall vases, oil paintings.

Servants came to take their coats and others wheeled in trays of cakes and savouries, while two manservants poured drinks.

The murmurs of conversation grew gradually to a happy exchange of news with much laughter and gesticulations. Richard and Jake, looking very pleased with themselves, were seated with two dark-haired beautiful girls who were discreetly flirting with them.

Although Mr van Neilson had ordered that English must be spoken there was, now and again, a lapse into their own language and, although Julie could get the gist of the subject, they spoke too quickly to grasp the whole.

A dramatic and a rather happy incident came when likenesses were being discussed. Mr van Neilson said to Richard, 'I would have said you were all van Neilson, were it not for your eyes. You have your mother's very beautiful eyes – you should win approval from the ladies.'

Richard looked startled. He glanced at Kitty then turned to the old man and smiled, 'Thank you, Grandfather.'

Mr van Neilson, with a rather proud look, bowed. 'I am delighted to make your acquaintance, my grandson. You are my *only* grandson.'

Julie expected some sour looks from the parents of his granddaughters but when one man said, 'Our daughters shall give you many great-grandsons, sir,' there was general laughter.

It was not until late afternoon that Julie was able to put names to each person and it was from Rosomunda, the daughter of Tyler's sister Caterina that she learned of the unrest among the young people.

'Our grandfather is what you call in England, a patriarch. He rules us, tells our parents what they must do regarding us. Oh, he is very charming, and had he not been related to us I think I might have fallen in love with him. Uncle Tyler was sensible to break away. I wish I could go to England. Do you have freedom?'

When Julie described that she was working and where and why, Rosomunda was entranced but, with a quick glance around, put a finger to Julie's lips. 'Do not mention that in this house. Grandfather would be horrified. He is a terrible snob.' Julie, annoyed, had more or less decided she would shock Mr van Neilson Senior when Rosomunda added, 'It would be your parents who would suffer. Do not spoil this reunion.'

The girl then turned her attention to Richard. 'I think my cousin Richard is most attractive. I must get to know him better, then perhaps we can marry and he will take me to England.'

Julie expected her to break into an impish grin but she was deadly serious. Julie thought she had better warn Richard he was to be pursued with a view to marriage!

There was a time during the evening when Julie began to feel the odd one out. Richard and Jake had the attention of all the girls while Fergus and Tyler seemed to be holding court to the rest of the party. She was sitting near a door that led into the garden and after a while she got up unnoticed and slipped outside. There she stood, taking in the scene and thinking she had never seen an evening more beautiful. Stars hung low in the midnight blue of the sky and moonlight touched flowers, greenery and small waterfalls with silver. She walked on under an arbour of trailing greenery and had stopped again to gaze into a rockpool when an image appeared close to her reflection.

'Don't you think we make an attractive pair?' Fergus said softly. Some small fish made ripples on the surface destroying their features and they both laughed.

'So much for conceit,' Julie said.

Fergus linked her arm through his and as they moved away he asked her if she liked her new family.

'I like them all – I think. I'm not sure about my grandfather. He's so courteous, so charming, but I should hate to live in the same house with him, I would feel trapped.'

Fergus stopped and turned Julie to face him. 'I think you would feel trapped wherever you lived, Julie.'

They were under trees and his face was just a pale blur. 'I don't feel trapped living with Tom and Ivy – well, perhaps occasionally. Is one ever free? Aren't we always answerable to someone? My parents are very much in love but my mother is always concerned about what my father thinks.'

'The perfect wife,' Fergus teased.

Julie moved away. 'I don't want to be perfect, it would be so boring. I think I would have liked to be an explorer and go into the jungle –'

'And be beaten up by a wild animal and I would never have met you.'

'I'm quite sure if someone told you in a month's time that I had died you would say, "Julie? The name's familiar, but I can't place her. Who was she?"'

'Oh, I would place you all right. You are not the type of girl who is easily forgotten.' Fergus paused then added gently, 'Why are you in such a depressed state, Julie? You're in these lovely surroundings –'

'I don't think surroundings have anything to do with moods. I could be in quite a happy mood scrubbing floors or serving in the shop; on the other hand I was in a happy mood when we visited all the fountains. And the night we –'

She stopped, embarrassed, and Fergus concluded for her, 'The evening in the gondola. Only you would not allow me to become too romantic.'

'You know why,' she said. 'There is not much romance in having such an evening arranged by one's mother.'

Fergus stopped again and knuckled her under the chin. 'Would it surprise you to know that I was the one to suggest taking you out?'

In the silence following this Julie was aware of the cool evening scents and the cascading sound of water. Fergus cupped her face between his palms. 'Tantalising Julie van Neilson, what am I going to do with you?' His eyes were dark pools, his voice a caress. He leaned towards her and kissed her full on the mouth. His lips were warm and she responded to their sensuous movement. Pushing her hair aside he trailed a finger round the back of her ear, sending a throbbing over her body.

Voices from a short distance away made Julie panic, but Fergus still held her lips, and when he did draw away his fingers on her skin made her long for more. She heard her mother saying, 'Oh, it really is beautiful,' then Fergus took her hand, whispered, 'This way,' and he ran her lightly along a path and stopped again under a group of Cypress trees.

He placed her with her back against the tree trunk and laid his hands on her shoulders. 'We have some unfinished business to attend to. I can't leave you feeling deprived on such a romantic evening.'

Julie tensed. Feeling deprived? Did he think he was doing her a favour? 'Thank you very much,' she said, 'but you can confer your favours on some other girl who you think needs them.' She pushed him away and began to run, not stopping until she came to some tall bushes. Then, lost in them, she stopped to regain her breath.

A moment later she heard Fergus calling her name softly. 'What's the matter with you, Julie? I didn't kiss you because I felt I had to – I *wanted* to. Perhaps I chose the wrong phrase, but then *I* am not perfect.' She detected a smile in his voice but she refused to respond. When she remained silent he said, his tone now cold, 'Very well, stay in there if you wish. I am certainly not going to plead with a girl who is behaving like a spoilt child.'

Spoilt child indeed! Julie was indignant until she realised he was right. A girl with more experience would have questioned his remark there and then instead of running away. She said, hesitantly, 'Fergus?' But there was no reply, and when she heard his receding footsteps she knew he had meant what he said.

She made to come out of the shelter of the bushes but after a while found she was going in circles. Keeping her gaze on the moon as a guide she set off again, only to discover that each path brought her back to a central spot. This was ridiculous. She listened for the voices she had heard earlier but they now sounded a distance away. How long would it take for them to find she was missing? Would Fergus tell them where she was?

Julie had been warm when she left the house, but now a creeping chill was seeping into her bones. Her teeth were chattering when she heard the voice of Mr van Neilson calling, 'Julietta?'

She answered him and he came for her, sounding none too pleased. If she had mentioned she wanted to walk in the garden, he said, someone would have accompanied her. Julie had to restrain herself from telling him that she had been with his wretched guest Fergus Damant. She apologised for being so thoughtless, adding she hoped she had not caused any worry.

'We were all worried, of course.' In the next moment he was concerned for her. 'You are cold, Julietta. Here, take my jacket.' Its body-warmth was like moving to a fire. She thanked him and he smiled down at her. 'You remind me of my wife, Julietta. She had the same beautiful features and lovely eyes and she would go into the garden and be missing and someone would have to go in search of her. You are a dreamer too?'

'I was. I think I am a little more practical now.'

'Ah,' he wagged a finger at her, 'a man prefers a woman to dream, she is more feminine, more loving.'

They were in the open where the moon was brightest and Julie glancing at him saw there was a kindliness in his eyes. She returned his smile. 'I shall remember your words – Grandfather.'

He tucked her arm companionably through his. 'Yet another granddaughter, I am indeed a lucky man. My only regret is that I did not meet you and your brother sooner.'

Julie no longer felt the odd one out.

Fergus was not in the room when they went in, but he came in a few moments later and began, 'I cannot find her,' then stopped on seeing her. Julie smiled, but there was no warmth of response. He added, his voice still cold, 'I'm pleased that Mr van Neilson found you.'

The following day, Mr van Neilson arranged little excursions around the area for all of them, travelling in three limousines. Whether by accident or design Julie was never next to Fergus. He included her in any conversation but the closeness they had shared before was gone. At first it worried her then she decided it might be for the best. A man who would take umbrage because she would not allow him to make love to her was best avoided. But even while Julie was thinking this it hurt because she hated there to be any animosity between them.

That evening, after dinner, Mr van Neilson suggested they take a stroll up the road and visit friends of the family.

It was an enjoyable evening. They had drinks, talked and left with the promise to call again. As it turned out this time Julie found herself walking with Fergus behind the rest of the party.

'Quite a pleasant outing, wasn't it?' he remarked.

'Yes, it was,' Julie replied but did not enlarge on it.

After a short silence Fergus turned to her. 'Oh, come on now, Julie, stop sulking.'

'*I'm* not sulking,' she retorted, 'although I do have reason to. I did my best to apologise to you last night when you came in from the garden, but –'

'Apologise?' Fergus spread his hands. 'I heard no apology.'

'I smiled at you,' she snapped. 'That was my way of letting you know I was sorry. I felt that I had behaved a little childishly. But what did I get in return? A cold stare. Today you've behaved so stiffly towards me it's a wonder you didn't crack.'

He laughed then. 'Oh, Julie, you're so funny, and like all females you exaggerate.'

'Well, perhaps I did a little, but you must admit you didn't behave too well last night. You did leave me lost in a maze. Nor did you tell anyone where you had left me.'

'What did you want me to say – that I had taken you to a certain spot for the sole purpose of making love to you? I didn't know the bushes constituted a maze. I did go to look for you, but you had gone. Mr van Neilson must have brought you back a different way.' Fergus moved closer. 'Julie, you must believe me, I would not have left you had I thought you were in any difficulty. What is more, I thought you would not want to be anywhere near me after the upset of last night.'

'You behaved like an adolescent getting all high and mighty because I wouldn't let you make love to me.'

'All right,' Fergus said. 'I behaved like an adolescent – now will you stop nagging?'

'I am not nagging, I'm simply speaking my mind.'

'Oh, yes, you are very good at that, Julie, and doing your best to diminish me. Did it not once occur to you that I left you because I couldn't trust myself to stay with you? If I had I would –'

Fergus stopped and Julie, feeling a stir of her emotions again said, 'You would have what – hit me?'

'Oh, I could have done that, believe me. There is nothing more destroying to a man than to have a woman respond to his advances and then for her to draw away and say, no, no.'

Julie glanced at him. Fergus was pushing his hands through his hair. 'I'm sorry,' she said in a low voice. 'It's just that I'm, well, I'm not experienced in – these things.'

He gave a sigh of despair. 'I know, Julie, I know, and that is why I hated myself. I've always considered myself to have an iron control and there I was, behaving, like you said, as a raw adolescent.' After a pause he added, 'If I promise it won't happen again, can we be friends once more?'

Julie, pleased to be restored to their former closeness, became pert. 'How will I get experience if it doesn't happen again?'

He stopped and gripped her shoulders. 'Julie, be warned, don't play games with me.'

More soberly she replied, 'I won't, I promise, I'll be as good as gold.'

Fergus grinned then. 'That is something I cannot imagine. Come along, we had better catch up with the others or I won't be responsible for my actions.'

This was a new rôle for Julie, to be so desirable to a man he had difficulty in controlling his emotions. She liked the feeling it gave her, yet she was sensible enough to know it would be dangerous to play the coquette with Fergus.

# Chapter Fourteen

When they arrived back the men settled for a nightcap while the women voted to retire. Julie went upstairs, had a leisurely bath, towelled herself dry and after pulling on a nightdress was standing in front of the mirror brushing her hair, and imagining herself in all sorts of romantic situations with Fergus when there was a knock on her door and her mother came in.

Without preamble she said, 'Julie, two things have happened since you came upstairs which have altered our plans quite dramatically. One of the maids told Mr van Neilson when we returned that a man she had met a few days ago, and who has taken her out twice, has been asking questions about us, wanting to know which place we would be visiting next.'

Julie's heart began an uncomfortable thudding. 'Violet? So she's caught up with us. How long are we going to keep on running away from her? She's sworn to get Richard in the end.'

'She won't,' Kitty said fiercely. 'We've told him about her, he had to know. He's annoyed, told us we're fools to keep on running. He's offered to meet her, to tell her he wants nothing to do with her.'

'Then why don't you agree to let him meet her?'

'Because I know my sister,' Kitty replied, her expression grim. 'Richard is vulnerable, I know she has an attraction for him and he wouldn't stand a chance with her. Sometimes I think she has a hypnotic power.'

'So what are we going to do?'

'Your father suggests we go to the Tiernes. It's quite a long journey but he said we would take our time and stop at places on the way.'

'What about Fergus and Jake – they won't want to come! Jake won't want to leave Rome, nor for that matter will Richard.'

Kitty assured her they did. In fact, both were excited at the thought of going to Monchau, it was very old. When Julie reminded her that Fergus was to attend a wedding in Rome Kitty told her he was willing to say it was impossible to attend. She added that of course Fergus and Jake would put up at a hotel in Monchau.

Julie's pleasure at that moment was not so much that at last she would be meeting her mother's side of the family, but that Fergus would be travelling with them.

Kitty drew her fingers across her brow. 'Your father will be getting in touch with the Tiernes in the morning then we shall decide when to leave. Good night, Julie. Have a good sleep.'

Julie lay wide awake in bed, going over the meeting with Violet in the art shop; her denial that she saw any resemblance to Fergus Damant in the carved head. It was the likeness that had drawn Julie to it – the strong, clear-cut features and the expression of a man who knew what he wanted out of life and was determined to get it. Violet had remarked that Fergus masked his feelings because of his work. Did he have a secret life? Julie had taken it for granted that the car following them had held someone Violet had engaged, but supposing it was someone else? Someone following Fergus . . . But for what reason?

Julie's thoughts ranged over several possibilities then suddenly the image of Angus came into her mind. Dear solid Angus, who in spite of not having the polish or sophistication of Fergus had a personality all his own. It was impossible to think of him as having a job where secrecy was essential. She could feel his feather-light touch on her cheeks, and hear him say, '*Girrl* –'. Julie smiled to herself. Had he received the postcards she had sent him? Had Tom and Ivy received theirs? She had sent a lot, extra ones for Tom because he was always so caring for her well-being. What pleasure she would have telling them all that had happened. Julie frowned. Well, perhaps not all . . .

A telegram had been despatched to Monchau before breakfast and when the meal was over a reply came from the Tiernes to say they would be pleased to see Kitty and her family. They would be at the house for another four or five weeks.

Tyler studied times of trains and routes while Fergus worked out yet another plan to get them to the station unseen. Due to his ingenuity and Mario's expertise they left Rome two hours later without their pursuer being aware of it.

Julie had a feeling that all but her mother were beginning to enjoy the intrique. Kitty was tense and, when the train steamed out of the station, she sank back into her seat and gave a deep sigh. 'Pray we can now have some peace.'

Tyler assured her with a smile there would be no more rushing around and he was right.

Sometimes when they left the train to break their journey they would stay in a town to please Richard and Jake, but mostly it would be in a village where there was no awe-inspiring scenery but a stillness, a quiet beauty where the pace was slow, the people relaxed and where a shepherd tending his flock could have stepped out of a Biblical painting. Kitty gradually lost her look of strain.

Julie enjoyed it all, but her greatest pleasure was in having Fergus to herself for a while. One evening when they were out for a stroll and they had dropped back behind the others, Fergus said, 'Well, and how would you like to live in this peaceful part of the world?'

'I'm enjoying it, but I don't know whether I would want to live here all the time. Perhaps if I was older it would be good to get away from all worries.'

'Wherever you live there are worries, Julie. These people must worry about droughts or storms destroying their crops, or their cattle being wiped out by disease.' Fergus shook his head. 'No, one can escape trouble, no matter the background.'

Julie glanced up at him and smiled. 'Not unless you were a saintly man and lived on top of a mountain.'

'And what would happen if storms broke out? Then he would have the worry of wondering if the people could get up the mountain to bring him food.'

'He wouldn't need food,' she protested. 'His faith would sustain him. Wouldn't it?'

Fergus grinned. 'I don't know, I'm not a saintly man.'

'I bet you aren't!'

'Now don't spoil it,' he teased. Then on a more serious note he added, 'I think this is the best thing that has ever happened to me, Julie. Always when I've gone abroad I've had the weight of business to contend with, but during these past two weeks I haven't even given it a thought.'

This last sentence made Julie realise how easily Violet had slid into the background. That morning she had heard her mother laughing at something her father had said. Even the Tiernes' name had been mentioned only when they discussed Monchau. Fergus was the only one who knew anything about the place but then he only knew it had a medieval air, was beautiful and a tourist attraction.

Fergus laid an arm across her shoulders and remarked on the contrast of the noise and bustle of Rome to this quiet backwater where the only sound was the distant barking of a dog. He picked up a strand of her hair and idly curled it around his finger. Most of the time their relationship had been a companionable one and Julie had told herself it was best that way, but at moments like these, when Fergus made actual contact with her she felt so drawn towards him it was an ache.

'Don't do that,' she said, 'you're tugging my hair.'

'I'm not, I was being quite gentle, but if you don't like it –' He drew his arm away. 'There, satisfied?'

Julie who had made the remark on impulse now regretted it. She gave him a pert glance. 'No, not really, I think I quite liked it.'

He wagged a finger under her nose. 'You're tormenting me again, Julietta van Neilson.'

'*You* are tormenting yourself, Fergus Damant,' she taunted. 'You're teasing me with your love play because there are no other girls around to make love to.'

'My dear Julie, aren't you aware that there are girls in every town and village who are willing to make themselves available to men, and who incidentally, are not always the professional kind. I noticed the proprietor's daughter this morning at breakfast making eyes at your father. He *is* a handsome man.'

'Mother would have had something to say if she had noticed it,' Julie retorted, feeling a little annoyed that the teasing had taken a different turn to the one she had intended.

'But your mother wouldn't have said anything,' Fergus replied. 'She knows your father would not want anyone else, she's secure in his love, and that is how marriage should be.'

'Heavens above!' Julie exclaimed. She stopped and eyed him belligerently, hands on hips. 'I started by saying I liked you wrapping my hair around your finger and end up with a lecture on fallen women, the fidelity of husbands and the smugness of wives.'

Fergus began to laugh. He laughed so heartily that the others in front stopped to ask what the joke was. He managed to say he would tell them later then shook his head at Julie, still chuckling.

'You are one on your own, Julie. You're funny and lovely.

Come on.' He linked his arm through hers. 'Lecture over. Tell me some more about your views on life.'

'I'm sure you would rather tell me *your* views. After all, *you* are a brilliant man of the world, while I am just a raw amateur who knows nothing!'

'Oh, no, I think you know a lot more than I give you credit for. You suggested that your mother was smug because of the fidelity of your father. What made you say that?'

The fire went out of Julie. How could she explain that she sometimes resented the deep love between her parents because she longed for that kind of love herself? She ended by saying it was a foolish remark to make, she had made it without thinking.

'I don't think you did,' Fergus said quietly. 'I think it's something you've given some thought to. Do you want to talk about it?'

Julie was saved a reply by Richard stopping to point out a tiny church on the hillside. They decided to visit it. They all seemed affected by the peace of the little church and no mention was made of the reason for Fergus' earlier laughter.

As the days went by Julie and Fergus slipped once more into a companionable relationship, but Fergus no longer tried to touch her, not even linking arms with her and Julie, longing for his touch, bitterly regretted bringing about this state of affairs by a slip of her silly tongue.

As they were nearing the end of the train part of the journey Richard said to Julie, 'Mother is beginning to look strained again. I feel guilty for having pressed to meet the Tiernes. I hated them when we left for what they had done to her, but now my hatred is gone. The thing is, what is this visit going to do to Mother?'

'I'm as guilty as you,' Julie said, 'but this is no time for recriminations. The visit will clear up the mystery and we can only hope that the meeting will be sociable and end amicably.'

For the journey to Monchau a car was hired but although Tyler had said it would be less confining than the train no one seemed inclined to get out of the car and take stock of the countryside.

When they had made their last stop two telegrams had been despatched, one to a hotel for accommodation for Fergus and Jake and one to the Tiernes. Both had been acknowledged, the hotel to advise that two rooms had been reserved and the Tiernes' saying they must come straight to the house, no matter how late they were in arriving. The welcoming sound of the telegram had Kitty looking less strained and eased the conscience of Julie and Richard.

Dusk was beginning to fall when they drove down the winding road to Monchau which lay in the valley. Halfway down Tyler brought the car to a halt and they sat in silence looking on the scene below. The windows of the tall, medieval timber-framed houses and hotels were warm with red-shaded lights; windowsills everywhere were adorned with boxes of daffodils, tulips and hyacinths and these flowers were echoed in tubs that stood on the narrow bridges over the town's river.

'Oh, how beautiful,' Kitty breathed. 'I feel quite moved.'

Julie did too, and she thought surely anyone who lived in such a beautiful place could not be vindictive.

Tyler drove on. They saw Fergus and Jake settled in at the hotel then Tyler said, 'I'm sorry we won't be together this evening, but we shall contact you tomorrow.'

'Now look, you are not to worry about us,' Fergus said. 'We'll find plenty to do here.' He laughed. 'I imagine Jake will be up at the crack of dawn and go scouting around.'

Goodbyes were said and Julie felt that the gentle pressure of Fergus' fingers on her arm as they drove away was a caress.

They had been in close proximity for so long it felt strange without the two men as the car climbed out of the valley. It was now dark and headlights picked out the narrow-hedged roads. They had been told that the Tiernes' house was built in the side of the hill and they would know it when they came to it by the waterfall that cascaded into a pool. It was lighted by lamps at night and the house was always well-lit.

Kitty said, 'I hope there's not too large a family to cope with. We've been so spoilt these past two weeks.'

Tyler assured her gently he was sure she would cope, no matter how many people there were, and Kitty turned her head and smiled at him, thanking him for his confidence in her, which made Julie feel the loss of Fergus more keenly than ever.

The lights of other houses guided their way but when they came to the Tiernes' house it was like seeing a fairy grotto. Skeins of water falling from the hillside were rainbow-hued by the coloured lamps that shone on them. The windows of the house were softly lit. It was built of wood with verandahs.

When they drew up outside the house the door opened and only two people were outlined in the doorway. They came out. Their welcome was warm, handshakes firm. 'How pleased we are you were able to come,' said the portly Mr Tierne in a hearty voice.

Mrs Tierne, in contrast with her husband, was a quietly-spoken, sweet-faced woman, who declared she had been in a state of excitement all day waiting for them to come. 'Please do come in,' she said. 'Helga will show you to your room and after you have freshened up we shall all have a meal.'

The walls and floors of the house were also of wood, reminding Julie of Crescent House, but here the rooms were of uniform shape.

Over dinner the talk at first was of the house and the waterfall, with Mr Tierne explaining it was an indulgence. As a child he had been given a plate by his uncle on which was painted a waterfall with rainbow colours and he had vowed then when he was old enough he would have such a waterfall where he lived. In their holiday home in Monchau, he had made his picture into reality.

Mrs Tierne asked about their journey and said she thought it delightful that they had made it so leisurely. When her husband was travelling anywhere he always had her rushing about.

'But not here in Monchau,' Tyler said smiling.

Oh, no, here was peace. She wished they could live here all the time, but of course that was impossible. There were the potteries her husband owned to be attended to.

The moment Mrs Tierne had spoken she looked at her husband in a worried way. He shook his head at her then described Monchau, talked about the history, the beauty, but although he spoke in a lively way, somehow a note of unease had crept into the conversation. Julie guessed it was because of the mention of the potteries, which her grandmother should have shared in, having been married to Richard Tierne.

This subject was not raised until the meal was over and they were all sitting round chatting. Mr Tierne said abruptly, 'The business side of your visit here must be on your minds, and I am quite willing to discuss it now, but if you are too tired after your journey – ?'

Kitty said she would prefer to discuss it now, then it could be put behind them. Mr Tierne agreed, but looked at Richard and Julie and asked hesitantly if she wished the young people to stay.

'Yes, I do, Mr Tierne,' Kitty said. 'They have been kept rather in the dark about my parents' marriage and I feel they are old enough to know the whole story.'

At this a look of embarrassment came over Mr Tierne's face. He coughed. 'You mention marriage, Mrs van Neilson, but our solicitor could find no record of your mother having been married to my cousin Richard.'

Kitty sat up, the colour draining slowly from her face. 'But this is ridiculous. Mrs Helder applied to Somerset

House to find out what name my birth had been registered in. This was when I was to be married. At least, her solicitor applied. I was told I was registered in the name Tierne.'

'Why did you need to apply, Mrs van Neilson?'

Kitty was silent for a moment then she said, 'For two reasons. My mother discovered that her first husband, who was named Harvey, had married her bigamously. Also, as I was fostered for several years I had been known by the name Leddenshaw.'

'I see.' Judging by the look on the portly man's face he did not see and Kitty tried hastily to explain further, and seemed to Julie to be getting into a muddle. When Julie glanced at Richard he was sitting wooden, pale too.

Tyler said quietly, 'My wife has not been well, Mr Tierne, but I can assure you that a marriage was performed between my wife's mother and your cousin Richard Tierne. Mrs Helder was an old friend of the family and a woman of integrity, she would not have lied.'

'So why should our solicitor have lied?' Mr Tierne enquired in a reasonable tone. 'He is considered to be a person of integrity, too.'

Kitty, who was beginning to recover from the shock of the news said briskly, 'I know this, Mr Tierne! My mother would not have lived with a man if there had been no marriage, and they did share a cottage on the Yorkshire Dales for their honeymoon.'

At this, Mr Tierne suggested they let the matter rest for the time being. He would go more deeply into it, make enquiries. In the meantime, they must enjoy their holiday.

Kitty gave in with a graciousness Julie felt sure she was not feeling. After this the conversation centred on the glass business and ceramics, with Mr Tierne suggesting they might like to visit one of their branches in Germany.

When there was a lull while wine was being poured Richard asked permission to walk in the garden. To Julie's relief he asked her to accompany him. Once outside Richard exploded.

'What exactly is going on in this family? Is my mother also a bastard?' As soon as the words were said he asked for them to be retracted. 'I'm sorry, Julie, but honestly, there's so much secrecy surrounding our family, what am I to think?'

She laid a hand on his arm. 'Whatever has happened, you can't hold Mother responsible. And anyway, I feel sure Mrs Tierne is right and the marriage was not acknowledged. You heard what her husband said about the family going back generations, originating from a noble family. Jonathan Tierne is obviously proud of it and does not want his family name sullied.'

'What about *our* name? I'm fed up with the whole thing.' He walked on, hands thrust into his pockets, kicking at the grass. 'I wish I had never come here.'

'Well, we have and it's no use spoiling the holiday.' Julie spoke sharply. 'We don't know what Mother had to put up with in her life. We've only seen the good side, enjoyed the luxury they were able to provide.'

Richard sighed. 'All right, you win, I won't say any more. Come on, let's take a look at the waterfall.'

The water cascaded from a high drop into a rockpool, the spray touched with all the colours from the lamps. The pool narrowed and the water tumbled over rocks and disappeared into the darkness.

Richard said, 'I understand that deer come down to the stream to drink during the afternoon. It must be a beautiful sight to see.'

'Yes, it must.' Although Richard was trying to speak normally she was aware of the underlying pain, and because she loved him so much she grieved for him. 'We shall come to watch the deer tomorrow,' she said.

'I won't be here.' To her startled enquiry of why he added gently, 'It's all right, Julie, I'm not leaving. It's just that I shall be with Jake tomorrow. I want to know everything about Monchau, I'm fascinated by it.'

When they went back to the house they found their parents and the Tiernes in animated conversation. Richard glanced at Julie and raised his eyebrows.

Tyler said, 'Oh, there you are. Mr and Mrs Tierne have invited Fergus and Jake to stay here, isn't it kind of them?'

Julie and Richard agreed it was most kind and Julie particularly felt pleased, having missed Fergus more than she had thought possible. After all, it was only a few hours since they had parted.

When they had all retired for the night, Julie stood at her bedroom window. To the left lay the waterfall. Although the lamps had been turned out the cascading water stood out clearly against the darkness. Normally she would have found the sound of the water soothing but this evening there was a restlessness in her and she thought she knew why. Apart from having upset Richard she had found herself longing to be with Fergus. And yet, after a visit to London she had longed to get back to Angus. There was also the fact that she was enjoying this kind of life. But then, travelling was something new to her. It would be impossible to go on living in this way and, if she went back home she would be doing the same things again, meeting the same people . . . being bored. Although she had grumbled once or twice about the hard work, living with Tom and Ivy she had never known a moment's boredom.

Julie sighed and began to undress. At least there was no longer any animosity on her mother's side about the Tiernes. How this had come about she had no idea. There was still the uncertainty of whether there had been a marriage between her grandmother and Richard Tierne. But if this no longer worried her mother why should she worry? Julie pulled her nightdress over her head and felt suddenly brighter. Tomorrow she would be with Fergus again.

The following morning Julie was aroused by the muted sounds of men's voices and laughter. For a moment she lay drowsily trying to place where they were coming from when she heard the name Fergus mentioned. Then, wide awake, she flung back the bedclothes and getting out of bed ran to the window.

There she stood staring in astonishment. Richard, Jake and Fergus were splashing about in the pool. She turned and looked at the small clock on the bedside table. Six o'clock! How did Fergus and Jake came to be here?

She began to get dressed, her fingers fumbling in her haste to get outside and find the answer. She had not bothered to put on her shoes and when she got outside the dew-soaked grass was icy cold underfoot. Although the sun was quite bright pockets of mist lay over hollows.

Before she reached the pool the men began to clamber out. And it was then Julie stopped abruptly, colour rushing to her face. They were all naked. She hid behind a rose arbour and when she peeped out the men all had towels draped around their waists. Droplets of water glistened on their hair. Jake had a boyish plumpness, Richard was quite well-built but Fergus had a magnificent body. He picked his way over small rocks to the other side of the pool and walked to where the water cascaded in the pool with the lithe grace of a jungle cat. She felt a thrill go through her. He picked up a dressing-gown, donned it and came back to the others, who by this time had also put on dressing-gowns. When they all started towelling their hair Julie came out of her hiding place and hailed them.

Richard and Jake quickly tied the cords of their dressing-gowns but Fergus came striding towards her, hands outstretched.

'Julie! You should have come earlier and had a dip.'

She gave a shiver. 'It makes me feel cold at the thought of it. What are you and Jake doing here so early?'

Richard came up then. 'I took the car and picked them up.

I thought it would be best to get them settled in.' Jake laughed and said she was not to worry, Richard had not got them out of bed. They had been up since five o'clock.

'And had a long walk,' Fergus said, 'with Mr Tierne. He came with Richard.'

At that moment Mr Tierne came out of the house beaming. 'I'm so glad that I am not the only early-riser among you. I never sleep after four o'clock. But, I am not so hardy that I want to go into the pool at this hour in the morning!' He then said he could arrange for them to have breakfast here, or they could go back into Monchau and breakfast at a pleasant little tavern he knew.

'The tavern sounds tempting,' Fergus said, 'but your wife – ?'

Mr Tierne assured him that his wife was never fully awake until after nine o'clock and that it had been agreed with Tyler and Kitty that they would have a lie-in.

The five of them decided they would go to Monchau.

The men were dressed in double-quick time and off they went with Julie excited. This was different from *anything* she had ever done!

In the morning sunlight the town looked even more beautiful. There was colour everywhere – in the golden yellow of daffodils, the crimson of tulips, the blue of hyacinths and in the pink of blossom.

The tavern at the top of a flight of stone steps was old and quaint. Mr Tierne warned them it would be coffee only for the time being, as breakfast would come later. He wanted them to see Monchau from the best vantage point and what he thought of as the best time of day.

With their coffee drunk they made their way through the town, climbed small steps and walked along narrow paths that lay between spruce and oak trees. Julie, a little breathless by the climb, would have stopped and looked back but Mr Tierne told her no, she was to wait until she reached the top.

When they stopped at the top, in the shadow of a ruined castle, Mr Tierne said, 'Now you may look.'

When Julie did so she caught her breath. The early morning mist mingling with the fragrance of wood-smoke from chimney pots, cast a haze over buildings and trees, giving the whole a magical beauty.

'It's like a fairy-tale town,' she said softly.

Mr Tierne pointed out various places of interest then he told them laughing they could now have their breakfast. Over the meal he said that he would return to the house but if they wished they could stay in the town. They agreed to this and eventually it was decided that Richard and Jake would go off on their own and Fergus and Julie could explore together.

Julie was delighted to have Fergus on his own. Richard and Jake tended to go too deeply into the technicalities of their work, which could become a little boring at times.

They all parted to go their separate ways after Mr Tierne had reminded them to be back at the house that evening for dinner.

Fergus said, smiling at Julie, 'A whole day to explore. Where shall we go first?'

All that day Julie lived in a fantasy world. There was enchantment in a tavern where they drank wine, the shelves packed with copper and pewter and old porcelain edging the low ceilings; a fairy-tale magnificence in a building known as the Red House, with its sweeping staircase intricately carved in the baroque style; a symphony of sound in the river that meandered through the town and under the bridges with their wrought-iron railings and tubs of flowers.

Julie stopped on one of the bridges and was looking into the sun-sparkled water when Fergus said in a deep voice, 'Beware a troll doesn't jump out of the water and gobble you up!' She glanced up at him laughing and he made claws of his fingers and drew himself up to his full height as though about to pounce.

'I am a troll, fol-de-rol,' he said, 'and I'm going to eat you for my dinner! Do you know the story of the Three Billy Goats Gruff?'

'Yes, I do and I was always terrified that they would be eaten.'

'Of course not!' Fergus protested. 'I was only pretending. A troll is a gentle, mischievous giant.' He grinned. 'Like me.'

Fergus' light-hearted mood reminded Julie of the Sunday morning when they had met at the Portobello Road Market in London.

She cocked her head, pretending to study him. 'Do you know – I think you are one of the wicked giants. I bet if you had half a chance you would run off with the young princess and carry her into the forest.'

Fergus lifted her hair away from her face and ran his fingertips lightly round the back of her ears, sending fire through her. 'And shall I tell *you* something, my beautiful *Liebchen*,' he said softly. 'You are the only princess I want to carry off into the forest, the only one I have *ever* wanted to.'

Julie, with every pulse throbbing and knowing how easy it would be to succumb to the seductive tones, pushed him playfully away. 'Sire, it is broad daylight, and we are in the centre of the town. The game is over.'

Fergus wagged a finger at her and said, a wicked gleam in his eyes, 'For now, my Julie, for now.' He took her by the hand. 'Come along, we shall follow the river.'

It was being beside the river that reminded Julie of the deer which came to drink at the Tiernes' stream, and because Fergus had his arm across her shoulders and was toying with strands of her hair again, she was beginning to have thoughts she ought not to have and suggested they return to the house.

Fergus agreed and said if they took their time they could walk back. A few minutes later they met up with Richard and Jake, and after that there was no chance of any more intimate interludes with Fergus.

When they arrived at the house they found the Tiernes and Tyler and Kitty sitting companionably at one of the front windows. They too were waiting for the deer.

Mrs Tierne had started to ask them about their day when her husband interrupted to say, 'Here they come,' and nodded in the direction of the stream.

A stag came into view first, followed by six does walking in single file and three fawns trotting sedately by the side of their respective mothers.

Mr Tierne said with a booming laugh, 'The Sultan, his entourage and his progeny!'

To Julie he had coarsened what she thought of as one of the most beautiful scenes she had ever witnessed and she knew then that she did not like Mr Tierne.

The does picked their way delicately, a shyness in their lovely eyes that were like liquid velvet. The stag drank first, but not before he had looked carefully about him for predators. An inborn instinct. The does then drank, but keeping an eye on the fawns which had become suddenly playful.

Fergus said, a smile in his voice, 'Have you noticed how the "aunts" take care of the little ones too, herding them back to safety when they stray? It's delightful to watch them, isn't it?'

Julie thought, Oh, Fergus, I love you for that remark alone, for the warmth and caring in it.

Later that evening Richard said, clapping his hands, 'Well, and what are we going to do tomorrow? Who's for an early dip in the pool?'

Kitty said, 'If you are going into the pool again, Richard, I suggest you wear a bathing costume.'

He gave an embarrassed grin and spread his hands. 'I wasn't to know that Julie was going to come out, now, was I?'

Julie shot up in her seat and announced, 'I didn't see them naked,' and wanted to crawl into a hole when after a split second's silence her mother said quietly:

'I didn't know they were, Julie. When I saw Richard he had a towel fastened around his waist.'

Julie was conscious of Richard and Jake trying to suppress laughter and of Fergus, sitting back, arms folded, gazing at the ceiling, a smile playing around his mouth. She felt like groaning.

Mrs Tierne spoke up then, saying with her sweet smile, 'Now then, there is no problem. If Julie or anyone else wants to go into the pool we have plenty of costumes available.'

Julie presumed the men were wearing bathing costumes the next morning when she heard their muted shouts and laughter coming from the direction of the pool, but she did not get up to see, she thought it wiser not to. She only wished later she had kept a check on her tongue because she was sure it was her remark that was responsible for her parents accompanying them wherever they went during the next three days.

When Julie did have a few moments alone with Fergus he teased her about the incident of the pool, saying with a laugh, 'You do realise what you did for us, don't you? We swam in Victorian woollen bathing suits that came below our knees, they weighed a ton when wet. You missed a treat not coming out.'

'I'm sure I did, but I didn't dare after what I had said.'

'We were surprised you had seen us in – let us say – a state of undress. Where were you hiding?'

Hiding suggested she had been enjoying watching them so she denied it. 'I came out, noticed you and retreated. When next I saw you all you were in dressing-gowns.' His amused smile made her add, 'You don't believe me, do you?'

'Well –' he raised his shoulders. 'What should a gentleman reply to that?'

She gave him an impish grin. 'As a *lady* I can say it was

quite an experience. A very interesting and a valuable one.' With that she left him, and when Fergus called to her to come back she ignored him, smiling to herself.

With true male conceit he would be curious to know what she thought of his – body. Well, as Ivy would say, let him put that in his pipe and smoke it! It would be interesting to know what he would have to say the next time they were alone.

# Chapter Fifteen

As it turned out, there was little opportunity for Julie and Fergus to have any time together the next day. A feeling of unrest had crept into the holiday. Jake was fidgety, hinting about them going back to Rome and Fergus said he felt he ought to be getting back to London. They could return to Rome at some future date. Then Kitty started talking about a return to London, but at this Richard objected, pointing out they had come to Monchau for one purpose only, to find out why the Tiernes had ignored his grandmother's marriage to Richard Tierne.

'And what happened?' he said. 'Mr Tierne told us there was no record of such a marriage but promised to go into the matter. And what has he done - nothing!'

Tyler spoke up then, saying quietly, 'I mentioned it to him less than ten minutes ago. He told me he was waiting for a reply from his solicitor and should have this by today or tomorrow. I think we should wait, don't you?'

They all agreed but Kitty did add that if no reply was forthcoming by then, any further business would have to be conducted by letter.

It was late afternoon the following day when Mr Tierne invited them all to his study. There he held out a letter saying, 'This is the news we were waiting for. It seems that a marriage *was* recorded between your mother and my cousin, Mrs van Neilson. I simply cannot understand how such an error could have taken place! I shall certainly take everyone to task who is concerned in this affair. It's a terrible thing to have happened.' He leaned forward. 'You do understand, of course, that this makes no difference to my inheriting the estate?'

'Yes, I do understand, Mr Tierne. My father willed it to you. The important thing to me is that my parents' marriage was valid. What I couldn't understand was the Tierne family ignoring my mother. Now I know the reason, the matter is settled.'

When Mr Tierne went on apologising and making dire threats to those involved in the mistake, Kitty got up. 'It's over, Mr Tierne, think no more about it. I certainly won't.'

Tyler then said, 'Now that the matter is settled, Mr Tierne, we must start thinking about returning home. It's been a wonderful holiday and we do want to thank you and your wife.'

When they left Mr Tierne to get dressed for dinner Richard exclaimed, 'There's something that stinks about this whole affair. He *knew* there was a valid marriage, I'm sure of it. The man is – well, smarmy is the only word I can think of to describe him. In my opinion, Mother, your father made a later will leaving everything to your mother and the family destroyed it!'

Kitty laid a hand on his arm and said quietly, 'Richard, listen to me. I don't care if there was another will. I only wanted my mother's marriage to be acknowledged by the Tierne family and this has been done. No, Richard,' she scolded gently, when he made to speak again. 'It's finished, I refuse to discuss it further. Tomorrow we shall make plans to leave for home.'

Richard said to Julie afterwards, 'I'm furious, because I feel we're still not getting to know the full story, neither from the Tiernes nor from Mother. And do you know something, I've just realised that I didn't like Mr Tierne from the first day we met.'

Julie stopped and looked up at him. 'I'm glad you said

that, for neither did I. I found that out when we were watching the deer yesterday and I wondered why I hadn't discovered it before. He is, as you say, smarmy and I think he's coarse, too.' Julie raised her shoulders. 'But if there is some mystery we're not going to get to the bottom of it here so we'd best just forget it.'

'I won't forget it,' he said grimly. 'Just as I can't forget that Violet might be my true mother.'

Julie looked at him shocked and Richard said in a more quiet tone, 'Don't worry, Sis, I'm not going to do anything about it. I don't want to. She belongs to the past. I have the future to face.' Then in brighter tones he added, 'Here, do you think we could persuade the parents to spend a few days in Florence before we return home? I'd hate to miss the chance. Jake was talking about it this morning . . .'

At that moment, all Julie wanted was to get away from this house.

They took their leave of the Tiernes the next day with Mrs Tierne shedding tears and saying how much she would miss them. Kitty and Julie hugged her, with Julie knowing that her mother shared the knowledge that Mrs Tierne was a genuinely warm and loving person.

Mr Tierne declared in hearty tones that once they were back in England they must all arrange to get together. Tyler said, yes, they must, but his words were addressed to Mrs Tierne.

Their homeward journey was planned with fewer stops than their outward one and for the first half of it there was a general air of gloom. Richard and Jake were disappointed because they had failed in their request for a visit to Florence; Fergus seemed to be deep in thought most of the time and Kitty and Tyler had little to say.

One day, when they were boarding the train after an overnight stay Julie exclaimed, 'Well, so far it's been as if we had had ten bereavements in the family. I can't wait to get back to Stoke to have a laugh and chat. I hope none of you will mind if I seek someone pleasant on the train to speak to.'

This had the hoped-for effect. It startled her parents out of their apathy, Richard and Jake began to joke and Fergus enquired, with a smile, if she thought him pleasant enough to chat to. Although none of them slipped back into their previous gloomy state it was a relief to Julie and, she was sure to everyone else, when they eventually arrived in London.

By then, Julie, in spite of having enjoyed the carefree life of the earlier part of their holiday, was determined she was going back to Stoke. She would just have to try and make her parents understand how important it was to her. It was late when they arrived and Tyler suggested they all stay overnight at the Savoy and sort themselves out the next morning.

Before they went to bed, Julie spoke to her parents about her plans. Tyler was gentle with her. 'I could insist that you come home, Julie, for you are under age – but I won't, because you would be resentful, then we would all be unhappy. We shall always be there if you need us.'

'I know, Daddy.' She put her arms around him. 'I'm grateful to you both for giving me this wonderful holiday. I think I grew up a little when I went to live with Tom and Ivy and I think I've grown up a lot more during this holiday.'

Kitty said, a sadness in her voice, 'I wonder if we ever stop growing up?'

Julie went to her and hugged her, too. 'I don't think I want you to, not altogether, because then you wouldn't understand the needs of your children.'

Kitty held her away from her. 'Words of wisdom, Julie. Yes, you are growing up. Come back to us when you are ready.' Julie was too choked to reply.

The next morning, Richard and Jake, who were now over their exhaustion of the journey, became excited at the thought of eventually going to live in the house that Tyler and Kitty had talked of buying.

'Just think,' Richard exclaimed, 'a housekeeper-cook to look after us. What more could we want?'

Fergus was planning to go back to his rooms in Lower Regent Street, but apparently not to stay. He had made a phone call earlier and told them after breakfast he would be leaving for China in a few days' time.

'China?' Julie said. 'What exactly *is* your work?'

Fergus grinned. 'Remind me to tell you when I come back.' He then began to talk about something else.

After breakfast he said to Julie, 'So you're planning to return to Stoke.' He tapped her lightly on the nose. 'I'm going to miss you, Julie van Neilson.'

'I doubt it! Not with all the lovely Chinese maidens around.'

'But you are special. No one would cheek me the way you do, or argue with me, or torment me, or –' His voice softened, 'or look at me in such an appealing way . . . as you are doing now.'

Julie drew her gaze away, feeling the ache of parting. When would she see him again? She said, trying to instil a lightness into her voice, 'There is one regret that I do have about the holiday.'

'Oh, and what is that?'

'That I didn't see you in the Victorian bathing costume.'

A slow smile spread over his face. 'And I regret that you didn't wear one too and come into the pool with me. You don't know what you missed.'

'Yes, I do,' she said, 'I –'

Tyler interrupted to tell Julie she must leave soon if she was to catch her train to Stoke. Fergus leaned forward and kissed her on each cheek in the continental way. 'Goodbye, Julie, take care of yourself. Don't be surprised if I pay you a visit one day.'

'Do that, Tom and Ivy would make you welcome. They're lovely people.' She left then, wondering how long it would be before she would see Fergus again. Perhaps never.

He could meet someone on his travels and settle in some other country. But even as Julie thought it she was praying that it would not happen. She wanted to see Fergus again, otherwise her life would seem empty.

And when she was in the train and waving goodbye to her family she had such a feeling of aloneness she wondered if she was doing the right thing, going back to Stoke. But as the journey progressed, she thought of the pleasure of seeing Tom and Ivy and Angus and telling them all about her travels, and of Tom saying eagerly, 'And what did you do then, Julie?' Or, 'What did you do next?' and knew that she was doing the right thing.

There would, of course, be the move to Echo Cove. They must already be in the throes of packing, ready to go. It would be interesting to have a change, and making the tea-shop a success was another challenge. And then there was Angus' little pottery business, it would be good to paint some of the items. She would miss the customers in the shop, of course, but then there would be a different kind of customer to deal with, the visitors to the cove. It would be lovely in the summer to be beside the sea.

By the time they reached Stoke, Julie had worked herself up into such a state of anticipation at seeing them all again that she decided to take a taxi. On arrival, she tipped the taxi driver lavishly, and told him she could manage her suitcase.

She humped it into the gas-lit shop, paused at not seeing anyone behind the counter and was about to call, 'Tom – Ivy!' when a figure came forward from a shadowed part of the shop and stopped under the gas-lamp. 'Hello, Julie, we weren't expecting you.'

'Ivy –' Julie stood, shocked by the gaunt face, the lack-lustre voice. 'What is it, Ivy, what's wrong?'

'Tom's dead. He died ten days ago. Dead . . . and buried.'

Dead? Julie felt rooted to the floor. 'It can't be – not Tom.' She ran to Ivy and put her arms around her and they clung together wordlessly, tears welling and sliding unheeded down their cheeks. Ivy was the first to draw away. She pulled a handkerchief from her pocket and wiped her eyes. 'I didn't think I had any tears left. Come on, love, I'll make you a cup of tea.'

The kitchen, always so warm and cosy, held a chill. The fire had burned low. Ivy filled the kettle and put it on the gas-stove. Julie stood a moment, uncertain, still not able to take in the news of Tom's death, then she took off her coat, went out to the back, brought in some pieces of wood, put them on the fire then piled coal on top. Ivy was just standing, staring at the kettle.

The jangling of the shop doorbell startled Julie. Although she had no wish at that moment to meet any customers she went in, and found Mrs Meadows taking off her shawl. The plump little woman stared at her. 'Julie! We didn't know you'd be back. Oh, dear, and what terrible news it is to come back to. I came to help out for an hour, Ivy's not herself, not herself at all. Look, you go and be with her, I'll manage here.'

Ivy didn't say another word until they had sat down at the table with their mugs of tea. Ivy milked and sugared hers and stirred it. Then she put the spoon in the saucer and looked up, and her eyes were dark pools of grief.

'Do you know what I used to say about death when I was young, Julie? If heaven's such a wonderful place why do folks bawl when someone dies? Now I know that no matter how wonderful it is, nothing can take away that unbearable ache inside you. Sometimes I feel I want to get a knife and cut it out. I knew I loved Tom, but I didn't realise just how much until he was taken from me.'

'Oh, Ivy, stop tormenting yourself, Tom wouldn't have wanted it. I only wish I had been here to – say goodbye.'

'He would know how you feel, Julie. You've no idea how much pleasure he had from all the cards you sent him.' She nodded towards the mantelpiece. 'He had them all standing up there but the day he was ill he wanted to have them in bed with him. He loved you, Julie, you were the daughter he never had.'

Julie felt so choked she was unable to reply.

'He was only ill for that one day,' Ivy went on. 'I know it was best for him to go like that but it's the sudden wrench. Poor Tom, he couldn't get his breath. It was the war that killed him.' Her voice had risen. 'May the people who invented gas for warfare be crucified!'

Her shoulders sagged suddenly. 'But it's done and I can't bring him back.'

There was the sound of the back door opening and closing then firm footsteps came up the yard. Angus! When he came into the kitchen he stopped. 'Julie –' He gave a pitying glance in the direction of Ivy then said, 'You've come back at a bad time, lassie.'

'I'm glad I came when I did.' Ivy poured Angus a cup of tea and he came and sat at the table. Julie asked if he wanted anything to eat and he said no, he had had a meal earlier at a friend's house. He stirred his tea for a long time then he said to Ivy, 'I called at the station. I can get a train to go North at half-past nine in a morning, eleven o'clock on a Sunday.'

She crossed her arms and rocked like a mother nursing a child. 'I don't think I ought to go to Echo Cove, Angus. I feel it's wrong. All my memories of Tom are here.'

Angus laid his hand over hers and said gently: 'Your memories will be with you wherever you go, Ivy.'

She got up and moved around the kitchen. 'Tom never even had a chance to see Echo Cove. He was longing to go, it had become a dream to him. Why should he have been denied it? If only he had spent *one* day there, he could have –' her voice broke. With a fist to her mouth she stood at the window, her back to them.

Julie made to get up to go to her but Angus restrained her. 'Let her be,' he mouthed. He then explained to Julie in a low voice that they had planned he should go back to Echo Cove, see again what needed doing structurally to the house, and take another look at the tea-room. He also needed another look over the little house and shed where he was planning to live and work. Then he explained he'd given in his notice at the potteries.

At this, Ivy came back to the table. She gave a sniff and sat down. 'Well, that's it, no more tears. You gave up your job to help me, Angus, and I think the least I can do is to give Echo Cove a trial. I suggest that you take Julie with you when you go to look around. She will see with a woman's eyes what is needed. I'm sure there'll be someone in the village you can board with. I'll pay for both of you. Yes, I will,' she added as Angus made to protest. 'I have a bit of money and I *want* to pay so just leave it, will you?'

And Ivy, taking it for granted that Julie would want to go to Echo Cove with Angus, got on to the practical side of the business, talking about what they would need. She could get all the crockery cheap from the potteries, good seconds. She would buy checked gingham in the market for tablecloths and cut and hem them herself. Billy Barker would get her the cutlery.

Julie must note what cooking facilities there were in the house, see if there would be room for two gas cookers. She could measure up the windows for curtains. The list of things to do and arrange went on and on but Julie made no attempt to stop her. Life had come back into Ivy's voice.

There were certain pieces of furniture that Ivy wanted to take with her, but other pieces could be sold and then replaced when they got to Echo Cove. Angus suggested looking around for auction sales – often a small hotel or a guest house would be selling up. Ivy agreed with this.

Once, when Ivy went into the shop to help Mrs Meadows, Angus said to Julie, 'You came back at the right time after all, lassie. You've done Ivy the world of good, she never shows her feelings as far as affection is concerned, but like Tom, she loves you like a daughter. I wondered while you were away whether you *would* come back.'

'There was a time when I didn't think I would. But somehow I suddenly knew I had to return. And I'm glad I did.'

'I'm glad too,' Angus said softly. 'You were a great miss, Julie. I haven't asked about your holiday, but we can talk about that tomorrow. You're tired, aren't you? You get off to bed if you want to, I'll help Ivy to clear away and lock up. And, Julie, if you don't want to come with me to Echo Cove – I want to go the day after tomorrow – you don't have to. I can manage.'

Ivy, who had caught the tail-end of the conversation as she came into the kitchen, repeated this. 'Would you rather wait and come with me, Julie?'

'No,' she said. 'I think it might be better if I went and laid the ground for you coming. But how will you manage here? There's all the packing-up to do.'

Ivy said they could do that together the next day, adding that the Liggetts had offered to come and take over the running of the shop as soon as she was ready. And then she ordered Julie off to bed. It was the old Ivy, bossing again, and Julie was glad.

The bed seemed tiny and hard after the luxurious hotel living, yet once Julie was under the clothes, cosy with a hot water bottle that Ivy had put in, she had a feeling once more of coming home. For a while she even wished they were not moving somewhere else. But soon she knew deep down it would be the right thing for Ivy, a different environment, a new business.

Julie was not conscious of having wept through the night but she must have done, because her pillow was damp the next morning. She lay for a while, unwilling to face the day, unwilling to face the thought of yet another train journey the next day. But once she was up and bustling around, talking to customers, she felt back in the swing of things.

So while the new owners of the shop took over, Angus got his pottery tools and wheel packed, while Julie helped Ivy to sort out items which were to go to Echo Cove. In spite of it being quite an exhausting day and in many ways an emotional one, handling Tom's small possessions, Julie felt this day had been good for her. There had been no time to dwell on Fergus and to wonder what he was doing. That would come later.

They were all up early the following morning, with Ivy issuing instructions from the moment she came into the kitchen till the moment Angus and Julie were ready to leave. And, in fact, they were on their way to get the tram to the station when she came running after them. She had brought them some candles – the gas might have been turned off in the house. Angus teased her, saying why hadn't she brought a tin of oil for the lamps and she gave him a push and said, 'Oh, you!'

Angus and Julie exchanged smiling glances, pleased that Ivy was behaving more like her old self. When they boarded the tram to take them to the station he said, 'It's having a new interest and I'm sure Ivy feels that Tom will be there with her in spirit in Echo Cove.'

It was not until they had started their train journey that he mentioned Julie's holiday. The strange thing was that although she had thought she would be able to talk about it with enthusiasm once they were alone, she found herself instead describing everything in a stilted way, and thought she knew why. Despite Angus still being dear to her, there was something extra about Fergus Damant that had captured her heart.

What Julie did concentrate on was in telling Angus about the art – the paintings, carvings and magnificent architecture. When he said it sounded as though she had had a wonderful time she told him yes, it had been a great experience, one she would not have missed; all the images would be with her for the rest of her life.

'And you fell in love,' Angus said quietly. Julie, who was sitting opposite to him in the carriage, looked up, startled.

'In love?'

'With Michel Angelo. Your face wears a rapt expression whenever you speak of him.'

Julie felt a surge of relief. 'Oh, yes, he was indeed a wonderful man, a genius. I do wish that you could have the opportunity of seeing his work, Angus. When I thought of the paintings I had done I realised they were pathetic! I know nothing.'

'We can't all be geniuses, Julie. He painted for love, but for bread, too. I paint because I like what I do, but I must also work for bread.'

Julie was immediately contrite. 'Oh, please don't think I was criticising what you do, Angus. It is the ordinary workers who are the salt of the earth.' When she saw a smile playing around his mouth she laughed. 'I'm making it worse, aren't I? All right, I'm a worker, too. And I feel we are going to find an awful lot to do when we arrive.'

When Julie did eventually get her first glimpse of the house she was appalled. In her mind, when Angus first described it she had imagined it to be standing on its own, a house in some small need of repair, and was totally unprepared for it being flanked on either side by what looked like derelict warehouses. There had once been a walled garden in front of the house but the walls had either been partially knocked down or crumbled. The garden itself was overgrown, and the front door and windows of the house were practically devoid of paint. Two window panes in one of the downstairs windows were missing.

The property stood back from the road on a slight slope. Julie had stopped at the bottom of the slope and now Angus said, in mild tones, 'It needs a bit doing to it.'

'A bit!' she exclaimed. 'It's a shambles! What about these – these old – warehouses?' Julie pointed to them. 'They make the *house* look derelict. You didn't tell Ivy about those.'

'There was no point. The council are to pull them down.

The men are starting on them soon. It'll all be cleared by the time she's ready to move in.'

'If I were to make a guess,' Julie said, 'I would say the council has been promising that for years. No wonder Ivy got the house and land cheap. No one in their right minds would set up a tea-room here and expect to get customers. I think *you* are out of your mind, Angus MacLaren, and I think you've been most unfair to Ivy. It's like cheating her!'

'Oh, you do go on, Julie,' he chided her gently. 'Stop worrying. You won't know the place by the time Ivy comes.'

He put his hand under her elbow to urge her forward but she pulled away. 'What about this cottage and shed where you are supposed to live and work?'

'It's at the back of the house. Now come on and take a look inside the house – you can't judge a book by its cover.'

Angus unlocked the front door with a massive key and stepping aside waved Julie ahead. 'There you are, Madam, ready for your inspection.'

Julie put a hand to her nose. 'Who has been living in here? Or should I say *what* has been living in here? It smells like a pigsty.'

'It's just an accumulation of dirt. Soap and water will soon work wonders. The hall is small but there's a good-sized kitchen.' He opened a door on the left. Julie walked in then stopped, feeling more appalled than ever. The floor was covered with rubbish – old newspapers, bottles, dozens of jam jars, rusted cake tins, old clothes . . .

'Thank goodness Ivy didn't come with us,' she exclaimed. 'One look at this lot and she would have turned tail and gone straight back to Stoke!'

'No, she wouldn't,' Angus said. 'She would have put on an apron and started to clear up.' The mildness of his tone made Julie want to pick up one of the bottles and hit him on the head with it.

'I suppose you expect me to clear it out then start scrubbing floors? I don't mind scrubbing normal floors but I object to cleaning what is no more than a pigsty.'

'You malign pigs,' Angus said, smiling. 'They're clean creatures. But don't you worry, I'll find someone to clean up.'

'We can't afford paid help,' Julie snapped. 'I'll do it, but right now I think we ought to start looking for somewhere to board. It'll be dark in another two hours.'

'I think I know where to try. Meanwhile, have a look around the house, I'm sure you'll find it has great possibilities. I'll be back soon.'

When he had gone Julie left the kitchen, went into a room across the hall, which in Victorian times, she thought, would be known as the parlour. This room was fairly large too, but wallpaper hung in strips and the iron fireplace was rusted. It was in here that the window panes were missing, and the draught whistled around her ears. There was no rubbish to clear from here, apart from two broken chairs.

Julie went next to a door at the back of the hall. She presumed it would lead to a scullery but when she opened the door she was met by a wall of junk – old bedsteads, broken chairs, sofas, sideboards, old mattresses. There was even a grandfather clock on top of the pile. Julie fumed. How could Angus say the house had possibilities? It was just a dump.

Then over the top of the rubbish she saw what appeared to be a biggish window. She edged her way round the pile then stopped and caught her breath. The window overlooked cliff-top and sea. The day was cloudy, the sea rough, white horses capped the choppy waves, but to Julie the scene had great beauty. Excitement rose in her.

It was the perfect place for a tea-room. She could see people sitting at small tables, enjoying Ivy's home-made teas of cream and jam scones, gingerbread, rice cake, fruit pies . . . Oh, this house could be made really attractive, that is, with the wretched warehouses demolished! Julie felt she could hardly wait for Angus to return.

She went upstairs. Two bedrooms were at the front.

From both the harbour could be seen, with fishing boats and small craft bobbing on the water. To the right was a small bay with rocks and a stretch of sand. At the back was the boxroom and another bedroom. From here, Julie could see a small, rather derelict-looking cottage and close by, a brick-built shed. Was this where Angus would live and work?

She had gone into the front again and it was from here that she saw Angus striding up the slope. She ran downstairs and met him at the door. 'I take back all I said about the house! It certainly does have possibilities.' Julie sobered. 'But what about the junk in the annexe? How can we get rid of that?'

'Everything that isn't usable I'll chop up for firewood and the rest, apart from the grandfather clock, I'll burn. I want to try and repair the clock. Have you seen the cottage and shed – they're at the back of the house?'

Julie told him she had seen them but thought the cottage looked derelict. He dismissed this – the place would look different when it was cleaned up and with some new paper on the walls. So who was going to do all this cleaning and papering, Julie wanted to know, and Angus said, 'Oh, Mrs Pinner knows someone who will help with the clearing out and the wallpapering. She also knows of a man who will build up the broken wall and another who will tidy the garden.'

'And does Mrs Pinner believe that the council will demolish the warehouses?' Julie asked, trying to keep the sarcasm from her tone.

Angus shook his head. 'No, she says they've been promising for ten years to pull them down. But – I'll get them to do it. You'll see.'

The odd thing was, Julie believed that he would.

# Chapter Sixteen

Twenty minutes later, Julie was being introduced to their landlady, who after showing them their rooms offered to make them a meal. Julie liked Mrs Pinner who, although having a quiet way about her gave them a lot of information. A farm nearby could supply them with eggs, butter and milk, and the greengrocer, bakery and newsagents all had delivery boys. It was a good place to live in, she said, neighbour helped neighbour.

She made them a meal and while they ate it she told them where to find the doctor, the dentist, the church and the hospital. They learned about the lives of many people in the area, but never once did she say anything malicious about any of them.

Julie told her about Ivy and the death of Tom and Mrs Pinner said that she had lost her husband at sea, three years before. A steel hawser on one of the winches had snapped while lifting the nets and her husband, who had his hand caught in the net, was dragged overboard and drowned.

'What a dreadful thing to happen,' Julie shuddered. 'Surely such accidents are rare?' Mrs Pinner replied, a sad note in her voice, that unfortunately there were many similar accidents.

When Mrs Pinner tried to persuade them to have another wedge of fruit cake Julie said, 'I would love another piece, the whole meal was delicious, but if I ate a crumb more I wouldn't be able to move and I do want to go to the harbour to hear the echoing cliffs.'

'Ah, yes, but that will not be until nine o'clock. It's only at high-tide that one hears the echo. The fishing fleet goes out then, and visitors consider it quite a sight to see. If you wish I can walk there with you and introduce you to some of the people.' Julie and Angus agreed.

The night was clear, the sky starlit and there was a stillness when they set out. But once they reached the road that led down into the harbour a murmur of voices met them. Julie thought it a lovely scene. From uncurtained windows of cottages and houses candlelight, lamplight and gaslight cast a warm glow over the cobbled quayside. In the harbour were the red and green navigation lights of the trawlers and smaller craft and the beam of the lighthouse swept in an arc across the water.

The trawlers were preparing to leave and the shouted orders of men on board mingled with the voices and laughter of the people on the quayside, the echo from the tall cliffs bouncing back in an undecipherable babel.

Mrs Pinner introduced Julie and Angus to people standing around in groups and they were given a warm welcome. One old sea salt gave Julie a toothless grin and told her she was the bonniest stranger to come to these parts for many a year, to which Mrs Pinner replied that Julie would not be a stranger for long.

When the trawlers began to leave with a chugging of engines a quiet came over the people and although a man began to play a lively tune on a harmonica Julie was aware of an underlying melancholy, as though the fishing fleet was going into battle. Oddly enough, it was only the music that echoed from the cliffs.

When the last boat had been swallowed up into the darkness the people began to leave. Mrs Pinner said, 'Shall we go? I expect you'll both be tired now after your journey.'

They all had a hot drink then Angus said he would be away to his bed, he wanted to be up at five o'clock the next morning.

'Five o'clock?' Julie exclaimed. 'I hope you don't expect me to be up at that time?'

'No, nor do I expect Mrs Pinner to get up at that time either. I'll have my breakfast later. Say half past eight, then I can show you my cottage and shed.'

Julie had a dreamless sleep, and at breakfast announced she was fresh and raring to go! Angus said, good, she would need to be for what was to be done that day.

The two-roomed cottage was in better condition than the house – there was no rubbish and no paper peeling from the walls. With a bit of a clean, Angus said, and a few pieces of furniture in, he would be fine.

The shed was quite large and sturdy. Julie could tell by the way Angus talked about it that he was very well pleased with it as a place of industry. There would be shelves for his work here, and display shelves there. When his wheel and tools came he would get started right away. They went over to the house.

After the smoky air of a town Julie found the freshness of seaweed-laden air exhilarating, but when they went into the house and she saw the rubbish once more she felt depressed, in spite of the fire burning brightly in the grate. Where on earth should she start? Should she throw everything away? Angus laid out several large sacks and from another bag brought out a kettle, milk, sugar and a variety of mugs. They would need a cup of tea later. Julie did not know then that an army of people would be arriving.

The first to come were two women who introduced themselves as Gertie and Gloria, they had come to help. Gertie was built like an Amazon, while Gloria, sadly misnamed, was as thin as a beanpole with false teeth that kept dropping as she talked.

Gertie informed Julie that they had better start in the kitchen. She put down a bucket and took out floorcloths, two scrubbing brushes and soap. 'Didn't know if you were prepared,' she said. She studied the mass of rubbish. Within five minutes she had it all organised. They would set aside the jars for the folks who made their own jam, she never had time, herself. The empty beer and lemonade bottles could go back to the off-licence, there was a penny deposit on each bottle. She and Gloria sorted through the pile of clothes, and one lot was put aside to go to the church jumble sale, the rest could go to the rag and bone man – the kids could get balloons for them.

Before Julie had a chance to take part in this clearance two men arrived, both elderly, and both weather-beaten. One had come to build up the wall and the other to start on the 'garding'. Angus dealt with them but hardly had they disappeared when two more men appeared, one to turn on the gas and the other to replace the broken window panes. By this time, Gertie decided a cuppa would be welcome. But before the tea had been made a van drove up and three men and a youth appeared. Angus came up with them. They had come to look at the warehouses, for a team would start demolishing them the next day.

Julie stared at Angus in awe-struck wonder. When on earth had he contacted the council? He had come in for breakfast at half past eight and had not been out of sight since.

With the gas laid on, another kettle went on the rusty stove and in the end ten people stood around with steaming mugs of tea. The men in the van had provided their own mugs, one saying it was always best to 'be prepared'.

They all discussed the possibilities of a tea-room being a success and there were Fors and Againsts. Those who were against pointed out that there were plenty of little cafés dotted here and there, but those for the tea-room said that none were large enough to cater for coach parties. This house would be ideal if Angus and Julie would display large signs near the road where buses and coaches and cars passed to go to the harbour.

Angus ended up by giving one of the men an order to

make the signs. This man drained his mug and said, 'Well, that sets me up now for some work.' The tea party disbanded.

By lunchtime Julie felt she had done a hard day's work, yet she had done practically nothing. She decided her feeling of exhaustion was due to the energetic activities of Gertie and Gloria.

They had dumped six full sacks outside, carried all the broken furniture outside too for Angus to sort out which he wanted to keep, then had scrubbed the kitchen floor to 'sweeten' it. After that they started stripping wallpaper from the wall of the largest bedroom. The bedrooms would have to be done first, Gertie said, to give the walls a chance to dry before the rooms could be slept in.

If Gloria had had her way all the walls would have been distempered but Julie said that Ivy liked rooms wallpapered, she thought they made them warmer. To this Gloria sucked back her teeth and declared that wallpaper harboured bugs. Julie shuddered but Gertie came to her aid.

'Don't you worry, hinnie, there ain't no bugs in this house. You have what you want. You go to Harry's Hardware, he has job lots, they're leftover rolls from hotels along the coast.'

Gertie then gave her instructions about patterns, too large a pattern meant wastage, and about matching colours, so that Julie wondered if she dare choose any wallpaper without Gertie being there.

Mrs Pinner had promised to have a hot meal ready at twelve o'clock and when Angus and Julie left Julie said, 'What a morning! Gertie and Gloria are like a music hall turn and the whole thing is turning out like a Keystone Cops film.'

Angus laughed. 'Yes, I know, but they're big-hearted people. Mrs Pinner told me that Gertie and Gloria, and the men who came to fix the panes and do the garden won't accept a penny. I wanted to insist but Mrs Pinner told me I would insult them. It's something they do for every newcomer to the community.'

Julie was silent for a moment then she said quietly, 'I'm glad that Ivy decided to come and live here.'

After lunch Angus gave her some money for the wallpaper and Julie set out for the village to find Harry's Hardware. The village led from the harbour along narrow, cobbled streets. It was a small shop and although the paper was in job lots there was an excellent selection. Harry, the proprietor, a small amiable man, treated her like royalty, bringing up a chair for her and displaying various rolls over a stand.

Remembering Gertie's warning about wastage with large patterns Julie kept the designs simple – and ended up paying ten shillings for enough rolls to do the four upstairs rooms and the parlour. Harry promised that the parcel would be delivered within the next fifteen minutes.

Julie dawdled on the way back, looking in shop windows and noting that the cafés she saw *were* too small to take coach parties. When she got back she would weigh up how many small tables would go in the annexe. There were also the windows, to measure up for curtains.

As Julie was about to pass the church the vicar hailed her. 'Miss van Neilson, isn't it? Yes, of course it is, you were described to me. How are you, my dear, and how are you getting on with my people in Echo Cove?'

'Very well indeed, in fact everyone is so friendly, so kind, I'm beginning to wonder if –' Julie smiled, 'well, if there are any unpleasant ones around.'

The vicar, a large man with a gentle voice inclined his head. 'Well, let me tell you a little story, Miss van Neilson. There was a house for sale and two ladies, let us call one Smith and the other Jones, were interested in buying it. Mrs Smith enquired at the little corner shop what the neighbours were like. The shopkeeper asked her what her present neighbours were like and Mrs Smith said they were terrible people, she had always had terrible neighbours. So the shopkeeper told her she would find these neighbours terrible too.'

A twinkle came into the vicar's eyes. 'You have probably heard this story before.' Julie said no and he went on. 'Well, Mrs Jones also went to the same corner shop and she wanted to know what the neighbours were like. To the shopkeeper's query of what her present neighbours were like Mrs Jones said they were lovely people, she had always had delightful neighbours –'

Julie laughed. 'And the shopkeeper said then she would find these neighbours delightful, too.' The vicar nodded and said, 'Exactly.' A woman with three small children came up and Julie left then with the promise she would be in church on Sunday morning.

She was thinking it was too good to be true with all these wonderful people, when on turning a corner she bumped into a middle-aged man who cursed her for treading on his corns. She apologised profusely but the man showed no signs of relenting and went limping away muttering that some stupid folks never looked where they were going. Julie, although sorry for causing the man pain, was satisfied that a balance had been struck. It would be terrible to live in a place where everyone was a goody-goody.

By the time she got back, Gertie had whitewashed the ceiling and Gloria was sorting through the rolls of wallpaper to find which would be suitable for the main bedroom. Julie picked out the white with a pale green satin stripe, which Gloria condemned as showing every mark. Julie smiled and said, 'I know that this would be my employer's choice.'

Both women stopped what they were doing and there was a short silence as they stared at her. Then Gertie said, 'I thought that you were the boss with your la-di-da voice.'

'No, I'm the employee, the worker.'

'Oh,' said Gertie. 'Oh I see!' said Gloria.

From then on their attitude changed, Julie belonged to the 'union'. The next day she was allowed to scrub a floor and make a bonfire of the stripped wallpaper. And was happy.

During the next few days other helpers appeared but Gertie and Gloria remained the 'gaffers'. Windows were cleaned, other rooms were papered and some painting done. On the fourth day Angus was offered ten café tables, forty bentwood chairs and a carton of various coloured paints at a low price. He bought them.

Julie asked, 'Why buy the paint? It won't be any use for your work and the colours are not the ones wanted for the house?'

'No, they're not but I thought of painting our tea-room with murals, a seaside scene. If the weather happens to turn stormy when people come out for the day picnicking they can do their picnicking in a bit of jollity.'

'I don't know,' Julie said, her tone doubtful. 'Would Ivy like it? I don't think she would.'

The next morning when Julie arrived at the house at nine o'clock one wall was painted and she eyed it in astonishment, not only at the life in the scene but at Angus' expertise. It glowed, she felt she was sitting in sunshine on a beach. There were red and white striped bathing tents and deckchairs, children playing, making sandcastles, some running towards the sea, arms outstretched, joyous. There were people on the beach in deck chairs, women gossiping, some dozing, there were men with newspapers over their faces, their trouser legs rolled up for paddling. There were women paddling with children, their skirts held high against the waves. There was a Punch and Judy show, a man selling ice cream cornets and children on the swings, being swung high, the boats looking as if they were going to loop the loop.

Julie turned to him. 'Angus, it's wonderful. You're an artist, a great artist. You should be painting canvases.'

He shook his head. 'No, I'm not good enough for that, but I'm glad you like this. I thought I would do a sea and cliff scene on the opposite wall.' He was glowing with the pleasure he would be giving to other people and Julie thought – I love this man, but in a different way from what I feel for Fergus. He continued, 'Here, you must come and see the grandfather clock, I got it going last night. Come on!'

He ran her over to the cottage and flung open the door. 'There it is – what do you think of it?'

It was not the clock Julie found herself staring at but at the furnished room. 'When did you do this?' she gasped.

'I didn't. Some of the women fixed it up when they knew I would be living here on my own.'

'Oh, yes!' Julie tried to make her tone teasing but wasn't sure that she had succeeded. '*Young* women, I presume.'

'Jealous?' Angus asked laughing. 'One was young, two were middle-aged and one was a grandmother. They sandpapered the floor, stained and polished it. They whitewashed the ceilings and walls to make the room lighter. Nothing has been done yet with the bedroom.'

'And the furniture? Who brought you that?'

'I bought the pieces from the second-hand shop.'

There was a small gate-legged table, two chairs with velvet seats and a leather armchair, which Angus said needed the springs attending to. There were horse brasses on the wall by the side of the fireplace and a picture of an inn, a scene of yesteryear, above the fireplace. 'All very cosy,' Julie said. 'How about your pottery shed?'

'Oh, that is waiting for the wheel and tools. Two men fixed up some shelves for me. *Now* will you look at my lovely clock?'

For the first time, Julie became aware of a gentle tick-tock. The case was walnut, and had been beautifully, lovingly polished. The dial had the days of the month, gave the tides and position of the moon, the sun and stars.

Julie ran her hand over the case. 'It's beautiful, Angus, really beautiful. You've really been working, you're to be admired.'

Angus said that he would, of course, give the clock to Ivy when she came. It was hers, it belonged to the house she had bought. But for the meantime he would have the pleasure of it.

Julie had written to Ivy every day, even if it was just a few lines, to tell her of their progress and Ivy had replied to each one, saying in the last one that she was now ready to leave, and would probably travel the following week. She added that now the time was near she was looking forward to living where Tom had wanted to be. This had Julie close to tears. She only hoped that the complete change and planning the tea-room would help Ivy over her grief.

Mrs Pinner had arranged to board Ivy too until beds were brought and put up and other furniture arranged.

That evening, Angus and Julie went for a walk on their own. They descended to the harbour and stood listening to the old fishermen who were seated on either side of the harbour shouting across to one another. The echoes came back jumbled, because most of them were talking at the same time. Some of them were puffing away at clay pipes and the pungent smell of tobacco lingered on the still night air. A few couples strolled around and one or two groups of shawled women stood gossiping. Angus suggested they walk to the lighthouse.

They had started to go towards the path that led to the lighthouse when Angus stopped and said he wondered if he shouted something out loud, would they get a clear echo? Julie suggested he try it and – to her astonishment he shouted: '*I love Julie!*' The echo came, '*I-I, l-love, J-Julie.*'

It came in a silence as though everyone in the harbour had been waiting for it.

Angus grinned. Julie laughed a little shakily, then grabbing her by the hand Angus ran her along the grass path.

# Chapter Seventeen

Angus and Julie didn't stop running until they reached the rocks in the little cove, then Julie was forced to stop to catch her breath. Until then she had treated the incident in the harbour as a piece of fun but now realised that Angus was watching her, waiting. For what? To see her reaction to his declaration of love?

She turned away from him and took a deep breath. 'Oh, isn't this lovely, so peaceful. Listen to the sea.'

'Not many men would declare their love for a girl in public,' Angus said, half-serious, half-joking.

'No, they wouldn't.' She laughed. 'I only hope the echo of your words didn't sound as clear to the people in the harbour as they did to me, otherwise you'll have the vicar on the doorstep wanting to know when you're going to call the banns.'

'Would you mind?'

Julie tensed. Below them, wavelets broke against the rocks and came running, cream-frothed, over the sand. When she made no answer Angus said quietly, 'You're in love with someone else, aren't you?'

Above them the beam of the lighthouse swept across the water. When Julie looked at Angus she saw pain in his eyes. 'I don't know, Angus, I don't know that I'm in love with anyone at the moment. All I know is that Ivy is going to open a tea-room and I want to help her to make it a success.'

'Yes, of course.' He stepped to a ledge of rock below and held out a hand to her. 'Let's walk, shall we?'

He talked about Ivy, wondering what her reactions would be when she saw the house, then he went on about getting his pottery shed fixed up and Julie was glad to let him talk, wanting to dim the image of Fergus which had sprung so vividly to her mind only minutes before. But Fergus would not be shut out and it was not until the next morning when a letter from Ivy came to say she would be arriving the following day that Fergus slipped once more into the recesses of Julie's mind.

When she walked up to the house later she tried to see it through Ivy's eyes, and was pleased with what she saw. Although everyone had been against her having the painting done white, because of the sea air she had insisted and had also asked them to paint the front door red. It had to attract from the roadway. With the warehouses pulled down there was now a view through to the cliff-tops and the sea. The garden wall was restored and the garden dug over and planted with a few green shrubs to give it life. Later, there would be flowers – a mass, if they all flourished.

'Yes,' Julie said aloud, 'I think Ivy will be pleased.'

Ivy was pleased. They took her upstairs first and from the moment of seeing the wallpapered bedrooms her pleasure increased with each move. When she went into the tea-room and saw the murals she said, 'Well! What do you know! No doubting who's responsible for this.' She turned to Angus. 'How did you manage to make this room look as if it were full of sunshine? Tom would have loved it.' When Julie and Angus exchanged glances at mention of Tom's name she said briskly, 'He's part of this and we are going to talk about him. My weeping is done. How about a cup of tea and something to eat? I've brought food with me.'

Ivy had travelled in the van that had brought her furniture and what she called her 'bits and pieces'. Now, she asked the driver to come in and share their meal.

Within two days the house looked lived in. Curtains were up, lino bought and laid, rugs down and tables and chairs set out in the annexe. Ivy then invited Mrs Pinner and all those who had helped with the house to a special tea. She took to them and they took to her. There was a constant lively chatter, with Gertie and Gloria declaring at the end of it that Ivy was quite a 'character'.

Angus offered Ivy the clock but she said she already had three clocks and would be only too pleased for him to have it. After this, she said she would open the tea-room the following weekend.

Ivy spent the next few days baking cakes and a rich fruity smell mingled with that of spices and ginger. It hung on the air and on the third day brought three hikers to the house, asking if they could buy some cake. Ivy told them the tea-room was not yet open, but she sat them down to wedges of cake and cups of tea, told them that this was on the house, but in return they were to tell all their friends. They grinned and said, 'You bet!'

By Friday afternoon, they were ready for the GRAND OPENING. The tables had been laid with red-and-white checked tablecloths, teapots and crockery were all laid out ready and a large board had been stood on the grass near the roadside announcing the opening of the tea-room.

Ivy had even arranged to have a tea urn in the parlour so that odd cups of tea could be served from the wide window to those wanting to picnic. Mrs Pinner's young niece was to attend to this part of the business.

At that time in the afternoon the weather was sunny. At eight o'clock it began to change and an hour later Mrs Pinner came to warn them that bad weather was on the way, there were all the signs she said.

Unhappily, her forecast was correct. A gale blew up and by the next morning rain was lashing against the windows and water was cascading into the water butt from the gutters.

'It would, wouldn't it?' Ivy exclaimed. 'But there's nothing we can do about it except watch the rain and grumble. We're not the only ones who'll be suffering.'

Julie said, 'If say, charabanc trips have been arranged they'll still come, hoping the weather will clear up later don't you think?'

Ivy nodded. 'You're right, there's still hope. And if they have been travelling in this weather they'll need something hot. I'll get a big pan of soup on the hob.'

No hikers or cyclists appeared, an odd car passed and a few vans but no signs of any charabanc. At least, not until twelve o'clock when one stopped beside the sign. Ivy and Julie held their breath. They could see people peering through the celluloid wide-screens but no one got out. The charabanc moved away, stopped, then reversed, turned and crossed the road and took the one to come to the house. Julie hugged Ivy. 'Our first customers. Come on, get prepared!'

Julie was at the door to welcome them. The driver, a little red-faced man said, 'It was the smell, love, that drew us. You've got something good cooking.'

'Soup,' Julie told them and they all trooped in. The murals delighted them. There were cries of, 'Here, our Jack, come and take a look, isn't that feller in that deckchair like your dad?' . . . 'Eeh, Phoebe, look at that sea, in't it lovely, I could go for a paddle in it.' A man guffawed and said he was going to start and build a sandcastle.

Julie thought it was a pity Angus was not there to hear all the praise, but he was working long hours at his pottery.

The party had healthy appetites and when they had finished the driver said they had come to hear the echo and would not be leaving until after it, so could Ivy do them a supper about eight o'clock? She offered them pies and mushy peas and they said great! After they had gone, Ivy put on her hat and coat to go to the village to buy the meat.

At ten o'clock that night, Ivy, Julie and Angus sat round the kitchen fire with cups of cocoa, Ivy declaring it had been a good opening. The driver had promised to tell other charabanc owners about the food and added that all the people he brought to Echo Cove would come to Ivy's tea-room.

The name stuck and 'Ivy's tea-room' became a byword with visitors. Even on the worst weekends the tea-room was always busy. Angus had also found a ready trade with his pottery. During the week when trade was more slack Julie helped him with painting the items.

Angus said one day, 'It's not really what I want to make, but it's important to have a bread and butter line.' The pieces he was making were mostly small jugs and bowls, and cups and saucers, with small flowers or designs on them and the words, '*A Present from Echo Cove*' painted on in gold lettering.

One evening, when Julie was alone with Angus she asked him what he would really like to make. He said, 'Busts. I like to study people's faces, learn their characteristics.'

'So what is my character?' Julie asked lightly. Angus sat looking at her for some time then asked her if she really wanted to know, for it would be the truth. She told him it was what she expected of him and Angus got up and moved around the kitchen before sitting down again.

'You need to be loved, Julie, and you have a lot of love to give but you're afraid to show it because you have such a restless spirit. You must always be on the move.'

Julie protested at this. He was wrong, look how she had stayed with Ivy and Tom and then moved with Ivy. Angus reminded her how she had been restless after living at Stoke for a few weeks, but then the London trip and the Italian holiday had come along. After that, there was another move for her. How long before she would be restless again?

Julie accused him of being unfair. 'Were you never restless when you were younger?' she asked.

He was silent as though weighing it up then said, 'It was not so much a restlessness as the need to earn my living. I came to Stoke because I was a potter. I would probably be there now had it not been for Ivy and for you, Julie. You know I love you, but I'm not going into that. You will probably end up marrying Fergus Damant.'

Julie's head came up. 'What makes you say such a thing? I've hardly mentioned him.'

'You're not aware of it. Whenever you have a letter from Richard or Jake you always say after reading them aloud, "I wonder where Fergus Damant is, neither of them mentioned him." Why don't you ask when you write the next time.'

Angus had stirred images again that Julie had kept tightly locked away, of Fergus in Venice, their night of romance on the canals, Fergus during their journeying to Monchau, and in Monchau itself. She remembered his laughter, his teasing and his love-making . . . Oh, yes, he had made love to her over and over again – with his eyes.

'You are stubborn too, Julie,' Angus said.

'Can't you find one good characteristic?' she asked.

'Yes, I can.' He spoke softly. 'You have warmth, tenderness and a great capacity for loving. To me, they erase any faults you have.'

'Oh, thank you very much! I asked for the truth and I got it, didn't I?' She got up. 'I'm going to bed. Tell Ivy when she comes back.'

In the darkness of her room, Julie wept. Why did Angus have to stir up memories of Fergus? It hurt her deeply that he had not written, never sent any word to her, and pride would not let her ask.

Two days later, as though she had transferred her thoughts to her home, she had a letter from her mother mentioning him.

'*Fergus came to us for the weekend. He was asking how you were getting on at Echo Cove. I told him you seemed to be enjoying yourself.*'

Julie read on, expecting more about him, but that was all. She could not believe it. He must have said more, must at least have said something about their holiday in Italy. But her mother just went on to tell her about their latest business deals and snippets of news about business colleagues. There was a postscript.

'*Richard has just phoned. He said he had met Violet unexpectedly in London. She got out of a taxi to speak to him. She was on her way to Paris. In one way I was glad he was honest enough to tell me, but any mention of my sister's name is like someone sticking a thorn into my flesh. I can't help thinking that their meeting was not accidental, but I didn't question him about it, he is always reticent about Violet . . .*'

As reticent, Julie thought, as her mother was about Fergus. What was wrong with everyone? Why had there always to be this secrecy? This was one letter Julie did not share with Ivy and Angus, she simple related the unimportant bits.

There followed a period of storms when even at weekends there were few visitors to the cove. One afternoon when Julie had a fit of restlessness on her Ivy said, 'For heaven's sake find something to do or go out for a walk, blow the miseries out of you.'

'I haven't got the miseries,' Julie retorted. 'It's this weather – it's depressing.'

'You'll go on feeling depressed if you're idle.' Ivy, who was making a batch of cakes, picked up a bowl and broke eggs into it. 'You can either whisk these, go and help Angus, or get out of my way.'

Julie said she didn't want to mix eggs and she didn't want to help Angus, she would clear out. She went to get her hat and coat and pulling them on, snapped, 'I'll go and drown myself, get out of everybody's way!'

'Blah, blah, blah,' Ivy said. 'Don't come back here drowned and wet all over my clean kitchen.' Julie slammed the kitchen door.

The wind came at her with gale force and she buttoned up her coat, then tugged her knitted bobble cap further down on her head. 'And blah, blah, blah to you,' she shouted, but the wind carried her words away. What was she doing here? For the past two days the only people she had seen were Ivy and Angus, for even Mrs Pinner hadn't called on account of having a chill. They should have stayed at Stoke, where at least there were always customers to chat to and have a laugh with. Then Julie thought of Ivy who always kept busy and had never once moaned about losing Tom. But then that was Ivy, a stoic, like Angus, who worked all hours to wrest a living from his business and without a word of complaint.

Every person was different. Angus had been right when he told her she would always be restless. At this moment she was wishing she had accepted her mother's offer to live in Longon. Richard and Jake raved about the house which her parents had bought in Mayfair. In one of the letters Richard said that Mrs Boswell, the housekeeper, was a treasure who anticipated their every need.

The harbour came into view and Julie paused. The sky was leaden and outside the harbour the angry sea chopped and tossed about, then nearer shore formed into waves which, gathering momentum, rolled along the foot of the cliffs and broke against the sea walls, forming seething cauldrons of foam in the inlets. Not a single ship was in sight and all the smaller craft had been beached.

Skirting the harbour, Julie took the path that led to the sandy cove. Here, where the land was more open she had to battle against the gusts of wind that at times brought her to a standstill, its howl mingling with the raucous screams of gulls which swooped and dived and skimmed over the water, snatching up food.

Reaching the cove, Julie climbed the rocks and stood on the topmost one, a large flat slab. The waves broke against the rocks below and rose in spumes of spray, making her step back. She began to feel excited. There was something magnificent, primitive, about the anger of the elements.

Ahead of her were cross-currents where the waves built up. When one massive wave came rushing shorewards she knew when it broke it could swamp her but she stood there, hypnotised by the scene.

Seconds before the wave broke, someone snatched her. She was aware of a man shouting something to her, but it was impossible to make out what he was saying for the roar of the sea.

Then she was set down on the sand and the voice shouted: 'Look! Don't you realise what could have happened to you?'

Julie glanced over her shoulder and saw a wave rise and swamp the slab, the residue cascading in miniature waterfalls over the rocks.

'It would have sucked you with it into the sea!' Julie turned her head and found herself looking into an angry face. She thought the man looked like Fergus Damant, but this couldn't be, Fergus was miles away and anyway this man was dressed like a fisherman in heavy knitted navy jersey and oilskin trousers.

'Julie, are you all right?' He gave her a little shake.

She eyed him in faint astonishment. 'It *is* you. What are you – where did you – ?'

A wild gust of wind buffeted them. Fergus put an arm protectively around her and hurried her near the cliffs where there was a piece of jutting rock. Then, as another gust came showering them with a cloud of fine sand he looked about him and asked if there was anywhere they could shelter. She told him about a series of caves further along and he took her by the hand and ran her in that direction. Her heart began to pound with a different sort of excitement. Fergus was no longer the immaculately-dressed man about town, but a pirate, his thick dark hair dishevelled and curling in the sea fret. She was his woman!

Oh, heavens, Julie thought, she was really letting her imagination run riot, but it was lovely, she was enjoying herself. She tugged at his hand as they drew near the entrance to the caves and gave a nod.

Once they were out of the teeth of the storm she pulled

off her hat and shook out her hair. Fergus peeled off the oilskin trousers, remarking he found them cumbersome.

Julie said, 'There's a small cave over there, and I have a fire laid ready to light.'

His eyebrows went up. 'Were you expecting company?'

'No,' she said, in a woeful voice. 'I gathered the wood when I was shipwrecked, then found I had no match to light it. But you being a pirate will, I'm sure, be equipped for any emergency.'

Fergus knuckled her chin, laughing softly. 'Lovely, crazy Julie, come along, let me see this cave.'

As Fergus put a match to the kindling he said, 'And now, satisfy my curiosity. Who was intended to sit around the fire?'

'A neighbour's small grandson and his friends. Johnnie had asked for it as a special birthday treat. They were to be pirates who would attack the rich merchant's vessel, carry off his gold and also his five beautiful daughters. The cave was to be their hideout.'

Fergus grinned. 'How old is this Johnnie and his friends?'

'Seven, eight –'

'They were starting young, weren't they? Gold *and* the beautiful daughters?'

'They see the swashbuckling films at the Saturday afternoon matinées. Unfortunately, poor Johnnie contracted measles the day before his birthday so the treat had to be postponed.'

'And happily, the beautiful girls escaped being ravaged.' He was now sitting back on his heels, an impish glint in his eyes. 'A quaint old-fashioned word – ravaged.'

'Yes, well –' Julie picked up a twig and threw it on the pile of wood where flames were beginning to appear, unwilling to admit even to herself that it conjured up something quite pleasurable – that is, if the pirate were Fergus. She said suddenly, 'We're chatting away here and you haven't told me how you came to be in Echo Cove.'

Fergus got up then. 'I had to go to Edinburgh and Richard suggested I break my journey and call and see you.'

Julie's head came up. 'You saw Ivy?'

'Yes, she told me you had gone rushing out in a temper, threatening to drown yourself. Not that she expected you to, of course, but she pointed out that the weather was rough and you were foolhardy and an accident could happen.'

'I'm not foolhardy!' Julie protested vehemently.

'What else would you call your behaviour, standing on a rock where a wave could have swept you into the sea at any moment? You gave me a shock, I can tell you.' His voice had softened on the last words and Julie searched his face.

'Why did you come, because Richard asked you?'

'No, Julie, I wanted to see you. I longed to see you.'

She turned away. 'I can't believe that. You never wrote, not even a card. A postcard would have been sufficient.'

He turned her to face him. 'It wasn't as easy as that, Julie. There were problems. I'm older than you, I go away a great deal – abroad – it would not be fair to you.'

Julie dismissed this as being no problem. Many husbands were older than their wives, and what about women who were married to sailors who went for long voyages? 'No,' she said, 'you're just making excuses. If you had wanted to see me as much as you say you would not have created even *one* obstacle.'

Fergus said gently, 'Some men have been known to sacrifice their own happiness for the girl they love.'

It was the first time he had even suggested he loved her but because Fergus was a man of the world and she felt it might be something he would say to other girls, she said, 'But not *you*.'

'Why not me, Julie?' He ran a finger lightly down her nose, a sad little smile touching his lips. 'You don't have much faith in me, do you?'

His touch sent a tremor through her. She wanted him to

hold her, ached for him to make love to her, so why was she not responding? Perhaps it was all the 'commonsense' talks delivered by Ivy. 'Always think before you act . . .'

'The fire is burning up,' she said, and drew away from him. She held out her hands to the now leaping flames, whose glow lit up the walls of the cave. 'Surprising isn't it, that the wood has kept so dry.'

He came up behind her and said softly, 'Do you want to talk about driftwood?'

'No, not particularly.' It was impossible to keep the tremor from her voice. She unbuttoned her coat, making the excuse that the cave was getting warm now, but knew this was not the reason. Fergus helped her off with the coat and laid it on a rock shelf. He then removed his sweater, which had Julie wondering if he had seen her gesture as an invitation towards a more intimate atmosphere. Her heartbeats quickened.

'The pirates had the right idea, didn't they?' he said. 'A nice warm cave to gloat over their gold and –' He paused and when he made no attempt to finish the sentence she gave him a pert glance.

'And what? To ravage the girls, is that what you were going to say?'

Fergus grinned. 'The films make it seem an adventure.'

Julie caught her breath as an image sprang into her mind – a rich, beautiful girl, struggling with the handsome master pirate who was carrying her off to his ship. The girl had soon succumbed to his passion . . .

Fergus lifted Julie's hair away from her face and drew his fingertips lightly around the back of her ears, sending little shivers of excitement running up and down her spine. 'Who would you prefer to be with at this moment, a handsome, gentle prince or a rough-necked pirate?'

'A rough-necked pirate, of course, so much more advanturous!' She laughed to show it was just a joke, but the laugh was definitely shaky.

'Right!' said Fergus, 'the lady must not be disappointed.' He drew her fiercely to him. 'You shall submit to me, woman, or I shall beat you.'

'Never, never!' she cried. 'You shall kill me first!'

'Kill you I will, but not before I make you mine!'

His mouth came down over hers, his lips moving sensuously, almost savagely. Then suddenly the play-acting was over. Julie found herself responding as emotions came to the surface, which she had experienced in a minor way when thinking of Fergus making love to her. What she had not been prepared for was a wild throbbing all over her body. Fergus' attitude towards her had changed. He began to undo the buttons of her blouse, not with any haste, but with a slow deliberation, as though he knew it was something he ought not to be doing. When the last button was undone he drew away from her, his gaze holding hers, his eyes dark and slumbrous. But he said nothing.

Julie began to undo his shirt and she felt him give a little shiver. He removed the shirt and she took off her blouse. 'Julie I –' his voice was ragged. He slipped the straps of her cami-knicks from her shoulders then drew in a quick breath as her breasts were exposed.

He buried his face against her neck, murmuring endearments. He kissed her eyelids, her throat, her breasts, then he began to finish undressing her and after he had stripped off he picked her up and laid her on the woollen sweater. By this time, Julie was shivering with excitement.

He explored her body, his touch so light it was as though his fingertips were hovering over her skin in a magnetic way, drawing every nerve end to the surface and bringing to Julie an agonising ecstacy . . . 'Oh, Julie, Julie, I love you, want you . . .'

The urgency in his voice, his need, her own need, blotted out all reasoning. Julie dug her fingers into his back. He took her then and above the pain she was carried on the crest of a wave to a height that made her unsure whether the moaning she heard was her own voice or the moan of the storm, echoing in the confines of the cave.

Afterwards, when she lay in Fergus' arms in that pleasurable languorous aftermath and watched the flames from the fire flickering on the wall Julie wondered what her parents would say when they knew that she and Fergus were going to be married. They would be pleased, she was sure, they both liked him, liked him very much. She thrust to the back of her mind the fact that she was no longer a virgin.

Julie glanced at Fergus and a wave of tenderness for him swept over her. His eyes were closed and his long dark lashes fanning his cheeks gave him the vulnerability of a boy. She touched his hair and his lids flew open. 'I thought you were asleep,' she said softly.

'No, I was thinking.' He got up and began to dress.

She panicked. 'Fergus, what is it, what's wrong?'

He got her coat and held it out. 'Put this on for a moment, I want to talk to you.' There was a sternness in his voice. She put on the coat and held it tightly around her, watched him wide-eyed, aching because she felt he was despising her for giving in to him. He turned to her.

'Julie, I hate myself for what I've done. I've always prided myself on my iron control yet here I am –' He flung out his hands in a gesture of despair. 'How could I have behaved so despicably?'

'Oh, please don't regret it,' she begged, 'otherwise I shall feel – feel wanton.'

'No, no, Julie, not you.' His voice had softened. He drew her to him. 'You're sweet and lovely and innocent –'

'Not now,' she said with a tremulous smile. 'I wanted you to make love to me, longed for it. I want you to make love to me again – and again.'

He put a finger on her lips. 'Stop saying such things! You don't know what you are doing to me. Here I am apologising for making love to you and wanting madly to make love to you *again* – and again.'

He drew away from her and picked up his shirt. Julie said in a small voice, 'Don't turn your back on me, Fergus. It may be a long time before I see you again.'

'Oh, God –' He swung round and pulled her to him.

There was no fulfilment for Julie this time, but she didn't mind. The important thing was that Fergus loved her – she was his woman. She was disappointed that he insisted they leave soon afterwards, yet she knew it made sense. Ivy would be wondering where they both were.

When they were ready to leave, Fergus traced a finger round the contour of her cheekbone. 'You are so beautiful, Julie. I think I began to fall in love with you the Sunday we were at the Portobello Road Market. You were wearing that funny sou'wester and over-sized macintosh. You looked adorable.'

'I looked dreadful, but somehow I didn't mind. I enjoyed every minute.'

Fergus took her by the hand and declared they must leave that very moment otherwise he would not be responsible for his actions. They left the cave laughing but on the way sobered up, with Julie deciding they would simply tell Ivy they had been walking, which was true. But even as the decision had been taken Julie felt uneasy, knowing how discerning Ivy could be. She must *never* know what had happened in the cave.

Julie was to think over her meeting with Fergus many times during the next two weeks. Ivy had accepted their explanation for being late, but thought them fools for staying out in such weather. She also accepted Fergus and to Julie's surprise Fergus and Angus got on well together.

Ivy called them the two 'Gusses'; until then, Julie had not noticed the similarity in their names. Her disappointment came when Fergus announced he had to leave that evening to continue his journey to Edinburgh. He kissed her on both cheeks in the continental way again when he left and promised to write. Julie read a lot into his expression as he said this.

But Fergus had not written and when Julie missed her monthly period the worry began.

# Chapter Eighteen

Ivy said to Julie one morning at breakfast, 'Something hasn't happened to you this month that should have done. Why?'

Although Julie had prepared herself for this she could not stem the colour that rose to her cheeks. 'I don't know. I used to be late sometimes – at home. I'm only two days over. I have been a week late before.'

The lie stuck in her throat. She had difficulty in eating her breakfast. Ivy sniffed and said if she didn't come on by that evening she would give her some hot ginger wine, it might do the trick. Her tone suggested it would have no effect.

Julie, feeling distraught, was glad when Ivy sent her to the village to do some shopping. Although she had taken it for granted that Fergus would marry her after making love to her in the cave, she was now full of doubts. He had not bothered to get in touch with her and that was not the action of a man totally in love and thinking of marriage. But whatever happened, no one must know that Fergus was responsible. She would not have him called names. After all, she had almost begged him to make love to her.

Instead of going straight to the village she went first to the cove. She had been several times before to relive the ecstasy, the intimacy of the firelit cave. Today, the cold ashes and the sullen sound of the sea seemed to register the death of her hopes and dreams.

She recalled the simple things, like how pleased she had

been to be wearing her pure silk cami-knicks instead of the fine lawn pastel ones she wore most days, and how Fergus had remembered their Sunday at the Portobello Road Market . . . It was the day he had begun to fall in love with her . . . *'You looked so adorable, Julie'* . . .

The words mocked her and she ran out of the cave, determined she would not come back again to torture herself.

When Julie got back, Mrs Pinner was there and was going to stay for the day. The two women chatted together and after lunch Julie said she would go and help Angus.

The weather was a little warmer than it had been of late but Julie felt cold all the time now and was glad of the warmth from the kiln when she went into the shed. She stood close to it. Angus, who was busy wedging clay looked up. 'Hello, Julie, come to lend a hand?' He paused then added, 'Are you all right? You look a bit peaky.'

'It's nothing, I'm just feeling a little chilled. There's a coolish wind blowing in from the sea. What can I do to help?'

Angus picked up a piece of wire to cut the clay then stood with it between his fingers. 'Something's bothering you, Julie, isn't it? You're not yourself,' he shook his head, 'not yourself at all. Is it – could it be Fergus you're fretting over?'

A pulse began to beat in Julie's throat. She put her hands behind her back and clasped them tightly. She was about to say no when she saw the gentleness in Angus' eyes.

'Yes, I am.' She was unable to keep the misery from her voice. 'I haven't heard from him since he left. He did promise to write.'

'And you're in love with him.'

'I am and it hurts.'

'I know,' Angus said quietly and Julie ached for herself and for this man who loved her. Then Angus said, 'Let's set you to work – it's the best thing for what ails you. I'll give you some butterfly dishes to do, nice and cheery and beautiful.'

Julie excelled at painting butterflies and she realised that Angus had been right. Once she had started she became absorbed in her work and also in what Angus had to say. He told her he was thinking of expanding, making larger pieces like vases and jugs. He had met a man who ran an art shop further along the coast and was interested.

'That's good,' Julie said. 'Why don't you try and do some paintings, Angus, perhaps seascapes, you have a flair for them. I don't think there is anyone who comes into the tea-room who doesn't pass a remark about your lovely murals. They really are excellent.'

Angus said a little wryly that he might if there were more then twenty-four hours in a day or, if Julie had been free to help decorate the vases and the bowls.

When Julie protested she was not qualified he said, 'Don't belittle yourself, love, you have a lot of talent. I always feel you have a reluctance to let your ideas flow. Look at yon butterflies you're painting, they're alive, free.'

'They're not free,' she said, a bitter note in her voice. 'Men capture them, stick pins in them and add them to their collections.' Julie became aware that Angus was watching her closely and although she longed for comfort she was glad when he resumed his work without making any comment.

They worked in comparative silence after that until they heard the ringing of the big handbell which Ivy used to summon Angus for a meal. But when Julie and Angus were crossing the field he laid his arm companionably across her shoulders and said, 'You'll hear from Fergus, never fear. He's a decent fellow. I felt he was a man of principles. All sorts of things could have cropped up to prevent him getting down to a letter.'

Julie was so grateful for the generosity of the words she felt she could have hugged him, and felt so much brighter she was able to join in the general conversation over the meal.

Afterwards, Angus went back to the shed but Julie stayed to help Ivy and Mrs Pinner with preparations for the next day when they were expecting four charabanc-loads of people, apart from others who might arrive. They baked until late and when Mrs Pinner went home she left with a promise to come and help the next day.

Ivy said briskly to Julie, 'I'll heat you some ginger wine. You can take it up with you and drink it in bed. If that doesn't do the trick I'll do you a brew of herbs tomorrow and if that doesn't work, then heaven help you!'

So Ivy knew! Julie felt as though insects were crawling over her spine. She was about to blurt out what had happened when she suddenly remembered Peg at Stoke telling her that some girls had their periods late after the first time they had been with a man. 'It's the shock to the system,' Peg had said, 'and the excitement.' Julie felt hopeful. Perhaps the ginger wine would put her right.

It had no effect, nor did the brew of herbs that stank the house out. Although Ivy went about tight-lipped she said no more until Julie started with morning sickness, then she railed at her.

'I can guess who's responsible! It's that Fergus Damant, isn't it?'

Julie denied it, she denied it vehemently. She had worked out a story and she told it now. 'It happened the night I went to the local dance with Minna Daley and her sister. I drank some rough cider and it made me feel ill. I left word for Minna that I was going home. A boy took my arm as I left. Then I don't remember much more after that. When I recovered I was on the dunes . . . alone.'

Ivy demanded to know who the boy was and swore she would see him in court. Julie declared she had no idea who he was and even if she did she was not going to have her name bandied about in public. Ivy then flung her arms up in a gesture of despair. 'What in heaven's name am I going to tell your parents?'

'I don't want them to know. They mustn't ever know!'

'Of course they have to know. They have a right. And

anyway they're the best ones to deal with this situation. There's things that can be done with money.' Julie wanted to know what money had to do with it then burst into tears. Ivy put her arms around her. 'Don't cry, love. Look, you sit down and we'll have a cup of tea and talk it over.'

With Julie calmer Ivy explained that there were clinics in Switzerland where girls could go to have an 'operation' to get rid of the baby. Either that, or the girl could stay with some nice woman in the country until her baby was born then have it adopted. Julie knew she would not resort to either of these possibilities. This living embryo inside her had been conceived by herself and Fergus. It was their child. She loved Fergus, always would, no matter what. She would keep the baby in spite of the disgrace.

When she told Ivy this there was a long silence then Ivy said, 'I don't think you realise what this entails, but then that is something you would have to discuss with your parents.'

The last thing Julie wanted was to discuss anything with her parents and she became agitated again. Then suddenly she realised this was her trouble – she had been too upset for coherent thought. She could still hear from Fergus, it could be today – or tomorrow. Angus was right when he said that all sorts of things could have happened to prevent him writing.

But a letter from Richard the next day destroyed her hopes. In it he asked if Fergus had visited her on his way to Edinburgh. Neither he nor Jake had seen him, yet he knew Fergus was back in London because Klara had seen him pass in his car when she was in the West End.

Julie sat numbed, knowing why Fergus had avoided them all. He was a man of the world, would have known when he made love to her that he could have left her pregnant, but had no wish to be involved.

That evening Julie was sitting over the fire, steeped in misery when Ivy said quietly, 'Julie, you must make up your mind what you're going to do. You *must* let your parents know.'

'I don't want to write to them, I don't want to go home, nor do I want to go to a clinic in Switzerland. I want to keep the baby.' Her voice broke. 'Oh, Ivy, what am I to do?'

Ivy sat down facing her. 'It would have been so different had it been a young man you were in love with but –' she paused then added slowly, 'Angus would . . . marry you . . . he told me so.'

Julie stared at her, shocked. 'You told him? How *could* you?'

Ivy straightened. 'Because I know he loves you and I know you're fond of him, that's why.'

'But it was not your place, you had no right, how many more people have you told? Mrs Pinner and –'

'No, Julie, I haven't. Angus is the only one and if I'm honest I was thinking of the child. I feel it's wrong to take a life but I also think it's more wrong to let a child be brought up to be known as a bastard.'

Julie felt suddenly choked, knowing how much Tom and Ivy had longed for children. She said, 'I couldn't marry Angus, it wouldn't be fair. I'll write to my parents tomorrow.'

All the next day Julie avoided Angus, even going out when he came in for meals. Ivy said no more but she went about tight-lipped.

The next morning, Julie was alone in the kitchen when Angus came in. She tensed and made to leave but he caught hold of her arm. 'I want a word with you. Don't punish Ivy because she told me about you. She's suffering enough already. She feels she's failed in her responsibility towards you and is making herself ill with worry. You must remember she no longer has Tom to talk things over with. She needed to tell someone.'

'I'm sorry,' Julie whispered. 'I didn't realise –'

'She loves you as much as I do,' he said gently.

'I know, and thanks for offering to – marry me, but I couldn't.'

'It's all right, Julie, I understand. After all, we are from different worlds.'

Julie's head came up. 'That has nothing to do with it, not as far as I am concerned. I simply think it's not fair to you to father another man's baby.'

Angus put his hand over hers. 'It wouldn't suffer because of that, Julie. It is yours, too.'

'I know you would care for it, Angus, but marriage is for a lifetime.' Julie pressed her fingertips to her brow. 'I can't decide anything, I'll have to think about it.'

For the next hour Julie could not eliminate the words 'a lifetime' and all its connections from her thoughts. Supposing she were to marry Angus and then Fergus came back into her life? Not only would she be denying herself the right to live with the man she loved, but denying her child the right to know his or her own father.

But then, never at any time had Fergus hinted at marriage. She had been a fool to expect it. She must pay for it, for the baby's sake. And yet would it be such a great punishment? She had once thought herself to be in love with Angus, they got on well together, they could perhaps build up a future.

Julie suddenly shivered. Is that what she would add to a marriage bowl after a year of being married? They got on well together? No, there had to be love on both sides, romance, otherwise it would be impossible.

In spite of this when Julie saw Ivy later she told her right away she had decided to marry Angus, adding she would send her parents a telegram.

'Why not a letter?' Ivy asked. 'It would be less of a shock.'

'Not the way I shall word it. I shall say, "*Need your permission to get married. Deliriously happy. Love Julie.*"'

Ivy looked puzzled. 'I can't see what you're achieving.'

'If I send it from the post office Mrs Milne will have the news to all corners of the village in no time. And by the time the banns are called it will seem to everyone that they had known about the coming marriage for ages.'

'Very clever of you, I'm sure,' Ivy said, disapproval in her voice.

'Don't you see what I'm trying to do?' Julie pleaded. 'I'm trying to prevent whispering going on that it's obvious I have to be married. Although, of course, they will know eventually I suppose, when the baby is born.' Tears filled Julie's eyes.

Ivy touched her arm. 'Don't cry, love. They wouldn't know for sure, not if you went home before the baby was born and stayed for a few weeks afterwards. There are plenty of premature babies about and yours could be one.'

Julie smiled wryly. 'With my luck it will probably be a twelve pound bouncing boy.' Ivy laughed and the unhappy moment passed.

Julie then went to tell Angus of her decision. He was quietly pleased but warned her there were still hurdles ahead. She would have to get her parents' consent. She told him about the telegram she planned to send and said she was sure she would have a quick reply. She did have a quick reply. It was from her mother – saying she would be arriving at Echo Cove late that evening.

Ivy was full of a mingled pleasure and apprehension. It would be lovely to see Kitty again after all these years, but what was she going to say about the whole affair? Julie felt surprisingly calm, probably, she thought, because she was sure her mother would not oppose the marriage, not when she knew there would be no getting rid of the baby.

Julie and Ivy were on the platform that evening to meet Kitty and fortunately all tension among them was immediately relieved by the reunion of Kitty and Ivy. They laughed and cried together and reminisced about their 'upstairs and downstairs' days. Did Ivy remember this . . . did Kitty remember that . . .

It was not that Julie was forgotten. Her mother gave her a

hug and a kiss and told her gently they would have a talk later.

It was not until they were sat down to a cup of tea that Kitty said quietly, 'Well, now, Julie, what is all this about wanting to get married? Unfortunately your father is in Germany at the moment so was unable to come with me.'

Julie told the story about the unknown boy who had 'seduced' her and after telling it for the third time was beginning to believe it had actually happened.

Kitty, naturally, was shocked and like Ivy wanted the boy brought to justice. Julie explained why this was impossible and went on hastily to tell her mother about the offer of marriage from Angus.

'He loves me,' she said, 'and I'm more than fond of him. He's kind and warm-hearted, a lovely man, everyone likes Angus.'

Kitty was beginning to look a little bewildered. She said it was certainly more than generous of Angus to offer marriage but a great deal would have to be discussed before this could take place. For one thing, her father would have to be consulted. One mistake now and Julie's life could be ruined. As parents they must take the responsibility.

Julie protested at this, she alone was responsible for what had happened. She had been warned about drinking rough cider but had ignored it. Ivy had told her she was not to drink and insisted that she come home with Minna and her sister, but she had ignored that, too.

Kitty asked about Angus' prospects, whether he could afford to support not only a wife but a child. Julie was not to forget she had been brought up in good surroundings. Kitty did concede that they would, of course, buy them a house and then they could live in London.

To this Julie gave a determined no. Angus had a house already. They would live here; they both liked Echo Cove and they would work together. 'Don't forget, Mother,' she said, 'you came from a working-class background and you married Daddy who was wealthy, but *you* created your own business. Well, in my case the positions are reversed. Angus has the working-class background, but I must stress he wants no help from you. We shall work up a business together.'

Kitty was silent for a long time then she gave a nod. 'I think you might be able to, Julie, but your father will still have to be consulted. I did speak to him on the phone before I left home and shall get in touch with him in the morning again, that is, if I can speak to him in private.' Ivy told her that she could arrange this.

Julie then said, 'And once Daddy has given his consent then Angus and I can see the vicar and arrange for the banns to be called?'

Kitty's eyebrows went up. 'You're very sure that your father will give his consent, Julie. And are you sure it's right to be married in church?'

Julie, who had given this a great deal of thought said, 'Yes, I am. I want my baby to be christened in church without any stigma attached. He or she has committed no sin. You, Mother, and Aunt Helder were always insisting that Richard and I went to church and to Sunday School, with Aunt Helder saying if we listened carefully to the word of the Lord we would not go far wrong.' Julie paused. 'Well, I listened and although I agreed with some things there were many, as I grew up, with which I disagreed. I accept without question that God made us all, so therefore was responsible for what we feel and, I think that girls who get into trouble should not be accused of sinning, should not be begging for forgiveness, but understanding.'

Julie, aware of a silence, suddenly realised she was pleading her own cause, not that of other girls. To her mother's slightly questioning look she said fiercely, 'I only want what is best for my baby!'

'Yes, of course.' Kitty looked at Ivy and raised her shoulders with a helpless gesture. 'I'm beginning to think that my rebellious, restless daughter might make a good mother.'

'And a good wife,' Julie said quietly. 'Angus will never suffer for what – happened to me.'

By this time, Kitty was beginning to show signs of strain and Ivy suggested they go to bed and leave whatever else had to be discussed until the next day.

After breakfast the following morning Kitty made her phone call to Germany and came back with the news that Tyler had given his consent to the marriage. He also said that with the situation as it was he would agree to whatever arrangements were made.

A few minutes later, Angus arrived and to Julie's relief he and her mother took to one another right away and had a long talk. Afterwards, Julie was sure it was because of Angus' sensible approach in all matters that her mother accepted they would be married in Echo Cove.

'I can see it's for the best,' she said, 'but of course I'm naturally disappointed that Julie is not being married from home.'

Kitty had two full days with them before she had to go back for Tyler's return from Germany. In that time, Julie took her mother around the harbour and the village, introducing her to all those they met. People smiled knowingly and said they had heard rumours of a wedding and Julie beamed at them and told them they were right, while Kitty smiled and said how pleased she was about the marriage and how much she liked Angus, who was a delightful man.

After that, the wedding arrangements went ahead. Minna Daley, the girl Julie had become friendly with, was to be bridesmaid, and Richard had agreed to be best man. He and Kitty and Tyler were to arrive the evening before the wedding and were to stay with Mrs Pinner. Julie was glad they had agreed to this, rather than stay in a hotel.

Ivy's present to Angus and Julie was the wedding cake and

the reception. It was to be held in the tea-room with willing neighbours taking charge. Julie was to wear cornflower blue with a matching Juliet cap and Minna would be wearing pale pink. Angus had bought a dark grey suit for the occasion.

Tyler and Kitty would have lavished gifts on them but all Julie would accept was a carpet square for the living room. When it arrived it was one of the famous, thick-piled Durham carpets in brown with a soft blue pattern. Accompanying it were velvet curtains and cushions in the same blue. Julie was delighted with them.

A joint present from Richard and Jake was a full china tea-set and dinner-set in Wedgwood. Then other presents began to arrive from friends at home, some of them quite extravagant. But the ones she received from the local people gave her as much pleasure – china dishes, towels, pillow cases, tablecloths, dressing-table mats – which Ivy declared were all very *useful*, her glance going towards a cocktail shaker and crystal glasses that had come from her friend Caroline and family at home.

The evening before her parents were due to arrive, Julie went to the cottage to check last-minute arrangements with Angus. When she went into the living room she looked about her with a warm glow of pleasure. She said to Angus who had come out from the small kitchen, 'It looks lovely, doesn't it, so cosy.' She looked up at him and added softly, 'It's our very own home.'

'You've no regrets, Julie?'

'None whatsoever. We'll be happy, I know we will.'

'I've something for you.' Angus had given her an engagement ring which had belonged to his mother. It was an emerald set in a cluster of pearls. The ring had come from a long line of MacLarens. Julie loved it. She had not expected anything else and wondered what it could be when Angus brought a parcel from the sideboard.

When she undid the wrapper she felt suddenly tearful. A

marriage bowl. It had all the figures representing the ingredients to go into a marriage to make it a success. The glaze was the lovely blue of the carpet and curtains. 'I wonder what ingredient I shall add at the end of a year, Angus?' she asked quietly.

He tilted her face. Tears had welled up and rolled slowly down her cheeks. Angus wiped them away with a gentle forefinger then held her close. 'All I want is for you to be happy, Julie.'

A knock on the door and Ivy reminding them it was time to go to the station had them drawing apart. Julie drew a quick breath. 'And now, for meeting Papa!'

She had been dreading meeting her father, but he was gentle with her, calling her his little girl and for the first time Julie had a feeling of guilt, not because of what had happened with Fergus, but because she had lied to all those she loved.

Richard chatted away to Angus and Julie knew it was something that came naturally. It wasn't just the desire to be pleasant to his sister's future husband. He was interested in the echo in the harbour and in the fact that it was a fishing village. They were to have supper at Ivy's before going to Mrs Pinner's and when Richard and Tyler saw the murals Angus had done they were greatly impressed.

'You've missed your vocation, Angus,' Tyler said. 'You have work there that could be exhibited.'

Angus smiled his slow smile. 'I like it as a hobby, Mr van Neilson, but I enjoy what I am doing now. One feels very close to nature when working with clay, shaping it into forms. It's something that goes so far back, doesn't it?' Angus began to talk about the early potters and Tyler joined in. They had to be begged to sit down for their meal. Julie and her mother exchanged smiles. Angus had been accepted into the family.

Richard said afterwards, 'He's a great chap, your Angus. You must both come for a weekend sometime, Jake would enjoy having a talk with him. Jake sends his love, by the way.'

Julie had forced Fergus to the recesses of her mind, but the fact that Richard had not mentioned him brought him to the surface. Why had Richard not spoken of him? Had he seen him and told him about the wedding? Had Richard guessed there was something between them? Should she ask about Fergus? After all, if there had been nothing between them it would have been a natural thing to do. Julie had made up her mind to question him when her mother came up and asked to see the recent presents that had arrived.

And Julie was left in torment. Tomorrow she was marrying one man and pining for another. Angus would be making love to her and she would be thinking of a firelit cave and she and Fergus lying naked in one another's arms, sated after their wild love-making. It could never be the same with Angus. She was mad, mad, to go through with it.

By bedtime her torment was almost unbearable and she was all for calling the wedding off when Ivy said something that brought her back to sanity.

'Be loving towards your parents tomorrow, Julie. Although they've given in to you on everything you wanted to do, or didn't want to do, I know that deep down they're upset because you wouldn't be married at home. You're an only daughter and you know what parents are about a daughter's wedding, a mother especially.'

'I couldn't be married at home, not under the circumstances.'

'Why not? You're not showing anything. Could it be because Angus is not of your class?'

'No, of course not! It's just that, well, I wanted to be married here because we're going to live here. They'll be our people, our friends.'

Ivy held Julie's gaze steadily. 'If ever you do anything to hurt Angus I'll never forgive you. He deserves the best. Always remember that he's given your child his name and that Angus is proud to be a MacLaren.'

Some instinct told Julie then that Ivy knew about Fergus. Her heart began a slow pounding, and as she felt colour rising to her cheeks she got up and carried the empty cocoa mugs to the sink. Ivy came up behind her and put a hand on her shoulder. 'There are some things that need to be said, love. You'll be starting a new life tomorrow, so it's best that it should be started with a clean slate - between us. I'll always be there if you need me.'

Julie felt she was crying inside. She turned to face Ivy, and said in a low voice, 'I'll always need you.'

Ivy gave her a quick hug then sniffed. 'Well, come on, get off to bed. It's a big day for you tomorrow.'

A big day, Julie thought, as she lay in bed. She wondered how she would get through it. It should be a big day for her parents, but what were their thoughts? Everything they had suggested buying for her, apart from the carpet, she had refused, never realising how much pleasure she had denied them.

Her parents had offered them a London honeymoon, saying they could stay in the Mayfair house. Richard and Jake would move out temporarily while they were there, but she had refused that too, saying they had planned to honeymoon in a little place further along the coast called Bamburgh. People who came to the tea-room always said how beautiful, how peaceful it was.

Was this the reason she had turned down the offer of a London honeymoon - or was it because she might meet people she knew there, who would be introduced to Angus and . . .

No, no, she was not a snob, no one could ever call her that. She would not have agreed to marry him if that had been the case. But then, they were going to live here in Echo Cove, among a working-class community. How would she have felt, had they been living in her parents' community, amidst business colleagues and wealthy friends? Angus would have fitted into it, he was knowledgeable, could talk on many different subjects. He would be an interesting guest at any dinner party. Interesting to whom? The men who talked stocks and shares and take-over bids? Or the women who boasted of the titled people who had graced their own dinner tables?

Julie knew then she was fooling herself, knew she would not want to walk with Angus into the Waldorf, the Savoy or the Ritz to dine with friends.

And was ashamed.

# Chapter Nineteen

The following day, Julie went through all the motions of being a bride, walking down the aisle on her father's arm, returning Angus' smile at the altar, making her responses in a clear voice, happily acknowledging the good wishes from the congregation who overflowed the church. She laughed as she and Angus cut the cake while someone took a snap with a Brownie box camera, made a show of enjoying the wedding breakfast and afterwards, left for their honeymoon in a secondhand Morris car, for which Angus had paid five pounds.

During all this time, Julie felt as though she had been merely an onlooker. When the car began climbing the rise and Angus said, 'Well, Mrs MacLaren, it's all over!' she looked at him, bemused. Mrs MacLaren? It sounded strange.

'Did the organ play?' she asked.

Angus laughed. 'I think it was about the most enthusiastic rendering of *Here Comes the Bride* I've ever heard. Where were you?'

'I don't know. I think perhaps I was worrying unconsciously about things going wrong – if Richard would lose the ring or the vicar would forget to turn up, or if the starting handle of the car would be missing! I can only vaguely remember saying goodbye to the family and to Ivy. Was it Minna who caught my bouquet when I threw it?'

'Yes, it was, and she was pleased, she's a nice lass.' Angus patted Julie's hand. 'But you're to forget what might have gone wrong. We're going to relax and enjoy the next four or five days. I say four or five because if we get bored with doing nothing we can always come back home.'

Back home . . . with a husband . . . forever. Julie made an effort to fight off depression. 'You are the one who will probably get bored,' she said with a forced lightness. 'I'm just looking forward to having some peace and quiet.'

'You'll get no peace, I warn you, *Mrs* MacLaren!'

Julie tensed, then relaxed as he went on, 'We'll be doing a lot of walking, over the headland, on the beach and the dunes. It's a beautiful coastline.'

Julie liked Bamburgh on sight, but she did not find the peace she was seeking until the evening when they walked along the beach. The sand, silver by day, looked even more lovely in moonlight. So did the castle, which stood on a rise. Before the moon came up there had been a starkness against the skyline, now it had acquired a beauty of its own.

Angus told her about a young woman called Grace Darling who had taken out the lifeboat and rescued people shipwrecked during a terrible storm, while her father tended to the lighthouse. This was back in the eighteen hundreds, Angus said, but Grace Darling was still revered as a heroine here in Bamburgh.

'She deserves to be.' Julie shivered. 'I would have been terrified battling my way through a storm.'

'I don't think you would,' Angus said quietly. 'I think you would have attempted it had you known how many lives were involved. You have courage.' He paused then added softly, 'You looked so beautiful today, Julie. I'll try and make you happy.'

She felt deeply moved. 'You've made me happy, Angus, I don't want a fairy-tale world. I want to share my ideas with you and not only try to build up a business but a good life, too.' A faint smile touched her lips. 'You might have trouble with me. If I get restless, slap me down.'

'Oh, I'll do that, lassie, never you fear.' The gentleness of his voice belied the threat. He moved closer, seemed as though he was about to kiss her then drew back. And Julie was glad, not yet in a receptive mood for love-making. Perhaps in a while.

They had booked in at a small hotel and were the only guests for that evening. Although the proprietors fussed over them a little because they were newly-weds they did not intrude.

Julie, following the custom of a wedding night went upstairs first to their room, leaving Angus to go for a stroll. She stood at the window which overlooked the sea, longing to feel loving towards him, but it still eluded her. It had been a mistake to come to the sea, for as much as she tried to suppress the image of a firelit cave it kept rising to taunt her, and every time this happened she gave an unconscious pleasurable shiver.

Was she going to have to think of Fergus to pleasure Angus?

No, that would be cheating and she had cheated him enough over the baby. Determinedly, she began to undress. If needs be, she must be honest with him, beg him to be patient with her.

She was pulling her nightdress over her head when she suddenly remembered Angus shouting in the harbour, '*I love Julie*' and the echo returning the words. Not many men would have had the courage to do such a thing. Although she had not realised it at the time it had set the scene for the wedding, everyone knowing they were in love. Or – thinking so.

Julie finished pulling on her nightdress then she smoothed her hands over the soft fine satin, knowing then she was ready for Angus to love her and for her to give.

Julie, inexperienced, had not expected one man's love-making to be different from another's, but there was a difference, a big difference. Angus was gentle, afraid of hurting her. He was patient, wanting her to gain enjoyment. Julie never did reach a point of estasy or fulfilment as she had done with Fergus, but it did one good thing for her: it sent Fergus to the recesses of her mind again. This was a man who really cared what happened to her, and she vowed then she would never deny him and do all in her power to make him happy.

When Julie roused the next morning the sun was streaming in at the window and Angus had gone from the bed. She then became aware of the little maid standing there with a tray of tea. The maid said, 'Your husband said to tell you, Mrs MacLaren, that he had gone for a swim, but that he would not be long.'

'A swim!' Julie shuddered. 'The water must be icy cold.'

'The North Sea is always very cold, ma'am, but your husband is a big, strong man. I doubt whether he'll feel it.'

A dreamy look on the girl's face had Julie seeing Angus through different eyes. It came to her then that many village girls and women who came to the tea-room had cast him admiring glances. Well! A man desired. For the first time in her life Julie knew a small feeling of possessiveness.

When Angus returned he was glowing. He was wearing an old, navy-blue flannel dressing-gown she had never seen before. As he began to towel his hair she said, 'You must be frozen!'

'It was exhilarating. Well, perhaps a wee bit nippy.' He grinned and came towards her. 'Move over, you can warm me up.' He peeled off the dressing gown and Julie found herself staring at the well-muscled body. As he flung back the bedcover she began a weak protest.

'Angus, you can't – *we* can't – someone might come in.'

Then he was holding her, his mouth covering hers. Little shivers of excitement ran through her, but although she still did not experience what she had known with Fergus, she was content that she could enjoy her husband's love-making.

Afterwards, Julie lay drowsily listening to Angus making

plans for their few days. Being newfangled with the car he wanted to drive her along the coastline to see other places. 'But tomorrow onwards,' he said, 'we shall do some walking, explore Bamburgh and the area round about.' Julie, feeling in a lazy state was about to say couldn't they drive everywhere when she suddenly remembered Ivy talking about Angus' finances.

'He had a bit put by,' she said, 'but what with coming to Echo Cove, setting up the pottery, buying clay and paints and things, his suit for the wedding and then the car –'

Julie had interrupted to point out that the car would be an asset. Instead of having to pay someone to deliver his pottery pieces to various places he could transport them himself.

'But is it a paying proposition?' Ivy had asked. 'With petrol at a shilling a gallon I feel the car is an extravagance.'

Julie had smiled to herself at the time, at the thought of five pounds for a car being considered an extravagance, but now she could understand Ivy's reasoning. If Angus had a lean time in selling his pottery a few shillings for petrol would be precious.

She thought then how selfish she had been. Her father had wanted to give her some money to help them get on their feet and she had also refused that in her desire to be completely independent of them. All she had thought about was herself. She could have helped Angus now. Not that he would willingly have taken money from them, but if it had come from her – to help build up the business – how foolishly she had behaved. If she was to ask her father now for money it would seem like begging, like admitting she had made a mistake in marrying a poor man.

Well, she would have to work hard with him, making sure that the sales and turnover were big enough so they would not need to beg. Julie, suddenly aware of Angus watching her, turned her head. He began to chuckle.

'And what were *you* thinking about? Your lovely face had

so many changes of expression I couldn't work them out. One moment you showed dismay, then sadness, then determination – I *think*!'

'Oh, I was just weighing up the possibilities of building up the business.'

'In bed, by the side of your loving husband? My dear girl, you insult me!' He made to draw her to him but she laughed and flung back the bedcovers.

'I know we shall be travelling in the car but if I don't get up now I'll lack the strength to climb into it.'

He jumped out of bed and seizing her, swept her off her feet. 'Then I shall carry you into it,' he said, then groaned at the sound of the breakfast bell.

'And I'm not even washed, much less dressed,' Julie wailed. 'They'll know what we've been doing.'

'I'd be suprised if they didn't, as we *are* on our honeymoon.'

Later, when they were driving along the coast Julie said softly, 'I wouldn't have wanted to go anywhere else in the world for our honeymoon, Angus, it's beautiful.'

The day was glorious. There wasn't a cloud in the sky, and there was the clarity that is seen in open spaces. The sea lapped on shore, on rocks and the coastline was rugged, its stretches of dunes bristling with the spiky marram grass that resists all storms.

They visited tourist villages along the coast and browsed around gift shops comparing Angus' work with those pieces displayed, with Julie declaring that his painting was far superior to any of the pots and dishes they saw.

In the afternoon they walked over the dunes, shading their eyes against the brightness, and with not a soul to be seen for miles around they made love, with Julie determinedly ignoring the spiky grass prickling her skin. Afterwards, she laughed about it. Angus teased her and said, pleasure was always more enjoyable if you suffered a little for it. Which immediately brought Fergus springing to her mind again, the ecstasy and the pain. She jumped up. 'Come along, we have a lot more to see.'

During the next couple of days Julie discovered she had a passionately demanding husband, but she could not get him to stop worrying about hurting her. 'I want you to be rough with me,' she complained. 'I would enjoy it more.' But it was not in Angus' nature and she had to be satisfied that he was able to meet her own demanding needs. She had not realised that a woman could be so passionate.

They explored Bamburgh. Then suddenly the honeymoon was over and it helped that the weather had changed, with leaden skies and a restless sea, and then downpours on the journey back. Angus had put the cover on the car and fixed the side curtains, which although making it cosy, spoilt the view.

Ivy welcomed them with a glowing fire and a hotpot for lunch.

'It's been lovely,' Julie said, 'we must tell you all about it, but it's also lovely to get back.'

Ivy looked from one to the other. 'It's done you both good – you needed the rest, you've lost that strained look.'

Angus grinned and said, 'I don't know about the rest,' but Julie shook her head at him and added quickly, 'We've walked miles over headlands, beaches, the dunes, we've been everywhere. We've brought you a present. It's a pincushion – as you're always saying you can never find a pin when you want it. And there's some special toffee from a little shop in Seahouses.'

The pincushion was of red velvet edged with gold braid. Ivy declared it was so beautiful she would be afraid to use it. But she would enjoy the toffee.

They had finished the meal and were sitting chatting around the fire when Ivy said suddenly, 'Oh, I nearly forgot, there's some letters for you, quite a pile, I suppose they're from well-wishers. One of them's from Germany, who do you know there? I put them in the drawer.'

Julie felt as though all the colour was draining from her face. Germany? It could only be from Fergus. She left opening it until last. She read briefly from the other letters, saying who they were from and that presents from some of the people were on the way. She had hoped to avoid opening the one from Germany but realised that Ivy was waiting.

She scanned the page and making an effort to sound casual said it was from Fergus – Jake's brother – adding, 'He too is sending a present. It'll be exciting waiting for the post.'

There was no opportunity to read the letter properly until she and Angus went to the cottage and Angus left her for a while to go to the shed. Julie took the letter to the bedroom.

It was short, a letter anyone could have read:

*'Dear Julie, Jake wrote to tell me that you were getting married. I'm so pleased for you. I hope that you and your future husband will be very happy. I may have the pleasure of meeting him sometime when I return to England. I leave Germany in a week's time to go to the USA again. A present has been despatched to you, and I hope you will both like it. My very good wishes for the future. Yours sincerely, Fergus.'*

Yours sincerely . . . Julie felt herself trembling. How cold it sounded after what they had been to each other. Yet how else could he have signed it? If only she knew what he had been thinking when he wrote the letter. Did he regret that she was married? Why, oh why, oh why had he written just at this time? If only he had written months ago . . . but would it have made any difference?

The present came the next day, a tapestry, a forest scene. Thank heaven he had not sent a sea-scene. Even then it was bad enough having to hang it on the wall. Every time she looked at it she would be thinking about him. Why had he not chosen something else? But then, he could have sent a sheepskin rug, as a friend of her father's had done, and with it in her bedroom she would have been thinking about Fergus every time she stepped in and out of bed.

Angus, who admired craftwork, declared it must have taken someone many hours of laborious work to have handstitched the tapestry. Ivy sniffed and said it was a pity he hadn't sent something more useful like a set of pudding basins instead of something to get dirty on the wall.

At this Julie could not help but laugh. It relieved the tension building up in her and eased the ache of wanting Fergus.

After this, Julie settled down to being dedicated in helping Angus with the pottery, assisting Ivy with the tea-room and being a housewife. As trade increased in both pottery and tea-room, Angus worried over Julie. He complained that she was doing too much, she must think of the baby.

'I am,' she said. 'A lazy mother when carrying is no good for her child, I read it. I'm naturally energetic and he'll know it by now and sleep when I sleep.' Angus teased her then, told her she had the baby firmly fixed in her mind as being a boy, and he hoped she would not be disappointed. 'I won't,' she said.

When Julie felt the first movements of the baby she stood, awed by the wonder of it. It was bedtime and she was getting undressed. She waited, almost holding her breath, and when the movement came again she whispered urgently to Angus, 'Come here, quickly.'

'What is it?' he asked. 'Are you all right?' She took his hand and laid it on her stomach. The movement was more positive this time and she looked up at him, her eyes brimming with tears.

Angus said, 'Oh, Julie,' and his eyes were moist, 'how wonderful.'

She loved him then for sharing her joy, for accepting the baby as theirs. Angus made plans when they were in bed, insisting that Julie heed him. Ivy must have someone else to help in the tea-room. No, he was not forbidding Julie to lend a hand but she had to realise how fragile a creature an embryo was. If she was foolish and overworked she could lose the baby and then she would be heartbroken, so would he. She was to go to her parents' weeks before the baby was due and she was to stay as long as she wished. He would manage and so would Ivy. The busiest of the tea-room trade would be over by then.

Julie, knowing it was sensible, agreed, but she wished she could have stayed at Echo Cove. She wanted Angus to be there when the baby was born. He had a right to be, he was the only father the baby would know.

One good thing for Julie, as far as keeping the time of conception secret, was the fact that she hardly showed she was pregnant. Her slight plumpness was referred to by some of the villagers, with indulgent smiles, as 'married life agreeing with her'.

Ivy made her calves' foot jelly and beef tea and insisted she had the white of an egg whipped up with milk every morning, saying she had to keep her strength up. Julie stopped insisting that she had never felt in better health.

One day Ivy said, 'That's no lad you're carrying, it's a girl, I can tell by the shape!' To Julie's pettish protest that she wanted a boy Ivy told her she would have to take what she got and be thankful if the baby was all right.

With a lovely fine summer the tea-room was always busy and Angus' trade had trebled. Julie loved it when a charabanc load of people would arrive and all was chatter and laughter. But she also enjoyed the quiet times when she sat painting the dishes, the jugs, the cups and saucers. Often Angus would say, 'That's it, you've done enough,' and Julie had come to know that nothing she might say would make him let her put on one more stroke. When she told him he was getting bossy he would grin and say, 'As long as you accept who is boss that's fine with me.'

When Julie was seven months pregnant and looking as though she were only five months she had a letter from her mother asking her to come home soon, it would be foolish to travel any later. Ivy and Angus agreed with this but Julie was reluctant to leave. 'After all,' she said, 'the baby isn't expected until the end of December.' Ivy pointed out it could be earlier but on this Julie was as stubborn as Angus. She would leave in another two weeks and not before.

Ten days later after a letter had come from her father saying he was coming to collect her that weekend, Julie half-heartedly began packing a suitcase. She knew that Angus would be all right with Ivy looking after him, knew she would be seeing them both at Christmas, but it was the weeks in between. She would be bored at home. Here there was always something going on, people dropping in.

Julie sighed. Being bored was a small price to pay for what she had done. She went to the wardrobe and was sorting through her dresses when Angus called from downstairs, 'Julie – we have a visitor from London – guess who?'

She froze. It was not her father . . . Fergus? Her heart began a wild beating. Would he have the nerve to come here? Yes . . . yes, he would. She went out onto the landing and saw from the top of the stairs not Fergus, but Richard. For a second Julie knew a swift disappointment then she went hurrying down to him.

'Richard! What a lovely surprise.'

He held her at arms' length for a moment, declared she looked positively blooming then hugged her, rocking her to and fro, saying, 'Talk about a secretive family. I didn't know about this baby until a week ago.'

'Is Daddy still coming?' she asked. 'He was coming to pick me up this weekend.'

'I know, but I had a few days off and asked if I could come instead. Jake's with me, he's talking to Ivy, he'll be over in a few minutes.'

'Well, sit down,' Angus said. 'I'll soon have a cup of tea on the go. You said you had come by car, Richard.'

'Yes, Father lent me his Rolls – did you hear that, Julie?

He thought it would make it easier travelling for you. I left it hidden in a wood on the road further back.' Richard grinned at his sister. 'I remember how you didn't want anything ostentatious at the wedding.'

'No, and I still don't. A Rolls in our midst would certainly seem like proclaiming the family's wealth.'

Richard caught sight of the tapestry and went up to it. 'I say, I like this. Where did you get it?'

'Fergus sent it.' Julie wondered if there would ever come a time when she would be able to speak his name or think about him without her heart racing or tremors going through her body. 'It came from Germany but he said in his letter he was more or less on his way to America.'

'Yes, so Jake was saying. By the way, the arrangements for Christmas have been changed. We're going to hold it in the Mayfair house. And it fact, Sis dear, that is where I shall be taking you. Mother thought it would be a bit more lively for you. Klara is delighted, she'll be able to visit you.'

'Oh, that's lovely. I'm so pleased.'

Angus made the tea and as he began to pour it Jake arrived. After that the conversation was general and lively, with Richard and Jake announcing they were not going to leave until they had heard the echo in the harbour. Angus told them it would be no problem, the tide would be high in just over an hour.

When they had gone to the harbour Angus said, 'Well, Julie, it'll be better for you being in London, especially with two lively chaps to keep you company. It'll soon be Christmas and Ivy and I will be with you and then after that –'

'The baby will be born,' she said softly. 'Oh Angus, you must stay for the birth. He'll be *your* son.'

'Or daughter. You know something, I think I would like a girl.'

They had discussed names but nothing had been settled. Julie said now, 'What are we going to call this son or daughter? I think I would like it named after your parents.'

'What about your own parents, they would be hurt if you didn't –'

'I don't think so, but in any case you are my husband, Angus. What were your parents called?'

'My father was Robert, my mother Lyndsey, but I still think –'

'I like both names. If it's a boy he shall be Robert Tyler MacLaren, and if it's a girl she shall be Lyndsey Catherine MacLaren. No one could find fault with that, now could they? Anyway, it's all settled.'

Angus grinned. 'And who is being the boss now?'

She put her arms around his neck. 'Oh, Angus, I'm going to miss you terribly.'

'I'll miss you, lassie, but the time –'

'I know, I know, it will fly over.' She wept and he held her close and for the first time called her his *darling* girl. She smiled at him through her tears. 'And you're my man and I love you very much.'

On looking back over the drive to London Julie marvelled how she could have driven so many miles in a car and not felt the slightest bit tired at the end of it. She said to her mother who was waiting at the Mayfair house to greet her, 'I thoroughly enjoyed the ride and the picnics we had on the way. Ivy packed enough food to last a family for a week! She sends her love and says she's looking forward to being with you for Christmas. Angus, too. Oh, the house is lovely, Mother.'

'I thought you would like it. It's not as large as the one where I was in service when I was young, but it has a lovely big kitchen, and Mrs Parker is in her element.'

'Mrs Parker? I thought there was a Mrs Boswell?'

'Mrs Parker offered to come and be with you when she knew that the present housekeeper had to leave on account of ill-health.' Kitty smiled. 'You always were a favourite with her, she'll keep an eye on you but she won't fuss you, never fear. Come along and I'll show you your room. It's on the first floor.'

The room they entered overlooked a small back garden. The carpet was dark green, the satin quilted bedcover a deep peach colour, which was echoed in the shades on lamps and wall lights. Julie said, 'This is the master bedroom, isn't it?'

'Yes, it is, Julie. Your father and I wanted you to have it while you are here, and the small room adjoining can be used as a nursery. Oh, Julie,' Kitty gave her an impulsive hug, 'we're delighted we're going to be grandparents. Yes, we are, it wasn't easy at first, we couldn't get used to you being married, but now, well – it's a lovely feeling!'

Julie smiled. 'You don't look old enough to be a grandmother. No one will believe it.'

'I want them to, I'm thrilled. And Julie, you will let me buy the layette, won't you, *please*? It will give me so much pleasure.'

There was no need this time for her mother to plead with her to accept the gift. Julie said yes, of course, and Kitty's face lit up. They would have a lovely shopping morning once Julie had settled down.

Julie got a warm greeting from her father too when he arrived. She was to take things easy, ask for anything she needed. Had Richard behaved himself and driven carefully? Julie told him yes, marvellously.

Jake had said that his aunt Klara would love to come and see her and when she arrived the next day she beamed and said they must have a look round the shops so she could buy something for the 'little bundle' to come.

For two days Julie lived in a euphoria of being cosseted, of everyone being happy, full of life, and then suddenly she became aware of a change in Richard. While conversation was going on around him he would be withdrawn into a world of his own. After a while, Kitty asked him if he was all right. Was he sickening for something? He said no, he was fine, and took part in the conversation.

But one evening when Richard had taken Julie into the little library to find a book he thought she might like to read, he stood in the middle of a row, his finger on a book, lost once more in this other world. She began to feel uneasy. Fergus' name had not been mentioned since they were at Echo Cove. Did Richard know something about him, did he know that the baby was his? No, surely not. But supposing he did know? She moved closer to him.

'Richard, what's wrong? You keep going into a daydream.'

He let his hand fall to his side and stood looking at her. 'I wasn't aware of it. It's just that –' he turned to the shelf, 'I can't think where that book can be. It was here a few days ago.'

'*Richard*! What's wrong – tell me. Is it the baby, do you resent me being here?'

He eyed her in faint astonishment. 'No of course not, why should I? I do have something on my mind, but it's something I can't talk about. It's –' He gave a sigh of despair. 'Well, I may as well tell you, I suppose you'll get to know sooner or later. It's Violet . . .'

The cold shiver that went up and down Julie's spine at any mention of the name repeated itself. 'What about Violet?'

Richard pulled a book from the bookshelf, opened it at random, flicked through some pages then looked up. 'I've been meeting her recently.'

'Oh, no! How could you, Richard? You know she's a liar – think of that tale she told about the miniature.'

Richard thrust the book back on to the shelf. 'She had to get me interested. I don't blame her. You don't know her as I do. I find a great loneliness in her.'

'She's a *great* actress!'

'Look, Julie, sit down and let me tell you *her* story. We've only heard the parents' side of it.' When Julie declared she would prefer to hear her parents' version than that of Violet he became angry. 'There might be fewer criminals in the world if people had listened to their side of the story in the first place. A boy who picked up a halfpenny in the gutter was branded as a thief because he pocketed it. And the name thief stuck.' Julie said, all right, she would listen.

'Violet had a terrible life as a child, she was the slave of the family.'

'She was her father's blue-eyed little girl and couldn't do a thing wrong!'

'That's what your mother told you. Violet had to make her own way in the world. She married, thinking her husband had money, but all he left her when he died were debts and a pregnancy.

'She was desperate –' Richard's voice had softened. 'She wanted to keep the baby but it was impossible so she took it to the only place she knew it would find a good home. To the home of her sister Kitty and her husband.'

'And left it on the doorstep in the freezing cold to die,' Julie said harshly. 'I'm sorry, but I just can't believe a word that Violet says.'

'And what was she told?' Richard demanded. 'That the baby had been adopted by a couple who were emigrating to Australia, and what was that but all lies.'

'Richard, let me say something important.' Julie spoke more quietly. 'We might never get to know the full story but remember this, you could not have been more loved or more cared for than you've been by Mother and Father.'

'Because it suited them. Well, I am only going to say one more thing. I know that Violet is my natural mother. She's asked me to go and live abroad with her and I'm seriously thinking about it. And I'm warning you, if you tell the parents and they try and stop me, I shall – well – I don't know, but –'

Julie, in despair, covered her face with her hands and began to cry. Richard dropped to his knees, apologising for upsetting her.

'I had no right to go on at you, forgive me, I don't want to harm the baby in any way. But please, please, Julie, don't say anything to the parents. I'll wait – I'll wait until after the baby is born. Now dry your eyes, we don't want Mother to start probing to know what is wrong.'

Julie felt at that moment, it was a more desperate secret to keep than the one about Fergus' baby.

# Chapter Twenty

During the next few weeks, Julie was tempted many times to talk to Mrs Parker about Richard, to try and find out the truth, but then she decided against it. If Richard kept on seeing Violet he might eventually find out the kind of person she really was and lose his obsession with her. He never mentioned her and in fact, by his usual bright manner it could already be over.

The early weeks dragged by but once December was in Julie got caught up in the excitement of Christmas, the fact that Angus and Ivy would be coming and then the baby would be arriving. Klara was sure it was going to be a boy because Julie was carrying it 'all around'. Mrs Parker said every mother was different, it was impossible to tell by shape. All Julie wanted was for the baby to be born.

Angus wrote a weekly letter and so did Ivy. They both gave varying news of things happening; with Ivy it was mostly about the people who were asking about her. They all thought it was a shame she hadn't had the baby at home, but accepted it was right for a daughter to be with her mother to look after her. Angus wrote about his work and the orders coming in but always ending his letters with love and saying how much he missed her.

A nurse was engaged to come in right after Christmas, but had promised to be on call before then if needed. Julie said fervently she hoped it would not be necessary.

The doctor had pronounced that everything was all right

with Julie and she did feel very fit until a week before Christmas when she found she became easily exhausted and had developed a backache. Mrs Parker told her it was nature's way of telling her she needed to rest.

Ivy and Angus were to arrive on Christmas Eve. Julie felt she could hardly wait to see them. The house was decorated with holly and mistletoe and there was a huge Christmas tree in the hall, draped with tinsel and full of coloured shining baubles. Julie had done her shopping early and had her presents all packed. She had put them all under the Christmas tree about an hour before Ivy and Angus were due to arrive, and had straightened when she felt a gripping pain in her back. It lasted less than a minute, and taking it as all part of carrying a baby Julie said nothing, but when it came again ten minutes later she mentioned it to Mrs Parker. Mrs Parker looked at the clock and said they had better time the pains in case she was going into an early labour.

'Oh, no!' Julie wailed. 'Not when Angus and Ivy will be arriving soon.'

Mrs Parker remarked that babies arrived whether it was convenient or not and went upstairs to find Kitty, who was dressing. Kitty came down at once and telephoned both doctor and nurse. Both were out, but in each case Kitty was told messages would be given to them the moment they returned.

By this time, Mrs Parker had Julie in bed with her pains coming every two minutes. When Kitty came in with the news she said, 'Don't worry, Mrs Van Neilson, my mother was a midwife and I've helped bring plenty of babies into the world. This one is going to arrive before doctor or nurse can get here. I'll see to her if you get Mary to bring hot water up, then perhaps you can help me.'

Julie, who was lathered in perspiration and trying desperately not to shout out, bit her lower lip, drawing blood.

As the car containing Ivy and Angus and Tyler and Richard was on its way towards the house, Julie's baby was being delivered.

'It's a girl,' Mrs Parker announced and, lifting the child up by the ankles gave it a slap. Julie, watching the tiny scrap of humanity with a mixture of wonder and panic, released her breath when an indignant yelling filled the air. Julie and Kitty laughed and cried together. Then Julie said, 'Oh, Mrs Parker, *please* let me hold her.'

'When I've seen to you and she's cleaned up. I know your mother's dying to do just that.' Kitty took the baby lovingly and Mrs Parker went on, 'She's a little 'un, but she's got a good pair of lungs on her.'

Kitty said laughingly, 'She's you all over again, Julie, only you were not quite so tiny.'

The doctor arrived then and seemed surprised the baby had been delivered. He did not congratulate Mrs Parker, but unbent enough to smile and say after he had examined her, 'She's perfect, small but she will soon put on weight. A very demanding young lady. Nurse Freer telephoned to say she will be with you in about twenty minutes.'

At the door he turned. 'Oh, incidentally, your husband has arrived, Mrs MacLaren and he's biting his nails. I shall send him up, but he must stay only a few minutes, you must rest.'

The baby dropped off to sleep as Angus came tiptoeing in. Julie said, smiling, 'You've no need to be quiet, Angus, she's asleep. I think she exhausted herself screaming.'

'We heard her downstairs, it was the most beautiful sound I've ever heard. Oh, Julie, how are you?' He leant over and kissed her gently.

'I'm fine,' she whispered. 'Isn't she just beautiful? She's only five pounds six ounces but the doctor said she's perfect. Would you like to hold her?' Julie had not really expected he would but he held out his arms eagerly and handled the child as if he had been cuddling babies all his life.

'A perfect father,' Kitty said happily.

Ivy came in next with Tyler and Richard, but this was all too much for Julie, whose cheeks became flushed. The nurse, who had arrived, was younger than Julie had anticipated and seemed nice. She shooed the visitors out, saying that Mrs MacLaren must rest, then settled her patient in the bed, and within minutes Julie was asleep.

When she roused, Kitty and the nurse were sitting in the firelight talking quietly. She lay still, wanting to think over the reactions of her 'family' on seeing the baby. The eyes of all had been misted with tears, but with Richard she had seen pain and she wondered if he was thinking of his own birth and wondering where it had taken place.

Ivy had brought six tiny matinée jackets which she had knitted herself and had looked inordinately pleased when Kitty praised her for catering for the tiny baby.

Julie soon became impatient at having to stay in bed. She said later to Ivy, 'I wonder when I'll be allowed to travel? It would be lovely if I could go back with you and Angus.'

'Well, you can't, so stop grumbling. You should be thankful the baby is all right.' Ivy grinned suddenly. 'And doubly thankful she's small enough to be taken for being premature.'

'She won't be,' Julie declared, 'if she keeps on feeding the way she does.'

Ivy looked into the cot by the bed and smiled indulgently. 'She's a survivor, this one, adventurous I bet and restless like her mother.'

'And you'll discipline her, like you did me,' Julie teased.

'I will if I get half a chance. It's a good thing you won't be living here, your father is as daft as Angus is over her. She would be ruined. And when you do get home you'll have to watch Angus or he'll be picking her up the moment she makes as much as a hiccup, and you too, probably.'

Julie denied this. She might not know many things but she did know it was necessary to discipline children from the day they were born. To this Ivy said, 'You'll do, you'll manage.'

When the time came for Angus and Ivy to return to Echo Cove Julie clung to them, declaring tearfully she wanted to go with them. Angus soothed her. Her parents would be upset if they could hear her, for this was her home, too. It wouldn't be long before she would be back with them and in the meantime, she should take advantage of the rest. He would write and so would Ivy.

When Julie did return to Echo Cove she soon realised it was a very different thing living in luxurious surroundings, having her every want attended to and with a nurse to look after the baby, from coping in a two-roomed house, with the baby screaming for attention, nappies to be washed and all the other jobs that needed to be done.

Ivy had insisted on them both coming for their midday meal until Julie got her strength back. But even then Julie often arrived during the morning feeling harassed.

'If only Lyndsey wouldn't scream so much,' she said one day. 'She's taken to waking all hours of the night and I'm tempted to feed her, but the doctor said –'

'Never you mind what the doctor said. If she wants food give it to her. She's put on weight but very little. I believe in discipline but not starving a baby. All this newfangled stuff about being fed at set times. Our mothers never fed their babies at set times. They got to recognise when it was a hunger cry and when the baby was just yelling for attention. And so will you, so take my advice.'

Julie did and at last there was some peace in the house and her frayed nerves began to heal. It was not that she minded looking after the baby, she would have done anything for her, but deep down she knew she was hankering to get down to working in the shed again. Her fingers were itching to hold a paintbrush. She tried to work out a plan. She decided that after she had put Lyndsey in her pram for her afternoon nap she would take her to the shed and paint for an hour.

Angus was not too pleased about this, not because he was against the actual painting, but because he felt that Julie was not ready to do any extra work. 'You have to feel your way back into the daily grind,' he said, teasing her. 'You had very little exercise when you were at home. Take Lyndsey for a walk in her pram and increase the distance you do every day.' Julie was about to retort that she did not have time for long walks and stopped herself in time. She ended up by begging Angus to let her work for a while and then see how she got on. He gave in to this.

It was sheer joy to Julie at first handling the paints, doing designs, and she was surprised when after only twenty minutes her hand became shaky. Not wanting Angus to know this she sat back for a while, saying she had an idea for a design and wanted to work it out. By doing this at intervals she was able to complete an hour, and at the end of it was able to discuss a new design.

'How about a children's breakfast bowl with birds on it?' she said. 'Not only birds such as robins and sparrows but humming birds, parrots, birds of paradise. The children would not only be intrigued by them but be educated at the same time.'

Angus said he liked it, they would talk some more about it later. During the next few days Julie was not only able to work through the whole hour without a rest but had come up with more ideas. They would have zoo animals on bowls – giraffes, reindeer, polar bear, zebras. Angus grinned and asked her if she was thinking of mass producing and Julie, feeling happy and fit asked, 'Why not?'

The following afternoon she pushed the pram towards the shed thinking, why not mass production? They could enlarge the shed, employ people. Perhaps she would relax her own rigid rules about being independent and borrow some money from her parents. They would be only too delighted to help.

The baby, who appeared to be asleep began to whimper and Julie said, 'Now you can stop that, Lyndsey MacLaren, I have work to do.' The next moment she felt a lump come into her throat. She brought the pram to a halt and looked at her daughter. Although like a little doll she was frowning in her sleep, as though she had all the problems of the world on her mind. One hand lay on her cheek, the tiny spread fingers reminding Julie of daisy petals. Because Lyndsey was so small and fragile-looking women oohed and aahed over her, the 'sweet little mite'. Was she gaining weight?

Julie tucked the tiny hand gently under the cover and whispered, 'Sorry I scolded you, darling. I love you, I won't neglect you because I want to work.'

She left baby and pram outside the shed. Angus had made a wooden screen which would protect the baby from any strong winds but yet give her a chance of being out in the fresh air.

When Julie went into the shed Angus was absorbed in placing minute Egyptian figures in clay onto a tall, narrow-necked vase. The moulds for the figures, perfect in every detail of dress and features, had taken Angus many hours to make, but it was a subject close to his heart. He had studied Egyptian hieroglyphics and had once been asked to talk on the subject in a museum. Julie was beginning to learn a lot of things about her husband.

She found herself comparing Fergus' slender hands to the square, blunt-tipped fingered ones of her husband and knew that hands need not be slender and artistic-looking to create beautiful things.

She no longer suppressed thoughts of Fergus. Every now and again she would let his image surface, but she had sense to know it was unwise to dwell on him and he was soon relegated to the inner regions of her mind once more.

That evening when Lyndsey was settled in her cot and

Angus was at home sketching, Julie said she would walk across and see Ivy. It was a clear cold night, and on the air came the muted shouts of the trawler men who had just landed their catches. Elsewhere was a stillness that seeped into Julie. She thought of all that had happened since she had first come to live with Tom and Ivy, meeting new people, some of them characters, like Billy Barker and Peg. Peg had written a week ago saying, *'Guess what? Me and Alfred are getting married. No, we don't have to. I must be mad. Sometimes I can't stand the sight of him and yet when we fall out I can't wait to make it up. Can you understand it? I can't.'*

Julie thought she could understand it. Fergus had let her down badly, but he would always have a close place in her heart. Life was strange.

There was a light on upstairs in Ivy's house, as well as the kitchen and when Julie went in Ivy came downstairs, a large envelope in her hand. 'Hello, love,' she said, 'I was just sorting through some papers. You keep stuff that'll never see the light of day, so why hoard it?'

Julie knew by the look in Ivy's eyes the papers had to do with Tom. 'If they are of no use,' she said, 'throw them away, but if you feel there might come a time when you might regret destroying them, then don't.'

Ivy laid the envelope on the table and said she would think about it. She made tea, poured it, then passed a mug to Julie. 'Actually, I'm thinking of going back to Stoke to live.'

Julie eyed her in dismay. 'Ivy, you can't! I thought you had settled here.'

'So did I. I enjoy having the tea-room, meeting the people, but Tom isn't here with me, Julie, he's still at Stoke.'

'You're wrong, Ivy. Tom's spirit is with you wherever you are and surely you remember how much he was looking forward to coming here.'

Ivy nodded slowly. 'Yes, I know, perhaps you're right, I don't know. It was fine when we were busy but now the days seem so long. At Stoke we were always on the go, there were always people coming into the shop to chat to. I'll tell you this, if it wasn't for you and Angus being here I would pack up tomorrow.' Ivy looked at her hopefully. 'I don't suppose you two would like to go back? You were talking a while ago about trying to build up the business.'

'Yes, but we meant at Echo Cove. We like it here and as Lyndsey grows up she'll be able to play on the beach, build sandcastles.' Julie reached over and laid a hand over Ivy's. 'I do hope you'll stay, Ivy, we would miss you dreadfully. This slack time will soon get over.'

Ivy sighed. 'I suppose so, I'll think about it.'

When Julie reported this conversation to Angus she was surprised when he said that he had been contemplating such a move. She was angry and accused him of plotting behind her back. This Angus strenuously denied. He had not discussed anything with Ivy, he had simply thought, as Julie herself had done, that there was scope for expansion.

'I agree,' she exclaimed, 'but never at any time did you mention moving back to Stoke.'

To this Angus suggested it might be worth discussing, but Julie refused, sure that the whole thing had been talked over with Ivy first. She went to bed in a huff, and made a pretence of sleep when Angus came up. 'All right, Julie,' he said. 'We'll have no silent villa antics in this house. Now just sit up and hear what I have to say.' When she made no move he flung back the bedclothes and threw her her dressing-gown. 'You'd better put that on because I can see this is going to take some time. At once, do you hear?'

Although still annoyed Julie found herself responding to the mastery in his voice and in fact, she had a small feeling of sensuous excitement. She sat up and donned the dressing-gown then said, 'So, say what you have to and let me get back to sleep. And you had better keep your voice down or you'll have Lyndsey awake!'

'In the first place I haven't even started to raise my voice and in the second place Lyndsey, these nights, would sleep through an earthquake. Now then, when I say something it's the truth! I detest liars. If Ivy and I had had any conversation about going back to Stoke you would have known about it. Going back to Stoke was no more than an idea in my mind. I would never have mentioned it had you not told me about Ivy. We're not in a position to make a move, we need money before that could be done and it would be *our* money, money we had saved.'

Julie felt a certain guilt because she had been contemplating borrowing from her parents, and she lashed back at him. 'I'm glad you mentioned it would be money that *we* had saved. I've done my share in trying to earn it!'

'And haven't I just acknowledged that fact? Anyway, that's it. Apart from one more thing. I don't want a long face or any sulking in the morning.'

Julie shot up in the bed. 'Well, of all the nerve! Who do you think you are to give me orders? If I feel like pulling a long face I'll pull it, and that's that!'

'You won't, Julie, I won't have it. I've seen too many marriages ruined because husband and wife refuse to communicate. I've had my say and you've had yours, now let's forget it.' He began to undress.

One part of Julie wanted to give in but the other part was shot through with resentment. She began to shiver and she slid down into the bed, still wearing the dressing-gown. When Angus got into bed beside her minus his pyjamas, and tried to draw her to him she pushed him away.

'Oh no, don't think you're going to win me over with sex!'

'Then how about being won over with love?' he said softly.

When she lay unresisting he leaned over, pulled the collar of her dressing-gown away from the back of her neck and blew warm air gently down her spine. This always had the effect of sending delicious tremors through her body, but determined that Angus should know she would not be won over by caresses she forced herself to lie rigid.

'So,' he said, 'you want to be stubborn. Well, we'll soon cure that.' He tried to get the dressing-gown off her but she clung to it. The bed heaved, the bedclothes got into a tangle and Julie, thoroughly enjoying the romp, began to giggle. Angus tossed back the covers and pulled her out of bed. He managed to get the dressing-gown off, and her nightie, then after giving her a sharp slap on the buttocks he picked her up, dropped her back on the bed, and got in beside her.

Julie, with every pulse now throbbing, waited with an urgent excited anticipation for the onslaught from Angus, but instead found him lying passive beside her. She leaned up on her elbow and exclaimed, 'Angus MacLaren, don't tell me you're going to sleep on me after all this build-up! Do you realise the state I'm in?'

He stifled a yawn. 'Sorry, I'm tired, and I've got a headache, it's all this hard work.' Hearing the laughter in his voice she pummelled his chest.

'You wretch! This is no time for joking. I'll give you a cure for headaches!' She teased him with fingers, her lips, gave him gentle bites on his ear lobes, his throat; trailed her fingers down the length of his body until she touched his most sensitive part, then when he immediately responded she laughed and said, 'Now *you* can take over.'

She revelled in the feel of his strong, well-muscled body pressing against hers, gasped when *his* teasing fingers brought her whole being to the throbbing, sweetly agonising, need of fulfilment, but although his need was as great as hers, when he penetrated her she still did not experience the joy she had known with Fergus.

*Why, why?* As she lay cradled against Angus' shoulder she knew a feeling of despair. Were there two kinds of love? Or was it that first love would always seem the best?

She could see again the firelit cave, hear the roar of the sea, its thunder as it crashed against the rocks. The setting was as old as time itself and the wildness of their love-making primitive. Would there come a day when the image would fade into nothingness?

Angus was breathing gently in sleep. Julie put her lips to his cheek, vowing she would do her very best to erase that image from her mind.

# Chapter Twenty-One

The days and the weeks went by and with Ivy and Mrs Pinner taking care of Lyndsey for a good part of the day, Julie could turn out more work. She was throwing pots now regularly, their bread and butter lines, leaving Angus free to make the more expensive vases and bowls, which were finding a ready sale at art shops; owners were coming to see Angus with their orders.

Although Julie enjoyed the work she felt guilty at times, knowing she was doing exactly as her mother had done, becoming obsessed with it and leaving her child in the care of other people. There was also something else that worried her. It was Angus saying on the night that she thought of as their 'romp night' that he detested liars. What if he ever found out that Lyndsey was Fergus' child? He would not reject the baby knowing she could not be held responsible, but what if he rejected her? The thought was unbearable. She loved him, even though it was in a different way from what she felt for Fergus.

Julie put this last worry behind her. As Ivy would say, it was no use worrying about what might never happen.

Two months later, when Julie and Angus were selling everything they could make and Ivy was beginning to get bookings for coach parties, she had her third and much more devastating worry. She was pregnant again.

She wanted to rail at Angus for being so careless but it was impossible because he was so upset. 'I can't understand it,

Julie, I've never relaxed taking precautions, you know that. There must have been a fault in the sheath. Oh, Julie love, I'm so sorry, you not only have Lyndsey to look after but the house and –'

'It's all right, Angus, it's not the end of the world. I did want us to have another baby but well, I thought perhaps in a year or so. It's the business. I shall be able to work for a while but then Ivy will be getting busy for Easter and won't be able to look after Lyndsey. Can we afford to employ someone to help you?'

Angus said he would see about it and left it at that.

A few minutes later Ivy called. She was going to the shops and would take Lyndsey along in her pram. The baby was still small but she was filling out and was a lively child, hands ever reaching to catch a sunbeam or grab a finger or a brooch.

Ivy said to Julie, 'And what's up with you this morning? You look as if the butter had gone rancid on you.'

Julie gave a wry smile. 'Worse that that, or better, whichever way you look at it. I'm pregnant again.'

'Oh, good Lord, I thought you would have waited.'

'Your good Lord decreed otherwise.'

'Oh, like that, was it? Well, there's nothing you can do about it so you'll just have to grin and bear it.'

'I do want Angus' baby, Ivy, but it's just that it's come at an awkward time.'

'How many come at the right time? Come on, get the baby's hat and coat on, I'll have to go, we'll have a talk this afternoon.'

The baby was on the settee, feet pushing against a cushion, hands twisting and turning. She gurgled when Julie picked her up and cuddled her. 'Now you be a good girl for your Auntie Ivy, do you hear? No making eyes at the little boys in the village.'

'It won't be long before she'll be doing just that,' Ivy said, the note of sadness in her voice that always tugged at Julie's heart. 'She'll be crawling soon, then toddling and before you know where you are she'll be at school and –'

'Heavens!' Julie exclaimed. 'You are having her off my hands before she's even had her first birthday.'

'Yes, that's me, pushing the days, the weeks, the years ahead and for what?'

Julie, determined not to let Ivy get into a depressed state said, 'Ivy, we'll get a bottle of gin and drown our sorrows in drink this afternoon, how about it?'

Ivy grinned then. 'Chance would be a fine thing.' She held out her arms for the baby. 'Come on then, little charmer, let's get going.'

Julie watched Ivy pushing the pram over the field, straightbacked, walking in a determined way as though she were heading for the harbour to walk straight into the sea with her charge. Poor Ivy. Would she ever get over Tom's death?

Angus found a man called Walter Jennings to come and help him. Walter had once worked in the potteries but when his wife died he came to live at Echo Cove with his daughter and her husband. They were all right, he said, kind enough to him, but he needed to be out from under her feet during the day and was glad to have a job to do.

Walter turned out to be an excellent worker and more important, he was not worried how many hours he worked. 'It's a treat for me to be working with clay again,' he said.

'And he's a treasure for us,' Angus told Julie.

Julie had no morning sickness with this pregnancy and prayed that the child would be a boy, for Angus' sake.

She needed to paint, and knowing it would be impossible to work in the shed with the two men, asked Angus to bring her some work to do at home. Although Ivy was getting increasingly busy as it neared Easter there were days when she, or Mrs Pinner, would take Lyndsey for a few hours. On these days Julie worked joyously, making the most of her feeling of freedom. Not that Lyndsey was normally fractious, but Julie was always conscious of her being there and just had to give her some attention. If the baby had one of her screaming sessions and Julie knew it was just to get attention, she would scold the child, then be ashamed and make up for it afterwards with kisses and cuddles.

Letters came regularly from home, mostly from her mother, but her father wrote an occasional note and Richard often put a longish letter in with her mother's. Odd times she would get a separate letter from him and then she would feel she was getting a bonus. He would tell her all that he and Jake had been doing, all about London life, and what this Cockney or that one had said in the pub that they both still visited. Only once did Richard mention Fergus and then it was to say he was coming home to take Jake to Italy for two weeks. Richard added that Fergus had asked him to go too, but it was impossible as he had other plans. Richard did not say what the other plans were, and the fact that he had omitted to tell her had Julie a little worried. He had never mentioned Violet in any of his letters, but supposing he was planning to go abroad and live with her, as he had once told her he would?

Julie wished he had not sworn her to secrecy over Violet and then she could have confided her worries to her mother. But perhaps she was worrying too much. It was some months now since he had talked about going away with Violet. The whole thing could have fizzled out.

Julie had not told her parents yet about the baby, feeling that her mother would condemn Angus for the pregnancy, but knew they would have to be told sooner or later.

It was the week before Easter when Julie had a letter from her father. It was short: '*Dear Julie, I have some unhappy news for you. Richard has left home, gone away with Violet, abroad somewhere. Your mother is devastated, made herself ill. Richard, I feel sure will write and tell you. If he does and gives his address, would you please let us know. Not that we would try and force him to come back home, but only so we know where he is and to know that he's well. I'm sorry to have to be the bearer of such news. Write a few lines to your mother, she will welcome contact with you, we do miss you so. Your loving father.'*

When Julie first read the letter she felt she wanted to rush home and comfort her mother, but then she thought no, I have responsibilities here – a husband, baby and a pregnancy to cope with. If they had been honest with Richard about his birth this might not have happened.

No sooner had Julie thought this than slow colour crept into her face. How dare she talk about honesty? She had told everyone a flagrant lie about Lyndsey's conception. She had kept telling herself it was for the baby's sake, but it was also to protect Fergus. Had her mother kept the secret of Richard's birth to protect him *and* perhaps, his father?

Julie folded the letter and put it on the mantlepiece. She would show it to Angus when he came in. In the meantime she would forget it. She had enough to worry about.

Forget it? The problem nagged at her. Was she to keep her secret for years as her parents had done, and then in future years it would come out and cause terrible heartache, end up in Lyndsey rejecting her, wanting to find her real father? Oh, God. Why had she not been honest in the first place? Should she confess to Angus now? If she left it this guilt would be with her always, taunting her. If her father were actually Richard's father and Violet his mother her own mother had forgiven him. They were very close, deeply in love.

But Angus had rigid principles about certain things. He detested liars. This would not make for easy forgiveness. No, it would be impossible to tell Angus now. Perhaps when the baby was born she would try and explain how she had wanted to protect Lyndsey. With a child of his own he might have more understanding.

When Julie gave Angus the letter to read he said, after scanning it, 'Well, Richard is not a child. If that is what he wants to do who can stop him?' He laid the letter down and picked up his knife and fork to start on his meal. Julie stared at him.

'Is that all you are going to say? My brother has gone off with a woman who claims she is his mother, but he doesn't really have any proof.'

'Richard obviously has some reason for accepting her as his mother. There's nothing we can do about it, Julie, nor can your parents. They can't drag him back home. He's a grown man.'

The following day there was a letter from Richard. It was postmarked London but there was no address heading the letter. He said that no doubt Julie had heard from their parents about his leaving home, and added he had no regrets. Violet needed him: she was such a gentle person and had been so lonely and making herself ill with longing for him to be with her. He hoped by being with her he could give her the happiness she had missed in her life.

At this point Julie flung the letter down, saying to Angus, 'I feel I can't bear to read any more. I can't believe that Richard who *is* intelligent, could be so taken in by such a woman.'

Julie repeated what she had read so far and Angus said gently, 'You only know about Violet what you've been told, Julie. You don't really know her.'

'But I do, Angus – oh, yes I do! I met her in Rome, remember. Richard speaks of her as being gentle. He's obviously never seen the vicious, sneering side of her. Violet was determined to get Richard away to spite Mother, and she's achieved it.'

Julie picked up the letter and read the rest of it . . . '*Try and understand how I feel, Julie. I love you, and I have a certain affection for the people who brought me up as their own son, but Tyler and Kitty have never needed me as my own mother does. I'll try and keep in touch with you. My kindest regards to Angus, and much love to you and dear little Lyndsey.*' It was signed simply '*Richard*'.

Julie laid the letter down this time and said to Angus with a cry of anguish, 'He calls our parents "the people who brought him up". Angus, how could he? They were loving parents, he had everything – education, caring – yes, I know they were both busy people with their work, but we never did lack for love.' She paused and shook her head. 'Violet was talked about as keeping one of the wealthiest brothels in Paris!'

'A whore could still have a deep love for a child she had to give away because of being unable to provide for it,' Angus said quietly. 'Don't judge her too harshly until you know all the facts.'

'Will we ever?' Julie said on a sigh. 'I doubt it. I feel so terribly sorry for my parents. Perhaps it might help a little if I tell Mother about this coming grandchild.'

Julie wrote that day and had a letter from her mother by return saying how delighted they were to hear about the baby. She said they were becoming reconciled to Richard having left their London home and they could only pray he would find the happiness he was seeking. The rest of the letter was about business and the hope that Julie would come to them again when she neared her time for the baby to be born.

Julie had already made up her mind she would have the baby at Echo Cove; she was not going to leave Angus on his own again.

She was fit all the time she carried the baby but she worried because there was very little movement. Ivy said, 'This is a lazy one. I bet it will be a boy, and he'll be as good as gold. My mother used to say that boys were much easier to manage than girls, and she should know, she had five of each!'

On a blustery day at the end of November, after a six-hour labour, Julie was delivered of a son, a sturdy golden-haired child, whom the midwife declared was a 'regular Daniel'. Julie, who had decided to call a son Robert, now thought she would like the name Daniel, if Angus was willing.

Angus, who was only too pleased that mother and son were all right, was more than agreeable. 'You're a clever girrl,' he said softly. 'After you've had a sleep I'll bring Lyndsey in to see her brother, get her used to the idea that she's no longer queen of the household.' Angus smiled fondly as he said it. He adored Lyndsey, who was now toddling all over the place, and at such an amazing pace she had to be constantly watched if she was out of her playpen.

When Angus knew that Julie was pregnant again he had asked the landlord's permission to have another room built on the cottage, at his own expense. The man had agreed at once and now the room was finished. It had been Julie's idea in the first place, thinking it could be used as a combined playroom for the children and a place where she could work. She had found a girl who was willing to take the children out for walks, and help generally, but after news of Richard leaving home she wanted to have the children close to her. Yet it was essential that she had scope for her ideas.

Lyndsey took to her brother more readily than Julie and Angus had anticipated. Both had thought she would be jealous, but instead she chuckled when he was being bathed, and helped by handing Julie a flannel or a towel. When he was asleep in his cot she would watch him with the odd little frown she had when she was absorbed in something. The first word she spoke was not 'Mummy' or 'Daddy' but 'Daniel', and she would shout the name, as though relishing it. She had an infectious chuckle that made people laugh when they heard it.

Kitty, who had intended coming to be with Julie for the birth of Daniel had caught a chill a week before, which had developed into pneumonia, and it was not until Daniel was four months old that Tyler would allow her to travel. He came with her for a few weeks' visit to Echo Cove.

Julie was shocked at the change in her mother. She was

painfully thin and all her sparkle had gone. But she was greatly taken with the children and seemed especially drawn to Daniel, who was a placid child.

'He's lovely,' she said. 'What a handsome boy he's going to be.' She praised Lyndsey too, an adorable child, so affectionate.

Lyndsey, who was affectionate towards most people, seemed to have a special affinity with Tyler and he with her. She would follow him around, or clamber up onto his lap. Ivy said one day, laughing, 'Well, he was the one to bring her the big doll, wasn't he?'

Julie had a feeling this was not the reason. It was as though the child sensed he needed someone to love. Kitty was the one who got all the sympathy over Richard but Julie noticed that whenever her father talked about him there was pain in his voice.

Tyler had hired a private detective to try and trace Richard and Violet and he had found them, but there never was a settled address, since they were constantly on the move, travelling Europe. An elderly man travelled with them, ostensibly the husband of Violet, but according to the detective they were not married.

One evening when Julie found herself alone with her father she said, 'Daddy, I need to know something and I want the truth. I'm a married woman now and feel I'm old enough to know. Is Violet Richard's mother and are you –'

Tyler looked up. 'I'm not Richard's father, and that is the truth, Julie. I don't know if Violet is his mother, but the story of Richard being found on the doorstep in a basket is true. I regret now not having told Richard the story of his adoption at an early age. Kitty begged me not to, she loved him so much and felt like his own mother, just as I felt he was my own son. I worry about Kitty, how do you think she is looking, Julie?'

There was a pleading in his voice for reassurance and she was able to give it. 'I was shocked when she first arrived at the change in her, but I do feel she's much better now, with the sea air and the different company. Why don't you let her stay a while longer, Father? She could sleep at Ivy's and they could chat away about the old days to their hearts' content.'

'I would, if she's willing to stay,' he said eagerly. 'Anything to take that awful look of sorrow from her face. You suggest it and I shall back you up.'

Although Kitty was reluctant at first she agreed eventually, saying she would love to spend some time with the children.

It worked perfectly. Kitty not only took the children for walks but helped Ivy with the tea-room and was in her element. It was a radiant Kitty who eventually returned to Crescent House, with the promise she would persuade Tyler to come with her and spend a summer holiday in Echo Cove.

Julie missed her, not only for taking the children off her hands but for the first time she was really understanding her mother, her need to work. 'You are just like me in that respect, Julie. I didn't realise until I was older what a restless spirit I have. I've been fortunate that your father eventually came to accept that. Angus has yet to be coaxed that you have this need to be working at something other than housework and looking after children all the time. But he is such an understanding and loving man and I think he will in time come to accept it.'

Julie had never had words with Angus over her painting but he had tried to persuade her many times that she must not neglect the children. These were their formative years and were important.

Angus was marvellous with them. He had great patience, yet could stop one of Lyndsey's sudden tantrums simply by saying quietly but firmly, 'That's enough, Lyndsey.'

As the children grew older they loved going to the harbour and then on to the sandy cove where the caves were. Although Julie never went into the caves she would often sit and daydream for a while of the visit there with Fergus. At times it seemed as though the incident had never happened and at others Fergus would be so vivid to her she would feel an ache of longing to see him again.

Odd times, she would get a letter from Jake and always he would say how he still missed Richard, but only once had he mentioned Fergus and that was to say he saw him so rarely he had forgotten what he looked like! Fergus the mystery man. Julie wondered if she ever crossed his mind. Probably not.

When Lyndsey was three years old and Daniel two, Julie had the worst feeling of restlessness she had ever experienced. She felt she could have packed up and run away. Instead, she dressed the children and took them to see Ivy. Lyndsey went running ahead, skipping and jumping, with Daniel trotting behind her, laughing happily thinking it was a game.

By the time Julie went into the kitchen Lyndsey was begging Ivy to take them to the beach to make sandcastles. 'Well, and I might at that,' she said. To Julie she added, 'How about it? I have no bookings and Mary will stay in case of anyone dropping in.'

Although the cove was the last place Julie wanted to be, with its memories, she agreed. She could talk to Ivy there as well as anywhere else and the children would at least be kept absorbed.

It was the end of the season, a lovely mild day in October, with not a cloud in the sky and the sea with barely a ripple. They called at the cottage to collect buckets and spades and Daniel's pram and set off, with Lyndsey insisting on pushing the pram. Ivy said, 'She's skinny, but she's wiry.'

'Yes she is. She could do with a bit of Daniel's sturdiness.'

'Oh, I don't know, not on a girl. You have two lovely kids, you're lucky, Julie.'

Julie agreed, but it made her feel no less restless. Lyndsey's hair, which had been so dark at birth, was now a rich chestnut colour and curled at the ends. Daniel, golden-haired at birth, was turning darker; his was much finer hair.

They went to the harbour first to let the children see the boats and chatted to the old men on the seats. They were a great favourite with the old fishermen, with Lyndsey calling everyone Grandpa and Daniel trying to copy her but only managing to say Pa.

They then went along the path to the cove, with Julie pushing the empty pram as the children, excited, ran ahead.

Ivy said to Julie, 'You're quiet, what's on your mind?'

'I don't quite know, Ivy, I only know I'm appallingly restless. Perhaps it's the future I'm unconsciously thinking about. I don't feel we're getting anywhere.'

'Not getting anywhere? What're you talking about? You have a good business going.'

'Not as good as it should be. I'm doing a certain amount of work and Angus is working a sixteen and seventeen-hour day, and for what? We have a three-roomed *rented* cottage and nothing extra in it since the time we were married. It's not that I want luxuries but I would like to feel I could give the children more.'

'What more do they need? They're well-fed and well-clothed. If you knew the way some of the people live, like the miners, who struggle along on a pittance and –'

'I know, Ivy, I know all that. I can't help the way I feel, though.'

'I think you should be grateful for what you have got,' Ivy said gruffly. 'You don't know how lucky you are.'

Julie knew it was useless saying any more. She called to Lyndsey to wait and ran to catch hold of her before she jumped from the path to the beach.

The children romped about for a while then settled down, Lyndsey to build a castle and Daniel to make sand-pies. Ivy spread a rug on the sand and she and Julie sat on it and gazed out to sea, both silent, with Julie hoping to find some peace in this quiet place. But it was denied her. She said to Ivy, 'Do you still hanker after going back to Stoke, taking another shop there?'

'Sometimes, but I'm more settled here than I was. It's just the winter that's so quiet.' She smiled wryly. 'It would be ideal if I could spend the summer here and the winter in Stoke selling hot pies and peas and what-have-you. It was a good life, wasn't it?'

They became so absorbed in talk of the shop and the customers they had known that Lyndsey had to tug at Julie's sleeve to get attention. She stood hands on hips, her stance aggressive. 'If you don't come and look at my fairy castle, Mummy, I'll stamp on it.'

Julie got up right away and Ivy, too. They were both smiling as they walked to see the castle. Then they stopped and exchanged glances. Julie said, 'Do you see what I see? Someone must have helped her.' But there was no one around.

The castle was excellently fashioned, complete with turrets and ramparts. Julie said, 'It's beautiful, Lyndsey! Where did you see such a castle?'

'It's a picture in Auntie Pinner's bedroom. It's a fairy castle with dragons, but I can't make a dragon.'

Ivy said, 'I know the picture, and it's an exact copy. Your child has talent, Mrs MacLaren, and you grumble about being restless!'

'Yes, she has talent,' Julie said, but it only made her feel worse than ever because it brought Fergus vividly to her mind. What traits, what talents had the child inherited from Fergus' side of the family? Fergus had once casually mentioned when explaining Jake's love of architecture that their great-grandfather had been a well-known architect in his day.

But then there was Richard with the same love of the subject, and who was *his* real family? Julie, who had been hesitant about mentioning the expertise of the sandcastle to Angus, told him that evening and he said at once, 'Well, look at how creative her mother is.' He smiled. 'She's got her talent from you, my love. We shall have to nurse it.'

Julie said no more.

When the weather remained mild she took the children to the cove either morning or afternoon. Sometimes Ivy would come with them, sometimes Mrs Pinner, but more often than not there was just Julie with the children. Lyndsey not only built castles, but fashioned cottages, and farmyards, and when Julie tried to help she would say, 'I want to do this myself, Mummy. Help Daniel, he's not very good at making sand-pies.'

Daniel, ever amiable, would allow Julie to make one or two 'pies' but after flattening them, chuckling as he did so, he would want his bucket and spade back, 'Daniel would make them'.

One day Julie sat watching them, thinking she had two lovely children, a husband she loved, doing work she enjoyed (when she could), so why should she be so restless? If she could have a different life, what would she choose? Not one of luxury. And yet, she longed to expand, to test herself, to have a factory, prove herself. For what? For whom? Who would be impressed? Fergus . . . yes, yes, it would always be Fergus, to the end of her days he would be there in the inner recesses of her mind, waiting to be brought to the surface. Why had he stayed away from her, never written? There had not even been a card from him from some foreign place. It could only be guilt.

She got up and after checking that the children were still absorbed in their games she walked towards the group of rocks from which Fergus had carried her from the onslaught of the waves. There she climbed the ledged rocks slowly, pausing before reaching the top slab, feeling a momentary guilt for wanting to recapture a time that should have no place in her marriage.

That day had been stormy with waves building up into wide rollers which, gathering momentum, had broken against the groups of rocks, sending up rising spumes of spray. Although the sea was much calmer today there was a turbulence where the currents met, with waves rushing shorewards as though in an angry race. Julie compared the greyness and the turbulence to her own mood.

For some reason the marriage bowl that Angus had given her on her wedding eve came into Julie's mind. He had said she was to add another ingredient at the end of a year, an ingredient that would help to make for the success of a marriage. At the end of that year she had told him that a year was not long enough. That it was simply a settling down time; he was to ask her in another three years. Angus had said in his quiet way to make it the fifth year – by then she would be sure to know what she wanted to add.

There was a sudden break in the clouds and a thin shaft of sunlight slanted on the water. The greyness had gone and there was a clarity in the air that brought a tiny ship on the horison into clear focus and with it, as though the opening of the clouds had brought a divine message, she knew then the one ingredient that should have been on the marriage bowl from the first day of her marriage.

*Truth.*

How could she ever get really close to Angus with the barrier of lies she had told between them? But it was too late to tell the truth now; it would serve no purpose, only bring animosity, perhaps hatred. She would have to go on carrying the weight of her guilt for evermore. Oh, God, what a mess she had made of her life. With a feeling of wanting to run away and hide, she turned swiftly to leave.

In that split second of turning she stumbled over a small figure who said, 'Mummy' before hurtling backwards. She stood, numbed with shock, then with a sob she clambered down. Daniel lay on his back, one dimpled fist against his cheek as though in sleep.

She dropped to her knees, laid an ear against his chest. There was no heartbeat. She felt his wrist, but there was no pulse.

There was the sound of someone shouting. Two men

came running up. One said, 'We saw the boy fall, is he all right?'

'He hit his head on a piece of rock, I think he's dead,' she said, but the voice was that of a stranger coming from a long way off. And after that the nightmare continued.

# Chapter Twenty-Two

For over a week Julie shut herself off from everyone, apart from her mother and Ivy. She refused to see Angus and Lyndsey, but would not give a reason.

Then one day Kitty said, 'Julie, I am now going to do some plain speaking, as Ivy once did to me when I went through a terrible time. You've been cosseted and cared for but you now have to face the world of reality. You have a husband and a child who need you.'

Julie shook her head. 'They don't want me, they'll hate me for what I did. I killed Daniel. Yes, I did,' she persisted when Kitty tried to protest. 'If I hadn't been so wrapped-up in my own guilty thoughts I would not have been on the rock and Daniel would not have climbed up to me. I'm paying now for my sins.'

'If you have committed some sin then for heaven's sake get it off your chest, Julie!' In a softer voice Kitty added, 'Don't think I don't feel for you, I do, we all do, we all feel grief-stricken but I ache unbearably for Angus who is suffering for something he's not responsible for. He has not only lost his son, but his wife and the mother of poor little Lyndsey, who is upset and bewildered. *She* feels guilty because you accused her of not looking after Daniel, inferring if she had cared for him he would not have died.'

The shock of her mother's words brought feeling to Julie's limbs, sent blood pounding through her veins. 'I didn't say such a thing! I couldn't, I wouldn't!'

'You did, Julie. I know you were in shock at the time, but Lyndsey is not old enough to understand such things. For the past three nights she's cried herself to sleep. If you don't tell her you don't hold her responsible for Daniel's death, then I hesitate to say what will happen to her.'

Julie began to tremble. 'I didn't realise, I'm sorry, sorry. But I must see Angus first, I have something to tell him. I must, I should have told him before now.'

Kitty took her in her arms, soothing her. 'It will be all right, Julie, I promise, we want you back with us. I'll send Angus to you.'

When Angus came into the bedroom he made no attempt to come to Julie. All he said was, 'Hello.'

She sat, her palms pressed together for several moments then she looked up – and saw the anguish in his eyes. 'Oh, Angus,' she wailed, 'what have I done to you, with my selfishness, my stupidity? I was so full of guilt over Daniel. It would never have happened had it not been for me thinking of someone else at the time.'

She paused and looked away. 'I have something to confess. You'll probably hate me, but it has to be told. I let you and everyone else concerned think that Lyndsey was the result of being seduced by an unknown boy. Well, it's not true, he was a figment of my imagination.'

'Yes, I know,' Angus said quietly.

Julie turned her head quickly and stared at him. 'You knew? How long have you known?'

He came and sat down opposite her. 'I should have said I guessed it in the first place, then I was sure as time went on. You're not a good liar, Julie. You were always asking casually about Fergus and I knew by the expression on your face that you loved him. And also that he was Lyndsey's father.'

'Yet you married me.'

'I loved you too, Julie. And I love Lyndsey, as much as I – loved Daniel. You are not to blame yourself for his death. It was an accident that could have happened at any time.'

'But why, why an innocent child? *Why not me?*' The tears came then and Angus gathered her to him and stroked her hair.

'We cannot question the Lord's ways, lassie. There's a scheme in things we don't understand, nor, I'm sure are we intended to. Is there another world somewhere, with people in it of all ages? Is there a couple there who needed a child? Has Daniel fulfilled that need? I like to think so.'

Julie was deeply moved by Angus' simple faith. She could not accept it, but could find nothing to better it. Perhaps if she thought of Daniel playing happily in some other world. . . .

Angus brought out a handkerchief and dried Julie's eyes. 'When you feel better you must see Lyndsey.'

Julie had only to say, 'I'm terribly sorry, Lyndsey darling, for blaming you, I didn't mean it,' for the child to fling herself sobbing into her arms. Julie could only hope that her terrible accusation had not left a scar. From now on she would make it up to her daughter.

Outwardly, Lyndsey showed no sign of having suffered any permanent damage; she talked about Daniel, laughed when she remembered some funny little incident, but now and again Julie would catch the odd little frown that gave such a look of maturity to the young face, then she would wonder if Lyndsey was grieving inwardly.

Angus was gentle with both of them, but in spite of their lives seeming to resume a normal pattern, Julie knew it was not the same. When Angus made love to her it was quick, without any love-play beforehand, and she had the feeling it was just something that was a necessity to him. Then she would wish she had never confessed her 'lies'. With them unspoken they had appeared not to exist.

Before Kitty returned to Tyler, she begged Julie to come to London with her and bring Lyndsey. The change would benefit them both. At the time Julie would not leave Angus, but now she began to wonder if it might be wise to be parted for a while. She talked it over with Ivy who agreed it could be a good thing, especially for Lyndsey's sake, for Ivy thought she had become a little withdrawn at times.

'I've heard her talking to Daniel once or twice lately,' she said. 'I know that many children have an imaginary playmate, but somehow because it's Daniel I feel it could be a bit worrying. If she was in a different environment, like London, there would be so much to divert her. Have a word with Angus.'

Julie did and the result was a letter to her parents saying the two of them would like to come and stay for a while. By return came a telegram telling her how delighted they were; she was to let them know day and time of arrival.

Julie felt there was nothing that could excite her ever again, but she found a pleasure in Lyndsey's excitement at the thought of travelling on a train. London, of course, was just a name to her.

When the time came for leaving Julie felt a pang. Angus was so quiet nowadays. If only he would have come with them, but he said he had too many orders to fulfil. 'You two enjoy yourselves, that will be my pleasure. Write and let me know how you get on.'

When Angus kissed her before parting, it was to Julie the first real, loving kiss she had had since Daniel's death. She clung to him. 'Oh, Angus, I don't want to go, I must have been mad. I'm coming back home with you.'

He laughed a little shakily. 'And do me out of some boozy nights at the local with my pals! Off you go, the pair of you.'

Julie was still regretting leaving when the train was on its way. Then she was distracted by Lyndsey's excited squeals at seeing some sheep in a field. She concentrated on giving the child her attention, explaining later about the close living of people who lived in towns, about factories. And Lyndsey gave it all her rapt attention.

An awful moment came during the journey when the train

made a scheduled stop and Julie saw a little boy who resembled Daniel, with the same chubbiness and same chestnut hair with golden highlights. Lyndsey, who had seen him too, exclaimed, 'There's Daniel! Look, Mummy, look.' She began knocking on the window then she slid off the seat, saying she would go and fetch him.

Julie caught her and lifted her on to her lap. 'The little boy is like Daniel, but it is not him. See –'

There came the odd little frown then a desolation in Lyndsey's eyes. Julie, who had steeled herself to control her emotions, felt grief almost swamp her. She held the child close. 'Daniel is in heaven, darling, but he's happy there, playing with other little boys and girls.' Now Lyndsey wanted to know why *she* could not go to heaven to play with Daniel. It was an elderly woman in the carriage who was able to divert Lyndsey's attention by bringing out a picture book.

'This belongs to my little granddaughter,' she said, 'but I'm sure she won't mind you having it. There's a little story in it about a mischievous kitten. I'll read it to you. I know it'll make you laugh.'

Their benefactor read more of the stories and Lyndsey eventually fell asleep. Julie thanked the woman and said how grateful she was, they had gone through a difficult time.

'I understand,' she said. 'I lost a child, and he was a little older than I take your boy to be. I still think about him, but God has been good to me, He gave me three more children and I now have five grandchildren. We all have something to be thankful for, don't we?'

'Yes,' Julie said, looking at her sleeping child. 'We do indeed.'

There was not only her parents waiting to greet them at London but Jake and his Aunt Klara. It was good to have Jake and Klara there because it eased the meeting after the tragedy when she had last seen her parents.

Lyndsey's sleep on the train had been short and she had exhausted herself with all the excitement of everything she had seen so it was a sleepy child who was lifted by Tyler and carried. 'Bless her,' he said, 'she's ready for bed.'

'She's gorgeous, isn't she?' Klara enthused. 'Oh, what fun it will be taking her round the shops. And you too, Julie. Do you remember our last little expedition?' Klara would have gone on chattering had not Jake interrupted with a laugh:

'Can I have a turn to greet my favourite girl? Julie, how good it is to see you again!' No mention was made of Daniel and she was relieved. She was also glad that he had not spoken of Richard. They would have to talk about him later, but she wanted to get settled in first.

Julie was surprised to have a feeling of coming home. Perhaps it was because of Mrs Parker who was there in the hall. And it was she who took Lyndsey from Tyler's arms, saying, 'My niece will get her to bed, I have a meal ready for you all.'

Over the meal the journey was discussed, Lyndsey's reaction to it, Angus' work and Echo Cove and although it all sounded easy and pleasant Julie was aware of a constraint, and knew it was not because of Daniel but because they were all careful not to mention Richard's name. Julie was wishing they would say something about her brother when Klara said right out of the blue, 'Guess who is coming home this week? Fergus!'

Kitty said, 'Well, and where has he been to this time?' and Klara laughed and replied, heaven only knew where, but it would be lovely to see him, while Julie's heart began to beat in painful thuds. Why after all this time had he chosen to be here? Was it fate? No, she would not allow it to be fate, she would avoid him at all costs. He had no place in her life, no right to take any part in it. Yet, even as she thought it Julie knew she would not make a point of avoiding him.

Tyler said gently, 'You look tired, Julie. Would you like to sit back in the armchair for coffee?'

She forced herself to smile. 'No, I'm fine, enjoying all the chat.'

Before Jake and Klara left it was arranged that Julie, her parents and Lyndsey would all go for lunch the following day to Klara's house.

Kitty said after they had gone. 'We had to accept the invitation but I sometimes think that Klara has a struggle to live.' To which Tyler replied that Klara was well looked after. He did not mention by whom, but Julie guessed it was Fergus.

Lyndsey was sleeping in Julie's room, so she would not feel strange if she woke up during the night, and when Julie went up she stood looking at her small daughter, wondering what Fergus' reaction would be if he knew she was his child. There was no resemblance to him, and she would never tell him. Julie leaned over and kissed Lyndsey gently on the cheek. What would her future be? She was an exuberant little thing, given to tantrums if she was not kept under control when she wanted her own way, but so loving. In what ways would her creative ability develop? Would she be a lady architect perhaps, and set a new fashion in jobs for women? Or were there already lady architects? She must ask Jake.

When she did ask him the next day he said, yes, there were, but they were not popular with the men. Julie was indignant and wanted to know why. 'Because we want our women to be feminine,' Jake said, 'not mixed up with concrete and stone.'

'And I agree with Jake,' said a voice quietly from behind Julie.

For one heart-stopping second Julie was unable to move, then she turned. 'Why, Fergus, what a surprise! Klara told us you would be home.' Julie was surprised that she sounded so normal.

Jake made some excuse to leave them and Fergus laid a hand gently on her arm. 'I was sorry to hear about your little boy.'

'Thank you. Are you in England for long? Klara was

telling us you seem to be here, there and everywhere, like the elusive Pimpernel.'

Fergus smiled. 'But not such an intriguing figure.' He paused and his dark eyes, serious now, were searching her face. 'I've thought of you often, Julie.'

She wanted to shout at him, call him a liar, remind him he had not even bothered to send her a picture postcard. Instead she said: 'And I've often thought of our visit to Italy – it was good, wasn't it? I understand that you and Jake went back.'

'All in connection with his studies. I felt I owed it to him. He was missing Richard, he still is. They were such good friends.'

It was strange, Julie thought, they had all been carefully avoiding mentioning Richard's name, yet Fergus had done so and it had come naturally, making her ask if he had heard anything about him.

'Yes, I have, only recently, but I'm not sure how much your parents want to know. Perhaps we could have a stroll, after lunch, and discuss it.'

'I would very much like to know about my brother, if we can leave without – well – making it seem contrived.'

'I'm sure I can arrange it.' His amused smile made Julie annoyed.

'I don't doubt it. I'm quite sure with your expertise you can talk your way in and out of every situation!'

If he was aware of her annoyance, her sarcasm, he gave no sign.

Lyndsey came hurtling in. 'Mummy, Mummy, a lady has brought Aunt Klara a parrot to look after, it can talk. Come and see it!' She took Julie's hand and attempted to pull her.

Julie said, 'In a moment, Lyndsey. This gentleman is Uncle Jake's brother, say hello.'

'Hello,' she said, and would have been away had not Fergus caught her by the hand.

'A parrot, you say, and it can talk. What is its name?'

A smile lighted Lyndsey's face. She began to giggle. 'Chopsticks! Isn't it a funny name? Will you come and see it, too?'

'Yes, of course.'

Of all the pain Julie had suffered over Fergus' abandonment of her, this was the worst, seeing Lyndsey's hand firmly clasped in that of her father, a man she would never be able to call 'Daddy'. They went to the kitchen to see the parrot, and to the child's delight it called out as they went in, 'The ship's sinking, take to the lifeboats!'

Klara laughingly explained that her neighbour's son had bought the bird from a Chinese sailor, and added that at times he was a naughty bird and used swear words.

Fergus laughed heartily at this and Julie looking at the attractive face thought with despair – Oh, Fergus, how different it could all have been! Then Jake was there taking up their earlier discussion on 'lady architects' and the moment was gone.

The suggested after-lunch walk came naturally by an unconscious gesture from Julie. The room was warmer than usual and as she pushed her hair away from her brow Fergus said, 'It is warm in here, Julie, and of course you are missing the fresh air of the coast. I shall walk you to the park. It's quiet and there's plenty of space to breathe.'

Jake said he would go with them but Klara put a hand on his arm. 'No, let them go alone, we've been talking an awful lot and I think Julie needs to be quiet for a while.' To Julie she added, 'Wrap up, it's cold today and a bit damp. I wouldn't be surprised if we have fog later. And don't worry about Lyndsey, she's happy here with us.'

Lyndsey, who had been unwilling to leave the parrot was delighted to have her meal with Mrs Parker in the kitchen.

Fergus talked about London to Julie as they strolled through the streets towards Piccadilly, and it was not until they reached Green Park that he brought up the subject of Richard.

'I saw him when I was in Germany. He was with Violet and an elderly man whom he introduced as Baron von something or other. We exchanged pleasantries for a while then Violet and her – friend, excused themselves, leaving Richard free to talk to me.'

'How is he? Is he happy? Why won't he come home, or even for a visit? Did you tell him how unhappy he was making us all?'

'He knows it, Julie,' Fergus said quietly. 'I'm afraid that he is unhappy, too. We went to my hotel and we talked over a drink. He's come to realise that Violet's beauty is no more than "skin deep" but he won't leave her.'

'Why? Surely if he's found out what a liar she is –'

'He says she is not well and in fact inferred she might not have long to live. To me she was the picture of health, but she can put on an act of pathos. She put one on when she was leaving Richard. "Don't be too long darling," she said, then remarked to me with her pathetic smile, "I've missed so much of my dear son's life I feel I cannot bear to be apart from him." I noticed a wry smile touch her companion's lips at this and it was he who urged her away.'

'This baron, is he another one of her – ?'

'He is her present "bread and butter". Richard admitted it and hates all these lovers she has, yet he remains besotted with Violet. No, I'm wrong,' Fergus shook his head slowly. 'Besotted is not the right word – he's protective towards her, believes the way she lives is due to her earlier life. He said there was a depth to her that no one else seemed to have discovered.'

'It's terrible,' Julie exclaimed. 'My parents won't even discuss him now. Not because they no longer love him but because they love him so much. My mother once said as long as he remained in the background she could cope with life. If she talked about him the pain was unbearable.'

Fergus glanced at her. 'That is unlike your mother, Julie. I've always thought her a very balanced person.'

'She is in many ways but I think where a deep love is involved one can behave out of character.'

Fergus was silent. Had her words touched a chord, made him recall the firelit cave, their love-making? Made him perhaps, more conscious of his desertion?

There were few people in the park, some strolling couples, an elderly man and a woman. Julie could smell the dampness in her hair. She thought of Echo Cove and imagined she could smell seaweed. The day had never been light, not from early morning and she was aware of an air of melancholy. Fergus said suddenly, 'Julie, are you happy with Angus?'

She stared determinedly ahead. 'Very happy. He's a wonderful man, I couldn't have wished for a better husband or a more loving and caring father for my – for our child.' A tremor in her voice at the last few words had Fergus grip her hand.

'Julie – there's so much I would like to say to you, so much to explain, but it's impossible. Perhaps someday I shall be able to tell you and then you will know that I was not wholly responsible for my neglect of you. I'm only glad you found a man like Angus.'

Julie found it impossible to tell just what was in Fergus' mind. There were no inflections in his voice. She recalled her mother once saying about a man they had met as having a diplomat's voice and face, he gave nothing away. And that was how Julie felt about Fergus at that moment.

She said, 'Do you think that Richard might return home sometime?'

He shook his head. 'I doubt it. He doesn't want to come home – he stressed it, that is why I haven't mentioned him to your parents. I think it might be best not to say anything for the time being.'

Julie agreed. It would only be rubbing salt into their wounds . . . just as Fergus had rubbed salt into hers, although he may not have realised it. It was so easy to dispense his obligations by saying it was impossible to explain his neglect of her. She decided it was just as well they had met; it had destroyed this terrible longing to be taken in his arms, to be loved.

There was a silence between them after this. In the ever-darkening afternoon a mist put haloes on lamps and drifted in wraithlike swirls across the park. Fergus suggested it might be best to make their way back home, for the mist could thicken into fog. They were retracing their steps when he stopped.

'Julie, I'm going abroad again soon and may not be back for a very long time. I just wanted to say to you that I am glad I've seen you again and very pleased that you and Angus are so – suited.'

Fergus was not speaking this time with a diplomat's voice but with the voice of love. Julie knew that she had been fooling herself. This man would always be a part of her life. She said in a low voice: 'Tell me one thing, Fergus. Did you regret that afternoon in the Cove?'

'Only because I was not able to get in touch with you. Otherwise, no, it was the most –' There was pain now in his voice and he stopped abruptly. 'I must leave it at that. I think you understand.' He touched her cheek gently, 'We must go.'

It was only because Fergus kept the conversation on general topics after this that Julie was able to quell the turmoil of emotions he had aroused. She tried to think once that he had been showing off his expertise in handling women, yet she knew deep down that his feelings for her were genuine. Then she was tempted to tell him about Lyndsey, but knew she must not. He would be going away and she might never see him again.

In the three days he was in London they met several times and every time they did meet Lyndsey would hurl herself at him, squealing 'Uncle Fergus, come and see this', or 'Come and see that'. He seemed to delight in being with her and spoke to Julie of her as being a most adorable child. There seemed to be such an affinity between them Julie wondered why he had not guessed she was his daughter.

The evening he was due to leave she was with the rest of the family and all she received from him was a kiss on each cheek, but the strong grip of his fingers on her arms told her of his emotions.

In bed that night she wept for what might have been . . . and felt ashamed to be weeping for a lost love instead of crying for the tragic loss of poor little Daniel.

Julie had intended to stay in London for two weeks or more. It had been Angus' suggestion, saying she saw so little of her parents and it would not only give her time to catch up on all the news but allow her parents to get to know their only grandchild. But after Fergus had gone she became restless; she missed the sea, missed Angus.

One morning at breakfast she said to her parents, 'I'm thinking of returning to Echo Cove. I'm homesick and that is no reflection on either of you. I worry about Angus. He puts a brave face on Daniel's death but he grieves inwardly. I don't think I ought to leave him any longer.'

They told her they understood but said how much they would miss her, with Kitty adding, 'Lyndsey has wrapped herself around all our hearts. We must come and visit *you*.'

When Lyndsey knew they were leaving there were loud wails; she did not want to part with the parrot! Tyler lifted her on to his lap and said, 'I tell you what darling, when Gran and I come to visit you we shall bring you a parrot of your very own. How is that?'

The tears stemmed and Lyndsey was all smiles, bestowing loving hugs and kisses, which brought the comment from Julie that it was a good job they were going home or Lyndsey would be ruined.

The following morning there was a letter for Tyler and Kitty from Richard. It was brief. He asked their forgiveness for ignoring them for so long, blaming his lapse on the need to sort things out. He would come and see them sometime, but not yet. It was signed, *'Your loving Richard'*.

'Not loving son,' Kitty said tearfully, 'but at least he still does love us. It's a start.'

Julie thought, well at least Fergus had done one good thing – he had reunited her parents with her brother in spirit if not in person, and for that she was grateful. It would help to ease the parting when she and Lyndsey left.

# Chapter Twenty-Three

On the journey back to Echo Cove Julie felt a joyousness at the thought of her reunion with Angus. Once, picturing their love-making, her emotions were so strong she felt embarrassed and was glad that Lyndsey was there with her bright chatter to take attention from herself with the other passengers.

When they arrived, Angus greeted them both with a quiet pleasure but Julie knew by the smile he gave her and the warm slumbrous look in his eyes what was in *his* mind. She said, 'Oh, it's so good to be back!'

Lyndsey talked him to death, telling him about the parrot, repeating all the sayings of the bird, which had Angus laughing – also Ivy, who had a meal ready for them.

Ivy asked after Tyler and Kitty and wanted to know what they had all been doing in London, then Julie asked questions about the people in Echo Cove and about trade in the café. It was all happy and cosy until Lyndsey began to talk about 'Uncle Fergus' and the atmosphere changed.

Angus became withdrawn and Ivy regarded Julie with strong disapproval. Fortunately, Lyndsey kept the conversation going with talk of her visit to the zoo and other places.

It was not until they went home and Lyndsey was in bed that Angus broached the subject of Fergus, asking Julie if she had known that he was going to be in London. She said, 'No, I thought he was abroad. He stayed only for a few days and left to go abroad again.'

'Did you tell him about Lyndsey?'

'No, I didn't. To me, Angus, you are her father and always will be. That is, if you will accept it.'

'I have accepted it, Julie. I did so from the day she was born.' He paused, 'One day before you went to London, I scolded her for touching a vase that I had just finished painting. When she did it for the second time I put her outside the shed and told her she was not to come in until she had learned to do as she was told. I was harsh with her –'

'Oh, no, Angus, you're never harsh with her and she has to be disciplined.'

'When she came in about two minutes later she put her hand in mine.' Angus covered his left hand with his right as though feeling the tiny hand in his. 'Her eyes were brimming with tears as she said, "I'm sorry, Daddy, I won't do it again." '

He walked over to the window and added, a catch in his voice, 'Then *I* felt like crying, I love her so much.'

'Oh, Angus –' Julie went over to him. 'I'm sorry for even suggesting that you might not have accepted Lyndsey as your daughter.'

He reached out to her and she went into his arms, revelling in his strength and responding to his sensuous murmuring of, 'Oh, God, Julie, how I've missed you, how I've longed for this moment.' He leaned over and pulling the collar of her blouse away from the back of her neck he blew warm air gently over her skin. Shivers of ecstasy ran up and down her spine and she cried out. He gave an exultant shout as though he had conquered her against her will and began to undress her. Julie, her whole body throbbing, started to unbutton his shirt, her breathing as ragged as that of Angus.

When her blouse and camisole were on the floor he drew back and stood looking at the small firm breasts in an almost reverent way. His lips moved gently over the delicate flesh then with a rousing passion he kissed the column of her throat. Pushing back her hair he explored the inside of her ear with the tip of his tongue, making her cry out again.

With the last of their garments discarded, they explored one another's bodies, in a frantic way as though it would be for the last time. Then Angus laid her on the rug and after turning out the lamp he came to her, a Scottish warrior, proud of his masculinity, and dropped to the rug beside her.

Even then, although Julie knew that Angus was in the same sweetly agonising state of needing fulfilment as herself, they made further love-play.

The room was warm and the glow from the fire brought a sudden image to her mind of a cosy firelit cave, but it was gone as Angus made the penetration. She gasped, and as the rhythm increased Julie knew that this was the strongest emotion she had ever experienced in her love-making with Angus.

They were building up to the climax and she shouted, 'Oh, Angus, Angus!'

Then suddenly the rhythm stopped; Angus withdrew and rolled away from her. Frustrated and puzzled she exclaimed, 'What happened? Don't tell me you're punishing me for something that –'

'Punishing *you*? Do you know what you've just called out? Your lover's name. Oh, *Fergus*, *Fergus*, you shouted.'

Julie was appalled. She couldn't have done. 'I didn't,' she said. 'I wouldn't have done, you imagined it. Fergus must have been on your mind.'

'On *my* mind! Oh, no,' his tone was angry, bitter. 'He was on *your* mind, obviously.'

'No, Angus, no, you must believe me. It must have been the similarity of the names, we were talking about Fergus earlier.'

Angus refused to accept this. He dressed and went downstairs, and so began the first rift in their marriage.

To outsiders they appeared normal but when they were alone they spoke only when necessary. Lyndsey, still full of her London visit, seemed not to notice anything wrong but Ivy did.

One morning when Julie called Ivy said, 'So, what's up? What have you and Angus fallen out about?'

Julie explained what had happened and received from Ivy what she thought of later as the biggest 'dressing down' in her life. Who did Julie think she was? God Almighty? Had Julie ever given thought to all the lies she had told about the imaginary youth who was supposed to have seduced her? No, of course not, she was lily-white, and didn't give a damn for her husband.

Julie strenuously denied this but Ivy was relentless. It was time that Julie grew up, took on her responsibilities and stopped living in a dream world, instead of spitting into the face of a man who had given her a home and her child his name.

At this Julie burst into tears. She jumped up and made to leave but Ivy pushed her back into the chair. 'I've said all I'm going to say, now we'll have a cup of tea then I want to hear you say you'll apologise to Angus for the way you've behaved.'

It took two cups of tea before Julie agreed she had been wrong and promised to speak to Angus.

In bed that night she turned to him. 'Angus, I'm sorry – I've been a fool.' He drew her to him with a groan. They made love but for Julie it was just an act, lacking that lovely sweet rush of desire. And she wondered then if it would ever return.

The weeks drifted into months with a monotony that had her eventually experiencing the familiar restlessness. She wanted to expand the business, but Angus said it was the wrong time, there was talk of the miners coming out on strike and if they did things would be bleak in the North East. Ivy broached the same subject, complaining that already coach bookings had dropped off and the weekend hikers and cyclists were getting fewer and fewer. She added that if people stopped coming altogether to the tea-room she might as well close.

When Angus nodded Julie exclaimed, 'Oh, stop it, you two! You're a couple of defeatists! There hasn't been a strike, might never be one. I'm going to the quayside to get some fish, do you want me to bring you some, Ivy?'

Ivy hemmed and hawed, she'd gone off fish a bit and it didn't keep – well – perhaps Julie could bring her a little and would she bring some for Mrs Pinner who wasn't too well.

Julie stormed out. Was this to be her life for evermore, an important issue being whether Ivy wanted fish or not? There had to be *something* different. She could leave this place tomorrow and no one would care. Lyndsey was always wanting to be with Angus. He took her to the shed every morning and gave her pieces of clay to make into figures. She made passable animals and birds and Angus allowed her to paint them. The painting was not too good but he glazed them to please her and there was a collection of them in Julie's workroom.

By the time Julie reached the harbour she had worked off her temper. She always enjoyed the scene, especially when the trawlers were in; there was so much liveliness, so much activity. Most of the catches had been unloaded and the women and girls were gutting the fish ready to be packed into boxes, their raucous voices mingling with the shouts and quips of the men. Gulls shrieked and dived for the fish entrails and their cries and the voices bounced back from the echoing cliffs so that it was like the Tower of Babel.

Julie had got to know the women and girls and admired them for their cheerfulness and endurance, especially when they gutted fish in freezing weather with hands that were red and chapped.

An elderly man on one of the boats hailed Julie, 'Morning to you, Mrs Mac. I have some lovely lemon soles for you, some of the last of the catch, you can taste the sea in them. Here, give me your bag.'

He gave her enough for all of them to last two days or more, for just a shilling. Julie thanked him then said, 'Angus told me to tell you he'd take you up on your offer to have a trip out to sea, when it's convenient.'

'An' he'll be more than welcome if we can get out. Might not, if the miners come out on strike.'

Julie was puzzled as to how the striking miners could stop the trawlers going out. When she asked Angus he said, 'Spending power, love. If they come out they'll be determined to stay out until they get more pay, but the owners will be equally certain they won't give them any more, so there'll be a deadlock.'

'But I still don't see –' Julie began, and Angus went on, 'If the men strike there'll be dire poverty. The fishermen won't get the price they want for their fish and so the ripples in the pond will spread and spread.'

The miners did eventually come out and it affected many trades, including that of Angus and Ivy. Some people said it would soon be over but it went on for months, with a General Strike in between. Fortunately this lasted for only nine days.

Kitty wrote to say that the Bright Young Things in London were driving buses, with some of them getting beaten up. Girls did menial tasks and acted as porters at railway stations, but they treated it all as fun.

'Fun,' Ivy said grimly, 'and miners and their families in the North East and Wales are starving. And so will I be,' she added, 'if trade doesn't perk up soon. I've taken orders for one or two christening and birthday cakes, but they could stop if things get any worse.'

Julie asked Angus what they could do if his orders ceased.

'We'll wait until that time comes,' he said. 'Dave is still taking my better vases and bowls. He had an outlet in the South, but transport is getting difficult.'

Julie looked thoughtful. 'Why are the more expensive ones selling and not the cheaper lines?'

'Because the people with money can afford them. They haven't been affected so far. They buy them for wedding presents because they're different. Dave did say he might be able to sell a good-class novelty line, but didn't say what.'

Julie looked up. 'How about making marriage bowls? They *are* a novelty, I haven't seen any of them anywhere else.' She became excited. 'You could experiment with glazes, and instead of painting on the symbols make them in moulds. You are so good at that.'

Angus shook his head. No, the marriage bowl was his father's idea, his patent, as it were. Julie pointed out that surely if his father was alive he would be only too pleased for his son to produce his idea, but Angus was adamant. He would try and think of something else. Julie flung up her hands in despair. A good idea, a selling line going to waste because of stubbornness . . .

Julie still felt annoyed that evening at Angus rejecting the marriage bowl and was handling her own when he came in.

'Well, Julie,' he said quietly, 'have you found another ingredient to go into the bowl to help towards a successful marriage?'

'We haven't got patience on, have we?' she snapped. 'It needs patience to deal with a stubborn man who seems determined not to progress.'

'Julie, can't you understand my feelings about the bowl? My father made it for my sister, with love, wanting to help her marriage along.'

'Then can't *you* understand that distributing them would help other people in their marriages?'

A look of sadness came into Angus' eyes. 'It hasn't helped our marriage very much, has it?'

Colour rushed to Julie's face. 'If you're going to bring it up about Fergus again, I–'

'Julie, Julie–' It was a cry of despair. 'You know I wouldn't do such a thing. We've gone over all that, it's finished with, as far as I'm concerned. I was meaning that you never give of yourself to me now.'

'I've never refused you when you've wanted to make love!'

'No, you haven't, but there's a difference between lying passively and giving.' Angus got up and taking the bowl from her replaced it on the sideboard. 'We'll say no more, Julie, otherwise we might both say something we shall regret for evermore.'

In bed later she lay tense beside Angus, hoping he would not try to make up their quarrel by wanting to make love to her. This was one time when she would refuse.

Then she found herself recalling the time early in their marriage, when she was angry and had got into bed in her dressing-gown and Angus had tried to get it off under the bedclothes. What a tangle the clothes had got into! She smiled. They had ended up giggling.

Julie also remembered how Angus had drawn the collar of her dressing-gown away from the back of her neck and had blown warm air gently down her spine. He had stopped doing this lately. Was the fault hers? She turned to him, prepared to snuggle up to him then was aware of gentle snores.

Well really! She flung herself onto her back, fuming for having felt responsive. He had been the one to stir things up but she would be the one to suffer. No doubt she would be awake for the rest of the night.

And lie awake she did, her thoughts then centred on Fergus who she was sure would never have done such a thing as falling asleep with anger between them. If only she had had the sense to know that a marriage with one man would not work, not when she was in love with another. If only she had told Fergus about the baby. But then he had not been there to tell. Oh, why did she go on torturing herself? Ivy had accused her of living in a dream world and that was exactly what she was doing. But how could she change – it was her nature to dream.

Was it Tom who had once said that it was impossible for a person to change his or her nature; it was a question of recognising one's faults and trying to rectify them. But did she want to change? No, why should she? Dreaming of Fergus coloured her life.

She dreamt about Fergus that night, a muddled dream, and when she woke the next morning and lay thinking about it the longing to see him was no longer so acute. Perhaps in time his image would fade.

The pungent smell of burned toast drifted up the stairs. Angus was always up first and invariably he took Lyndsey down with him. Lyndsey was shouting, 'Daddy, Daddy! You're burning the toast.' He said something to her which Julie couldn't quite catch, then the child was giggling helplessly.

This made Julie pull herself together. She must be grateful for what she did have and stop feeling sorry for herself.

Angus did not make love to her for another week, and when he did Julie simply gave in. And so their lives went on.

As the strike continued the poverty increased, the ripples in the pond widening yet further. In Echo Cove the fishermen's families were suffering. The prices offered from the herring catches were so low that the angry fishermen tipped their catches back into the sea. This caused an uproar from the people, some who were without food, but the men said it was the only way to get their plight noticed.

In letters from home Kitty and Tyler offered help, begged them to accept it, but Julie refused, saying they were managing, but added that if there was a time when they were really short of food they would let them know.

Whenever people met the talk was solely of the strike and its repercussions. One evening when two of Angus' friends called, one of them said, 'I went last week to see my brother and his family in Jarrow. God, what a shock I got, they were like scarecrows.'

The other one said, 'I think one chap summed it up very well when he said that every man who had a job in a mining area was a king, and that some of the wives of the unemployed looked like their mothers.'

'How awful,' Julie said, 'but what can they do?'

The miners were out for six months and were eventually forced to go back because they were literally starving – and for less pay than they had received previously. Angus declared it was the biggest disgrace and tragedy of the century.

A recession, which Julie learned had begun before the strike, escalated. More and more people became unemployed, and orders were dropping off from abroad. Dave told Angus he couldn't take any more of his pottery, not until he could produce a novelty line.

One morning Julie came into the kitchen to find Angus staring into the fire. She came up to him. 'Angus, I'm going to accept help from my parents. I don't want to any more than you do but we must, for Lyndsey's sake.'

Angus gave a weary sigh. 'No. Before we do that I'll make marriage bowls. We'll talk it over this evening, discuss glazes, relief figures.'

When Angus had gone back to the shed and Ivy had taken Lyndsey shopping with her Julie sank into the armchair and looked around her. There were moments like this when she felt she had lived here a lifetime. Yet, it was such a small part of her life. She rubbed her toe over the pile of the lovely Durham carpet which her parents had brought them for their wedding present, their one luxury. But did she want anything else? Sometimes she was surprised at herself for finding pleasure in polishing the walnut sideboard, which Angus had picked up second-hand at the auction room. The patina of the wood glowed in the firelight. A log shifted, sending a shower of red sparks shooting up the chimney. Julie thought of the poor people who were without fires. They were lucky living by the sea, for there was always plenty of driftwood.

Julie stared into the heart of the fire then felt her heart give a lurch as she saw Daniel's image, his amiable round face, his small plump figure. *Oh, no, not now,* she pleaded silently, *don't taunt me.*

She wondered how often Angus thought of their small son. He never mentioned him, respecting her wishes not to discuss him. Lyndsey at times 'played' with Daniel, but she always talked in whispers as though she knew it was a taboo subject. Was it wrong to shut the child out of their lives, Julie wondered? Would her feeling of guilt be any less if they did talk about him?

A knock on the front door startled Julie. Friends who called would knock then look in but when no one appeared she went to open the door. Then she stood staring. 'Richard –'

'Hello, Sis.' He moved closer, then they were holding one another tightly, both too emotional to say any more.

When they separated Julie said, 'Have you been home? Does Mother know you're back? Come on in, what am I doing keeping you standing here on the doorstep? Sit down, I'll make some tea. Oh, Richard, I can't believe it, what happened?' Julie pushed back her hair. 'Sorry, I'm gabbling, I don't know what I'm saying, but *do* sit down.'

She filled the kettle then after putting it on the fire she turned to face him. He was the same attractive, well-dressed Richard but he looked more mature and there were dark shadows under his eyes.

Richard made small talk, as though wanting to avoid the main issue. He asked after Angus, enquired about the business and how they had fared during the strike. But when the tea was made and poured he said on a sigh, 'No, Julie, I haven't been home, I wanted to see you and Angus first. So much has happened, so much has changed. I've learned so much.'

'About what?' she asked, eyeing him almost warily.

'About my birth. I know now that Violet is not my mother

. . . but then neither are Tyler and Kitty my parents.'

Julie set down her cup, her heart beating in slow, uncomfortable thuds. She waited and after a moment Richard went on, 'Violet lived a life of deceit but I didn't know the full truth until a few days before she died.'

Violet dead? Julie had never liked her mother's sister but the fact that she was no longer alive somehow shocked her. She said, 'What happened?'

'She had a growth. She was terrified of dying.' Richard's hands were tightly clasped and his eyes showed pain. 'It was terrible to see her fear. Because of all the lies she had told she imagined herself going through all the fires of hell.' His voice lowered. 'I was just so sorry for her. She was her own worst enemy, a woman I realised later, who was so full of hate it warped her life. She wanted to be somebody and it ate into her that she was illegitimate.'

Richard sat silent, rubbing one hand over the other for a few moments, then he raised his head. 'It's strange, isn't it? I couldn't bear the thought at one time that *I* might be illegitimate, yet now it no longer bothers me. I remember how desperately I wanted the miniature that Violet said was of her first husband to be my father and how –'

'Oh, Richard.' Julie stared at him, appalled. 'And we went out of our way to prove that Violet was lying! How terrible – if only we had realised.'

'I'm not blaming you, you all did what you thought was best. I found out who my real parents were and I can understand Tyler and Kitty not being open with me. I think that they must have suspected that Violet was not my real mother.'

'Who was?'

'My father was the son of a squire and my mother a parlourmaid. Violet told me before she died. She bought the baby from the disgraced girl and left him on the doorstep of Crescent House, wanting your mother to think that I was Tyler's and her child.'

'Richard, I'm sorry.'

'It's all right, Julie, I really don't mind. I've learned so much during the past few years. I lived off Violet, knowing where her money came from. I felt that she had been badly done to when she was young. And even later, when I began to sense that she was not all she made out to be, I stayed, yet I longed to come home.'

'Why *didn't* you? Why did you never write? It was cruel. Mother was heartbroken.'

'I know, I know. That is why I came to you first. I want to see them, want to thank them for all their care, and to tell them that I love them both, but I won't stay. I can't. There's now a wanderlust in me. Violet left me her money, left me property and I've accepted it – that's the kind of person I've now become.'

'Oh, Richard, please don't talk like that.'

'I have to, I must purge myself. All Violet's early money came from brothels with a wealthy clientèle. I should have given it all away to help the needy, but I want it. Knowing this do you think I could possibly regard Crescent House as my home any longer?'

Julie began to cry and Richard came over and drew her to her feet. 'Don't, Julie, it hurts. I've never stopped loving you or the parents but I'm a different person inside. Don't you see? I did want to see Angus, but if you would rather I didn't stay –'

'Of course you must stay. I'll just tidy myself and we'll go to the shed.' Julie dried her eyes, not sure of anything any more. Not that her love for Richard would ever be any less, he would always be a brother to her but because he had been someone she had always looked up to she was bewildered by the fact that he was willing to live on immoral earnings. How would her parents react to this? Julie wished at that moment that they were here.

Angus' greeting of Richard was warm. 'Well! One does get surprises. You were the last person I expected to see.'

Angus cleared some pots from a wooden bench and dusted it. 'Take a seat and tell us what brought you back.'

Although Richard gave a more brief version of his life with Violet and her death, it seemed to Julie on a second hearing that he had lost an inherent sense of decency. Would he recover it if she could persuade him to either stay here for a while, living in a small community among hard-working people, where the air was fresh and clean, or go to her parents and the open country that he had enjoyed as a boy?

Richard, having explained about Violet, moved on to everyday things, business, the state of the world, the recession. And while the two men talked Julie moved round the shed studying work that Angus had done, beautiful work that could no longer find buyers. If only they knew how to export. Her parents could tell them. But even as Julie was thinking it Richard was saying, 'And of course America is in a worse state . . .'

Julie ran her fingers over a tall vase with a blue and green glaze, and mocking birds in relief work on branches. The birds were so alive one could almost hear them singing. There were plant pots with fluted edges on stands in autumn shades that had been a regular seller, but the outlet had now dried up. Surely there must be a market somewhere!

They stayed in the shed until dusk. Angus had just lit the gas-jet when Ivy arrived back with Lyndsey. 'Anyone at home?' she called as she came in, then stopped as she saw Richard.

'Well – Lord Almighty, I can't believe it.' To Lyndsey she added, 'This is your Uncle Richard, say hello.'

They all went back to the house and Julie thought that the nicest thing about being all together was seeing the tension ease in Richard and his delight in Lyndsey. She was in her element with a new uncle who was willing to play with her.

Later that evening, Richard said yes to Julie and Angus' invitation – he would very much like to stay for a few days until he could sort himself out. Ivy had offered to give him a bed but he was to come to Julie and Angus for meals.

At bedtime Julie said to Angus, 'I wonder what Ivy will have to say to Richard? She won't mince her words.'

'And perhaps that is just what he needs. He's been steeped in Violet's atmosphere and hate for so long that some of it has clung to him. Look, Julie, why don't you send a telegram to your parents in London in the morning, telling them that Richard is here? I think they should come. It might help their reunion if it takes place away from their home environment. It should help Richard anyway, he's very mixed up at the moment.'

'You don't mind, Angus? Oh, thanks, I think that's a great idea. I'll do that first thing.'

In reply to Julie's telegram word came to say that Tyler and Kitty would be arriving late afternoon.

It was a quiet, tearful reunion, tearful for Julie too, who had not realised until she saw her parents again just how much she had been longing to see them. Ivy kept Lyndsey out of the way until they all had a chance to talk and talk they certainly did. Kitty said that although she would not wish death on anyone she was honestly relieved that Violet would no longer turn up in her life to torment her.

Although Kitty was quietly overjoyed that Richard had come back she could not accept the fact of him wanting to live off Violet's ill-gotten money. 'Give it away, Richard,' she begged. 'Come back home, we can give you money until you get settled in work of some kind.'

He refused and was adamant about it. He would very much like to come home for a while, but he wanted to travel.

The following afternoon, Kitty suggested to Julie that they go for a walk, leaving the men to discuss world affairs. Julie was only too glad to have her mother to herself. She wanted to ask her advice about business without Angus being there.

It was late February with a touch of ice in the wind. But it was invigorating with white horses on the water and a clarity in the air that always gave Julie a feeling of uplift.

Kitty said, 'This is lovely. We've been in London for a month and we were talking about going back to Crescent House when your telegram came. I couldn't believe it when I knew Richard was back. But I feel we've lost him, Julie.' There was grief in Kitty's voice. 'Violet's left her mark on him as she did on everyone she came into contact with. I can never forgive her, not only for what she did to me but to our mother. Violet actually blackmailed her. She must have thought that I was illegitimate, but never realised that she and my other half-sisters were the bastards, not me. Mother was worried sick, always in debt to get money for Violet to buy fripperies and to protect me and the others from her. The worry killed her in the end. No, I cannot share Richard's feelings of pity for her.'

They walked in silence for a way then Kitty turned to Julie. 'Tell me, Julie, is everything all right between Angus and you? There's a feeling of – estrangement – between you.'

'It's the business. Everything is at a standstill.' Julie explained the position and Kitty said there must be markets that could be found, for Angus was excellent at his work. Julie then told her about the marriage bowls and Kitty showed interest.

'I think that would be an excellent selling-line. People are always looking for something different for presents and it does have a talking point. There is a recession but although your father's optical side has dropped off a little my side is still selling well. In fact, when we go out socially it's difficult to believe that there *is* a recession.'

They by-passed the harbour and made in the direction of the village. Julie had forced herself to go to the cove in the summer, not wanting it to be an out-of-bounds place for Lyndsey because of the tragedy of Daniel. But she was glad that today her mother had suggested the village.

They were stopped by a number of people who greeted

Kitty warmly and Julie realised how easily her mother fitted into any company. Although her parents had brought masses of food with them Kitty bought more and they were on the way back when she suggested they stop and have a cup of tea in the little café next to the haberdashers.

The tea had been poured, milked and sugared when Julie noticed that her mother was still stirring hers in a detached way. 'What's on your mind, Mother?' she asked.

Kitty looked up. 'We had some rather disturbing news about Fergus the other day.'

Julie wondered if there would ever come a time when she would be able to hear his name without a feeling of desolation, 'What news?'

'That's just it,' Kitty said earnestly. 'There isn't any. It's just as though he's disappeared from the face of the earth. It's months ago since anyone heard anything about him.'

'But what do you think could have happened to him?'

'Your father says he's only guessing at what could have happened but I think he knows more than he admits. According to his "guessing" Fergus works for the government, investigating corruption in high places. He said that a group of people might have found out and . . . well,' Kitty raised her shoulders in a helpless gesture. 'Pray heaven your father is wrong.'

Julie felt numbed. She had always hoped she would see Fergus again. She had to force herself to concentrate on what her mother was saying.

'I often wondered why he never married. But of course it could have been the danger of his work. No man would willingly marry under such circumstances, knowing he could make his wife a widow at any moment.'

This explanation had never occurred to Julie, and somehow it made the situation seem so much more poignant.

It was only later that anger replaced the feeling of poignancy. If Fergus felt he was unable to marry her then he ought not to have made love to her. He was no callow youth! But her anger did not make the pain any less.

Her parents and Richard spent a week with them and in that time Tyler was with Angus in the shed for long stretches, discussing the marriage bowls, and also his other work. 'Your work is excellent Angus,' he said. 'What is wrong is lack of marketing expertise. I'll get someone to deal with this. Your hands are full, creating, making.'

To Julie he said, 'And you go on making your butterfly dishes. I don't know how you've managed to create a feeling of mist in your glaze, but it does deserve acknowledgment.' Tyler smiled. 'I had not appreciated until now just what a talented daughter and son-in-law we have. This is what happens of course when husband and wife are both absorbed in a business of their own. Lyndsey has a certain talent,' he added quietly. 'Don't neglect it. She's a darling child, a little imp, of course.'

'But with an angel-shine.' Angus said. He paused then added, 'Like her mother used to have.'

Used to have? Julie glanced at him. There was a sadness in his eyes. She thought how far apart they seemed to be straying.

The door suddenly burst open and Richard came in. 'Where's my best girl? We're going for a walk.'

'I'm here Uncle Richard,' Lindsey squealed, and running to him held out her arms to be picked up. When Richard told her she had to walk she began whining that she wanted to be carried. He delivered an ultimatum. She walked or she stayed behind. Lyndsey slipped her hand into his and smiled up at him. She liked walking.

'Come on then, Gran and Aunt Ivy are waiting. See you,' Richard called as they went out.

Tyler said quietly, 'I think he's recovering. Perhaps another two or three weeks at home.'

The night before they were due to leave Kitty asked if she could take Lyndsey with them. 'Only for about a month,

Julie. She might help Richard to realise there is more to life than wandering aimlessly over the Continent. In Violet's world there was no room for children. It would also give you and Angus a freedom to go thoroughly into your work, until you get organised. You have a lot to do.'

'Yes,' Julie said, but stifled a fear that if Lyndsey was not there as a link between them she and Angus would grow further apart. Already he had rejected some ideas she had put forward. But she agreed to Lyndsey going to London because Angus had agreed to it. But he had stipulated it would be for no more than a month.

When they had all gone Julie knew a loneliness worse than any she had ever known in her life, because that night Angus slept apart from her, making the excuse he wanted to work through part of the night and did not want to disturb her. Julie recalled that disturbing her through the night had been a lovely part of marriage in the early days.

But then . . . as Angus had said, the angel-shine had gone.

# Chapter Twenty-Four

Julie came to realise the next day that if their marriage was to survive, she and Angus would have to have a long talk. The day before, she had suggested they do some Majolica work, the lovely bright pottery she had seen in Italy. He had turned it down without even giving an explanation. She could see now it was because of the Italian connection with Fergus, but surely they could not discard a good idea because she had seen the pottery in Italy? This was one thing she would discuss with him. And they must, of course, discuss the marriage bowls.

When she mentioned them he said, 'Later. I have other jobs to do.'

'What jobs?' she asked.

Angus, who had been about to walk away turned and met her gaze squarely. 'Why the sudden interest, Julie? You haven't shown much enthusiasm for my work over the past few months.'

Julie was about to protest hotly at this then realised it was true. She had hardly been to the shed, simply left Angus to his own devices. Since the sales had dropped off for the smaller items she had not even attempted to create anything. She held her hands out with a helpless gesture.

'I'm afraid I didn't inherit my mother's ability to make a successful businesswoman.'

'I didn't expect it when we married,' he answered quietly. 'All I hoped for was a loving wife.' With that he turned and left, leaving Julie feeling as though a chill wind had swept through the room.

It was not that she had seen herself as the perfect wife – how could she – but she had thought she fulfilled all the usual obligations, like meals ready for her husband when he came in, the house always spick and span and never once denying him when he wanted to make love to her.

Julie found herself trembling, realising just how much she had taken for granted. She had accepted, almost as if it was her right, that Angus should forgive her for all her lies about Lyndsey's conception; he had helped her over the grief of Daniel's death when his own heart must have been breaking. There had been times when he had asked her to give him a hand with the pottery and she had said she was not in the mood. Never once had he complained at her selfishness. He had had to work whether he felt like it or not to keep the home going. Shame made Julie's cheeks burn. How tarnished her angel-shine had become and the awful part of it was that it could never shine again. All she could hope for now was to earn Angus' respect. She would work with him, if he would accept it. She felt she wanted to go to the shed right away and tell him, but commonsense told her it would be better to wait until after they had had their midday meal, when there was less chance of distractions.

There was one thing about Angus: no matter if there had been words between them he would never allow a silence to settle between them, not altogether.

When he did come in he passed the remark that the weather was a little warmer then, after a pause added, 'Oh, by the way, I've had an order this morning.'

Julie looked at him in surprise. 'That's a bonus these days. Who from – Dave?'

'No, from a man who owns a hotel further along the coast. It's actually inland and trade has been practically nil lately. Then, during some digging workmen came across an underground spring. The water, according to an expert, has some medicinal qualities so this chap Miller is going to make a feature of it. He's going to give it an olde-tyme setting, with maidens carrying pitchers of water to the people who will be waiting with their goblets for their daily "medicine".'

Julie laughed. 'Do you think the hotel guests will believe in the medicinal qualities of the water?'

'The wealthy suffer from a lot of imaginary ailments and yes, they'll believe in the water if they're charged enough for it. I thought of making dark green goblets on a stem with a relief of acanthus leaves. I have to make ten pitchers and a hundred goblets.'

'Oh Angus, you'll need some help. Can I help?'

'I'll be glad of it. I've also put forward a plan to give this well some authenticity – a rock setting, with plants. I have some sketches in the shed, perhaps you can take a look later?'

Julie knew that Angus was excited about the project and when she discussed his plans later with him she became caught up in his enthusiasm. For the first time she understood how her parents got carried away when discussing ideas. She said, 'I especially like the designs of the goblets. We'll have to work hard to get them done because you must do some work on the marriage bowls and let Father have some samples.'

Angus told her he had already been working on them and produced moulds and some finished symbols to go on the bowls. He brought out a tray and laid them on the bench. The symbols had already been painted and glazed.

'Oh, Angus, they're lovely,' Julie enthused. There was the clown, to depict humour as one of the ingredients towards a successful marriage, the couple on the love seat . . . the clasped hands of friendship . . . the window box of flowers . . . the fairy-tale castle . . .

Julie ran a finger gently over the couple. 'You've caught such lovely expressions, Angus, they really do appear to be in love. And the handclasp seems to be so firm, so resolute, as though they are determined that no one shall come between them.'

'That was the idea,' he said quietly.

The fairy-tale castle brought a lump to Julie's throat. It was exquisitely made and coloured in delicate shades of pinks and blues and pale green, each tiny turret perfect. The castle had been Angus' suggestion because he said that everyone must dream.

But now she no longer had a dream . . . not unless she could count earning Angus' respect.

He began to talk about glazes and said he wanted to do some of the bowls with a simple white glaze. Julie was about to say, 'Oh, yes, for purity,' and stopped herself in time. She said, 'Yes, it would make all the lovely colours of the symbols stand out. But I do think we would need a variety of colours for the glazes, to suit all tastes. We need to appeal to a wide market.'

She hesitated a moment then went on, 'I had an idea last night, Angus, I wonder what you think about it. I thought if wooden plinths were made to stand some of the bowls on, there could be musical boxes incorporated into them. They could play a lively or a sentimental tune.'

Angus tugged at his lower lip, looked thoughtful for a moment then gave a nod. 'I like it. I could have a word with the clockmaker in the village, I'm sure he would be interested in that side of it.'

With a new rapport between them Julie felt sure that their earlier differences would disappear at bedtime but to her great disappointment Angus did not come to their bed, nor did he on subsequent nights.

After a week, full of despair, Julie took her complaint to Ivy . . . and was taken aback at her reply.

'It's all right discussing making marriage bowls and what ingredients to put in them to make for a happy marriage, but how can your marriage be a success if you miss out one of the most important ones?'

'What's that?'

'Sinking one's pride. How are you going to get Angus back into your bed if you won't ask him why he's staying away from it?'

'I couldn't. I'm not going to beg for – sex.'

'Then couldn't you beg for a little love?' Ivy queried, gently for her.

Julie sat hesitant for a moment then shook her head. 'No. If I had left Angus to sleep on his own then I would have gone back and said I was sorry. He was the one to leave and he will have to be the one to make it up.'

'But if you're not willing to sink your pride the whole idea of the marriage bowl fails.'

Julie gave a brief wry smile. 'Can you tell me how to depict sinking one's pride on the bowl?'

'Yes, write PRIDE in big letters on a big weight and show it being lowered down a well.'

Julie said she might suggest it to Angus as another ingredient and see if it would register with him. She did. He simply said he thought it was a good idea – and would add it to the others.

And so they worked. They worked long hours, slept apart but Julie was so exhausted each evening that she had very little time to moan about the breakdown of their marriage.

The goblets and pitchers won praise from the hotel proprietor, who told Angus that he and Julie were very talented and if he could recommend them for any special work he certainly would. Julie suggested he display a few marriage bowls in the reception hall in the hotel and to this he agreed. And before any of the bowls could be despatched to London for Tyler to find markets Angus was handed money for the first ten bowls from the hotel, with orders for several more, in different colours.

'Oh, Angus, that's marvellous,' Julie exclaimed. 'We've made a start, I'm sure now we're on our way.'

There was no hug from him, no kiss, as there would have

been at one time and Julie wondered how long Angus intended to distance himself from her. Forever?

Angus employed another elderly man who had been a potter before retirement, explaining that it might only be temporary if the marriage bowls did not sell.

When the samples were completed they were packed carefully and taken to the railway station to travel to London, with Angus saying pray heaven they would arrive intact. They did and within a week of their delivery Angus received a telegram from Tyler saying: '*Marriage bowls taken off. Kitty and I arriving with Lyndsey on Wednesday afternoon.*'

Julie did then throw her arms around Angus but his response was no more than a brief hug then he was saying, 'That's good news. And won't it be lovely to see Lyndsey? I have missed the little imp.'

Julie had missed her too, but she concentrated more on the fact of the sales. 'Daddy has done really well. I feel I can't wait to know who he has the orders from. If the orders are big, we'll have to employ more workers. You'll need to extend the workspace.'

'Don't get too carried away,' Angus cautioned. 'Let's see what we'll have to do, first. You'd better let Ivy know that Tyler and Kitty are coming.'

At times like this Julie regretted not having a larger house so she could put her parents up, but at least they were comfortable and happy staying with Ivy, especially Kitty who always seemed to be in her element going over her early life with her old friend.

Julie was on her way to tell Ivy the good news and met Ivy coming to tell *her* some good news.

'What do you know!' she exclaimed, 'I have a booking for a coach party! Some wealthy old chap decided to give a group of poverty-stricken housewives a treat and booked a coach to bring them to Echo Cove for a day. Isn't it great?'

Julie then told Ivy her news and there was jubilation with Ivy saying it was true about every cloud having a silver lining. She was going to the shops to stock up then she would have a big bake. 'Your mother will enjoy helping me, I know. See you later!'

When the family arrived from London Julie noticed with a pang how Lyndsey rushed first to Angus and flung herself at him. It made Julie recall how she had always greeted her father first after her parents had been away and she wondered if her mother had felt as hurt as she did now.

Then Lyndsey was flinging herself at Julie, chattering away excitedly and Julie held her close for a few moments before Lyndsey wriggled to be away, to go and see Ivy.

When Julie saw the expression on Ivy's face and that of Angus she wondered how she could have been so mean as to be jealous of the child's attentions.

Tyler was full of talk of the marriage bowls. 'It's fantastic how chance can play a big part in success. I was unpacking the bowls when one of my glass buyers arrived. He was intrigued by them, said he had a brother in ceramics – and from that man came the first order. Your mother had some of the bowls on display and lo and behold she took six orders for them, one of them from Germany. This could grow, Angus. You might need to enlarge your working space, engage more staff.'

Angus told him it would be no problem. He knew many people who were out of work and who would be glad of a job. He did add, however, that he did not want the business to grow too big. This had Tyler and Kitty and Julie looking at him in bewilderment.

Kitty said, 'But this is the whole purpose of business, Angus – building up, expanding.'

He nodded slowly. 'I know I have a family to support but I enjoy experimenting, both in design and with glazes.'

'And so you can,' Tyler said. 'I'm constantly experimenting with optical glass but you must have your bread and butter lines, and let other people handle the mass-producing side of it.'

'I'll see to that.' Julie spoke firmly. 'I want this business to be a success. If we can get orders during a recession how much are we going to achieve when trade improves? I shall enjoy the challenge.'

When they had got over the first talk of business Julie said, 'And now, tell me the home news. How is Richard? Didn't he want to come with you?'

There was a moment's silence then Kitty sighed. 'I'm afraid he's left us again. I suppose it was inevitable. He has this wanderlust on him again. But he has promised that he won't stay away for so long this time.'

'I give him six months and then he'll be back,' Tyler said firmly. 'Although he may not realise it he needs an anchor. And at least he knows we shall always be there when he needs us. By the way, Julie, did you know that Fergus Damant is back in London?'

Julie was amazed at how dispassionate she felt about this sudden news. 'I'm glad to hear it,' she said. 'What had happened to him?'

'Well, he said he had been taken ill at some outlandish place, but I feel we'll never get to know the complete truth from Fergus. Apparently he, too, is itching to go abroad again.'

'I'm not surprised. I think he just lives for himself. It's odd,' she added, 'but I can hardly remember what he looks like. He's like a stranger.' She was aware of Angus watching her and, wanting him to know how she felt about Fergus, without labouring it, she glanced at him and raised her shoulders in a dismissive way. 'That's how it is with some people, isn't it?'

Although Angus acknowledged this with only a brief nod she felt he understood what she had been trying to tell him.

To give Angus his due he wasted no time in getting the alterations organised. By eleven o'clock the following morning the shed was a hive of industry.

It was during this upheaval when some cupboards had to

be emptied that Julie found the extent of some of Angus' experiments – items he had never shown her, never talked about.

There was some Majolica ware, that surprised her, with the rich Italian colours. Then there was a vase with carved decorations, the carving so fine, so exquisite Julie wondered how Angus' large hands had managed to fashion them. A tall porcelain bottle in blue had venerable-looking men in white robes on it drinking wine; each face was a character study.

These beautiful pieces of work did more to make Julie realise that she had been the one to distance herself from her husband, and yet the odd thing was she found it impossible to tell him. Perhaps by working together they would get close without any advances or apologies having to be made.

Ivy had offered to make meals for all of them and Julie accepted, glad not to have anything to interrupt their work. Tyler and Kitty were only too pleased to look after Lyndsey and already they had half-hinted at taking her back with them again, to leave Julie and Angus free. 'We thought of spending a month at Crescent House,' Kitty said. 'Lyndsey would have a chance to meet many animals, with all the farms round about.' Julie had said they would have to talk about it, but she knew she would be willing for Lyndsey to go, and felt guilty knowing she was behaving exactly as her mother had done, letting someone else take care of Richard and herself. But then their whole life was at stake. If they did not get the opportunity to build up the business when they had the chance they could lose everything. It was these initial stages that were so important, the necessity of establishing themselves. And, after all, they owed it to her parents for getting them the orders.

Sometimes Julie felt that this was something Angus resented. And she mentioned it one evening when the kiln had cooled and they were taking the bowls out and stacking them.

'I'm sure you would rather have built up the business on your own, Angus, but you can do all your experiments once we can leave people working on their own.'

He straightened, picked up a cloth, rubbed the palms of his hands and said quietly, 'I imagined when we came to Echo Cove the two of us working together, without haste, you working out designs, for which you have a flair. And then when we had a small business established, we could go for a stroll in the evening, to the harbour, to the cove.' Angus suddenly threw down the cloth. 'But it hasn't worked out that way, has it? We have to mass produce, make money, become wealthy!'

'No, we don't have to become wealthy!' she retorted. 'We only have to make enough money to live on. I've never asked for a big house or a fancy car, but you're managing very well to put me in the wrong. I've made one mistake in my life and it seems you're determined to punish me for the rest of it.' Julie turned and ran out of the shed, hating Angus, hating what their life had now become, full of animosity. She ran on towards the cliff-top, a place she seldom came to; it was always the harbour that drew her.

The evening was a contrast to her emotions, the air balmy and the sea calm. She was stiff with resentment and felt she had good reason to be. But why should Angus be so resentful? He could do as he wanted, he had always been the boss. If he had no wish to mass produce then all he had needed was to say no.

Had the fact of Fergus still being alive and back in London reacted on him? Did he think he would always be there in her thoughts? She could tell him, stress that she honestly did not want to see Fergus again. But then why should she? Angus ought to be able to trust her. Deep down she had hoped he would follow her and apologise but she remained alone with the expanse of water and a feeling of desolation.

The cottage was empty when she returned and Angus did

not come in until the early hours. Once more Julie slept alone.

The following week they were kept constantly busy and Julie was sure it was this that kept her parents from becoming aware of the ever-widening rift between them. Lyndsey, of course, was a great help with her bright chatter.

When her parents suggested again that they take Lyndsey back with them to Crescent House Angus refused, and suggested putting it off for a while. At the moment another parting would be too close; he did not want the child to forget them. Kitty and Tyler said they quite understood, but Julie felt her mother especially was disappointed. It did one thing – it made Julie realise that Angus was right. Her mother was wanting to give the concentrated love to her grandchild which she had been unable to give her own children, because of her dedication to business. Julie vowed then it was something she would avoid.

There were tears from Lyndsey when the time came for Kitty and Tyler to leave and Julie felt tearful too, wondering how her marriage would be by the time she saw her parents again.

'Keep sending the marriage bowls,' Tyler said cheerfully, and to Julie, 'What about those little butterfly dishes you were going to make?' She promised to tackle them soon, but felt in her own mind they would never get made. Her heart was not in them.

And so Julie and Angus went on working in a dedicated way. Lyndsey spent a part of every morning in the shed but Ivy and Mrs Pinner helped to take her off their hands. It was essential if they were to supply the orders that kept coming in. The proportion of musical bowls ordered was quite high and kept a number of clockmakers along the coast busy. Some played *Here Comes the Bride*, others played *The Blue Danube* and a quite popular tune was *When You and I Were Seventeen* – these marriage bowls being destined for wedding anniversaries.

Then, about two months after Kitty and Tyler's last visit came a telegram saying they were coming for the weekend. It was essential; it concerned the marriage bowls.

Angus said if it was to increase the orders he would not do it; they were doing more than enough already. Julie felt it would have nothing to do with this, but was unable to pinpoint what it could be.

Tyler did not keep them in suspense when he arrived. He was angry, bitter. George Tierne, whose house they had stayed in during their visit to Monchau, was producing marriage bowls at his potteries in Germany.

'Turning them out night and day,' he said, 'and there's nothing we can do about it. You never did patent the idea Angus, and you ought to have done.'

'It was not my idea,' Angus replied quietly. 'It was my father's. Let Tierne turn them out. I can go back to what I want to make. I think I've established myself now with my work, and can afford to look after Julie and Lyndsey. That's all I want out of life.'

Julie looked at him with hope.

Tyler thumped a clenched fist into his palm. 'That dastardly Tierne! He not only did Kitty's mother out of her inheritance but –'

'Was it important?' Angus asked, eyebrows raised. 'Kitty's mother experienced a very beautiful thing. Her marriage with Richard Tierne was short but there existed a love between them that few people are privileged to share.'

In the silence that followed this Julie was aware of the slow ticking of the grandfather clock. Had her grandmother experienced the best kind of love, a lifetime condensed into one short month? Or was it false? There had been no time for quarrelling, no poverty to endure, no trials of any kind. How could one judge a marriage like that?

Kitty said slowly, 'I think perhaps Angus is right. Her memories were important to her. Mother must have lived her short marriage over and over again through my father's beautiful letters, I think these would be worth more to her than any inheritance.'

'*Poverty* killed her,' Julie said grimly, then added, looking from one to the other, 'and I suppose that is the most practical statement I have ever made.'

Tyler smiled suddenly. 'I think it is, Julie, and it's taken the anger out of me. Perhaps it's wrong to speculate what someone else's life would have been, had this happened, or that happened. A lifetime's happiness can hinge on one small thing. If I had not left home I would never have met your mother and so –' he spread his hands. 'If you had not made up your mind you wanted to earn your own living you would never have gone to work for Ivy and Tom and would never have met Angus.'

'No, I wouldn't, would I?' Julie said and got up. 'Ivy has a meal ready for us all, shall we go? We can talk some more about the business later.'

# Chapter Twenty-Five

While Julie's parents were with them she mulled over Angus' statement that all he wanted out of life was to be able to support his wife and child. On the surface he made it seem as though she, as well as Lyndsey, was of the greatest importance to him. But if this was so, why did he no longer attempt to make love to her? She decided that when her parents returned to London she would have a straight talk with him.

Kitty and Tyler left early on the Tuesday morning but there was no opportunity to speak to Angus on his own until eight o'clock that evening. The workers had left at half-past seven and when Angus did not come home Julie went to the shed. Two gas-jets were burning. She stopped at the window and looked in.

She found something primitive about the scene, looking at the old kick-wheel, the type that had been used for centuries. Angus, strong, well-muscled, was shaping a tall vase with his large hands – a vase with a delicacy about it. Sensuous emotions brought a weakness to her limbs. He was her man, earthy, passionate – yet tender. She longed to feel his arms about her, to be imprisoned by him, to feel his lips moving tantalisingly over her skin, arousing her to the agonising ecstasy that had been denied for so long . . . too long. With her blood now on fire she walked to the door and opened it. Without looking up from his work Angus said, 'Hello. I'm planning to work for another two hours.'

The lack of welcome, or even interest in his voice cooled her blood. She walked over to the bench. 'I felt it was time we had a talk.'

She might not have been there for all the notice he took of her. He finished the slender-necked vase, removed it from the wheel and after picking up a cloth he turned to her, wiping his hands.

'Yes, what about?'

A number of phrases ran through Julie's mind but she ended up by saying, 'Why don't you want to make love to me any more?'

'I would have thought that was obvious.' He picked up a piece of wire and cut a wedge of clay.

'Will you please stop working for a moment!' Julie clenched her hands. 'Why should it be obvious? I've never denied you.'

Angus sighed and flung down the wire. 'Haven't you any idea, any idea at all that the biggest insult a woman can offer a man is to lie passive when he wants to make love to her – like a cow!'

Hot colour rushed to her cheeks. 'Now who is insulting who?'

'Can you deny it? I would rather you had made the age-old excuse about having a headache than to submit. Yes, *submit*, and you're so damned smug about never having refused me. Night after night I've lain beside you and you've never once reached out a hand to me, or cuddled up close. And when I've made advances you've gone all tense. Well, I've had enough of being frozen out.' He picked up the wire again. 'And now, unless you have anything further to say, anything that's important –'

Julie stormed out, slamming the door behind her, the words 'like a cow' running through her mind. How dare he use such a coarse phrase to her! Of all the insults that was about the worst.

It was not until she was back in the cottage and sitting

over the fire that she began to accept his words. Wasn't it his very earthiness, his passion, his mastery, that she used to enjoy? Would she want him if he was any different, over-gentle, fastidious? No, she did not want him to change but he would have to apologise for what he had said if they were ever to get together again.

She sat up until midnight but Angus did not come in. By then she realised she would never have the feeling for pottery-making that Angus had. It was something she had done as a challenge. She enjoyed the painting of the pottery but did not feel anything, even in the handling of the clay as he did. It was as though his whole soul went into the work – as though it was something that had been passed down to him through the centuries – an ageless beauty.

Julie sighed, made preparations for bed. She would have to see how things turned out, but she was still determined that he would have to come to her.

He did not come to her, and day followed day with a regular monotony.

At the beginning of June there was a heatwave. It did not bring the usual rush of visitors but there was a trade that kept Ivy reasonably occupied.

Mrs Pinner had her niece and children staying with her and Lyndsey spent practically the whole of the day with them, either helping Ivy or on the beach. Then one morning early there was great excitement. Two dolphins had come into the cove. Mrs Pinner and her visitors had already taken Lyndsey to see them, but at nine o'clock Ivy came to the shed to see if Julie wanted to take a look at them.

'They're funny to watch,' she said laughing. 'We think they've fallen out and the male is trying to make it up with the female.'

'It's more likely to be the other way around,' Julie retorted. 'It's always the women who have to do the crawling.'

'Not on our marriage bowls,' Angus said mildly.

'Nothing on those marriage bowls has any reality,' Julie snapped. 'They're fairy-tale things.' She pointed to a bowl. 'Look at that – have you ever seen a man kneeling to a woman begging forgiveness?'

Ivy said, 'Come to think about it I've never seen a woman kneeling to a man. But then neither should have to, not if there's any love at all between them.' She grinned. 'However, as I'm not going to be drawn into an argument, I'll go and take a look at the dolphins. Coming Julie?'

Julie shook her head. 'No, sorry, we have an order to complete and I want to get as much done as I can before it gets too hot. Perhaps later.'

But even if she had wanted to see them they had gone later. Lyndsey was very excited at first after seeing them but when she returned from the beach in the afternoon she was quiet. Julie, hoping she had not had too much sun ruffled her hair and said, 'Are you all right, love?'

Lyndsey looked up from her toys. 'Do Mummy and Daddy dolphins fall out like real Mummies and Daddies?'

Julie felt startled. Had Lyndsey in her young discerning way been aware of the rift between Angus and herself? 'Of course they do,' she said brightly. 'All animals do and the birds, they all get bad-tempered at times. *You* get bad-tempered and throw tantrums.'

'But you give me a smack and I don't have one any more do I?' Lyndsey replied solemnly. Julie, lost for words for once picked her up and gave her a hug.

'Come along, we'll put you in the bath and get all that sand washed off you.'

As usual, Julie stayed up until after midnight and as usual Angus did not come in. She lay wide awake in bed, knowing that something would have to come to a head soon. They could not go on in this way. When he came in she would have to try to talk to him.

The grandfather clock in the hall had struck two sonorous strokes before Angus came in and deep down Julie was glad it was too late for discussion. It would have to be tomorrow.

She tossed and turned and eventually got up, pulled on a coat and crept downstairs. After hesitating, she went out and walked towards the shed. Making a cup of tea in the kitchen could have disturbed Angus.

Although it would soon be dawn there was not a pre-dawn chill. It was only the grass that felt damp. She went into the shed and noticing two items on the walls covered by cloths she lit a gas-jet. Slowly, she removed one of the covers. Then stood, staring at the ceramic piece exposed. A group of mounted Tartars, their scimitars flashing, galloped across the wall, the horses, nostrils flaring, tails and manes flying, looking as ferocious as their masters. Flung across the horse of each man was a young, captive maiden.

It was a wall-piece of cruelty, of terror, yet Julie felt moved by the sheer genius of the work. What had prompted Angus to fashion such a piece? What had been in his mind to want to portray such cruelty, such terror? Had he seen himself as one of the Tartars carrying her off? But then she had married him willingly and they had been happy, very happy. At least, at first.

When Julie removed the cover of the second wall-piece she drew in a quick breath. This was a complete contrast to the first, a gentle scene of deer coming to a stream to drink. It was a scene she had witnessed at the Tiernes' at Monchau and she had described it to Angus. How lifelike it was – he had even captured the maternal concern of the deer for the young fawns.

There was a sudden draught as the door opened and Angus came in. 'Julie – what are you doing here at this time in the morning?'

'I couldn't sleep. I didn't want to disturb you by making a cup of tea so I came in here.' She raised a hand indicating the Monchau scene. 'It's beautiful, just as I saw it.'

'I portrayed it as you described it, with tenderness – from the heart.'

'And the Tartar scene?'

'I had to get rid of my anger. It was eating into me.' He spread his hands. 'It was the only way I knew how.'

'I was going to make some tea,' Julie said, 'but I feel I want to walk.'

'I'll come with you.'

She did not want him to come. She needed to be alone to think. Then he said, 'The dolphins might be in the cove,' and she felt annoyed. What had dolphins to do with their marriage? There was something childish about the remark. She walked to the door and Angus followed.

They walked in silence and breasted the headland just as the sky was lightening; hues of pink defused the greyness but Julie shivered. They stood close, but still without speaking. She felt she had said everything there was to be said and thought ironically that there seemed little hope now of them ever finding the last ingredient to complete the marriage bowl, nor of regaining the intimacy that their marriage so sadly lacked.

She gazed almost stonily at the growing grandeur of the dawn. The gold rim of the sun finally showed itself all above the horizon and the sky was lit with a splendour which flushed not only the long thin layers of cloud with deepening hues of gold and pink, but also seemed to run in a liquid path of gold across the calm morning sea to where they stood. Julie realised it was a flood-tide, when nothing moved – or stalemate she thought, with grim humour, like our marriage.

She almost turned away but something in Angus' attention to the view made her take a final look. And there, cutting across the sea, coming inshore, was the unmistakable hump of a dolphin's back. It came slowly, but as if with purpose, right in under the headland beneath their feet, swimming along the line of the sun's path. Then she gasped as a ring of ripples seemed to encircle the dolphin, like a kind of watery halo. She saw the beak and back of a second dolphin swimming in circles around the first, which seemed to be completely ignoring it – like Angus she thought ruefully, and she running in rings to make him aware of her.

The second one turned on its side, coming ever closer to the first, which swam on in its uncompromising straight line; the second dolphin did not give up, and as though unable to restrain itself any longer, came close and brushed itself so gently, so sensuously, along the side of its unheeding mate. For long seconds the contact was ignored, then as it came near again the first dolphin at last turned its head and half-nuzzled, half-pushed at its insistent companion. Julie found herself smiling as the second one went into an ecstasy of delight at the recognition, diving down, then leaping far out of the water to express its joy.

Almost without thinking she found she had reached for Angus' hand, exclaiming aloud as the first dolphin finally turned and headed back out to sea, the two playing and gambolling together, each now taking turns to touch and tease the other, diving, leaping, circling towards the rising and strengthening sun.

She suddenly felt Angus' hand tighten meaningfully around her own. They did not speak, but from the corner of her eye she saw Angus stand taller, throw off the dogged look that had plagued him. The sun gilded his features as he looked upwards, the sun now a full golden ball above the horizon.

Julie recalled Angus saying, 'I've had enough of being frozen out,' and 'You've never once reached out a hand to me or cuddled up close . . .'

*Touch . . . Communication . . .*

It was the last ingredient for the marriage bowl.

As though by a signal they both moved away and, still hand in hand, walked slowly in the direction of home.